W9-CLW-788
3 3288 10175497 8 DEC 2020

Praise for *Lies of Descent*
by Troy Carrol Bucher

"The opening salvo in what promises to be a dramatic and inventive new fantasy series." —Peter McLean, author of *Priest of Bones*

"Well-written and compelling, Troy Bucher's *Lies of Descent* depicts how factual accuracy, military culture, and religion all conceal a long-standing historical deception about to implode into a conflagration fueled by the lust for power and fanned by mythic misconceptions." —L.E. Modesitt, Jr., author of the Recluce novels

"Bucher launches himself into epic fantasy. . . . This coming of age story will appeal to fantasy readers of all ages." —*Booklist*

"Troy Carrol Bucher deftly twists all of your expectations into new and innovative directions. Unpredictable; readers will not know what to expect from this epic fantasy as the lies that the world lives by begin to unravel." —Joshua Palmatier, author of the Ley trilogy

"Troy Carrol Bucher's debut novel shows how much promise he offers to the literary world with an inspiring imagination of secrets only touched upon." —*Irish Film Critic*

LIES OF
DESCENT

DAW Books proudly presents
the novels
of Troy Carrol Bucher

The Fallen Gods' War
LIES OF DESCENT
FAILURE OF DESCENT*

*Coming soon from DAW Books

LIES OF DESCENT

THE FALLEN GODS' WAR: BOOK ONE

TROY CARROL BUCHER

DAW BOOKS, INC.
DONALD A. WOLLHEIM, FOUNDER
1745 Broadway, New York, NY 10019
ELIZABETH R. WOLLHEIM
SHEILA E. GILBERT
PUBLISHERS
www.dawbooks.com

Copyright © 2019 by Troy Carrol Bucher.

All Rights Reserved.

Cover illustration by Ryan Pancoast.

Cover design by Katie Anderson.

Interior design by Alissa Rose Theodor.

Edited by Sheila E. Gilbert.

DAW Book Collectors No. 1832.

Published by DAW Books, Inc.
1745 Broadway, New York, NY 10019.

All characters and events in this book are fictitious.
Any resemblance to persons living or dead is strictly coincidental.

If you purchased this book without a cover you should be aware that
this book may have been stolen property and reported as "unsold and
destroyed" to the publisher. In such case neither the author nor the
publisher has received any payment for this "stripped book."

The scanning, uploading, and distribution of this book via the Internet
or via any other means without the permission of the publisher is illegal,
and punishable by law. Please purchase only authorized electronic
editions, and do not participate in or encourage the electronic piracy
of copyrighted materials. Your support of the author's rights is
appreciated.

First Mass Market Printing, July 2020
1 2 3 4 5 6 7 8 9

DAW TRADEMARK REGISTERED
U.S. PAT. AND TM. OFF. AND FOREIGN COUNTRIES
—MARCA REGISTRADA
HECHO EN U.S.A.

PRINTED IN THE U.S.A.

DEDICATION

TO DAVID BISCHOFF (1951-2018)

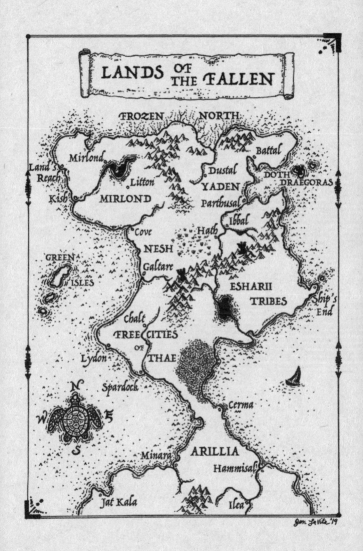

Together the Gods of Light and Dark created the universe, but those of light came to hate the darkness for the death and destruction it bestowed upon the worlds of man, so they tricked the Dark Gods, sacrificing hundreds of stars to create holes in the universe where the dark ones were pulled down through the fabric of existence and trapped outside time.

Although they could not conquer chaos and death, for those were built into the essence of the cosmos, the Gods of Light were free to act without balance. They built wonders that defied the laws of nature, ended disease and famine, and all but eliminated catastrophe and war for countless millennia.

Then, the Dark Gods found a way to return.

—Edyin's *Complete Chronicle of the Fallen*

CHAPTER 1

The dark-haired boy sat quietly at the table, dinner already eaten. He didn't want to draw attention to himself, so he stayed as still as possible while the grizzled old man across the table put down his fork and eyed the bone in front of him. Most of the meat had been stripped away though traces still dangled from the white knobby end. The man opened his mouth and placed the bone between spotted gums and missing teeth before swiveling it around, smacking and snorting as he angled it this way and that to tear off the last strands of flesh. When those were gone, he bit down with his molars, filling the single drab room of the house with the crunch of shattering cartilage.

The boy cringed at the sound, but he was careful to remain silent. Father's attention wasn't something he or his brother ever wanted. The bloom on his cheek was proof of that.

His father pulled the bone from his mouth with a slurp. Leaning forward, he spat cartilage and gristle onto his tin plate and wiped grease from his mouth with the back of a wrinkled hand. With a grunt of dismissal, he tossed the bone onto the tin, making a loud clang that announced the end of the meal. He thumped his chest until he belched and picked up his dinner knife to scrape at the underside of a fingernail. "Clean this up, Riam. Then go see what's takin' your brother so long in the barn."

"Yes, Father." Riam's chair screeched against the wooden floor, and he froze, half standing with his heart in his throat. It didn't take much to get Father going, and the scratch of the chair always irritated the old man. Thankfully, his father was too preoccupied with his nails to notice.

Careful not to make any more noise, Riam slipped sideways from his seat and made his way around the plain, sturdy table, stacking the tins and utensils. His hair was long, having gone all winter and through low summer without a cut, so he used one hand to brush it from his eyes whenever he bent forward. He left a plate with the remaining chicken leg, half a sweet tuber, and a burnt piece of flatbread for his brother Lemual.

Lemual was seven years older and had ridden to town earlier in the day. Once a month Father hooked up the wagon to purchase supplies from the mercantile. Lemual always rode in the day prior and placed the order so it would be ready. Riam envied his brother's solo ventures. One day he'd be old enough to make the trip, and it couldn't come soon enough.

With a sigh, Riam finished placing the last of the cutlery on the single wooden platter they owned and hurried toward the back door. He needed to make it outside before Father noticed the plate left behind.

"Boy . . ."

He jerked to a halt. He was an arm's length from the back door, but it might as well have been a full homestead away. His shoulders sagged. He knew the words that would come next.

"Take Lemual's plate with you," his father said in his calm, cruel voice. "He shoulda finished by now. He's lucky we let it sit as long as we did."

There was no *we* in the decision, but Father always spoke in plurals when being spiteful, spreading the blame. Riam couldn't hide the food either. He'd tried that before and had paid for it with a swollen lip and loose tooth.

I'm sorry, Lemual. I tried.

He wiped the disappointment from his face—he wouldn't give the old man the satisfaction of showing his true feelings—and returned to the table to add Lemual's plate to the top of the stack. It was his chore to feed the scraps to the pigs and scrub the tins in the water trough. He hated it. The rusted hand pump only sputtered out a trickle this far into summer and the handle went up higher than his reach, but at least it was getting easier. He'd hit a growth spurt this year and was closing in on his brother's height.

Before Riam could retrieve the tin from the table, the front door opened with its familiar creak. Father's back was to the door, so he didn't see Ferrick, the town magistrate, step inside. Ferrick's immense, round belly draped over his wide brown belt, and his second chin shook with his steps. Everyone knew serving as the local magistrate was Ferrick's first love. He wore a white shirt without wrinkles under a brown vest that matched his belt, and the truncheon of his office dangled from his side next to woolen trousers that were ironed crisp and straight. No, the man wasn't lazy. His weight was simply the manifestation of his second passion—food.

Why hadn't Ferrick knocked? Father barely tolerated the magistrate on the rare occasions they spoke, and he always grumbled about it afterward. If the magistrate thought Father was short with him when taxes and rent were due, he was about to get a full barrel for barging into their home. Father's temper was like a caged marcat. If you unlocked it, for Fallen's sake, you'd better not be in the cat's path when you lifted the gate.

Hopefully, it wouldn't go too badly. Despite his father's contempt, there was a strength and honesty beneath the magistrate's soft flesh most others lacked. Ferrick always snuck him sugar hardened with flavored syrup or, on special occasions, sweetcakes whenever Father wasn't looking. He didn't want Ferrick to stop. Father wouldn't spend a single dreg on sweets if he were the richest man in Nesh.

A thin man, almost as tall as the doorway, stepped from behind Ferrick's bulk. His hair was tied behind his head, revealing deep red-and-blue tattoos that twisted down his neck and disappeared under his shirt. The one under his left ear, an angry-looking owl with menacing red eyes, glared at Riam. The owl's sinister face scared him nearly as much as the newcomer himself. Riam tried not to look at it, but the owl remained at the edge of his vision, watching him.

Beyond the tattoos, the man wore loose trousers tucked into knee-high boots and a long-sleeved shirt with the sleeves rolled and held above the elbows by narrow straps that buttoned to the sleeve. Both the trousers and the shirt were the threatening deep gray of a storm cloud. Most striking, however, were the twin, leather-wrapped sword handles jutting out above his hips.

Riam didn't know who the man was, but he knew what the man was—a Draegoran. On more than one sleepless night Lemual had frightened him with tales of the demon men. Always dressed in gray and covered in tattoos, the demon men could read minds and killed people for their impure thoughts. His brother's tales usually ended with the Draegorans dragging children away, but the really bad children—those, they executed. He'd never quite believed his brother's tales, but here stood a Draegoran, exactly as described—a demon come to life—right in his own home.

The Draegoran looked Riam up and down, and the corners of his lips lifted into a satisfied smile that was anything but friendly.

He's come for me, just like in the stories. The tins slid from Riam's hands and hit the floor, filling the room with the clangs of bouncing utensils and tin plates.

Startled, his father jabbed the knife under his fingernail. "Faen's balls, boy!" He dropped the knife to the table and rubbed at the end of his finger. Finding nothing bleeding or damaged, he reached out with a greasy hand and snatched up Riam by the shirt. He yanked Riam close, so hard a button popped free and clattered along the floor. "You got the graces of an Esharii tribesman. Maybe a few nights in the barn will make you a little more careful."

Normally, Father's anger made him cower, but this time Riam ignored it. His attention remained fixed on the demon in the doorway. He tried to say something, but the words wouldn't come out. He could only stand there, mouth opening and closing like a landed fish.

"Look at me when I'm talkin' to you." His father drew back a hand.

Riam tensed for the blow and the words that had failed him a moment earlier came flowing out. "But the door—"

"I heard it. Your brother ain't gonna save you from . . ." He caught sight of the men, and his words trailed off. His hand lowered. The smile left the Draegoran's face, and for a long, awkward moment the only sound in the room was the soft hiss of the wind through the shutter slats.

Finally, the Draegoran broke the silence. "You were told the test was today. Why was the boy absent?"

Riam's father glanced at the knife on the table. He licked his lips.

"Don't be stupid, Ingis. Just answer the man so we can get this over with," Ferrick said. "I told him you were old, and it likely slipped your mind." He gave a slight nod of encouragement.

Ingis stared at Ferrick, his mouth slightly parted, contemplating the way out the magistrate offered. He shook his head slightly and folded his arms. A smirk lifted the corner of his mouth. "He won't be twelve until winter."

Riam gasped at his father's thin words. Even he knew you couldn't lie to a Draegoran, and he'd never seen one before.

The Draegoran moved, fast as an arrow. One instant he was at the door and the next he stood beside Father, holding him by the hair. He wrenched Father's head over the chair back, exposing his throat.

Riam's father kicked at the floor, trying to get his feet beneath him. He fumbled at the Draegoran's arms.

The man slapped Father's hands away as if wrestling a small child. He leaned down until they were face-to-face. "I could remove your right hand for lying." The words were low and flat.

The Draegoran would do it, too. He would cut off Father's hand with no more thought than someone gave to chopping wood. Riam could see it in his eyes and hear it in the emotionless, monotone words. Father spoke the same way when the beatings were the worst, telling Riam how everything was his fault and how if he were only a better child, then he wouldn't have to be punished so much. It was always his fault.

Is that it? Are Lemual's stories true? Is the Draegoran here to drag me away for my mistakes? He took a step back and found himself blocked by the ladder to the loft. He pressed against the rough wood, but it seemed to push him back toward the demon man.

"The truth this time. Why was the boy absent?" The

Draegoran drew one of his swords with his free hand. The weapon slid out of the worn leather sheath without a sound. "Think carefully before you answer." He waved the blade back and forth. It swayed like a thorn snake before striking, hypnotizing its prey. There was no looking away.

Ferrick took a step forward and opened his mouth to speak, but a hard look from the Draegoran stopped him. Ferrick held his hands together with his thumbs at his lips, too afraid to do anything more. A Draegoran's authority far surpassed a small-town magistrate's.

"I . . . I . . ." His father stammered. He looked back and forth between the Draegoran and the blade. "I . . . decided not to bring him."

"And why is that?"

His father trembled. "Because . . . I didn't think anyone would notice."

Riam had never seen his father scared of anything, and a part of him liked what he saw. *How many times have I cowered in the loft, shaking with that same cold fear?* He liked that someone was showing his father exactly how the man made him feel—terrified of the next blow. But, at the same time, it was his father. He didn't want anything bad to happen. Scaring him so he understood would be enough. Then maybe Father wouldn't hurt him anymore.

"And?" The Draegoran looked with hunger at his father's hand. He sniffed the air. "You aren't lying, but you aren't telling me something." The blade drifted higher, preparing to come down.

Why wouldn't Father answer? The Draegoran would do it if he didn't answer. For Fallen's sake, say something!

His father swallowed and licked his lips again. He looked to Ferrick for support, but the magistrate turned his head and studied an empty wall. Father's shoulders slumped, and his hands dropped to his lap. "Because you Draegoran bastards deserve to be stood up to. You take everything but give nothing in return. Why should I have to abide by agreements made generations before my great-grandfather was born?"

Ferrick sucked in his breath.

"It doesn't matter anyway." His father sagged. "Go ahead. Get it over with. Your kind ruined my life long ago."

For the first time, Riam saw his father for what he truly was, an old man—older than a man raising two boys ought to be—a tired man who hated his life and made his children pay for it. Disappointment and sadness filled Riam. Father would never change, not even with the Draegoran threatening his life.

"We give you peace. We give you freedom. We die to keep the Esharii from burning your homes, but it's not enough." The Draegoran cocked his head back toward Ferrick. "You see, Magistrate. People thrive under our protection, but they're unwilling to pay even the smallest price."

Defiance flared back onto his father's face. "Thrives! No one thrives. We barely survive!"

The Draegoran shook his head. "My words are wasted on you," he said. "You choose not to accept, or even understand, and so you never will. It's the same in every town and village from the plains to Mirlond." He let go of his father's hair and wiped his palm on his father's shirt. He took a step toward Riam.

"Don't be afraid, boy," the Draegoran said. "I'm going to touch you with the crystal, the same as I've done with a thousand others your age." He held up the leather-wrapped hilt. The silver pommel held a large, white-clouded gem. "You may feel nothing, but if my instincts are right, you'll feel a strange tug and see and hear things. It won't hurt you, though. I swear."

Riam wanted to run, but Father had taught him long ago that running only made things worse. Once, he'd torn his good shirt, the one reserved for going into town, while playing in the barn. His father's face had gone completely red, and Riam, scared of his anger, had run. He couldn't remember the beating when Father found him hiding in the grain field, but he remembered waking up in the barn bruised and sore. It was a lesson he'd never forget. Yet, despite this, it still took all his strength to stand and watch the hilt move toward his face.

A buzzing noise filled the room, growing louder the closer the sword came. The milky clouds moved within the gem, slowly swirling, hiding a distorted face—or maybe an animal of some kind. It was hard to tell. Riam's heart raced, and the gem pulsed in time with his heartbeat. He strained to make out the figure.

The Draegoran's lips moved, but the buzzing drowned out the words. The gem pulled at Riam's mind. There was no pain, but it frightened him more than anything he'd ever known. He would've bolted if not for the ladder holding him in place. He fought against the fear, willing it to go away. For a moment, the sensation ceased. Then the pommel touched his forehead, and the room exploded into light.

When it faded, the Draegoran, the magistrate, his father, all were gone. The room, normally dusty and drab, was clean and dressed with bright orange curtains and a flowery tablecloth. A young woman sat rocking a baby. *Mother.* She'd died when he was so young that he couldn't remember her face, but this was her. He didn't know how he knew, he just knew.

The room lurched and twisted. It was dark, and his father cursed. His mother huddled in a corner. Tears streaked down her face. The room twisted again. Father, Lemual, and Mother sat at dinner with an older woman. The room twisted once more. Crying and wailing. His father held the old woman by the collar of her shirt and hit her over and over. The wet smack of the blows made Riam gag. The room spun. His mother sat with a knife, her wide, glossy eyes staring into the fireplace. The wood cracked and hissed. The knife fell to the floor. Blood trickled from her outstretched fingers.

The scene changed. Lemual held the baby, telling it to be quiet. Yells came from the other room—Father, drunk and ranting. Again, it changed, and again and again. On and on it went, with each scene slipping by faster than the previous and each taking some small portion of him with it. He could no longer keep up with the images. The blur of sights and sounds made him dizzy and nauseated.

Riam needed to get away from the sword. It was draining him. He fought to break free, to come back to the present, but he wasn't strong enough. He tried again, concentrating on moving his head away from the pommel. With a loud pop, the images ceased. The Draegoran stood before him once more. The room swayed and bobbed around him.

The Draegoran held the sword before him. A piercing, bright light radiated from the crystal. "You have the blood." There was pride in his voice, and his eyes were wide in triumph as if finding something old that was lost.

Riam doubled over and puked on the Draegoran's boots. "Easy, boy. It'll pass." The man in gray held Riam's shoulders, steadying him until the room stopped trying to throw him onto the floor.

Riam wiped his mouth on his sleeve and muffled an apology.

"Hold off right there," his father said. "He's my boy, and I won't have—"

Pride turned to anger. The Draegoran spun back to Ingis and grabbed the old man by the throat. Lifting him out of the chair, he threw Riam's father to the floor hard enough that he bounced on the hardwood planks. The Draegoran didn't let up. He knelt in close and slammed the pommel of the sword against Father's head. The gem turned from white to a bright, angry red. His father went rigid.

"Magistrate!" he yelled back over his shoulder.

Ferrick jumped, startled at the use of his title.

"You are witness to a judgment of death."

Father's hands came up, palms out, as if they could ward off the Draegoran's words. "No. Wait." He looked to Ferrick. "He can't—"

The Draegoran turned the blade with a quick twist. It hung there, frozen for an instant, before descending.

"No! Don't!" Father yelled.

The blade plunged into the old man's chest, and it didn't slow until it bit into the wooden floor with a dull thunk.

Father struggled to focus on the blade buried in his chest. There was an odd look of curiosity on his face, like he couldn't quite grasp what had happened. "Wasn't my fault . . . hers," he wheezed. "Stupid whore." He spasmed, and his head lolled to the side with his empty-glass eyes coming to rest on Riam.

Riam wanted to scream but found his throat swelled shut. He could only stare at the blood spreading across the floor. He felt the sword's pull, soft at first, and then stronger. Father's face puckered and wrinkled like an old apple left in the sun. The crystal was absorbing him. Not his physical body. Something indefinable from inside was being leached away, siphoned up through the blade and into the pommel of the sword. The skin darkened and shrank, tightening up like dried leather. The blood on the floor crusted over and browned.

The Draegoran tore the sword free. The weapon came away clean and gleamed in the light.

Pain and fear squeezed and burned Riam's heart, but behind those feelings came another sensation: relief.

He's gone. He's really gone. He'll never hit me again.

Riam felt ashamed and guilty for those thoughts, but he couldn't help the release that came with them. There were so many times he'd wished his father were gone, and even a few times he'd wished him dead, although he'd never actually meant it. Regardless, his wish had come true. He dropped to his knees next to the husk that had moments earlier been a living man. "Father," he said, "I didn't really want you to die." He knew there would be no response, but he needed to get the words out, to say them aloud and make them real, even if no one listened or cared.

The Draegoran sheathed the blade. From his pocket, he produced two coins and tossed them onto the table. They clacked across the surface before sliding to a stop. "Payment for the child." Stepping over the remains, he caught Riam by the wrist and pulled him, unresisting, past the astonished magistrate.

"You killed him. You just . . . killed him. Right in front of the boy."

The Draegoran ignored the magistrate. He dragged Riam out of the house and across the dirt yard to his horse where he tossed the boy up onto the saddle. He checked the cinch strap before untying the reins and mounting up behind.

He shifted his weight back and forth, settling himself. "You coming?" he said flatly to Ferrick.

"But . . . but . . . why?"

"Better I killed the old man while he watched than to sit here and discuss the reason in front of him. You'll have a formal edict to post before I leave town." He lifted the reins and paused. "Oh, and I'll need another horse for the boy by nightfall." The Draegoran snapped the reins, leaving Ferrick standing in the yard.

They rode down the dirt rut leading to town. When the path made a sharp turn, Riam had a last look at the only home he'd ever known. Other than Ferrick struggling to pull his bulk up onto his horse, the outside of the house looked the same as it did every other day.

CHAPTER 2

D avisha was broken, and Father wasn't home to fix her.

Nola slipped the small yellow dress off the doll's delicate body and spread it out beside her on the porch swing. She frowned at the pieces in her hands. Mother had helped her name the doll years ago, which explained why it had an Arillian name—well, that and because the wood was the color of oiled bronze, a close match to her and her mother's skin.

Davisha was one of her oldest dolls, too, and it was the only one she owned that came from her mother's homeland. All the ones made here in Steading Rock were carved from lighter wood or were painted in creams or whites. She'd had Davisha for nearly as long as she could remember, but she didn't cry. She was far too old to shed tears over a doll—that's what Mother told her.

Nola looked down the road that led away from her home, peering between the rows of nut and fruit trees, wishing her father would appear in the sea of green leaves and gray-brown trunks. He was supposed to be back tonight. He would fix the doll—he could fix anything—as long as Mother didn't throw it out first.

She hoped he wasn't delayed. Father traded all across

the lands of the Covenant and beyond sometimes, depending on the time of year, and his return was never precise. But this time was different. Tomorrow would be her twelfth birthday, and—by chance—it would also be the day the Draegorans tested her.

Not that the test mattered. Her mother was Arillian, and the Draegorans never chose Arillians. In fact, no one from Steading Rock had ever been taken for as far back as old Lemara could remember. Nola still had to go, but it didn't make her nervous or scared. She would go in the morning and then return home for presents and sweets.

As if thoughts of Lemara summoned the old house servant, the front door swung open. "Nola, come inside. It's time to wash up for dinner." The white-haired woman held the door wide with one hand and waved Nola inside. She paused. "Oh, you've broken Davisha. Fallen's grace, what happened, child?" The old woman left the door standing open and hurried to Nola's side.

"She fell off the swing while I was watching for Father. He's supposed to be back tonight."

"Let me see her."

Nola held the pieces tightly in her hands, afraid the woman would decide there was no saving the doll.

"Come, come, child. I won't hurt her."

Nola knew that. It was a doll, not a person. *I'm about to be twelve, not five. I'm not a baby.* To prove it to herself, she took a deep breath and placed the broken doll into the woman's hands.

Lemara pulled the pieces close to her face. A dull, white film had thickened over the house servant's pupils through the last few years, making her sight poor. She twisted the pieces this way and that, lining up the jagged edges. She tsked her tongue several times while she worked at it. "I don't see why a little hoof glue won't hold her together. She'll have an awfully big scar, but scars aren't such a bad thing." Lemara reached out and tapped Nola's nose with a bony finger. "Scars help us remember who we are and what we've been through."

Nola nodded solemnly at the woman's words, but she didn't exactly agree. She certainly didn't want any ugly scars or the pain that came with them.

"Pick up her dress, and we'll take her inside. I'll put her

in the kitchen for your father to look at when he gets home, but don't you go bothering him the moment he arrives, especially if it's late. He'll be tired from traveling, even if he pretends otherwise."

"Yes, ma'am."

Dinner came and went, and they were eating dessert when the rhythmic clomp of horse hooves and the creaks and jangles of wagons and harnesses came from outside the house. Throughout the meal her mother hadn't said a word and barely touched her food, but all thoughts of the pudding and her mother's unusual silence were pushed aside by the sound of the wagon train returning.

"Father's back!" Nola shouted. She jumped to her feet.

"Of course he is. Now sit back down and finish. You are a young lady now. If you want to impress your father, show him how grown up and proper you are."

Nola frowned, but she plopped back down. Normally, she and her mother would run to the porch, play fighting and teasing one another to be the first outside—and Mother always let her win. *Why the change? Is it because I'm going to be twelve or because of the testing?*

"Lemara!" her mother called.

The old servant poked her head into the dining room. "Yes, Mistress Menovar?"

"Could you please prepare a plate for my husband? I'm sure he'll be thankful after such a long time away from your kitchen."

Nola loved the sound of her mother's voice, especially when she was trying to sound proper. Despite her years in Nesh, she still spoke with an accent. Nola's friends said it made her sound dumb, but to Nola, it made her exotic and special.

"Yes, ma'am. Started as soon as I heard the wagons. My vision may not be what it used to be, but I can still hear a butterfly scratching at a flower." She winked at Nola. "I'll have a bath drawn up after dinner as well. Can't have him soiling clean linens with dust from the road."

Nola finished her pudding, barely tasting it even though it was her favorite. Her foot bounced next to the chair, moving faster as time went by. She knew there were things Father had to oversee before coming inside. Wagons would need unloading into the storehouse and animals fed and stabled. He would also make sure the men who didn't have homes nearby were situated in the bunkhouse and that the work kitchen was preparing enough food for them. *But he's been gone so long, and it's taking forever!*

It seemed like half the night went by before she heard his boots tromping across the porch.

"Father!" Her chair slid halfway across the room, and she was running to him as soon as the door opened. She threw her arms around his wide waist, not caring if her mother was angry or what she'd said about being proper. "I knew you'd be back for my birthday!"

"Hello, Kit," he said. His rough beard rubbed the top of her head as he lifted her into the air and twirled her around in a quick spin. "By Sollus, you grow a hand every time I leave and return. You're almost too big for me to lift!"

"You were gone so long this time."

"I went all the way to Hammisal." He leaned in close to her ear and his beard tickled her cheek. "That's Arillia's capital. You have an uncle and a grandmother there."

"I know, Father. You tell me all the time."

"And how is Tamuhd?" her mother said coldly. "Still trying to rob us blind?"

Father chuckled. "Your brother would take the horse and wagons in payment for 'all the good deals' he's given us over the years if I let him. Four years since I saw him last, and he's still complaining about my stealing you away and what it's done to your mother. She is fine, by the way, though she still refuses to say your name. Instead, she asks how 'my wife and the child' are doing. She's a stubborn woman."

Mother pretended not to hear the last comments, but Nola could see the way she stiffened. Mentioning Feyza, her foreign grandmother, was never allowed. Nola didn't know what had caused the fight between her mother and grandmother, but she suspected it had to do with marrying Father. She had no idea why that was such a bad thing. Mother and Father loved each other. That was all that mattered.

"Did you remind that backstabbing, goat-smelling thief that he still owes you for saving his life? He'd steal the boots off your feet and not even show you the courtesy of hiding them if you let him."

Father held up his palms. "Peace. We did well, and your family treated our dealings fairly."

"You only think you did well because that's what he wanted you to believe. There's no such thing as 'fair dealings' when it comes to trade in Arillia, *especially* between family members."

"Enough, woman. I didn't drive two horses lame hurrying home to argue about family and trade. I came for a birthday . . . and to bring this." He pulled the pack he carried off his shoulder and withdrew a small, plainly wrapped package.

Nola clapped her hands together. "Thank you, Father!" She pulled the package from his hand and gave it a shake. It rattled softly. "What is it?"

"You'll have to wait until tomorrow to find out."

"Father! Please . . ." she whined. "It's mean to show it to me and not let me open it. It's nearly my birthday already."

He plucked the package from her hand and held it out of reach. "Tomorrow, Kitten," he said, using the full word instead of the usual "Kit" for short as he always did when pretending to be stern.

"Perhaps she *should* open it tonight." Her mother said. "What if . . ." She let the words hang instead of finishing.

Nola's mouth fell open. Mother never bent on anything.

"Nonsense. We've nothing to worry about. We'll go into town for the testing and be back by midday." He set the package on the table. "Now, what is there to eat? I'm starving, and it smells fantastic. I haven't had a decent meal since I left. I'd eat a maston if you put it in front of me. Sit down, Kit, and I'll tell you all about my trip. You won't believe what happened when we crossed the desert."

Between mouthfuls of Lemara's stew, Father told her about a one-armed man who played the saddest, most beautiful music he'd ever heard, and how they'd nearly lost a wagon to bandits before his men fought them off. Then, the most amazing thing happened at an oasis. A whole band of Esharii had arrived in the middle of the night.

"I thought there would be a battle for sure, but none of them will fight near water in the desert. It's against their rules—their edicts or some such. Never knew the swaugs had any laws, but I thank the Fallen they do, or I don't know how many men or wagons we'd have lost. Maybe everything.

"I even spoke to one. I tell you, except for the accent and face paint, I could have been talking to a fellow landowner, not savages. It was a peculiar thing—as if raiding and killing our people for a thousand years never happened. They were willing to trade, too, but they owned little of value other than the rings in their beards. And their women . . ."

"What about *their* women?" Nola's mother said.

"Easy, love. They stayed to themselves and well away from us. Palest skin you ever saw, though, and so little clothing . . ."

Mother's eyes narrowed to slits before Father realized what he was saying.

". . . it was shameful! Disgusting, even. Who would want skin so pale and ugly?"

"Uh-huh."

Father quickly changed the subject. "Made a fortune in Galtare off your brother's goods. The ivory and rope went so fast I should've charged double what I did, but we paid for the whole trip with half the wagons still full." He went on about goods and market prices up and down the coast.

The rest of the time he spoke, her mother sat in silence, staring at her tea. She didn't even say anything when Father cursed about the tariffs in Thae. Something was definitely wrong. Mother never ignored talk of money.

Nola's thoughts drifted elsewhere when Father dove into the countless small details of the trip. She stared at the small wrapped package, imagining a jeweled necklace, then an ivory brush, a fine worked bracelet, and a silver locket—so many possibilities it drove her crazy. Her thoughts never returned to the broken doll that needed fixing or to tomorrow's testing.

CHAPTER 3

"They are all here?" The Draegoran handed the reins to Riam and strode toward the children without waiting for the magistrate's answer.

Fourteen children stood lined up in the town square with family members close behind. The sun blazed above them, the season just turning into high summer, and mothers and sisters fanned themselves to keep the afternoon heat at bay. No more than ten or twelve faded buildings surrounded them, forming a rough square around a communal well, but a crowd of over a hundred gathered around the edges. The yearly testing brought in all the outlying farmers and landowners, even those who didn't have children. No one wanted to miss the chance of something new to talk about. Riam, however, was bored.

"They are all here, sir. Same as every year. All the children in Steading Rock and the outlying homesteads who turned twelve during the past year." The magistrate spoke in a rush while hurrying to keep up. Unlike Ferrick back home, the magistrate was a thin, hairless man with a narrow nose like a sparrow's beak. Sweat beaded on the man's bald head.

Riam drew lines in the dirt with his foot while he waited.

This was the third town in the last tenday, and he still didn't
know what the Draegoran wanted with him or why he'd
been taken. It felt like he was the only one who didn't know
by the way people stared at him. He'd tried talking to the
Draegoran, to ask him, but the man who'd killed his father
didn't speak much. He gave commands mostly, telling him
when to eat, when to sleep, and what to do. About the only
things Riam had learned were that the Draegoran was not,
in fact, a demon and that he had a name—Gairen.

The days with Gairen were far different than the company
of his father and brother. While they'd never been a happy,
cozy family, they'd still spoken to each other throughout the
day. Gairen issued his commands and kept to himself.

It hurt when he thought of Father, and he both worried
about and missed his brother Lemual terribly, but in some
ways, he was getting used to it. All he'd known his whole
life was his father's anger, even when he'd done what he was
told. He'd spent his childhood learning to avoid Father's
wrath and the back of his hand. So far, Gairen never threatened or struck him.

The only emotion the man had shown, besides that first
day in the farmhouse, was when Riam had reached for a
sword one night at camp. He wasn't going to take it or anything. He'd merely wanted to touch it to try and puzzle out
the unusual crystal. It pulled at him all the time, and he
wanted to know why. He'd thought Gairen was sleeping,
but before he could get close to the sword, Gairen seized
him firmly by the wrist.

"Don't ever touch a Draegoran's blade. That's a fast way to
a bad death. Besides, you'll be tired of blades soon enough."

There was no anger in the words, but his face had been
cold and dark in the dim light of the campfire. Riam didn't
understand what he meant, but he'd kept quiet. That was
another lesson he'd learned from his father, how to hold his
tongue and not ask questions.

Gairen drew one of his swords and stepped up to the
first child. Around the square, the crowd stirred and pointed.
He held the blade reversed, like a knife, with the blade
pointed down and the pommel above his thumb and forefinger. As usual, he said nothing to calm the children or
reassure the nervous parents behind them. There were only
the controlled, purposeful movements with which he did

everything. It was as if he wore a mask. He could have been dressing a rabbit for the skewer for all the emotion on his face. The children were simply items that needed to be checked and discarded. The one he tested now had sandy brown hair that was cut unevenly, like Lemual's.

Riam groaned. *Why does everything have to remind me of Lemual?*

He went back to drawing on the ground to distract himself, but it didn't help. *Where is Lemual, and what has he been doing for the last tenday?* He couldn't picture his brother remaining to work the farm, especially if there was a choice in it. Farm work wasn't something Lemual liked very much.

With no one to pay the rent, the landowner would take the land back. That meant another family would come. It was like the farm would be replanted, just like one of the fields, only with people. Riam liked that thought. Maybe it would become a nice place with a real family.

From there, Riam's thoughts turned darker. *What if Lemual is dead?* He'd heard his brother return from town before Gairen and the magistrate arrived, so he'd assumed Lemual had remained hidden in the barn. *What if he hadn't? What if Gairen had seen him first? Would Gairen have hurt him?* Gairen didn't do anything without a purpose, and Riam could see no reason for hurting Lemual. *But he did kill Father. . . . Stop it!* Riam told himself. Lemual was fine, and he was old enough to take care of himself. *But what had he done after finding Father dead? Is he following us from town to town, trying to get me back?* He should have caught up to them by now. *So, then, where is he? What if he'd been injured or robbed?*

"This one has the blood."

Riam's head snapped up to see Gairen standing in front of a girl with bobbed hair and dark-colored skin. The crystal in the sword glowed yellow, nearly as bright as the afternoon sunlight, and it created long shadows behind the other children in line. The girl slumped backward, and a big, bearded man caught hold of her. The girl's mother, a dark Arillian woman in an expensive dress, grabbed the arm of the bearded man, and the people on either side moved as far away as they could without getting out of line, distancing themselves from the family.

Riam felt bad for the girl. If it was anything like his experience, he knew she felt like emptying her stomach.

The glow from the sword faded. "The girl goes with me in the morning. You have until then to say your farewells." Gairen withdrew two coins from inside his shirt. "Your payment." He held two gold dregs out to the bearded man—a small fortune, even to a landowner. Neither the man nor the woman moved toward the money.

"I don't want the money," the woman said in a thick accent, her voice rising as she spoke. "I want to keep my daughter."

The husband stared at the ground between his feet. His face was red above his beard. Riam knew anger when he saw it. The man wasn't angry. It was something else.

"We have no choice," he said. He kept his head down to avoid looking at either his wife or Gairen.

"I don't care what your Covenant says." The woman waved her hands in the air frantically.

"Woman, this isn't the place—"

"But he's going to take her—"

The man's head came up. "I said, not here. Look around. You'll only make it worse."

The woman slowly took in the crowd and the hushed conversations that surrounded them. "But, Dar!" she pleaded.

"No!"

She searched the onlookers for support. When no one stepped forward, she pulled herself up tall and lifted her chin, salvaging what dignity she could. She wiped the tears from her face. "I should never have come to this forsaken place. My family will hear of this."

The bearded man flinched, but he pulled his shoulders back and faced Gairen. He took the dregs from the outstretched hand as if they were far heavier than only two small coins.

The girl rubbed at her forehead. "I saw myself as a baby, and you and Mother were so young. We were riding across the desert to escape something." She saw the coins in her father's hands. "What is happening? Why is he paying you?"

"Have her back here a sandglass after sunrise tomorrow and no later. Make sure she eats first and has on suitable clothes for traveling—trousers or breeches, not a dress. No more than a small pack she can carry to hold anything you want to send with her. She'll receive new clothing in Hath, so don't waste space for a spare set."

"What does he mean? Where am I going?" The girl looked back and forth between her parents. "You can't let him take me away!"

"Hush, Kit. We'll talk on the way home."

"I'm not going with him! Why aren't you telling him no?"

"Yes, tell her why you cower and do nothing," the mother said.

"Stop it! Both of you!" the bearded man's voice boomed out across the square.

The girl flinched away and slid under her mother's protective arm.

"Not more than a glass after sunrise," Gairen repeated. "Do not seek to flee or make me come for her." Gairen moved to the next child in line.

Just like that, the exchange was over, and the bearded man hustled his family down the street.

Gairen touched the hilt to the remaining children one by one. He said nothing more, and after he finished, he and the magistrate returned to the horses where Riam waited.

"They can all go. I'll take the boy to an inn and meet you at the hall for our remaining business." He took the reins from Riam.

The magistrate pointed down the wide dirt track that served as the town's main street. "The Bull is a good place. Stay away from the other inn."

"I saw it when we arrived. It'll do." Gairen paused to look at the drawing in the dirt—it was obviously a sword—and frowned before leading the horses away.

Embarrassed, Riam rubbed his foot across the drawing to erase it. He hadn't even thought about what he was making.

"Arrogant bastard," the magistrate mumbled, then remembered Riam. "You didn't hear that." He gave Riam a hard stare to make sure he understood before addressing the people on the street. "You may all go. The testing is complete," he yelled out. The crowd largely ignored him, and knots formed to gossip.

"Poor Darrel. I hope he knew this might happen," a nearby woman said.

"There'll be problems in that house tonight for sure if

he didn't," a man with a pointed beard and a thin mustache said and chuckled.

"Serves him right for marrying an Arillian. They're notoriously unfaithful," the woman replied. "And with him away so much . . ."

"Could have been passed down. Skips a generation sometimes."

"Bah, never had one in his family before, and I've never seen a dark-skinned Draegoran. Done it for the coin. I'm sure of it," said an elderly man with white hair. "An Arillian will sell anything if the price is right. Can't ever trust 'em."

Riam finished scratching out the drawing and ran to catch up with Gairen.

If the Bull was the better of the two inns, Riam hated to see what the other looked like. From the outside, the inn was past its prime, with a washed-out, dingy appearance that came from too many seasons and too little care. Several boards were cracked and split, and the roof of the porch bowed down in more than one place. Few could afford paint on the plains, even if it saved money in the long run. The owner of the inn was no different, with the exception of a faded, life-size image of the inn's namesake painted on the wall of the second floor. At one time the mural might have been black, but the years had faded the powerful-looking bull to a dull brown. Yet even with the neglect, the inn had to be better than another night on the ground.

Gairen handed the horses off to the inn's stable boy, a lad no older than Riam with bright red hair that was unlike any color Riam had ever seen. Riam tried not to stare as Gairen flipped the redhead a copper dreg and led the way through the open double doors.

Inside, the main room of the inn was well lit by open-framed windows. Benches and chairs sat around the room's eight or nine tables, and a small stairway climbed to rooms on the second floor. Like the outside, the walls of the room were unpainted, but at least there was oil rubbed into the furniture and the floors were clean. Riam had scrubbed the wooden floor and the table back home enough to know that someone cared a great deal for at least the inside of the inn.

Even with the windows open, the room was warmer than was comfortable, and the smoke of burning torgana leaves made Riam's nose itch. The sweet odor almost hid the smell of old food and sweat that permeated the room. Father had smoked torgana leaves when he could afford them. Ferrick had asked his father why he smoked the things when they caused your gums to rot and your teeth to fall out. His father had told the magistrate where he could shove his teeth and his advice.

The other inns they'd stayed at while traveling had been empty. Not this one. Men and women sat and talked or gambled with small tiles. Riam had never been in a room with more than four or five people in his life. This one was crowded and loud. Between the town center and the inn, it seemed nobody had anything to do.

"Doesn't anyone work in this town?" Riam asked.

"Today is Tenth Day. Most shops are closed, so the tradesmen and workers have the day to themselves." Gairen approached a small man wearing a grease-stained apron. A jagged scar ran down the man's cheek, and his jaw sat at a crooked angle. The man's beady, close-set eyes narrowed when he caught sight of them.

"I need a room for a night and food."

"Ye'sir." The words ran together. "Up stairs, lath' on the right's open. Comes with a meal for one and clean water. I'll throw in food for the boy since I've plenty prepared for the crowd, but the mornin' meal'll cost you extra." He pointed at a small empty table. "Sit, I'll bring food and the key. Stewed lamb today." He turned away.

"Wait," Gairen said. The word wasn't spoken loudly, but it was clearly a command.

The man was obviously busy with the crowd, but he stopped. His eyebrows scrunched together in impatience.

"I'll return in a sandglass or so. Until then, keep an eye on the boy."

"This isn't—"

"A glass. Maybe two. Make sure he eats. I'll take my food in the room when I return."

The man clearly didn't agree, but before he could argue,

Gairen disappeared out the door. He stood, mouth open, as if considering whether he should yell after the Draegoran. He decided against it.

"No trouble, boy." He gestured to the small empty table. "Sit."

"He can sit with me. I'll take care of him," a well-tanned man with foam in his beard called out. The customers nearby laughed.

"Hey, Jeba, I didn't know you took care of children. Could I bring my two little ones over?" another man called. "Haven't been able to get the wife's skirts up in daylight since they were old enough to walk." This brought more laughter.

Jeba's face puckered around the scar and reddened. "You're both real funny. How 'bout I call your tabs due 'fore I serve you another drink?"

Both men opened their eyes and mouths wide, feigning shock.

"And what are you grinnin' at?" Jeba asked Riam.

Riam sat down quickly and turned his eyes to studying the four men who sat gambling at the next table. They wore baggy colored shirts that laced at the sleeves and hung loose on the arms, brown or black trousers, and plain leather shoes with leather laces. Riam knew farmhands. He'd seen plenty back home. While these men were not richly dressed, they were too well dressed to be seasonal farmhands.

Father always complained of the large farmsteads that were wealthy enough to hire the seasonal labor that came up from the Free Cities of Thae at the end of winter. He'd always said that if he had the dregs to hire a few Thaens, then he'd be able to raise enough crops to make a profit. But Father had never wanted to work harder than he had to, and he'd never planted more than enough to get by and pay the landowner. It didn't matter now in any case.

The last thought slipped in and punched him in the stomach. His eyes watered. He gritted his teeth and held the tears back. He hadn't cried yet, and he wasn't going to let himself do it here in front of these people. *Father never allowed me to cry over anything while he was alive, so why should I cry over him now?*

Clenching his teeth, he concentrated on the tiles the men gambled with. With matching pictures, dots, and dashes, they built houses that weren't really houses and wheels that were actually spokes. Puzzling out how it worked slowly pushed thoughts of his father to the back of Riam's mind, and the tightness in his chest eased.

Aside from the bearded man who'd made the joke about Jeba watching his children, there was a man with a dangling silver earring who didn't say a word. The third was thin and puffed on a rolled torgana leaf. When he opened his mouth to speak, sure enough, there were gaps from missing teeth. The last was an ox-size man who had a wide face and big, meaty hands. He continually frowned and tapped at the table, counting in his head. Only a few copper dregs remained in front of him. In fact, most of the money on the table was in front of the man who'd made the joke, and the others looked to be enjoying the game about as much as Riam enjoyed shoveling pig shit back home.

"Bah! Fillo, you're an idiot and smoke too much. It's rotting your brain. When was the last time we needed the Covenant? Forty . . . fifty years ago? Not in my lifetime." The wide-faced man paused long enough to lean over and spit on the floor. "It's high time we followed the example of those up in Mirlond. Heard they got a new high landowner at the beginning of summer when the old one fell out of his chair dead. The Lion of West, they call him. First thing he did was break with the Covenant and exile all the Draegorans."

"Where'd you hear that?"

"A peddler came by my shop a few days ago to replace a broken strap on a harness. Told me all about it while I made a new one."

"I didn't hear anything," the man with all the money said.

"He was only passing through and in a hurry for some reason or other. Something to do with his family in Chalt. He didn't stay to sell anything."

"What else he have to say?"

"Not much. Only that they were hiring anyone with a sword or bow they could find and that Mirlond's army was already double what Draegoran law allows."

"That'd be the Church of Man's doing. Too many of them crazies up in Mirlond. This 'Lion' has signed his own death warrant. All the soldiers in the world won't stop the Draegorans." It was the first time the one with the earring spoke. The others seemed to agree with his assessment.

"Doesn't bode well. If Mirlond tries to break away from the Covenant, it'll be folk like us end up paying the price."

"It won't be us. Even if they're dumb enough to rebel— and I'm not saying I believe it—they're not going to attack anyone. They'll be too busy trying to hold off the Draegorans."

"Might be us. If they build a big enough army . . . well, then, where do you think the Draegorans will get an army of their own? They'll levy it from the other lands, and we're the closest."

"Well, it's only a rumor. Most likely they're only gathering men to try and retake the Green Isles when winter comes like they do almost every year."

Jeba returned and set a bowl of stewed meat and a cup of water on Riam's table. "Eat up," he said. He looked at the floor, his eyes narrowing. He turned to the wide-faced man. "And you, you screet's ass, stop spittin' on my floor."

"Sorry, Jeba." The man rubbed his foot over it.

"Oughtta make you scrub the whole Fallen place."

Riam took a bite of the stew and dove for the cup of water. The meat had begun to turn, and they were using hot pepper to cover the sour taste. He snatched the cup and drank half of it before the pain subsided. He blew out between his teeth to cool his tongue. The meat wouldn't hurt him—Fallen knew, he'd eaten enough half-turned meat back home—but he was going to need more water and to take smaller bites. He ate slowly, following it with sips from the cup while watching the men talk and play. The subject of Mirlond and the Draegorans didn't come up again, moving instead to complaints about wives and work.

Long after he ate all the stew he could manage, a new group entered the inn—three young men wearing soft linen shirts and knee-high boots that were shined black with only a hint of dust from the road. They were only a few years older than Lemual, and they carried blades.

Landowners . . . or at least the sons of landowners.

Where Gairen's weapons where short and sturdy, these were long and narrow, with ornate metal bands that swirled about the hilts. Even with their length, they didn't look like they'd do much good against the simple strength of Gairen's heavier blades.

"I told you, Mardin, nothing but farmers and fleas in

this town, and no whores," said one. He had short brown hair and round cheeks, and his face and neck looked like he'd never lost any of his baby fat.

"Probably only do it with sheep around here," Mardin said. Like the first, his blond hair was also short, but where the first man was pudgy, Mardin was big without the fat. His muscles bulged under his shirt.

The wide-faced man at the table next to Riam started to rise, but the man with the earring put a restraining hand on his shoulder.

The third and tallest newcomer scanned the inn and saw Riam. "They've got a boy. Maybe you could rent him." The other two laughed.

"Wouldn't mess with the boy," Jeba said. He limped toward the newcomers. "He's with the Draegoran."

"Well, I'm sure the man can share," the short fat one said. "We've just come from seeing him dispatch *justice* on a few criminals." He drew out the word *justice* sarcastically. "He seems like an efficient fellow, and sharing makes life more efficient. Now why don't you be efficient and bring us a bottle of wine." He smirked, pleased with his own simple wit.

"Maybe you've had enough already," Jeba said.

The tall one ignored him. "Efficient." He chuckled as he led the three to the only empty table in the room and spun the chair backward before straddling it. He rested an arm on the chairback. "That's a good word for the man. Stabbed those bastards through the heart and sucked the life out of them. One-two-three, just like that while they were tied up." He made three quick stabbing motions in the air.

"Magistrate should have done it himself. No one deserves to be drained like that."

"If the magistrate did, he'd end up with his hands behind his own back waiting to get stuck like the others."

"That's my point. We don't need them. All the magistrates and landowners should stand against them."

"You're all talk, Orin. You've never faced the Esharii," Mardin said. "My family's lands are near South Pass. Ask the people there, and you'll hear a different story. A Draegoran's about the only thing in this world that'll make the tribesmen think twice about raiding our lands, and even that doesn't keep them away all the time."

"Pshaw," Orin said. "You've never actually seen an Es-harii either. It's all a big scam to keep us under their heel. The Esharii haven't gathered with any real strength in years, and Arillia is crumbling to nothing. So what do they do that's so important?" He spoke louder. "I'll tell you. Nothing. All they do is get rich and fat off the taxes we pay."

The tall man looked nervous. "Shut up, Orin."

"A wise idea," came a voice from the doorway.

The newcomers' heads whipped around as Gairen entered the inn. He strode calmly by the young landowners, brushing up against the fat one as he passed.

The fat one kept his gaze on the table.

"We didn't mean anything," Mardin said. "My friend is a bit loud when he drinks."

Gairen ignored them but kept his eyes on the fat one while motioning to Jeba. "Bring my food and water upstairs. The key to the room, if you please?"

"Last room on the right. Bring the food right up." Jeba pulled an iron key from his pocket and tossed it through the air.

It was a bad throw. The key would sail well behind Gairen, but at the last instant he reached back. He never took his eyes off the three young landowners. The key smacked his palm, and he closed his fist around it.

"Would be nice if everyone were that efficient," Gairen said.

The fat one swallowed hard. There was sweat on his forehead.

"Upstairs," Gairen told Riam.

By the time he climbed out of his chair to follow, Gairen was already moving up the stairway.

"Son of a bitch scared the piss out of me."

"Must have been right behind us when we came in."

"You boys're lucky," Jeba said. "That Draegoran is as high rankin' as I've ever seen. Tell by the marks on his skin."

CHAPTER 4

Five days passed, and already Riam hated the girl. Her name was Nola, and on the first day she'd sobbed continually. Riam knew what it was like to be sad and alone, so he'd said nothing that day, allowing her to come to terms with leaving. He even let her cry against his back, although it made him feel uncomfortable and foolish. Now he envied that first day and wished she'd fall off the back of the horse they rode double so he could simply ride on without her.

She would not stop talking. She went on and on about her parents and her home, she asked questions about everything, and she wouldn't leave him alone.

It didn't help that they were moving east, away from the farmlands of Nesh and through the Dry Plains. Few lived in the high desert between Nesh and Yaden, and Riam could see why. Just looking at the baked earth told him the soil wouldn't grow crops even if there was enough water to irrigate, which there wasn't.

Worse, for the last three days the weather had been oppressively hot with no wind, so they both smelled, and their clothes remained wet where they pressed against each other. Yet the stifling heat only gave Nola another subject to talk about.

Riam was miserable, and even Gairen had given up on

telling Nola to be quiet and made long scouting trips ahead and to their flanks. He was on one of these now, having told Riam to ride toward a tall hill on the horizon.

"I love horses. My father only started letting me ride alone during the last year. What about you?"

"Sometimes," he said. He answered all her questions with only a word or two and an occasional short sentence. They were about the only things he could get out before she would start up again. He was convinced that her questions were designed only to create short, regularly spaced pauses in which to breathe.

"We have a big orchard with a pond at the center. Not like here. We haven't seen a tree or any trace of water since we left Steading Rock. Just grass. Oh, and rocks. I wish we'd see trees soon—or a whole forest. I've never seen a real forest before, and it would certainly be cooler riding in the shade."

Riam guided the horse around a clump of the tall grass. It was the only thing that grew in the area aside from a few thorny shrubs. This far into summer, the grass was dead and brown. Large patches were scattered out across the plains for as far as he could see. In some places they reached the foot of the stirrups, which was dangerous since they hid holes that could snap a horse's leg. Not to mention the snakes or marcats that hunted in the rocky, sparse grassland. Marcats generally avoided people and horses, but if they rode through a den, the cats would fight to defend their young. Tricolor—brown, black, and orange—and bigger than a farm cat, they were about the size of a dog or knee-high to a man. While their claws probably wouldn't bring down a horse, they could easily lame one.

He remembered his father cursing and throwing everything he could get his hands on the morning they'd lost all the brush hens they kept for eggs to a pair of the cats. The cats had bent the wire enough to gain access to the coop, but instead of going in and creating a commotion that would have woken the whole house, they'd come around to the other side and scared all the birds out into the fields. Lemual and Father were able to get a few of the birds back, enough to repopulate the flock, but most were scattered to the winds and hunted down over time. Instead of eating for one night, the big cats had kept themselves well fed for a season.

"I used to fish in our pond when Father was away. Did you ever fish back home?"

"Not really." Sweat trickled down the back of Riam's neck. Of course, seeing a marcat would break up the monotony of the plains and droning of Nola's voice. He hoped it wouldn't be many more days until they reached wherever they were going.

"Too bad. It really is fun, especially when you catch one that fights hard. Lemara, that's our house servant, she rolls them in flour before frying them in fat. Sometimes she lets me help. Once you get them into the flour, they don't smell so bad. Do you like fish?"

"Sure." In truth, Riam loved fish—it was a rare treat back home—but it didn't matter what he answered. Nola wasn't really listening. He used the same answer for most of her questions, and she never paused for an instant. He knew she was nervous and scared, but that didn't make it any easier. She wanted to talk, and he wanted to be left alone.

"I wonder if they fish where we're going. I'm sure they do. Once we get there, maybe we could go fishing sometime. I could teach you if you want."

"Sure."

"I bet servants do the fishing for the Draegorans. They must have lots of servants. They're richer than landowners. Father says the richer you are, the more servants you have. Maybe that's why we were taken, to become servants. How long do you think it will take to get there?"

"Not sure." They would leave Nesh when they made it to the end of the plains. Beyond was Yaden, where the long trains of empty wains came from every year to buy crops. He thought maybe the ocean and the Isle of Draegoras were on the other side of that. He'd spent close to two tendays riding with Gairen, but much of that had been zigzagging from town to town and not in a straight line. He had no idea how far they'd gone.

Nola continued talking about servants and what she thought they were supposed to do and not do.

He still didn't know why Gairen had taken them, but it seemed like an awful lot of trouble to go through for servants. Plus, the Draegorans had enough money to do anything or hire anyone they wanted. Whatever they'd been tested for, it definitely wasn't to be servants. Once again, he wished Lemual were here to explain things.

He checked the sun. It was straight above them, and the hill seemed to be just as distant. Nola chattered on behind him. He steered the horse around another clump of the tall grass. The day would never end.

They crested a small rise, and Riam brought the horse to a halt. Behind him, Nola described how best to care for hens in order to get the most eggs.

"There are riders coming this way," he said, interrupting her.

"What? Where?"

"Riders." He pointed off ahead and to the right.

Nola squirmed to look over his shoulder. "What should we do?"

The riders were still far enough away that it was anybody's guess how many there were. They'd obviously been spotted since the riders were coming straight toward them. It would be useless to try and hide.

Riam stood up in the stirrups and scanned the horizon. There was no sign of Gairen. He chewed on his bottom lip a moment before deciding that there wasn't anything they could do. "We'll keep moving. I'm sure Gairen knows where we are and has seen them."

"I wonder who they could be? Maybe there's another town nearby. Mom says . . ."

Riam groaned as Nola started off again. He did his best not to listen and watched the dust rise into the air behind the approaching riders. A short time later, Riam spotted a dust trail to his left, closer than the first and smaller, a single rider, and likely Gairen. Still unsure of what to do, but remembering his instructions, Riam continued forward.

Before long, the wavering image of the lone rider clarified to confirm it was Gairen, and a sandglass or so after that, Gairen was reining in next to them.

"There are riders coming," Nola blurted.

"It's a taulin. A Draegoran patrol. We'll wait for them near that low knoll." He pointed to a boulder-crested hill and kicked his horse.

They didn't wait long. Six men, riding in three pairs,

wound around the rocks to the top of the knoll. Lather and sweat outlined their saddles, and foam dripped from the mouths of their horses. They'd been riding hard.

The Draegorans all wore the same style of clothing, and all save one wore their hair long and tied back by a leather thong. Tattoos decorated the visible parts of their bodies. Most of the symbols were different, and there was no pattern, except that four of the six men had the same head of a wolf on the left side of their necks.

No, not six men. The lead rider was a woman wearing a tight leather vest that hid the outline of her body. It was her high cheekbones and sharp features that gave it away as they neared. She drew her horse up in front of Gairen, and the others formed up behind her. She may have been a woman, but there was nothing soft about her. Her face looked chiseled, with hard angles like the stones that capped the knoll around them. The outline of a war hammer marked her neck, and she was the only one with a tattoo on her face—a small crescent moon with a thin line completing the circle on her left temple.

He'd assumed that all Draegorans were like Gairen, carrying the same dual swords that he'd stared at for so many hours while riding, but the group carried a variety of blades in different sizes and lengths—two even had bows strapped to the backs of their saddles. Despite the variety of weaponry, however, all carried at least one blade with a white crystal in the hilt.

The woman spoke first. "Iya guyun sendol, kamutanil."

Riam's mouth hung open. He didn't understand a single thing she was saying.

"Karahm ferendum," Gairen replied.

Riam knew people spoke other languages in faraway places, but it was a shock to hear it for the first time. He could identify sounds, but it was as if someone had mixed up the order they were supposed to be in. It was both fascinating and frightening, and he was more than a little disappointed that he couldn't understand the conversation.

Nola fidgeted behind him. "I wonder what they're saying."

The Draegorans spoke rapidly and pointed in different directions. There was some kind of debate going on. One of them, one of the wolves as Riam thought of the four with wolf tattoos, kept pointing to the northwest. After several loud outbursts, the woman said something harsh and the man closed his mouth tight and stared at the back of her head with a sour expression.

Gairen listened to them for a time, but when he spoke, the newcomers went silent and sat up straight and attentive. Then they all turned to face him and Nola. It was uncomfortable, and he had the impression that they were all looking at him, not Nola. Gairen made another comment, and several of the newcomers appeared to agree with him before they returned to their discussion.

Riam baked in the sun while he waited for them to finish. There was at least a little wind when they moved. Sitting still in the heat made it much worse. Another obvious reason why nobody farmed this part of the plains—it was too Fallen hot. He unhooked a waterskin from the saddle and took long swallows.

"Don't drink it all. I want some."

Riam shook his head. It was a large skin. He couldn't drink it all if he wanted to. They passed it back and forth a few times before he put it back, still half full.

After what seemed forever sitting in the heat, the woman bowed her head respectfully. "Safe journey, Gairen."

"To you also, Shalla."

She turned her horse and led the group back down the knoll.

"They're searching for a band of Esharii that slipped over the mountains near North Pass. There's a stream a short distance ahead. We'll stop there to water and rest the horses. The taulin leader believes the Esharii are north and west of us, but we'll stay out of sight for the remainder of the day just in case. Once it's dark, we'll veer a little to the south to be safe and then ride fast until we make the outpost near Hath. We don't want to run into the Esharii out here on the plains."

"Where is Hath?" Nola said.

Gairen frowned, but he answered, "It's a small town a little over a day to the west, upriver of Ibbal. There's a Draegoran outpost near it that collects supplies for North Pass. It's also where those with the blood from Nesh are being gathered. Once there, the remainder of your travels

will be by boat." Gairen kicked his horse before she had
the chance to ask another question.

"Well, that was—"

"Yaw!" Riam snapped the reins. Nola grabbed his shirt to
keep from falling off. It was too bad the silence wouldn't last.

Riam stood next to the stream, keeping an eye on the
horses while they drank. Even near water, little grew—
mostly tufts of the tall, sharp grass. Nola was relieving herself behind a small hill, and Gairen knelt upstream, refilling
their waterskins.

Riam mulled over the words of the landowners back at
the inn while the horses drank. Gairen had killed again,
although killed wasn't exactly the right word. Riam understood that they were criminals and had done something to
deserve their deaths, but he had no idea what type of crime
merited death. *It would have to be something really bad, or
were they simply evil men?* He supposed this meant that
Father must have done something just as bad, or worse. *Did
that make Father evil?* For certain, he was callous and bitter, and he could be harsh when his mood was foul, but
Riam had never thought of him as evil. *He was . . . well, he
was just Father.*

Every story his brother ever told him held that the Draegorans were the evil ones, but—so far—Gairen didn't seem
like a bad man. Quite the opposite, actually, and while the
man wasn't exactly kind, his firm-but-fair behavior was far
better than the unreasonable fits of anger and punishment
Riam was used to. He kept waiting for that to change, for
Gairen to turn cruel and nasty, but it hadn't happened.

By the Fallen, he needed Lemual. Without him here to
explain things, that left only Gairen. Riam wanted to talk
to the Draegoran. No, that wasn't right. He *needed* to talk to
him. But he was scared—scared of both the man and the
answers. Riam stewed for a time chewing on his lip. Finally,
he couldn't wait any longer.

"Why'd you kill my father?" The question came tumbling out. It wasn't what he'd intended to ask, but his tongue
seemed to have a mind of its own.

Gairen paused from filling a waterskin. He scrutinized

Riam, sizing him up while deciding what to say. It was obvious he'd been caught off guard by the question.

Riam's confidence melted under the scrutiny, but he held his ground. He needed answers.

"I suppose you have a right to know," he said. "There's no easy way to say this, so I'll come right out with it. The man I killed wasn't your father. He was your grandfather."

Riam let it sink in. *What did the man mean, grandfather?* That couldn't be right. Lemual would have said something. Not once had his brother ever hinted at it. *Grandfather.* The word didn't feel right. *How could my father be my grandfather?*

"From what I felt, he killed your grandmother. He'd been drinking and it wasn't his intent. A man, however, is responsible for his actions no matter his intentions."

Riam had no words. His father . . . or grandfather was mean-spirited, but to kill his wife, Riam's grandmother. *How could that be?* Riam remembered the vision of the unknown woman being beaten. He remembered the smacking sound, and his stomach turned.

Fallen! I watched it happen.

"Your mother—"

"What about my mother?" Riam said defensively. "She died from a fall while riding when I was a baby." As soon as he said the words, he knew they weren't true. In the vision she'd sat by the fire, her eyes empty. He'd seen the knife. Even with the heat of the Dry Plains, he was suddenly very cold.

"Best to hear it all and get it over with. Your mother killed herself not long after your grandmother was murdered. He deserved execution for that as well. A man is also responsible for the consequences of what he fails to do."

Riam's chest tightened. He could barely breathe. "Why would she do that? That doesn't make sense. I still needed her."

Gairen shrugged. "Who can tell? Maybe to punish your grandfather or to get away from him. Maybe because she couldn't get over your grandmother's murder. When it comes to love and family, it's hard to understand what people do and things seldom make sense." There was pain in Gairen's voice—something deeper to his words.

Riam cared little about any deeper meaning. "But why

would she leave me?" He concentrated on the stream and the way the water churned along the bank. If he faced Gairen or looked him in the eyes he wouldn't be able to keep from sobbing. He bit down hard on his lip to keep it from quivering.

"There's no way to ever know the why. The crystal lets me feel some of the memories—the really strong ones—but it can't tell me what people think. I'm sure it had nothing to do with you and that she loved you. All you can do is try to understand it the best you can and make peace with what little understanding you come to." Gairen capped the waterskin and stood up. "Then you move on."

Somehow, there must be more. Gairen was holding things back, but everything the man said tore away the few memories he held true. *If he knows more, do I really want to hear it?* He couldn't bring himself to ask anything about his mother. He thought of asking about Lemual, but no, that might also lead to something horrible if Gairen had hurt him. It was safer to ask about things he had no memory of. He grasped at the first thing that came to mind. "Who was my grandmother?"

"I don't know. The magistrate said her name was Sen'lai. That's an Esharii name. Which is odd, because she couldn't have been Esharii, although I suppose it is possible that she was of mixed blood. Some Esharii captives escape and make their way back north, over the mountains. It's rare, but it happens—even more rare for one to do so with a child, but not impossible. Whatever the circumstances, it had nothing to do with her death. Your grandfather told the magistrate that she died milk sick, but the magistrate always suspected it was a lie."

"And my real father? I didn't see him in the vision. Do you know who he is?"

"He drowned when his ship sank a short time after you were born." Gairen looked away, out toward the horizon. "Best to leave it at that. Some things are better left alone, even when they're the truth. That's a hard lesson to learn, and even harder advice to follow."

"But—"

"We leave shortly after dark, and it will be a long night. You should get some rest." Gairen moved upstream, leaving Riam to his thoughts.

How could Gairen just leave it at that? Riam hadn't seen

so much as a glimpse of his real father in the visions. *Did Gairen learn more when he touched the sword to . . . to Grandfather? How did my real father drown? Had he even known about me, or had he known and left anyway? Did my real father know how bad it would be with Grandfather?*

Riam knelt at the water's edge. The ripples the horses made as they drank distorted his features. *What made Father . . . Grandfather so angry? So hateful?* In the span of a few moments, he'd been given glimpses of a grandmother he'd never known, a mother he barely remembered, and a dead father who'd abandoned him to a man who'd pretended to be his father. None of it made any sense.

Why hadn't Lemual ever said anything? Oh, Fallen, no. Lemual. The implications of the Draegoran's words cut him to his core. *Lemual isn't my brother! He lied to me, too.*

The answers only made him more confused and hurt, with more questions than before. It had to be a lie, an excuse to kill his father and take him away. He stood, fists clenched, preparing to tell Gairen that all Draegorans lied and were evil, that the man who'd raised him couldn't be his grandfather.

But he couldn't do it. Not once in all the days they'd been together had Gairen lied. The man simply answered questions the way he handled everything else, directly and openly. The truth was, Riam wasn't really angry with Gairen. That was the wrong person. It was his father . . . no, not his father. He would never think of him as Father again. But by any name, he was the man who deserved Riam's anger.

"Grandfather." He scrunched his nose at the distasteful word. That vile old man had destroyed his family. He'd even made Lemual, the only good thing he'd ever known, into a lie.

And now everything and everyone is gone. He picked up a rock. "I hate you. You ruined everything." He threw the rock as hard as he could at the stream. It skipped off the water and crashed into the grass on the far side.

"What are you doing?" Nola said from behind him. She couldn't see how red his face was or how close he was to tears.

He swung around. "Don't you ever stop asking questions? All you do is talk all day long about your *wonderful* family, or about your *big home* with orchards and fishing, or about whatever enters your empty head. When you're not doing that, you're asking stupid questions or stating the obvious. Can't you shut up for a change?" The wetness of his eyes made them feel larger. He was close to tears. He didn't want her to see him like this.

Nola stood rigid. "I'm soooo sorrrrry." She balled her hands into fists. "I was only trying to be nice and make friends with you, and I talk when I'm nervous! You don't have to be so mean!" She stomped off downstream.

"I'm not the mean one!" Riam yelled at her back. *I am nothing like my grandfather!*

CHAPTER 5

R iam sobbed. He yelled. He threw rocks at an imaginary grandfather until his arm hurt, and then he
flopped to a seat in the dirt by the stream. His anger
spent, he watched the sun fall and let the tears roll down
his cheeks. He was a hollow shell with little left inside, and
he would never get to tell his grandfather how he felt or
what he thought of him. In all likelihood, he would never
see Lemual again either. Lemual might really be his uncle
and not his brother—he wasn't sure what he was—but he'd
been something more than family. He'd been a friend. His
betrayal hurt the most, but he could forgive Lemual.

Riam threw a last rock at the water. "But not you,
Grandfather. You deserved more than a sword through the
heart."

He wasn't sure what that was, but the death seemed far
too simple and final. Through all of his life, the man had
never shown any remorse or sorrow for his actions, only
anger and blame. He should have given something back
before he died—something to make up for his shortcom-
ings. Instead, he'd been bitter to the end.

Riam was still sitting by the bank, well after dark, with
tears long dried, when Gairen came and put a hand on his
shoulder and told him softly it was time to ride.

He climbed into the saddle and put his hand down to help Nola. She ignored it and struggled to mount up behind him. After slipping several times, she managed to climb up using only the stirrup. She didn't put her arm around his waist to hold on. Instead she sat behind him with her arms crossed, and her elbows dug into his back painfully whenever the horse lurched.

The riding was slow and rough. Riam could barely see anything, so he gave the horse its head, trusting it to follow Gairen's mount. The unexpected dips and turns tossed them around in the saddle, threatening to throw them, and he could feel Nola stiffen the few times she was forced to hold on to him. Her elbows continued to dig into his back. He was sure she was doing it on purpose, but he didn't say anything. *What does she expect, that I should apologize? It isn't my fault!* He felt a pang of guilt at this. *It isn't hers either.* He still said nothing, though. He didn't know what to say, so they rode on in the heavy silence.

Sollus, the swift moon named for the last remaining God of Light, rose for its second trip across the sky. Almost full, it was bright enough to see by although it was still difficult to make out the ground in the shadows of the rolling hills. Sollus sped its way to the top of the sky as the ride went on. Riam hovered around the edge of sleep, and the night became a daze. Several times he fell asleep, and each time he would wake up when the horse lurched or when Nola hit him on the arm. Once, he dozed off and his head dropped backward, cracking Nola on the nose. He was sure it didn't hurt half as much as she complained it did, but he took her anger without saying anything other than mumbling an apology. Later, she was the one who kept falling asleep, and he held her arms to keep her from sliding off.

It was near morning, the sky behind them filling with early morning twilight, when Gairen stopped. Sollus was down to the opposite horizon, and something large and dark loomed in the direction they were traveling. Gairen stood in his stirrups and looked around before sitting back down. He moved his horse beside theirs and leaned in close.

"There are Esharii nearby, on both sides. I can't tell how many," he whispered.

Riam checked left and right. All he saw were shadows that could be anything.

Nola was excited. "What, where—" Gairen flattened his hand over her mouth.

"Hush! They have an okulu'tan with them—you call them spirit-takers here in Nesh—and the bastards can sense a hummingbird dodging through a hailstorm. He's using some trick I've never seen before to dull my sight, or I would've known they were there long before riding into an ambush." He turned his attention to Riam. "With luck, we'll slip by them, but if I tell you to ride, you ride as fast as you can. The forest isn't far, and the river is only a stead or so beyond. Keep going in this direction and you'll come to it. Once you get there, it's a day's ride downstream to the outpost. Don't wait for me and don't stop. I'll catch up. Understand?" Gairen's firm tone left no room for argument.

"Yes, sir. Ride hard for the river. Follow it downstream. Don't wait for you."

Gairen led them on as if nothing were out of the ordinary. They wound through the low ground around the hilltops to avoid being seen, but luck was not with them. The sunlight was just kissing the tops of the taller hills, lighting them up in gold, when there was a loud, high-pitched whistle behind them. Three riders came into view. One of the riders let out a loud, undulating yell, and all three drew long, curved blades and spurred their horses to full gallops.

"Go!" Gairen yelled. He drew one of his swords and turned to meet the oncoming Esharii.

Riam kicked his horse into a run, but at the top of the first rise he reined in to look behind them. Gairen rode straight for the oncoming tribesmen. The sun's rays reflected off his sword, highlighting both man and beast.

The Esharii warriors that barreled toward Gairen wore painted faces of faded green-and-black lines that continued down their arms and chests, standing out sharply against the pale skin of their bodies where it was exposed, and the swords they held were wide and heavy—the kind of weapons that would break bones as well as cut. The tribesmen raised their swords high into the air, ready to tear Gairen from the saddle.

The gap between the Esharii and Gairen shrank.

"What are you doing? Go!" Nola yelled.

The distance closed—fifty paces, twenty, ten. Gairen dropped his reins and drew the second blade. The ringing of metal striking metal filled the air, and the riders were past each other. One of the big Esharii blades spun through the air, a severed, green-striped hand still holding it. Its owner tumbled out of the saddle. The other two kept riding, straight toward Riam and Nola.

Nola pounded furiously on his back. "Go, you idiot!"

Riam kicked the horse, and they bolted down the far side of the hill. The rhythmic pounding of the horse's hooves and its labored breathing quickly drowned out the world around them. They went in a straight line, up and down the hills instead of around them. Riam could barely see the forest ahead.

They crested a rise, and an Esharii appeared on their right. He was close enough to see the white of his teeth against the green-and-black lines on his face, and Riam could almost count the rings woven into his narrow beard. Riam turned the horse to the left, angling to make it to the forest before the tribesman could cut them off. Once there, they might be able to lose the Esharii among the trees and vegetation.

Another Esharii with a wide black stripe across his eyes came into view on their left, and Riam turned the horse back to the right. He and Nola were now trapped, with tribesmen on both sides and pursuers behind. It was a flat-out race for the trees with the Esharii closing in.

"We're not going to make it!" Nola yelled.

Riam wrapped the reins around one hand and kicked the horse over and over, urging it to go faster. He held on to the saddle horn with the other hand while Nola's arms threatened to squeeze the air from his lungs as they galloped madly for the woods, trying to outrun the tribesmen.

They nearly made it. The forest was only a short distance ahead, when two more Esharii with swords drawn emerged from the tree line. The Esharii flanking them had driven them into these two, just like the wolves that hunted the farmlands back home. There was nowhere to go, except to try and race by them.

The gap closed. They would never make it by those blades, but the Esharii were riding side by side, and it gave Riam an idea. Riam nudged the horse to his right, the Esharii's left, in an attempt to stay away from the blades they carried.

Instead of trying to race by, Riam pulled hard on the reins at the last instant and slapped the horse on the opposite side of the neck with all his strength. The horse shied from the blow, putting the two Esharii directly in front of them. The horse tried to stop, but it was too late. They slammed into the first Esharii's horse at full speed, knocking it back into the second. Bones snapped and horses went down. Momentum threw Riam and Nola through the air, over the pile of animal screams and kicking legs. He landed hard, bouncing several times before sliding to a stop in the rough grass.

Riam climbed to his feet. His ears rang and his hand burned from the reins tearing free. Nothing felt broken, but his foot and hand throbbed. Nola lay nearby.

He pulled her to her feet. "Come on!" She stood blinking behind a mask of dirt and blood from sliding face-first on the ground. "We have to run!" He used his hand to swipe away as much of the blood and dirt from her face as he could and tugged on her arm. She began to move, following him in a slow, limping jog.

The other riders caught up with them. Riam glanced over his shoulder as one of the riders stepped from his horse in mid-gallop. The tribesmen timed it well, and he leaped through the air, tackling Nola and pulling her away. The second prepared to do the same to him. Riam cut to the left in front of the horse, barely escaping being trampled, and the tribesman misjudged his jump. The warrior landed and rolled. Coming to his feet, the Esharii charged after Riam.

Riam ran as fast as he could, but the tall grass tore at his arms and legs. There was no way he could outrun a full-grown man. When the tribesman caught up to him, Riam dropped to the ground and curled himself into a ball. The tribesman, still running at full speed, tripped and went sprawling. Riam darted off in a different direction.

He heard a horse behind him and changed direction several times, dodging through the grass. He expected the rider to do the same thing as the previous two, but this one anticipated his movements. A hand grabbed him by the back of his shirt and lifted him into the air. He swung his arms and squirmed, trying to break free. His shirt tore, but not enough to escape.

"Stop it, boy!" Gairen yelled. The Draegoran lifted him up over the front of the saddle and sped up, racing toward the woods. Riam did his best to hold on and keep the saddle from digging painfully into his side, but each bound of the horse slammed the saddle horn into his ribs.

They galloped into the trees with the Esharii behind them. Wind whipped Riam's clothes, and pine needles slapped his face and legs. He could only hang on limply, bouncing like a sack of vegetables, while the saddle jabbed into his side over and over again. His ribs were on fire, and each step of the horse was pure agony that made him whimper. Finally, when Riam thought he could take no more and would pass out, Gairen slowed the horse to a walk and then stopped.

"They've turned back." Gairen slid Riam to the ground and dismounted. He carried Riam to a bed of needles under a tree. "I'm going to water the horse, and then I'll take care of your hand."

Riam tried to sit up and stopped when pain shot down his side. His left hand was raw and bleeding, so he wiggled up against the tree trunk and used his other arm to lever himself into a sitting position. He panted from the effort, taking short breaths to ease the pain. One of his old leather shoes was torn open, and his foot was bruised and scraped. He could feel dirt and pine needles inside. He lifted his shirt gently. Dark bruises were already forming from his armpit to his hip. He touched one and winced. Gairen returned, carrying a saddlebag and a waterskin.

Awkwardly, Riam pulled off his torn shoe with his good hand. "You're not going back for Nola?"

"No use." Gairen dug around in one of the saddlebags and removed a small glass jar sealed with wax. Whatever was inside was thick and brownish yellow in color.

"What do you mean, no use? We can't leave her."

"We didn't leave her. She was taken." Gairen drew a short knife from his belt and carefully cut the wax around the edge of the jar. "Best hope now is that they are caught before they get back over the mountains."

Riam didn't like Nola much, but that certainly didn't mean he wanted to leave her with the Esharii. "Why didn't you stop them? There were only a few more."

"An Esharii warband has twenty to thirty warriors. This one had the spirit-taker with it, so there would be another ten or so pachna as his bodyguards. I'm good, boy, but not that good. I killed two and wounded a third. It was a close thing saving you."

Riam hadn't realized there were so many. "There must be something you can do."

"There is. We'll ride on to the outpost. Dying or getting captured won't get her back." He had the wax out now, and he laid it carefully on the pine needles. Using the knife, he stirred the pasty substance.

The words made sense, but, somehow, they felt wrong. *What if the Esharii had taken me instead of her? What if they had taken both of us? Would Gairen have ridden away and left us to be . . . to be . . . ? He didn't know what the Esharii did with children.*

He turned his attention back to Gairen. "What will they do with Nola?"

"Take her home and make a wife out of her. Trade her to another tribe. Make her a slave. Sacrifice her. I doubt even Sollus knows. You can never be sure what the tribesmen will do, but it was the Ti'yaks that took her, and they aren't the worst tribe as far as the Esharii go. At least they don't believe in torturing or eating people like the more remote tribes." He withdrew the knife. It was coated in the paste. "This will dull the pain and speed the healing. It'll also keep your hand from getting the rot. Don't let any get in your mouth. There's a fair bit of deathroot in it. It won't kill you, but it'll knock you out faster than a horse kick to the head."

Gairen spread the thick salve on Riam's side. He used only the flat of the knife and was careful not to touch the stuff with his hands. Riam caught a whiff of it and coughed. It smelled worse than a cage full of hens after a downpour, but everywhere the man applied it tingled and went numb.

Riam replayed the escape in his head. If he hadn't paused on the hill, or if he'd attempted to make it by the last two Esharii instead of barreling into them, Nola wouldn't have been captured. *It's my fault she's gone.*

Gairen seemed to read his thoughts. "Don't blame yourself, boy. You did as much as anyone could. You make the best choices you can, and then, right or wrong, you live with them. That's part of living. Worrying about 'what ifs' will only make you hesitate and fail."

"But it's my fault. I'm responsible."

"Maybe you are. Maybe you're not." He lowered Riam's shirt and took his hand to examine it. "I made a choice today, too. It was save you or her, but not both. You were still running, she was caught, so the odds were better going after you. If you need to blame someone, blame the Esharii for taking her, or blame me for dragging her from her home or for rescuing you instead of her." He turned Riam's hand palm up. "Open and close your hand while I wash it off."

Wincing, Riam did as he was told. Gairen uncorked the waterskin and used it to clean the wound. The cool water burned like a hot coal on Riam's palm.

He wasn't sure what Gairen was saying about who was to blame and who was at fault. His grandfather always blamed everyone else for his problems. He didn't want to be like that, but Gairen was nothing like the old man. It was confusing. He didn't know what to think.

"Good. Nothing damaged but the skin." He used Riam's shirt to blot away most of the water and blood. Picking up the knife again, he used it to spread the paste on Riam's palm.

"I still feel like I failed and that it was my fault."

"What you're feeling is guilt that you're here and she's not. That's normal. But you didn't make the Esharii come over the mountains. You didn't make Nola come with us. You ran like I told you to, and when it was obvious you wouldn't escape, you attacked by charging into them—hold your hand up."

"You saw that?"

Gairen pulled a small cloth from the saddlebag and tore it in two. With one half he cleaned the knife, careful not to touch the paste.

"It was both brave and foolish and lost a good horse, but the mere fact that you attacked when trapped tells me your grandfather didn't ruin you. You will do well when you reach the island." He tossed the dirty rag aside.

He picked up the other half of the cloth and wrapped Riam's hand. "I'm not telling you that you've no responsibility for what happened, far from it. What I'm telling you is that you didn't put yourself in the situation, you had the right intentions, and you made a decision. Can't ask for much more than that, and there's no changing what's done.

You can only come to terms with it and move on." He finished wrapping the cut and handed Riam the waterskin. "Drink as much as you need, but make sure you piss before we leave. We have a day's ride ahead of us once the horse is rested."

They ate a small meal of dried meat and hard bread. Riam sat with his stomach knotted, unable to stop thinking about the last words he'd spoken to Nola. He kept hearing her say she was sorry for talking so much. She didn't deserve the things he'd said, and—just like with his grandfather— he'd never be able to tell her what he truly felt. He'd been stupid and selfish.

When it came time to ride, the two mounted and followed the river downstream. The journey took them the remainder of the day, and it was dark by the time they arrived at the gates of the outpost, or at least what had once been the gates. Along with most of the wall, they'd been burned to the ground.

The Dark Gods did not return at once. The hole that opened was a fluke, created when two massive stars collided. Even with so much power released, the way back was no wider than a grain of sand, but it was enough for the dark ones to slip back into the universe.

When Parron, greatest of the Gods of Light, discovered the rift, it was already too late. There would be no tricking the enemy this time. The millennia outside the cosmos had made the Dark Gods insane, and only the destruction of all creation would sate their vengeance. There was but one solution to preserve the worlds of man.

The gods would have to fall.

—Edyin's Complete Chronicle of the Fallen

CHAPTER 6

R iam and Gairen reached the end point of their long ride, but by the damage, the outpost didn't look much safer than facing the Esharii on the plains. The front wall, originally built from timber, was nothing more than charred stumps lined up like the short, broken teeth of a bare-knuckled fighter. Sentries, spaced ten paces apart for the length of the missing wall, stood watch with soot-stained faces. All that remained of the gate was a set of twisted iron hinges that hung limply from the ruins of the frame.

Two men stood guard before the missing gates. They held spears instead of swords and, like the others manning the wall, wore leather vests over red undershirts. Riam and Gairen rode between them, and the men stood up straight and saluted, each touching the fingers of his right hand to his opposite shoulder and dipping his head.

Inside, the outpost was lit with iron pots of burning oil. Smoke drifted above the remains of at least two of the inner buildings, and it made Riam's eyes water and sting. A large warehouse on the far side of the compound looked as if it might have been damaged by fire as well, but it could have been a trick of the shadows in the dim light. Beyond this, the rest of the outpost, composed of nine or ten buildings besides the warehouse, appeared to have escaped any damage. The compound was roughly square around the buildings, and the stripped-timber of the remaining walls narrowed to sharpened points at the top. Ladders were spaced evenly around the walls to allow men to climb to a walkway that ran the length; here and there, a lookout peered into the darkness. Overhead, the stars looked hazy through smoke that lingered like a blanket of fog.

Riam and Gairen wound their way between the buildings to stop before a narrow, two-story structure. A green-and-white pennant adorned the top of the building, but it hung limply in the still air so that it was impossible to tell what was depicted on the fabric. A guard stood on the building's porch, and he ducked inside when he saw them.

"Wait here." Gairen slid from the saddle, leaving Riam mounted.

That was fine with Riam. His foot and side ached, and he had no desire to stand or try and walk.

An old Draegoran came out of the building, followed by the guard and a third man who carried a sword instead of a spear. The swordsman's blond hair was cut short on the sides and back, but it was long enough to form a nap of curls on top. Thick but neatly trimmed stubble ran from ear to ear that matched the yellow of his hair. Young and muscular, the man walked with the confidence of someone who was highly skilled at his duties. He was nearly as intimidating as Gairen.

The old Draegoran, however, made them both look soft as cubs. He had skin like wrinkled bull hide with tattoos faded and blurred with age, although Riam could still make out the owl on his neck that mirrored Gairen's. His long gray hair was tied back in the same manner most of the Draegorans seemed to favor, and the deep wrinkles in his cheeks made him appear withered and callous. Dark circles hung beneath his lower eyelids, but the eyes themselves were sharp and alert, and there was a power behind them that left no doubt he was in command. He didn't carry a sword, only a longknife, and for some reason this made him appear even more dangerous.

The two Draegorans met at the edge of the porch and clasped hands. Not like the handshake men used in Nesh, but palm to palm, fingers up, like two men arm wrestling or helping each other up. They pulled close and used their free hands to slap each other on the back. The guard went back to his post, and the blond man positioned himself nearby with his hands behind him at the small of his back. He stared straight ahead as if he were alone.

The old Draegoran was grinning when he and Gairen separated. "By Sollus, it's good to see you."

"Master Iwynd." Gairen saluted and made an exaggerated look around. "You've been busy."

"They hit us two nights ago. Rode in fast and threw some sort of explosive pitch before disappearing into the darkness. Burned so hot that more than one man lost his hair trying to douse the flames. Timed it right, too. I have only one taulin, and it is currently escorting the supply wagons up to North Pass. The regulars here are only foot soldiers—unsuitable for chasing mounted men." He looked to the swordsman. "No offense, Harol."

"None taken, Master Iwynd."

"Harol is the commander of the regulars assigned here. They're out of Thae and only arrived this past spring. Harol, this is Gairen. As you can see by the glyph, he's Owl Regiment. You can trust him."

"Warden." The man brought his feet together and his fingers to his opposite shoulder in salute before returning to his previous position, his eyes remaining fixed straight ahead all the while.

Gairen acknowledged Harol with a nod. "It was the Esharii, then?" he asked Master Iwynd.

"Well, they looked to be tribesmen and carried Arillian blades, but the Esharii have never attacked the outpost before—at least, not since the last invasion nearly sixty years ago."

"The boy and I were jumped by a band of Ti'yak at dawn, near where the river skirts the plains before turning northeast. It could have been the same warband. I spoke to a patrol that was following their trail, but they expected them to be farther west, deeper into the Dry Plains." Gairen paused a moment. "They had an okulu'tan with them. I didn't see him, but he was there, suppressing my vision with some new trick they've learned so that we rode straight into an ambush. I had two of the blood with me. I lost one, a girl. It's too bad. While the color of the crystal was a bit off, she tested quite strong."

"Most strange." The old Draegoran's forehead wrinkled even more than it did naturally. "That's the first spirit-taker to come over the mountains in years, and it's the first time the Esharii have gone after the children. Pity you lost one of the blood. We've gathered less than usual this year, and with how many are failing the tests these days, a single loss makes a difference." He turned to Harol. "I'll need another messenger for the pass, a fast one if there's to be any chance of getting the child back."

"Yes, Master Iwynd." Harol saluted and moved off at a run.

The old Draegoran rubbed his chin. "Something odd is going on. Doesn't make sense for the Esharii to attack the outpost. They don't gain anything. They barely damaged the warehouse, so there won't even be a delay in supplies for North Pass."

"Maybe they did it to make us waste more men guarding the supply route."

Master Iwynd shook his head. "No. That's not it. They don't gain anything from that either. Like I said, it's odd, even for Esharii, and that's saying a lot."

"What about this new high landowner in Mirlond, this Lion of West?"

"We're a long way from Mirlond. Lots of places closer to cause trouble."

"True, but it's in his favor to keep us focused here in the east."

"You don't really believe he's made some kind of deal with the Esharii, do you?" Master Iwynd said.

"No. Just grabbing at thoughts in the wind." Gairen waved toward the burned gates. "It's far more likely the Esharii are softening your defenses for a larger raid or distracting you from their real target—whatever that is."

Master Iwynd nodded in assent. "My thoughts follow the same logic. I sent a request to the commander at the pass for another company of regulars and a second taulin. Until I get them, I've hired men from the town to clean up this mess and rebuild the wall, and I have Harol's men building a palisade around the gap until the wall is repaired."

"With the Wolf Regiment in charge of North Pass, you won't get any help."

"I've been outmaneuvering the Wolves for a long time,

Gairen. I sent a copy of the request back to the council, and I made sure that the copy that went to North Pass said as much. If that idiot Renlin at North Pass turns me down, the council will overrule him. He'll look like a fool.

"He'll send me the reinforcements I asked for. He'll use it as an excuse to send me his problems and to get rid of those he doesn't trust, but he'll send them. In any case, I'll be sleeping with one eye open until I get the new wall up."

They were quiet for a time before Master Iwynd finally acknowledged Riam's presence. "So this would be the lucky one they didn't catch?" He spent a long uncomfortable moment examining Riam.

"Neshian, from a small town near Cove. The Esharii almost had him, but the boy thinks quickly," Gairen said. "Took down a pair of tribesmen with his horse."

Riam studied the saddle. He'd lost Nola. He didn't deserve the praise.

"Near Cove . . . I see." There was a note of distaste in his words. "Your brother again."

Gairen changed to the puzzling language from the day prior. "Hesta arganel ev noran i yoral. Diyoruk ev kora kyol."

"Entum," Master Iwynd replied. He turned to the guard and snapped his fingers. "Gairen needs to give me his report—in private. Take the boy to an empty room and get him fed, even if you have to wake Brin or Jon to get a plate."

"Be easy with him. He didn't escape the tribesmen without injury," Gairen added.

The guard saluted and leaned his spear against the wall before moving to help Riam out of the saddle.

"I'll find you when I'm finished," Gairen said over a shoulder as he and Master Iwynd moved toward the building.

"Come." The guard gestured for Riam to follow.

Riam was stiff and sore, but he limped as best he could behind the man. He didn't make it far before he was forced to stop and rest.

"I'm sorry," he told the guard.

"There is no shame in being injured fighting an enemy."

"I wasn't trying to fight them. I was merely trying to get away and had no choice but to charge two of them."

"You sell your actions short. Many would soil their breeches at the thought of charging the swaugs."

"Swaugs?"

"It is what we call them in Thae. It's . . . not a term for children to use. At any rate, it is my honor to wait for one who has faced the Esharii and survived to face them another day."

Riam examined the guard's face for signs that he was only humoring him. There were none. Embarrassed, he forced himself to hobble on despite the pain.

The guard led Riam to a small room. It was dark and contained only two woven mats stuffed with straw. Like everywhere else, it smelled of smoke.

"I'll be back with food. Wait here."

Since there was nowhere to sit, Riam eased himself down onto one of the mats to wait.

"What's your plan for the boy?" Master Iwynd said. He poured a dark liquid from a decanter into two glasses. The rich, sweet smell of liquor drifted through the room.

Gairen faked surprise. "Plan?"

Master Iwynd forced a smile. "You're as transparent to me as the day I started training you . . . so, again, what's the plan?"

They were on the second floor of the building with the pennant above it, inside Master Iwynd's modest personal quarters. A sturdy table with six chairs for dining sat at the room's center, and a large hanging cupboard was pushed against the wall behind it. Two comfortable-looking chairs faced a rock chimney with a simple wooden mantel. On the mantel rested a single arrow. It was Esharii, as anyone who'd ever faced the bastards could tell by the bright red-and-yellow feathering, and it had a nasty-looking broadhead with one edge broken. Gairen knew the arrow well. It'd sat on Master Iwynd's desk back on the island, but that had been a lifetime ago.

Master Iwynd stood by the cupboard. Dim light from the firepots outside filtered in through the room's two windows and danced on the ceiling.

"You still have this thing?" Gairen ran his finger along the shaft of the arrow. It'd been snapped into two pieces and wired back together. The broken tip was rusted, and the feathering frayed away from the wood at the ends.

"It keeps life in perspective." He handed Gairen one of the glasses. "Besides, the missing piece is still in here somewhere." He patted himself on the chest and took a sip from his glass. "Seems right to keep them near each other."

Gairen raised his glass to Master Iwynd. When the alcohol hit his lips, he closed his eyes, savoring the rich taste, and made an exaggerated sigh. *The advantages of civilization.* He'd risen through the ranks as a scout, but that didn't mean he'd spent his whole life in the wilds. "Where'd you get Arillian brandy out here?"

"Harol carried it all the way from Thae. It was a gift from him and his men when they arrived. You going to answer the question?" He said it good-naturedly, but there was a sober tone behind the words.

Gairen moved to one of the chairs and plopped down. He stared into his drink and swirled the liquor around, forming a whirlpool that threatened to spill over the top of the glass. *How much should I tell him? How much has he already guessed?*

Master Iwynd kept at him. "That's Jonim's boy. I can tell by looking at him. He has your father's deep, probing eyes and sharp nose. It's what you've been searching for these past two years and why you left your command, isn't it?"

Gairen stopped swirling the drink abruptly. *So much for keeping anything from him.* He took a deep breath, preparing for the argument to come. "It is."

"You think your father will change his mind if he knows his grandson is coming to the island? That's your plan? He won't, you know. He's committed to his course of action. There'll be no new Draegorans with the mark of the owl while your father is kyden of our regiment." He tossed back the rest of his brandy. "By the Fallen, if it were up to him, none with the blood would ever be trained again . . . by any regiment."

My father is a fool. He barely kept himself from saying it out loud. There were lines Master Iwynd would not tolerate him crossing. He had to remain calm and courteous. "Our regiment is dying, Master Iwynd. If Father doesn't take new trainees, we'll die off one by one until our regiment is only a memory. And, while we're dying, the Wolf Regiment grows stronger. None of the other regiments will stand up to them except for the Stonebreakers, but their kyden won't lead the council forever. The Wolves can't be allowed to wrest control from them. The whole continent would rebel at a return to their methods, not just Mirlond." *Why am I the only one who can see what's happening?*

Master Iwynd ignored his explanation and moved to the cupboard to refill his glass. "He was here last season. Did you know that? I mentioned that it was time I returned to the island and started training new blood for the regiment. He wouldn't hear of it—told me those days were over. When I mentioned your name, he stiffened up and refused to speak of you at all."

Of course. There's no talking to Father. Ever since Jonim died and Father became kyden, the man refused to see reason. Their last conversation had turned to yells and insults. "I tried talking to him before I left, but he wouldn't listen to me either. It's more than my brother's death and me resigning my command. There's something he's not telling us. Something he learned when he became kyden and joined the council. You were the arms-master for the regiment before he sent you here, and he's never even told you why he stopped training replacements. Why? Why send his most trusted man away with no explanation?"

"He doesn't have to give me a reason. He's my kyden."

"Even when he's destroying us? My duty is to the regiment, not to him."

"Careful, Gairen. That's a dangerous line of thinking. A kyden and his regiment are one and the same. I've known your father a long time, and I owe him my life from more than one occasion." He pointed to the mantel. "When that arrow was sticking out of my chest, your father killed a dozen tribesmen and carried me twenty steads through enemy-filled wetlands to get me back to North Pass, all the while draining the life from himself with my blade to keep me alive.

"At one point, we were surrounded, and there was no way out. The Esharii had us trapped, and they had at least two spirit-takers with them. I knew I was dying. He knew I was dying. The arrow had punctured a lung, and I'd lost a lot of blood. I told your father to take my strength into his blade, to use it to escape, but instead he set me down in a clearing and drew his sword to protect me. I tried to get up and help but blacked out. When I woke up, we were halfway up the mountains to North Pass. I was in bad shape, but every time I grew close to dying, he'd put his hand on my blade, and I'd feel it draining him, giving me strength.

"I don't know what he's doing now, or why, but I trust him. I've spent most of my life following his orders in one way or another, and although I haven't always understood what he was doing or believed he would succeed, it's always come out well in the end. You have to trust him.

"Now, I understand, he's your father, and that gives you some leeway to question him, but the rest of us don't get to do that. If you were any other warden, I'd curse you out and tell you to get back to your duties. I probably should've done that a long time ago, but I've become soft in my age."

This was an old argument. *Master Iwynd lets his loyalty blind him. Something is wrong with Father, and the arms-master refuses to see it.* "I have to try something. That's why I had to find Jonim's son, and I have to make sure Father knows exactly who he is. It's the only thing I can think of that will make him begin training again. It'll be just like it was with Jonim and me. There's no way he'll allow his own blood to be trained in another regiment."

Master Iwynd held his glass out with one finger extended, pointing at Gairen. "And if he does abandon him? Did you think through what'll happen if your father doesn't resume training? What the other kydens will do when they find out who the boy is? Because they will figure it out, and they'll use him any way they can for leverage. You'll be throwing him into a boiling pot that he won't be able to climb out of, because any regiment that places their glyph on his neck will either be trying to get at your father or won't trust the boy because of your father. Either way, he'll never complete the training in another regiment, and you know it. He'll die, and it'll be your fault."

Gairen stood up and put his glass down on the table hard enough that the remaining liquor sloshed over the edge. *It doesn't matter. What is risking one boy—even if he is my nephew—in comparison to losing the regiment?* "That's a chance I'm willing to take. There's no other way." *I know Father will never abandon Jonim's son.*

"There is another way. Trust your father. Believe in him as I do. Tell the boy to say he's from Thae, and no one will put it together. Resume your command of the scouts at South Pass. That's the only way the boy has a fair chance.

I know your father. He won't train any more of the blood, no matter who they are. A Draegoran has no family. He's learned that lesson the hard way."

"No." Gairen shook his head. "I'm sending a letter with the boy. If Father doesn't train him, then so be it; the boy's death will be on his head, just like Jonim's."

"That's going too far, Gairen. Your brother's death wasn't your father's fault, and it hurt him as much as it did you. Trying to manipulate the man will only make it worse. Obey his orders. That's the best way to serve the regiment."

Gairen looked down at the floor. *If only Master Iwynd would help, then Father would listen, and the boy would be safe.* He knew what the answer would be before he asked, but he had to try. "It would help if you wrote a letter to go with mine. He will listen if it comes from both of us."

"No." Master Iwynd's response was immediate and firm. "He's given me my orders." Master Iwynd reached into his shirt and withdrew a folded piece of paper with a wax seal. "I'd hoped it wouldn't come to this. I figured you needed time to come around on your own, but it isn't working. You're obsessed." He held the paper out to Gairen. "These are orders for you to report to South Pass and take command of the scout company."

"Why? So I can personally watch as our regiment dies off? You know the Wolves give us missions that put us at risk. They're taking every advantage they can to hurry us toward extinction."

Master Iwynd pushed the paper into his hand. The wax seal was black with the impression of the sun rising behind a single blade. "The order comes directly from the council, not your father. You have no choice. Your father tolerated your disobedience for the last two years, but it's over, Warden." He emphasized the rank. "You cannot disobey the council."

Gairen looked directly into Master Iwynd's eyes. "Write a letter to go with mine and I'll do it." He tried not to sound as if he were begging.

"No. You'll do it or face your punishment from the council."

Faen take Master Iwynd and the council! "You'd hand me over to them?"

"You were one of the best students I ever trained, but

yes, I would. It's the law. Without the law, the Covenant has no meaning." He said it without a trace of emotion, and his expression gave away nothing. "But it's not going to come to that. It's over. You've found a child Jonim sired. Finding a second will make little difference. It's time to return to your duties."

Gairen looked down at the paper. He pressed his lips together and breathed rapidly through flared nostrils, trying to calm down. He squeezed the order until the wax seal crumbled in his hand, but he didn't put the order down or attempt to give it back. He couldn't.

"I can't stop, not after everything I've done to find the boy."

"You're as stubborn as your father. Go. Write your letter if you must, it's within your right, even though I think you're wrong. The day after tomorrow, however, as soon as the children head downriver, you ride for South Pass. If you don't arrive there in a tenday, they won't have to send any taulins out looking for you because I'll find you myself and drag you there."

"But—"

"That's all. You're dismissed."

Gairen's whole body tensed like a coiled spring. Arguing with his old master was one thing, but he could not refuse the order. He stood there, unmoving for some time. Finally, his shoulders sagged. He bowed his head and raised his fingers to his shoulder in salute. "Yes, Master Iwynd." *I will send the letter. It will have to be enough.*

"Oh, and Gairen." The words were softer. "Take the boy into town and get him cleaned up in the morning before he joins the others. While you are at it, draw enough coin to pay the tailor for all his services. He's had a busy week outfitting the children for their journey. I'd planned on doing it myself, but it'll save me the trip. I don't like sending one of the regulars. People need to see that we do more than order others around and execute prisoners. Your father taught me that."

CHAPTER 7

Riam woke from dreams of ash and fire. It took a moment for the memories of the escape from the Esharii and arriving at the outpost to separate themselves from the images of sleep. The smell of burnt wood still hung in the air, but above the pungent odor lurked the rich scent of roasting meat, making his mouth water. His stomach growled. He'd fallen asleep before the Thaen Regular returned with food, and he was starving. He smacked his lips at the thought of real food. Hopefully, the days of hard bread and dried meat were behind him. He rubbed his eyes to get the sleep out. A crust of dust, smoke, and tears clung to his eyelashes. He wiped the worst of it away and let his arms unfold into a stretch.

Yesterday's abuse from the saddle horn jabbed like a spear into his side. "Faen's balls!" he said between clenched teeth. He hurriedly looked around to make sure no one heard him. He was alone in the room, which was a good thing. If any of the townsfolk back home had heard him say the Dark God's name, they would've taken the hide from his rear end.

Lifting his shirt, he whistled. Mottled purple-and-yellow bruises ran from his armpit to his hip. His hand wasn't much better. A scabbed-over line crossed his palm where

the skin had been burned away by the reins. He let his shirt
fall and made a tentative circle with his arm, testing the
pain. *I survived worse at home with Grandfather. I'll get
through this.*

Pushing the pain away, he examined the room more
closely. It was smaller than it'd appeared last night—much
smaller. The walls and floor were solid and barren, made
of rough wooden planks. The canvas pallets were dingy. It
had to be a cell of some kind; otherwise there would have
been more than the small window in the door. He'd been
so tired when he came in that he hadn't noticed. Standing
slowly, he limped to the door and tested the handle. The
latch clicked. At least it wasn't a cell for him.

Outside, it was still dark, and the dim shadows of the
outpost's walls masked what light came from the horizon.
If they were roasting meat, however, it meant dawn was
close. He wished he could've slept longer. He was still tired,
but his grandfather had never let him sleep past sunrise, so
he usually woke early out of habit. There were even times
when he'd been up before Gairen on the long ride here.

Riam yawned again and went looking for a place to relieve himself. He had no difficulty finding the privy. Even
though it was early, he wasn't the only one awake. Uni-
formed regulars scurried about the outpost in pursuit of
their duties. They paid little attention to a boy hobbling
through the compound.

Gairen was standing in front of the cell when he returned. He smiled as Riam approached. If Gairen was a
fearsome man to behold in daylight, the white of his teeth
as he smiled in the dim light made him downright scary. If
Riam hadn't spent so much time with him, he'd have run
for the gate. He took a deep breath and forced himself to
walk calmly toward the man. Even after the fight with the
Esharii, Gairen's clothes were as fresh and crisp as the day
he'd walked into Riam's home. Riam's own clothing was
dirty and spattered with dried blood. The right knee on his
trousers was torn, and the leather laces of his shoes had
knots in them to keep them together. His left shoe had a
large hole, big enough that his toes slipped out if he wasn't
careful.

"You're up early. I didn't expect to find you awake."
There was a hint of approval in Gairen's voice.

Praise wasn't something Riam was used to, and it usually embarrassed him more than anything. Oddly, when it was just Gairen with him, it felt good. He stood up a little straighter and his side hurt a little less.

"I'm sure you're hungry. There should be something ready by now. We'll eat, and once the sun is up, we'll go into town to get you new clothes and a bath. You'll be leaving tomorrow morning, and I won't send you downriver looking like a beggar or a raker's churp."

Riam groaned. He wouldn't mind the new clothes since his own were ruined—though he had no idea what a raker or a churp was—but he didn't look forward to bathing. He hated being cold and wet. He'd tried swimming with Lemual a couple times, and it wasn't much fun when he could barely keep himself from drowning.

Gairen led him to a long building with a wide stone chimney rising from the roof. In the early morning calm, smoke hung weightless around it. Not the smoke of the fire that damaged the outpost, but the good kind—the smoke from roasting meat. This close, the smell was overpowering, making his stomach growl even more. Despite the pain in his side, his steps lightened, and he sped up. He didn't care what they were serving. He'd eat a screet if they put it on his plate.

They'd stayed at several inns while traveling, with common rooms large and small, but the inside of the long building dwarfed them all. More than a dozen tables in neat rows filled the room. The worn benches between them were empty, but the room must have held a hundred people when it was full. Two cooks, the room's only occupants, worked around the fireplace. A small pig was spitted over glowing coals below a metal hood that funneled the smoke into the chimney. On the table closest to the cooks lay an assortment of vegetables, breads, and cheeses. There was even a comb of honey. Wooden plates were stacked on the corner, and a variety of pots and pans hung in perfect order by size on pegs along the wall. One of the cooks had wispy white hair and long eyebrows, while the other was balding and missing most of his right arm. A metal cap covered the end below the elbow. He used his good hand to turn the spit.

"Bad luck today, boy," Gairen said loudly, even though the room was empty. "Brin is still alive. The food may finish the Esharii's work." The man with the missing hand stopped turning the pig. The other's lips split into a wide grin.

"I heard you ran into some tribesmen," the one-handed bald man said. He let go of the spit handle and wiped grease from his hand onto his apron. "Pity they weren't better fighters. I was hoping they'd taken your balls back across the mountains and thrown them into their sacred lake." There was no trace of humor in his deep voice.

"Not this time, and not anytime soon. Besides, it's the regimental glyph they prove their kills with, not the balls." Gairen waved toward the one-handed man. "This, boy, is Brin. He's a mean-spirited, hairless old badger, and with that one hand he cooks up the worst food in all of Yaden. The other is Jon. He's a *hair* better." He emphasized the word *hair*, and Jon chuckled.

"Well, you got the hairless part right," Brin said. "How was Nesh? You're not being assigned here, are you?"

"Nothing much changes out on the plains—full of tenant farmers and landowners that complain too much and understand too little—and no, simply passing through."

Jon took over the spit, winding it slowly. Dripping fat sizzled and flamed. "Don't see why anyone would live out there. No trees. No shade. Too Fallen hot for me."

Gairen nodded toward the spit. "That pig ready? We've only eaten hard rations the last few days, and not much of those."

"The pig's ready enough and so are the oats. Grab a plate, and we'll get you started."

Riam picked up a wooden plate and a spoon. He held it out toward Jon.

"I've seen many a child brought in over the years, but few that looked so rough, Gairen. You should get him cleaned up," Jon said, cutting meat from the haunch. He placed a slice on Riam's plate and added a ladle full of the oat porridge. Cucumber and tomato followed. Brin gave Riam a chunk of bread and put a generous dollop of honey on the oats.

"We're headed into town to remedy that after we eat." Gairen picked up a plate and waved Riam toward a table.

Riam quickly discovered that Gairen was joking about the food. The meat was the best he'd ever tasted, seasoned with spices of some kind, and bits of apple and the honey gave the oats a sweet flavor. Even the bread was soft. At home the cooking was always bland since they couldn't afford anything more than salt to season things with. Fresh bread was even rarer than spices. He'd eaten half the food on his plate before Gairen sat down. Jon came behind him with two cups and a pitcher of water.

"Your father came through in the spring, on his way back to the island." Jon filled the cups.

Gairen didn't look up from his plate and kept eating.

"He asked if I'd seen you."

"Well, I didn't ask about him, did I?"

"Fine." Jon thunked the pitcher down, shaking the table. "Your business."

The two cooks went back to work, and Riam and Gairen ate in silence until Master Iwynd entered with Harol. Gairen pursed his lips and his eyes narrowed. The old Draegoran paused from giving Harol a list of priorities for the day long enough to greet Gairen.

"Warden," Iwynd called out.

"Master Iwynd."

The words were formal and stiff compared to last night. *Something must have happened after I left. They'd met like long-lost friends, and now they're barely speaking.*

"It isn't personal," Master Iwynd said.

"Maybe not to you," Gairen said under his breath, far too quiet for the old Draegoran to hear, then louder, "I understand my duty, sir."

Master Iwynd stared at Gairen a moment before he and Harol retrieved plates and moved to another table on the far side of the room.

Gairen rubbed at the owl on his neck with the tips of his fingers, lost in thought as he stared after them.

Riam pointed at the owl. "You both have that same tattoo. What does it mean?"

Gairen stiffened. "Only Arillians mark their skin with ink. Do I look like a dark-skinned Arillian to you?"

Riam shook his head vigorously and cringed, expecting a blow. He hadn't meant to upset Gairen. "I'm sorry, sir. I didn't mean anything by the question," he said quickly.

"I'm not your grandfather. I don't hit children. But to keep you from saying something stupid later to someone who does, they're not tattoos. They're glyphs, and they're not placed with needle and ink. The one on the left," he pointed with his spoon to the strange, dark-blue owl with narrow, evil-looking red eyes, "shows the regiment a Draegoran belongs to. The other," he pointed to the right side where an arrow with two perpendicular slashes across the shaft rested, "is the mark of his kyden."

"Kyden?" Riam asked.

"It's a Draegoran word. 'Master' and 'teacher' are the closest translations, but it's also the title and rank of the commander of one of the six regiments. When you complete the first rites of your training and retrieve a crystal, a kyden will select you for his regiment. That's when you earn the first glyph, and it marks you as a member of a regiment. You earn the glyph of your kyden when your training is complete—if you complete it. No Draegoran may leave the island without that second glyph."

They ate quietly for a time, until Riam couldn't take the silence any longer. "How many glyphs are there? I mean, I've seen the wreath, the horn, and the uneven lines on your forearms, and the woman on the plains had the crescent moon on her face. Oh, and there was the wolf on several of the Draegorans with her." There were others, but Riam was unfamiliar with the animals or symbols they depicted.

"There are hundreds," Gairen said, "each representing an event."

"So how many do you have? I'll bet it's a lot if you have that many on your arms."

"Too many," he said under his breath, "but it's not the number that's important. Each glyph is embedded into the skin and written under your name in the rolls of your regiment. This way, every Draegoran's path may be read and honored long after the death glyph is inscribed. Many names in our hall have several hundred glyphs, but for each of those, there are a dozen with less than ten. There are more than a few with only two." He paused for effect. "The owl and the death glyph—those are the ones who fail to survive the training—of which there have been far too many."

Riam froze with the spoon in his mouth. *Death glyph? Failed training?*

"It's what we learn from the path after we bond with our crystal that's important, not how long or short it is."

"But you said before that some aren't able to retrieve a crystal. What happens to them? Do they get to leave?" Riam asked.

"Some serve on the island or elsewhere. Others are . . . not so lucky."

"So Brin and Jon are Draegorans, even though they don't have glyphs like you? They failed to get a crystal and now work here."

"What?" Gairen looked puzzled, then grinned when he figured it out. "I assumed you understood why you were tested, but I forget how little I knew when I was in your place. You will soon be a recruit for the regiments. Based on your lineage, I don't see you failing to retrieve a crystal from the vault. If you're good enough and work hard enough, then one day you'll be a Draegoran."

Riam's eyes grew big. "But I'm not a Draegoran. I'm from Nesh."

Gairen laughed. "No one's been born a Draegoran since the survivors of Draegora fled across the ocean a thousand years ago. Almost everyone on the continent has at least a trace of the blood, even the Esharii. The only ones who don't are either pure-blooded Arillians or are from the most distant tribes. But even that isn't what makes you Draegoran. It's the blood of Parron that marks you for training."

Parron? What did the Fallen God of Light have to do with it? "I don't understand."

"After Parron fell to continue his battle with Tomu on this world, he had eight children. You were selected because the blood of one of those children flows through you, and it's strong enough to allow you to use these—" Gairen twisted one of his blades so that the hilt was visible above the table. White clouds continued to swirl within the crystal in the pommel, tugging at Riam's mind as if there were something he should recognize—something he should know but couldn't remember.

"You can feel it, can't you? You don't know what it is, but it pulls at you."

Riam stared in fascination at the crystal. He nodded. "What does it mean?"

"It means your bloodlines are sufficient to link you with a crystal when you've learned enough." He let go of the hilt and the sword disappeared back below the table. "But that's a long way off, and after quite a few 'ifs.'"

"What does it do?" Riam asked.

Gairen held up his hand. "It's safe to discuss this here in the outpost, but it's best to wait until you reach the island to speak of these things. You'll have plenty of time to learn before entering the vault to link with your crystal. For now, hurry up and finish eating. I'm looking forward to that bath."

Riam had a lot more questions. *When will training begin? How many others will there be? What did Gairen mean by "link with your crystal" and Parron's children? That couldn't be true. How could anyone possess the blood of a fallen god?*

On top of it all, a larger issue rose to the surface. He was going to be trained as a Draegoran. He wasn't sure how he felt about that. Everyone across Nesh disliked and distrusted them, but Gairen seemed to be a good man. A sudden thought made his eyes widen with excitement. *I'll get my own sword. Or even better . . . two, like Gairen.*

"I said eat, not sit and daydream."

Startled, Riam returned his attention to his food, but his mind continued to churn with questions and thoughts of swords and glyphs. *Grandfather, Nola, the Esharii— Everything is suddenly life and death. A few days ago, Draegorans were no more real than monsters in the dark, and now I am on my way to becoming one.* He ate the rest of his meal without tasting it, picturing himself returning home dressed in gray and carrying a sword. Ferrick would faint if that happened. He giggled at the image of the big magistrate plopping to the ground and dirtying his crisp, clean clothes.

Riam and Gairen returned to the two-story building from the previous night. Two desks filled the room on the bottom floor, and a young Thaen Regular sat at the smaller one. The man obviously served as a clerk, but it was clearly not his true calling. Papers lay piled around in no discernible order. The clerk searched the piles for something, causing one of the stacks to fall and scatter across the floor. "Sorry, sir," he said and swept the papers under the desk with his foot, as if Gairen would forget his clumsiness once the evidence disappeared from sight. He continued to hunt through the stacks and at last held a single sheet up in triumph.

"Here's the account of debt." He handed it to Gairen and fumbled a key out from where it hung around his neck. Instead of taking it off, he leaned down awkwardly and used it to unlock a drawer while bent over. This was followed by an attempt to break his neck when he tried to stand with the key still in the lock.

Riam covered his mouth to keep from laughing.

"Sorry, sir. Harol ordered me to never take it off, and he takes his orders very seriously." He wiggled the key and it came free. "It gets stuck sometimes." He took a moment to straighten his shirt before withdrawing a leather pouch from the drawer.

"Fourteen silver dregs," he said, counting out the coins. "If you could bring back a chit with the tailor's stamp . . . er . . . for the records, you know . . . not . . . not for proof or anything. That is, if you don't mind . . ." The clerk kept his eyes on the desk while he stumbled through the words.

"Be at ease," Gairen said. "Even Draegorans have procedures. In fact, we complain all the time that our island floats on paperwork." He put the dregs inside a pocket at his waist and folded the paper. It followed the money into the same place.

"Guess that's true everywhere." The clerk stood up tall and saluted.

"I hope that boy manages a spear better than he does a desk," Gairen said once they were outside.

Riam didn't laugh. It wasn't funny. He knew how intimidating it felt when Gairen directed his full attention at you.

"We'll walk to Hath instead of riding. It's only a couple of steads, and it's not worth the trouble of saddling the horse. It'll be good for your side to stretch it out."

Riam had nearly forgotten the pain, but with the reminder his side ached once more. This, in turn, reminded him of his hand, and it began to throb as well. He doubted walking would make either of the injuries feel better, but he kept the opinion to himself. Complaining wouldn't solve anything.

They left the outpost through the same charred gates they'd entered the night before, taking a narrow dirt road north and west. In a short time the road met the river and followed it downstream. The deep green water ran slowly and steadily under the cover of the tall, thin pines and leafy oak trees. Birds chirped around them, and the morning air was cool and damp, almost chilly compared to the plains. The dusty road sent up small puffs with each footstep, but not enough to make a person cough. All in all, Gairen was right. He did feel better.

While they walked, Gairen told Riam about Hath. "The town is primarily a logging community, with several saw-mills shipping lumber downriver through Ibbal and on to the capital city of Parthusal. The timber is cut a hundred steads upriver, closer to the mountains where it's colder and the pines grow larger, before being bundled and guided downstream by rivermen who ride the logs like rafts."

He went on to explain that they would pass through the timber yard where the logs were pulled from the water to cure before being taken to the mills. "Once we make it to the yard, the road will be paved, and we'll be free of the dust."

That made sense to Riam. A loaded wagon or a heavy wain could turn a dirt road into deep ruts that stressed the wheels and axles in a matter of days, especially after a rain.

Riam looked for the logs in the river while they walked, hoping to see the rivermen. The river twisted and turned lazily, moving away from the road and returning farther on.

"See how it meanders?" Gairen said. "That means it's an old river. Rivers are like people. A young river runs straight and fast. An old river takes its time and winds its way along. This one is very old—here long before we landed on the continent. Once it hits Ibbal, it joins the Layren. That's when it speeds up and makes a line straight to Par-thusal."

Riam nodded, but he wasn't really listening. His mind kept returning to Gairen's words about swords and glyphs and regiments. *Who cares how old the river is, anyway?*

Gairen was still talking when they reached the yard. A massive chain, anchored by stone pillars, stretched from shore to shore. It held a bundle of timber with more than ten logs above the waterline fast in the middle of the river. Men in two boats and on top of the logs scurried to tie the bundle off to a thick rope that ran up a smooth dirt ramp and into the yard where it was fastened to a team of bored-looking mastons. Back home, the woolly brown beasts with thick black manes and forelocks were used to pull the large wains that came every summer to carry grain from the plains to the cities. The mastons' bulky frames were twice as wide as a horse and half again taller. They had horns like a bull, except that they were angled more forward and upward, and ended in dull rounded points instead of sharp tips. Nobody rode them much, or at least not for long. They were simply too big and wide to ride comfortably.

Some of Riam's best memories were of him and Lemual playing around the woolly beasts when they were younger. The owners would chase them away over and over again. They'd made it into a game until Grandfather put a stop to it.

Around the remainder of the timber yard, logs lay spread out and stacked. Hundreds filled the wide clearing. Brightly colored timberwains lined up with their sides to a loading dock. The dock rose higher as they went, so that the timberwains could be loaded with a row of logs and then pulled forward for the next row to be loaded without much lifting. The far end of the dock was nearly twice the height of a man. A line of mastons with harnesses dangling from their horns in front of them carried logs to the dock.

Teamsters supervised the loading. One squatted to check the heavy axles while another examined spokes as thick as Riam's leg. The heavy springs on the wains made the beds sit unnaturally high, like they might tip over sideways on the slightest incline. One of the men, wearing a floppy brown hat and leading a maston, waved at them. Riam waved back. While the men weren't farmers and wore different clothes, they were just as friendly as the people back home.

Strangely, the wains were a mix of colors, like they'd each been one solid color and then all were taken apart and put back together with the pieces mixed up. Some of the wagons were red with yellow spokes, others were green and white, and there was one that was the worst mix of orange, blue, and green Riam had ever seen.

"Why all the colors?" Riam asked.

"They paint the axles and spokes with bright colors to make it easier to see cracks in the wood," Gairen said.

"They use what's cheapest, and they don't always have the same colors available when they make repairs."

Already loaded, the lead wain stood alone on the paved stone road. There was a single teamster standing on the driver's bench hammering at something. He was partially hidden by the logs on the back of the wain, but he kept pausing in his work to lean out and watch them as they approached and then duck back quickly and continue pounding. Riam couldn't get a good look at what he was doing—fixing the seat, maybe, or trying to adjust a log.

A faint buzzing noise filled the air as they drew closer, almost like being tested with Gairen's sword. Only this time, it wasn't coming from inside his head. By the puzzled expression on Gairen's face, he heard it, too. The noise made Riam shiver. It was not a friendly sound.

The teamster pounded faster, almost frantically, the closer they came. The sound of the hammer striking the wood made a deep thud with each swing, the tempo rising like a heartbeat from heavy work.

He and Gairen were no more than a couple of rod lengths from the teamster when the man paused with the hammer above his head and stared at them. A sheen of sweat covered his face, and his skin was flushed. His eyes were wide with panic, but his mouth was set in a determined line. He turned back to the large pine logs on the back of the wain. The ends of two of the logs were capped with an odd, muddy beige material.

Riam tilted his head, trying to figure out what was on the logs and what the teamster was doing.

Crack . . . Crack. The man struck quickly and precisely two times, once on each of the caps. They shattered into pieces and fell away. Riam stared in horror. The answer to the buzzing noise became apparent—wasps.

Yellow bodies as big as two fists put together, legs as long as fingers, and stingers the size of cherry stems, they came out of the log in a writhing flood of yellow and black.

The first wasps out went straight for the teamster. Clamping onto clothing and exposed skin, they drove their massive stingers into his flesh over and over. The man screamed and crumpled down onto the driver's bench, twitching. In a flash, he disappeared beneath a mound of swarming yellow.

More wasps poured out, taking to the air and flying straight for Riam. He stood, transfixed by the sight. He had nowhere to run, no way to escape the swarm. The safety of the water flashed through Riam's thoughts, but it was too far away, the wasps too close. He could see his death reflected back at him in the black mirrored surfaces of a hundred bulbous eyes. Still, he didn't move.

It wasn't fear that held him in place. It was the overwhelming sense of the futility of doing anything else. In a moment, he would be dead, with those sharp, vertical jaws tearing at his skin and those stingers plunging into his flesh, and there was absolutely nothing he could do about it.

The wasps were nearly upon him when Gairen stepped forward with his blades swinging and turning so fast Riam couldn't follow them. The first of the wasps dropped to the ground, cut in two. Riam was so mesmerized by the wasps that he hadn't seen Gairen draw his swords.

"Get down and don't move!" Gairen yelled over his shoulder.

The commands broke Riam free. He jumped backward. His foot caught on a stone and he found himself complying with Gairen's order unintentionally, crashing to the ground on his backside. There was no way Gairen could fight them all off.

Gairen's blades twisted through the air. More wasps fell. He moved backward step-by-step, keeping the deadly creatures at bay, until he stood directly over Riam, his legs straddling him. Wasps swarmed all around, buzzing angrily as they darted in to plunge those deadly stingers into them. Screams and yells broke the silence of the timber yard. The wasps had reached the other workers.

Riam wanted to curl into a ball, but instead he lay flat, unmoving like he'd been told in fear of tangling Gairen's feet. Above him, Gairen wove a shield with his blades. There were dozens of the wasps circling them now, and each time one came within Gairen's reach, he would lash out, taking the creature down. The man never missed. Broken and severed pieces of the wasps lay scattered around them, their yellow bodies rapidly fading to a dull brown, drying and puckering as if they'd been dead for weeks. His grandfather's body had done the same thing, and just as happened back then, he felt the pulling sensation.

Riam's despair fell away. Gairen was invincible with his swords. The wasps would not reach them.

A faint, glowing mist floated above the dead and dying wasps. The mist concentrated and turned as it rose, funneling into tendrils that stretched into the air. The ends of the tendrils latched on to the pommels of the blades, and the crystals in the hilts glowed as the mist fed into them. The tendrils grew stronger and thicker, and the crystals grew brighter as more wasps piled up around them.

One of the wasps made it past Gairen's defenses and landed on his leg. With death no longer certain, Riam didn't hesitate. He grabbed the massive wasp by the wings and pulled, ignoring the pain in his injured hand. One wing snapped off, and his hand slid free. The wasp plunged its stinger into Gairen's leg.

"Aghh . . ." Gairen grunted. He stumbled but continued fighting.

Riam snatched at the wasp again, this time taking a firmer grip. Its body was cool beneath his hand and covered in fuzz, like a peach. He shivered and yanked it free. It wiggled like a baby marcat in his hand, trying to turn on him. It was stronger than he expected, but he didn't let it escape. The wasp's tail curled inward, but it was unable to bring its stinger close enough to stab into Riam's hand. Against its mandibles, however, Riam had no such luck. It clamped down on his finger with an agonizing pinch that wouldn't let go. He smashed the wasp headfirst onto a paving stone. There was a loud crunch and he felt the wetness of the wasp's guts splatter his arm. He smashed it down one more time for good measure and hurled it away. Another landed on Gairen's back.

Riam sat up, reaching for it. "Gair—"

A blur of yellow and black smacked him in the face, cutting off his warning. Riam jerked away and slammed the back of his head down onto the stone by accident. All he saw was yellow. Then his vision cleared, and he couldn't even scream. One of the wasps was on him, its stinger right in front of his eye. The creature's squirming limbs clicked, and its hooked feet tangled in his hair and scratched at his cheeks. A musty earth smell filled Riam's nostrils. The insect's bulging abdomen reared back, the stinger glistening in the morning sun.

Gairen's blade tore across the bridge of Riam's nose and cut the wasp in two. Green ichor and blood burned his eyes, blinding him. He swatted at the dying creature and shook his head to dislodge it. Warm blood from the cut on his nose ran down his cheeks. Another wasp landed on his shoulder. This time Gairen wasn't fast enough to save him. He felt the stinger slide into the meat of his shoulder, all the way to the bone.

Riam screamed as poison seared its way into his body and down his arm. Rage took over. He grabbed the wasp by the back of its head and twisted until the head came free with a pop. He flung it away.

Three more wasps made it past Gairen's swords. Riam couldn't see them, but he felt them land—one on his chest, another on his thigh, and the third near his waist. They struck in quick succession. His body filled with molten iron. The world went white. His jaw locked shut and his back arched while his heels scratched at the road. His chest constricted. He couldn't breathe. Nothing existed except blinding whiteness and agony. Then even those faded, and his vision darkened.

In the emptiness there was no more pain, no more wasps, no more anything except for two points of light that wove above him. He floated, detached from the world, watching them. At first, the movements seemed chaotic and disjointed, but then he saw a pattern to them, like a dance. He felt pulled toward the rhythmic movement of the lights.

The mists he'd seen forming above the dead wasps glowed ethereally around him. Suddenly, he understood. The lights were the crystals from Gairen's blades moving with his strikes and turns. Like his grandfather, the essence or energy, Riam wasn't sure which, that remained when the wasps died was being drawn into the crystals. He could feel himself being drained the same way. The mist materialized around his body. It was thicker, heavier, and it coalesced into a single strand that sought the leftmost crystal—the one in the blade that had cut him across the bridge of his nose. He was cold and alone with his strength fading. He didn't want to die.

CHAPTER 8

R iam drifted, surrounded by the soft glow of energy while the crystals continued to weave their pattern above him. The back of his mind tingled with the distant awareness of the poison working through his body, but the pain no longer reached him. The borders that defined him thinned and broke down, clouding his thoughts and leaking away his spirit into the strand that threaded out toward Gairen's sword. The strand snaked its way up, turning this way and that as it followed the crystal's movements. It drew closer and closer, until it met the crystal in the pommel, and a surge of energy flooded out from Riam. The gem flared brighter, and the lights increased their pace. His essence fed through the crystal to Gairen, allowing the Draegoran to move and fight faster.

The test in his home was a minor tug in comparison—a summer breeze compared to the buffeting winds of a thunderstorm. It wrenched at his soul, while at the same time suffocating him as if holding him underwater with his lungs empty and his strength fading. The crystal pulsed with his heart, and with each beat, more of him leaked away. He would soon be a dried husk, like his grandfather or the dead insects around him. In desperation, he reached out to tear away the tendril that linked him to the crystal. He was shocked when he felt it—solid, like grasping iron.

How is this possible? His body lay unmoving on the ground, paralyzed and constricted by the venom. He was two beings, the one unmoving in the physical world and the one of energy here. He needed to think, but it was so hard to concentrate with his strength pouring away. There had to be something he could do to save himself.

He pulled at the tendril again. It didn't budge. He tried tightening the boundary of himself, willing his body to keep his essence from leaving. He might as well have tried holding water in his hands. It didn't work. He gave in to the panic and thrashed and flailed at the tendril that drained him. Nothing he did made a difference. The crystal continued to pulse with his heartbeat, sucking away his life with each beat.

The crystal! He forced himself to calm down, to stop thrashing. The crystal captured the essence of those who were cut by the blade and fed it to Gairen. If he couldn't stop himself from being pulled into the crystal, maybe he could prevent his energy from reaching Gairen, maybe even take it back. Instead of fighting against the pull, he needed to be closer, to understand how it worked. Above him, the gem blazed, the tendril of mist spiraling into it ominously.

Riam was running out of time and didn't see much choice. He gathered together what little awareness he still possessed and shoved it down the tendril. His thoughts became part of the current of energy, rushing toward the crystal.

Before Riam, the gem burned like a small sun, and its pull grew stronger the closer he came. He barely stopped himself from being sucked into its fiery depths. This close, the tendrils were lines of solid energy. Unexpectedly, there were two lines leading out. The larger was white and led to Gairen. Riam saw the hazy shimmer of the man. The other was faint and tinted red, arrowing out into the darkness beyond his awareness. *Why were there two?*

It didn't matter. He had to stop the energy from reaching Gairen. He would either take control or die. Tentatively, he touched the line leading to Gairen, willing it to give him strength. He felt a trickle of power, but it wasn't

•

enough. He needed all the power the crystal had, and he
needed it now.

He pulled harder at the line of energy. It strained and
fought against him. He tore at it with everything he had,
willing it to break. With a deafening pop, the strand broke
free and dissolved. The crystal swelled with energy that
had nowhere to go. Riam eagerly gave it an outlet, channel-
ing it back down into his dying body.

Power poured into him, filling him with life. It was the
most wonderful thing he'd ever experienced, like every
small moment of joy and satisfaction in his life crammed
into a single instant—every piece of candy from Ferrick,
every word of praise from Gairen or his brother, every moment of freedom from his grandfather—all happening at
once. He smelled it. He felt it. He tasted it. He screamed.
He wept. He laughed. Power continued to fill him. It
burned away the poison. It mended the cut across his nose.
It even healed the damage to his side and hand. He pulled
in so much he thought he would explode into a blaze like
the crystal. He never wanted it to stop, never wanted anything else. With a gasp, his lungs filled with air, and the
world came crashing back.

Gairen stood above him holding a single sword at the
ready. The white clouds and blue sky were crisp and clear
above. In fact, everything was more lucid and focused than
it had ever been. He'd never even known he had poor vision, but the energy had improved his eyesight when it
healed him. He could see the smallest details in the clouds.
He could taste the air and the scents of the timber yard.
There was the musty earth smell of the wasps, the sweet,
damp smell of the mastons, and the overpowering tang of
wet timber. They smelled magnificent. Even the ground
beneath him smelled rich and comforting. Gairen's other
blade lay on the ground nearby. Riam didn't see it. He
didn't need to. He felt it. The blade was a part of him now.

Only one wasp remained, circling slowly around them.
The others were gone, either dead or off attacking the
workers. Riam looked down at his body and shuddered.
Dead wasps covered his chest and legs, but no blade had
touched them. Shriveled and drained, they crumpled like
paper when he brushed them away. The last wasp flew in
close and Gairen sliced it neatly in half. Where Gairen had

moved so quickly before, now the swing seemed slow and unhurried.

Gairen turned on Riam. "What did you do to the sword?" He bent down to pick it up and jerked his hand away as soon as his fingers touched it. "By the Fallen," he cursed. "What have you done?"

Riam sat up and stared helplessly at Gairen.

"Get them off! Help me!" The yells came from the direction of the river.

Gairen spun toward the sound. "Pick up the sword and stay close."

Riam scooped up the weapon and dashed after Gairen. The hilt was warm in his hand. He dodged a team of mastons that stood oblivious to the terror around them, their thick hides protecting them from the wasps.

At the riverbank, two men with hatchets stood back-to-back and a third writhed on the ground, screaming for help. Wasps clung to his clothing. Gairen kicked at the creatures, and those that took flight he cut from the air before they could climb out of reach. Riam stomped on one, and it made a satisfying crunch when he killed it. By the time all the insects were dispatched, the man on the ground no longer moved. Gairen felt his neck, but the man wasn't breathing. Gairen shook his head, confirming he no longer lived.

A single wasp circled them once, out of reach, and decided to ignore the remaining humans. It darted out over the water and into the trees on the far side of the river.

"Fourteen dead, not counting the man who did it," the foreman told Gairen, his gaze sweeping around the timber yard. "Never seen wasps that big." The man held an ax handle in his hand, and his fingers were white where they gripped the narrow end. The remaining workers had lined up the dead on a loading dock. Looking down the row of bodies, the foreman shook his head. "Teamsters were the closest, so they lost the most. Only five of them still living, and one of them's been stung pretty bad on the leg." He pointed with the handle to a group on the bed of the last wain. "We put a tourniquet on the leg to keep the poison from his heart, so maybe he'll live."

"Tell them to untie and retie the tourniquet every quarter of a glass. It'll let his body sort out the poison a little at a time. They can remove it after they do it eight times if he's still alive," Gairen said.

"I'll tell them," the foreman said. "We're still missing three. One was working the boat, so he may have let the current carry him downstream to escape. Hopefully, the other two ran away and will make their way back to the yard." He didn't sound optimistic. "We'll search for them after we get the bodies loaded and headed back to their kin. The ones that have kin, anyway."

"Anybody know this man?" Gairen asked the men around him. He knelt beside the body of the teamster who'd released the deadly insects. The workers looked back and forth from one to another. None knew him.

"Thought maybe he was a new hire by another mill. He was here and loaded when I arrived," said a teamster. "There are nine different mills. Drivers come and go, so we don't always know each other."

"Who loaded his wain?"

"That woulda been Theril." The foreman pointed to the third body in the row of the dead. "Wasps got him." Riam recognized the bloated face of the man in the floppy hat who'd waved to him.

"Theril wouldn't have missed the hollowed-out logs," the foreman said.

Gairen made a thorough search. He stripped the dead man of clothing and examined both the body and the clothes. There were large red welts, easily the size of plums, scattered over the man's pale corpse. The body had a few scars, but nothing of note. His dark hair was cut short, but not in a way that would make him stand out in a crowd. His only possession was a small blue-and-white charm held by a chain around his neck. Gairen tore it free and shoved it in his pocket.

Riam looked away in embarrassment as the dead man's private parts flopped around when Gairen turned him over and back while checking him. Many of the men did the same. When Gairen finished, he tossed the dead man's breeches onto the body irreverently, like piling up refuse.

These were the first bodies Riam had ever seen other than his grandfather. He thought it should bother him more than it did, but aside from the uncanny stillness he found disturbing, he wasn't sick or scared. In fact, he was intrigued. He could almost feel the energy seeping out of them. He glanced down at the blade in his hand. Somehow, he knew that if he so much as scratched one of the bodies, the blade would draw out whatever essence remained. The thought raised his pulse and made the hair on his arms tingle.

"Anyone check the wain?" Gairen asked. He deftly used the dead man's shirt to take the sword away from Riam. He slid it into its sheath and then wrapped the shirt around the pommel. The men around them were all shaking their heads no. None of them had been willing to go near the wain with the possibility of more wasps inside the logs.

Gairen moved his search there and climbed up to the driver's bench. "Logs have been split, hollowed, and then put back together. Used clay caps to cover the ends." He tossed down a piece of the hardened clay.

The foreman caught it. "Then they had to have been brought in on the wagon, too fragile for rolling it about and loading. Means Theril wasn't involved. I'm glad. He was a good man."

"Like to know how they got the wasps in there," a teamster said.

"Smoke maybe, like with bees," the foreman answered.

"Or at night. They go dormant at night," another worker added.

"Brave men to do that job. I've never seen them that big."

The foreman turned the clay piece back and forth in his hand. "Crazy is more like it."

"Can't imagine doing something like that at night. Think of the size the nest would have to be."

Riam shivered at the idea of collecting the massive wasps in the dark.

"They were after you, and they knew you'd be coming through the yard," said the foreman.

"I know." Gairen climbed down from the wain.

They remained until the logs could be unloaded and taken apart to ensure there were no more of the creatures left inside. The foreman thanked Gairen for that and for saving several of his men's lives.

Riam knew why the man thanked Gairen; he'd risked his life to save the workmen after protecting him, but if he and Gairen hadn't come through the yard, then all of the foreman's men would still be alive. Either the man chose to overlook this, or he hadn't thought of it yet. Riam believed it to be the first, but then wondered why this didn't bother the man. He didn't understand adults sometimes.

Riam was surprised when Gairen told him they were still going into Hath.

"Running back to the outpost won't solve anything, and we'd still need to go into town."

As they left, two men added the limp form of the teamster who'd been stung on the leg to the row of bodies on the dock.

Hidden among the wide leaves of an old softwood tree on the other side of the river, the last remaining wasp clung to a limb stretched out over the water. The insect's hooked feet held on to the gnarled bark, and its mandibles opened and closed mechanically, chewing at the air. It tilted its head left, then right, staring malevolently at the workers. It was a long way from its nest, but these were the creatures that had torn open its home and taken its queen. Its small, black antennae twitched with desire. It wanted to fly across the river and sting them. It wanted to kill them. The black wings against its yellow body sprung out, but it didn't take to the air. The okulu'tan controlling its mind wouldn't let it.

Steads away, out on the edge of the plains, the Esharii spirit-walker sat inside his tent, eyes closed, watching the Draegoran and the boy through the insect. A single wasp, the queen, was tied with string and suspended half submerged in a golden bowl of water on his lap. Not just any water, but sacred water from the Najalii, the lake of life in the center of the Esharii homelands. The okulu'tan held the bowl cupped in his hands with his thumbs curved over the edge and in the water. Red-and-yellow streaks of light darted through the water between the man and the insect. The light's reflection off the bowl's surface gave the water a forbidding glow.

The okulu'tan opened his eyes, revealing red pupils that shone nearly as bright as the golden bowl in his hands. Sitting in a half circle before him were three Esharii warriors. Two of them were anxious, he could tell by their breathing and the thin film of sweat on their striped face paint, but they said nothing and waited for him to speak. They knew the dangers of disturbing him while he used his power.

The largest was Pai'le, the warleader of the band of Ti'yak warriors who had escorted him over the mountains. Like most men with great strength, he was impulsive, believing that his strength made him right.

Next to Pai'le sat Ky'lem, the warrior's disfigured second-in-command. The jagged scars on the left side of the tribesman's face and his torn ear fooled many into thinking he was simply a fierce fighter. While it was true that there were few who could best him in wrestling or with a knife, his true strength lay in his thoughts. There were none who could outsmart him, and what made him remarkable was that he preferred to use his mind before fighting. It might have been better if he was in charge, but the okulu'tan had other plans for the scar-faced warrior.

The last tribesman was his pachna, and the leader of his bodyguards. Like all his bodyguards, his face was unpainted, marking him as chae'lon—of no tribe. The warrior had served him faithfully for many years, even though it meant that as chae'lon he could keep no wives.

The three sat cross-legged, their wide-swept Arillian blades next to them, on colorful rugs used to floor the tent.

"The old Draegoran still lives. He sent the younger one and the boy you failed to capture in his place," the okulu'tan said.

"They're dead?" Pai'le asked.

"No, the trap failed. The Church of Man's agent stirred the creatures up too much, making them difficult to control. I couldn't bring them all to bear on the gray demon, and he fought them off. The boy, however, is of more interest. He was stung several times and should have died, but I believe he used the gray demon's blade to save himself. He is quite strong."

"And the Church's agent?"

"Dead. He could not be allowed to survive the attack."

"So, both of the gray men still live." The big Esharii grinned. "More honor for my men when we kill them." He was eager to redeem himself for failing to capture the boy and kill the young Draegoran out on the plains.

"This is not about revenge or honor, Pai'le. I want the

children, especially this boy." The okulu'tan pushed the
wasp under the water with his thumb, squashing it against
the bottom of the bowl. Energy flashed through the water
like lightning in a thundercloud. He brought the bowl to his
lips and tilted his head back, swallowing the sacred water.
Then he closed his eyes and placed the queen between his
molars with two fingers. He didn't want to use the power
this way. It was dangerous and hastened the madness, but the
way events were falling into place could change everything
he'd planned before coming over the mountains.

He had to know the truth, and that meant searching the
memories his mind kept locked away to protect itself, memories from traveling the ways. One could not see the infinite possibilities of the future and remain sane in this
world, so the mind of a spirit-walker blocked them out, but
they were there, deep in the recesses of the spirit. The spirit
knew which were important, and day-by-day, piece-by-piece,
the memories he needed to save his people slipped through.
It was a dangerous balance. Too many memories, and he
would be lost and confused, unable to tell the difference
between what "was" and what "could be." Too few memories, and he would be unable to guide the other okulu'tan.
Using the magic to force those memories was not something he wanted to do. It hurried the madness that would
one day take him, but he had to know the truth. In all his
memories of the future, he'd never seen this boy among the
Draegorans. He had to know why. He bit down, crushing
the wasp. Power surged through his body, and he clawed
through the hidden spaces of his soul for answers.

When the power left him and his mind returned to the
world, he opened his eyes. The three warriors still sat pa-
tiently before him, waiting for his commands.

"We attack the outpost tonight. Capture the boy and the
other children. The gray demons must not be allowed to
possess him." He didn't want to think about what would
happen if they were unsuccessful. He reached out and took
hold of Pai'le's chin. He squeezed it firmly, sending enough
power through his fingers to jolt the big warrior's heart.
"You must not fail this time." There was but one small
chance to save his people if the boy escaped them, and it
would cost the okulu'tan his life.

"We will take the children and kill the gray demons,"
Pai'le said in a matter-of-fact tone, as if it were already done.

The okulu'tan let go of Pai'le's face. Despite the big
leader's boasts, there was a strong chance the attack would
fail. He must make plans for that. The boy twisted the possibilities around him, making the future unpredictable, but
there was a second path leading to the salvation of his people, and he already possessed the catalyst he needed to
force his people to follow it.

He turned to his left. At the far edge of the tent sat the girl
they'd stolen from the young gray demon. She sat blindfolded
and gagged, with her hands and feet tied in front of her. She
could not understand their words, but she twisted her head
this way and that, listening intently. Oh, yes, he had plans for
this one—plans that did not involve Pai'le or his pachna.

"Leave me. All but you, Ky'lem."

Back on the tree, the wasp vibrated and shook. Free to kill
the humans, the wasp dropped from the limb, attempting to
take flight, but its body was changing. Its wings would not
respond, and it tumbled toward the water, shrinking until it
was no more than a finger's width across. The wasp landed in
the river, too small to make a splash, only a small ring that
spread outward on the surface. What little intelligence the
creature had gained was now gone. It kicked and squirmed in
the water, trying to break free. There was something it needed
to do, but it couldn't remember what. A large, rainbow-
colored fish rose to the surface and snapped up the insect,
swallowing it before diving back down to deeper water.

CHAPTER 9

It was still morning when Riam and Gairen stepped through the carved wooden arch that marked the outskirts of Hath. The events of the morning pressed heavily on Riam, but at least he could think of something besides the wasps and the dead men on the loading dock. He never wanted to see another wasp again, and for as long as he lived, he would hate the creatures even if they were small. Gairen hadn't said a word to him since leaving the timber yard, and the silence left many unanswered questions in Riam's mind. Most of all, he worried that Gairen was angry with him.

Riam hoped he wasn't. As far as he knew, he'd done nothing wrong. He'd somehow taken control of one of Gairen's swords—maybe even "linked" with it, as Gairen put it. Yet he'd done it to save himself, not to try and steal the sword. For Fallen's sake, he'd give it back if Gairen would just show him how.

"I didn't mean . . ." He started to say as much.

"Not here," Gairen said.

"But—"

"I said, not here." Gairen quickened his pace.

Riam sighed. The discussion would have to wait.

The silence gave Riam the chance to take in the town.

Hath was very different from the towns on the plains. Besides the forest that surrounded it, it was larger, with rock-paved streets instead of dirt, and with buildings that were short and squat, built with logs instead of milled lumber. There were no pictures out front to show him what each building held within. Instead, signs carved with curious symbols and flowing lines hung over the doorways. There were no porches either, only short overhangs to keep the rain off the doors. It wasn't crowded this early, but a few people were out moving along the streets or preparing to open their shops.

"The buildings are so different here," Riam said. "How do you know what's inside each one? There are just a bunch of squiggles over the doors." He felt dumb asking the question, but he wanted Gairen to talk about something—anything to make things like they were before the timber yard.

There was a long pause, but thankfully Gairen answered. "We're in Yaden now. Customs are different, and it's cheaper to build with logs. Trees are scarce out on the plains, so wood has to be hauled in from here or Thae. A wainload of lumber builds more than a wainload of logs and is easier to haul. Here, rough logs are plentiful and cheaper than milled boards." He gave Riam a sympathetic half smile. "As for the 'squiggles,' those are words. Another failure of your grandfather, but you'll learn to read when you get to the island."

The buildings and the words—though he was dubious about them truly being words—weren't the only differences to the towns on the plains. The men they passed were bulkier with fairer skin, almost as pale as the Esharii. Many had hair that was light-colored or red like the stable boy in Steading Rock. Light hair was rare back home, and Riam had the uneasy feeling that everyone was staring at him until he noticed a few others with hair as black as his.

Two girls, close to an age where they would be called women, walked down the street toward them. It wasn't their hair that Riam noticed. Their skirts came down to just above the knees, and they wore sandals that laced up above their calves. The girls on the plains wore full dresses unless they were riding or working; then they wore breeches. None of them wore dresses this short. He blushed and pretended to read a sign when the girls caught him staring. Both gave him odd looks when they passed, and Riam found his head swiveling around to catch a glimpse of their calves.

He whipped his head back around when one almost caught him staring.

"Bit young for that, aren't you?" Gairen said.

Riam's face reddened. He wasn't looking at them in that way.

Gairen stopped at one of the log buildings. He tried the metal handle, and when he found it locked, pounded on the door several times.

"Not open yet," a voice called from inside.

He pounded on the door again.

"I said, 'Not open yet!'"

Gairen's fists opened and closed and his body tensed. He looked ready to kick the door in.

Riam slid a step back, out of the way. He'd never seen Gairen acting short or flustered, and he didn't want to be the target if it came to that.

Gairen took a deep breath and exhaled through his nose before knocking on the door so politely it was scarier than if he'd pounded on it.

"Are you deaf? We're not open." The voice grew louder, and the sound of keys rattling came from the other side of the door. It opened a crack. "If you come back . . ." the voice trailed off as the door opened the rest of the way, exposing a short man with sharp, squinty eyes and a close-cut beard. "My apologies." The man's tone was friendlier, but he wore the forced smile of one accustomed to serving others. He flinched when he looked at Riam.

"I need clothes and shoes for the boy, and I have the payment for the others you've already outfitted."

The man kept glancing at Riam. "Is he injured? Does he need a bandage?"

Riam touched his face. Dried blood and wasp guts flaked away from his cheek. He felt fine, but between his clothes and the blood, he must look like he'd wrestled a marcat before sleeping in a nest of screets. No wonder the girls gave him such peculiar looks.

"No. Had some trouble on the way here, but it's mostly superficial."

"Super-what?"

Gairen ignored the question. "We're headed to the baths after we finish here. He'll be fine once he's cleaned up." Gairen took out the pouch of coins and shook it. "Can we get started?"

If the man's grin had been faked before, it was real now. Just like back home, nothing made a tradesman more sincere than the sound of rattling coins.

"Well, I'm sure you know best. Come in, come in, and we'll get the boy some clothes to replace those rags." He stepped out of the way and motioned them inside with a sweeping bow. His voice slipped into the comfortable role of a shopkeeper who'd been at his work for years. "Same as always? Two shirts, one long-sleeved and one short, two pair of trousers, a pair of sandals, and a pair of boots?"

Riam whistled. There were enough clothes in the room to outfit his hometown several times over. The shop was overfilled with shelves and bins that held all manner of clothing in more colors than a field of flowers. There was hardly an empty space that didn't have something poked away. Clothing hung haphazardly on pegs down the support posts in the center of the room, and there were bins of sandals and shoes. Several pairs of leather boots were lined up on one of the shelves. An open doorway to the back revealed two boys near Riam's own age who were sitting at a table and sewing.

"I need at least one set of clothes and either the sandals or the boots now. The rest I'll need in a glass, or at most a glass and a half, unless you're willing to bring it to the outpost."

"Hmm. Let me see." The man eyed Riam up and down, sizing him. "I think I have some things that'll do." He combed through one of the bins, throwing clothing this way and that.

Riam watched one of the boys stitch while the tailor searched. The boy pierced the cloth he was working, pulling the needle through, then the thread. He tightened the stitch, and then he did it again . . . and again . . . and again. A door opened in Riam's mind, showing him the future. This would be the boy's life forever. The two boys would live and work here, doing the same thing day in and day out until the tailor grew too old or passed on. Then one of them would take over. The other, most likely the younger, would either work for the older brother or head out to start his own shop in another town. It didn't matter which brother left or stayed, they would both be doing the very same thing they were doing now for the rest of their lives.

Riam shivered. *No wonder Lemual wanted to leave home so much.* He hoped with all his might that Lemual was safe and had gone his own way. No one should be forced to spend their life doing something they hated. He almost felt sorry for the two boys, but they had a roof and food, and a father who didn't seem unkind. That was more than he'd grown up with.

It may have been only a pair of tendays since Riam left home, but it felt like seasons. The power he'd felt had done more than heal him. He'd confronted something more terrifying than anything he'd ever faced in his life, more terrifying than his grandfather, and he'd survived it. *No, not survived.* In a small way, he'd helped defeat it.

He wasn't sure that he wanted to be a Draegoran yet, but by Sollus, he knew that he didn't want to spend the rest of his life in a room pushing a needle or planting seeds on a farm. He was meant to use the power he'd felt for something more. He could feel it in the sword at the edge of his awareness.

Riam looked toward the blade. He wasn't the only one looking. Gairen stood staring down at the sword handle wrapped in the dead man's shirt with a scowl on his face. He lifted a hand to touch the sword, then hesitated before reaching it. He kept his hand there, a finger's breadth away from the hilt for a moment, before shaking his head in frustration. He rubbed at his temple.

"This might be a little big, but it'll do." The tailor stepped up to Riam with a plain gray shirt with short sleeves. "Big is good. Boys grow fast at your age. Put it on." He dug in another bin. "I think I have a long-sleeved gray that'll fit."

The cloth was a plain, heavy weave that would last, and it smelled far better than the shirt he was wearing. He put it on. The man was right. It was too big and hung loosely from his shoulders.

"Ah, here it is." The man pulled another shirt from the bin and tossed it onto a table.

"I've sandals that will fit, always make plenty for summer, but no more trousers that small. I can have my boys sew two pair, and they'll be ready in half a glass. Boots I can work on myself and have one of the boys bring them to the outpost 'fore dark. I'll have to charge you extra for the rush." He pulled out several pair of simple leather sandals and handed them to Riam. "One of these should fit."

"If you could have one of the boys bring a set of the trousers to the baths—"

"Sha'ra—sha'ra, as they say in Arillia. It is nothing. Captain Karlet told me he's headed downriver in the morning. Every year it's the same. Always a rush for the last few children you bring in." The tailor snatched up Riam's old, torn shoes and threw them onto a pile of scraps in the corner.

The second pair of sandals Riam tested seemed to fit. He fumbled with the laces until the tailor showed him how to tie them properly. He was embarrassed by how dirty he was, but the tailor didn't say a word. Riam walked around the shop like a marcat with wet feet, lifting and shaking each foot. The sandals felt light but comfortable—they were the first pair he'd ever worn, and the first of anything that hadn't been handed down from Lemual.

Next, the tailor grabbed a long, slender chain hanging from one of the racks. Red links were spaced evenly along it. "Let's see. You look to be about seventy-five links tall, so that means . . ." He measured from the floor to Riam's hip. "Yep. Thirty-one links. I'll have the boys make 'em thirty-four. You can roll the bottoms up, and I have a piece of rope you can use for a belt." The tailor whipped the chain around Riam's waist with a practiced flick of his wrist and caught it easily with his other hand. He pulled it snug and nodded to himself before letting it fall back around. "That's all I need. Have the trousers to you in no time." He stood with his hands on his hips.

"The total? For him and the others," Gairen asked curtly.

"Let's see. Six dregs for the boots, and eight for everything else . . . times ten . . . and of course a small fee for the rush . . . that's a hundred and forty-eight. Fourteen to a silver in the market, so ten silver and eight iron, or a gold and a half-silver."

Riam swallowed. The rent and taxes on the farm had only been fifteen silver dregs a season.

Gairen opened the pouch and counted out eleven silver dregs before shoving them into the tailor's hand. "Keep the extra."

"As always, it's an honor." The tailor slipped the coins into a pocket. "Let me get you a chit. Know you'll need it."

They left the tailor's shop, and Gairen marched them down the street. Riam had to run at times to keep up. Funny, he wouldn't have been able to run at all if the sword hadn't healed him. They turned down one of the side streets and followed it until they came to the last building on the edge of town. It wasn't exactly a building, more of a large roof with missing walls and a line of tubs separated by strung canvas. The tubs varied in size, with some large enough to fit several people. A small bench sat next to each, with split timbers laid out between the tubs to walk on.

A young man with pockmarked cheeks met them at the front. "Two dregs for a fresh tub, or a single for the use of a common."

Gairen paid two, and they were led to one of the smaller baths. "Pumped this one this morning. It'll be cold still, but it's clean." The young man placed a small bar of soap and a brush on the bench and pulled the canvas curtain closed.

Between the long ride, the escape from the Esharii and the fight with the wasps, there wasn't a single part of Riam that wasn't filthy.

This fact hadn't escaped Gairen. "I'll go first," he said quickly as he stripped his shirt off and threw it over one of the ropes. He unclasped his belt and stood both swords against the bench. He was careful when he put the wrapped one down, and he was slow to release it, as if it might disappear the moment he let it go.

Riam watched Gairen, in awe of the numerous scars and glyphs on his back and arms. The largest scar ran in a jagged white line from his shoulder, down along his side, to his hip, and the skin was puckered and uneven around it. There were dozens of glyphs, not just the ones Riam was used to seeing. Many of them were damaged or torn by whatever wounds created the scars.

Gairen caught him staring. "Hopefully, you can avoid having as many of these as I do. It was not my intent to give you your first."

Riam tilted his head, confused, and Gairen tapped on

his nose. Riam ran his fingers along the bridge of his own nose. He'd forgotten about the cut. There was a firm line running from one side to the other, and there was a slight notch where it crossed the bridge.

"I'll give you some advice to remember as payment for the scar," Gairen said. He climbed into the tub and eased down into the water. "Most people want a drink or a woman after facing death, but a bath is best." He laid his head back on the edge of the tub and closed his eyes. "I'll tell you why. First, a bath won't make you do something stupid, and it never asks for more coin if you stay in it too long."

Riam almost dropped his new shirt into a puddle of water by the tub. Gairen had never spoken like that before. It was . . . well, it was like Lemual or one of the other boys from town.

"Second, it washes away the blood and sweat so you get the smell out of your nostrils. Extremely hot or extremely cold—either will do. Makes it feel as if the water is burning away the past and you come out fresh."

Riam didn't want to get into the cold water no matter what Gairen said. He turned his hands over. There was blood and green ichor on them, and the sight brought the events of the timber yard back into his thoughts. Maybe the bath would help, but he doubted it.

"Hand me the brush and soap."

Riam did as asked automatically, thinking of the bodies on the loading dock. "Do you ever get used to it? To the dead, I mean, and the killing?" He was asking about more than the wasps and the dead men. If he was going to become a Draegoran, he wanted to know about the prisoners Gairen had executed and the Esharii he'd killed on the plains.

There was an awkward pause as Gairen weighed the question and how much he wanted to say. He glanced at the swords and ran his palms down across his cheeks till they were closed in front of his lips and nose like a man praying to Sollus. He took a deep breath and sighed, and when he spoke, there was something different about his voice that Riam couldn't put his finger on.

"You learn to see beyond the death and the dead—beyond the blood. In the beginning, it's easier if you look inside a person and know the crimes, like with your grandfather. Then you get angry, but it's an honest anger, and you use that rage . . . that wrath, to get through doing what needs to be done. It's harder when the innocent die, but it's the same. You use the anger over the injustice of the world to motivate you. After a time, you simply don't think about it much. As far as the Esharii, that's war. People die in war, and there's no use getting angry. It's simply you or them."

Riam's heart clenched at the unexpected reference to his grandfather, although he was more startled than hurt. Thinking of the old man wasn't nearly as painful as it used to be. That didn't mean he didn't feel anything. It was simply more distant.

"And afterward?" Riam asked. "How do you live with it?"

"If what you've done is right, it's no harder than getting over the death of the insects we killed today. It's the mistakes you remember. Those are the memories that follow you and keep sleep at a distance." Gairen slid under the water and came back up. He ran his hands through his long hair, combing it out.

If being a Draegoran meant protecting others, then Riam could live with that. He could see himself standing up against people like his grandfather someday. But he still wasn't convinced. Too many people seemed to hate the Draegorans. From what he'd seen, it didn't add up.

"I don't understand." Riam paused, trying to figure out how to get at the question. "If all Draegorans are like you, why do so many people seem to . . . well, hate you? I mean, you've been good to me, sir, and you've never hurt me or—as far as I can tell—anyone that didn't deserve it." He took a deep breath. "But are all Draegorans like you? And if they are, then why doesn't everyone love the Draegorans? It doesn't make sense. You've told me I have the Fallen's blood, and now that I am connected to the sword," he pointed to the blade against the bench, "I believe you, but I'm missing something."

It was Gairen's turn to look shocked, his eyes widening at the offhand mention of the sword. At first, he seemed to float between anger and discomfort, but to Riam's surprise, he tilted his head back and laughed.

"You've your father's direct logic, that's for Fallen sure. Well, you didn't pour sugar on it and neither will I. Far too few Draegorans are like Master Iwynd or me. Many enjoy the killing and the power, especially the Wolf Regiment. You saw some of them in the taulin out on the plains. That's the difference between the Owls and the Wolves—we serve the people of the Covenant. The Wolves see everyone who isn't Draegoran as maston or cattle."

Riam's head snapped up, all thought of the sword forgotten. *Father? Did Gairen say father?* His heart beat faster.

"The Wolves and their allies led the Draegoran Council for hundreds of years. They caused most of the resentment and hatred that exist today. To be fair, those were harder times with an Esharii or an Arillian invasion every year, and they called for harsher methods. Times have changed, but the Wolves have not. They no longer lead the Council, the Stonebreakers do, but they want to, and they haven't changed their methods."

Riam nodded as if he was paying attention, but his mind raced. Gairen had never mentioned Riam's father before, and Riam wanted to know more. He tried to slip in a question. "Was my father like you . . . or the Wolves?"

Gairen paused and stared off at nothing. "He was a far better man than I am." It was almost a whisper.

"So he was a warden? Everyone calls you that, but I don't even know what that is." Riam held his breath and leaned down to untie his sandals casually. He was afraid that if Gairen saw the eagerness on his face he would stop speaking.

"It's a rank. Like the kydens we spoke of earlier. Every Draegoran has a rank and position. Initially, it's easy to understand who commands whom, but later it gets more complicated. To keep it simple, after your training is complete, you'll most likely be assigned duties as an armsman or a scout. Armsmen can be sent anywhere, but scouts tend to go to one of the two passes.

"Five armsmen and a taulin leader make up a taulin, and a half-warden leads five taulins. From there, it goes to warden, senior warden and then a master. A master commands at both of the passes and in each capital with a senior warden as his second-in-command. Understand?"

"I think so." Riam wanted to talk about his father, not receive a lesson on Draegoran ranks.

"Good, repeat the order back to me."

Riam let go of the laces and looked up. He hadn't expected to be tested. "Um . . . armsman, then taulin leader, um . . . a half-warden, a senior . . . no, wait, a warden, then a senior warden. Last is a master."

"Good." Gairen scrubbed with the soap as he spoke. "Now, those are the primary ranks. There are numerous positions, like scout or inspector, or training the regulars. These are each a bit different. Scouts, for instance, are assigned directly to a warden who falls under the senior warden. They have but two positions—scout, which is equivalent to an armsman, and senior scout, which is equivalent to a taulin leader. There is one exception to that, and that's a free scout who carries the rank of a half-warden, but that's where it starts to get complicated."

It'd become complicated long before now. There was no way Riam would remember all of it.

"And the regiment a Draegoran comes from also makes a difference. For instance, most Owls start as scouts."

"So you're a scout?" Riam asked.

"Yes and no."

Riam groaned. There was no way to sort it all out.

"I've been something . . . different for a time." Gairen paused and bobbed under the water a few more times to rinse. "This will get easier. It's mostly a matter of understanding that many positions have the same rank. For instance, there are wardens who oversee city districts or are advisers to the high landowners." He wiped the hair out of his face. "Now, tell me the rank order for scouts."

This time, Riam was ready. "Scout, senior scout, free scout, and then warden." He could repeat the words, but most of it didn't make any sense.

"You've a good memory. Don't worry on it too much. You'll learn all of this later. What I'm really trying to tell you is that everyone and everything has its place and rank, and everyone knows that place." He smirked a bit to himself. "Or at least I thought it was that way. You taking control of that sword has put a bend in my thoughts."

Riam tried to slip in another question about his father. "What was my father's place? Was he a scout?"

Gairen's face sobered. "Your life is about to become more difficult than it's ever been. You can either embrace the order and structure of the island and your regiment, learning your place and becoming a working part of it, or you can fight it and chase your own needs and desires. Some choose the latter, but they don't live long. Don't waste your time worrying about things that are out of your control." He chuckled. "Would that I could heed my own advice."

Riam listened and did his best to understand. *I don't know if I can forget trying to find out about my real father.* "I'm just curious about him. That's all."

Gairen ignored him and climbed out of the tub. "Your turn," he said and sat down on the end of the bench to dry.

Riam stripped off the rest of his clothes and climbed in. The water was freezing. He grabbed the soap to get it over with. He'd thought the conversation over, but Gairen surprised him.

"None of this may make sense, but all you need to remember is that you will not succeed at anything you don't believe in. Forget your family. Forget your past. Forget worrying about your father and your grandfather. Commit everything to becoming a Draegoran, and you might survive long enough for the answers to find you."

Yes, but it's hard to decide something when I'm not even sure what that something is! He wasn't going to say that out loud, however. He simply nodded in agreement like he thought Gairen expected. *How can I forget my past?*

Gairen said nothing more than to point out areas to scrub harder for the remainder of the bath.

Even hurrying, Riam was shivering by the time he climbed out. A breeze blew in under the canvas, making it even colder. He certainly didn't feel "reborn," and he had the impression that there was a lot more blood and sweat ahead of him than behind. He stood by the tub, exposed and freezing, waiting for the water to dry and his new trousers to arrive. Thank the Fallen it wasn't winter.

CHAPTER 10

The outpost was busier when they returned near midday. The regulars under Harol's command, along with a good number of townsfolk, were digging out the burned section of the wall. A single harnessed maston pulled the charred stumps free of the earth. Nearby, a second work detail dug a trench and set stakes into the ground in front of the damaged area. The thunk of axes filled the air as men hacked away at the old timbers, either making stakes for the palisade or cutting what wasn't useful into firewood. Farther out, a second trench was dug in front of the line of pickets.

"Straight out of Nevil's *On Defense*," Gairen said. "Perfect for stopping a mounted formation. It needs to be done, but it's a waste of time. If the tribesmen return, they won't come against that. When you're fighting the Esharii, always assume they'll attack where you least expect. You'll be right nine outta ten times."

Gairen pointed to a small building. "The other children sleep there. You can join them later, but first, find the stable and check on my horse. Clean out his stall if it isn't done already, and when you've finished that, comb him down and give him an extra bucket of grain. He'll need it after the last few days. Join the others at the evening meal when you're done."

"Yes . . . Warden." Riam tested the word. It didn't feel right, but it seemed better than saying sir or using Gairen's name.

"I'll be at Master Iwynd's quarters. I need to let him know about the timber yard, and I have reports to write." As an afterthought, he added, "Come find me if the new boots don't arrive before dark. You'll be leaving at sunrise, and you'll need the boots."

The stable was between the warehouse and the privy. A Thaen Regular was cleaning the stalls out, but he hadn't reached the one that held Gairen's horse.

"Glad for the help, even if it's only for the one stall." He sucked at a tooth, making a sharp smacking noise. "It's a good day to clean 'em out. The taulin's horses and most of the drafts are out with the supply delivery, and most of the spares are bein' used for cleanin' up the wall." He handed Riam a flat-tipped shovel. "Only have the one 'barrow, but I'll work on the stalls closest to you and we can share it. Horse shit goes down the trail out the small gate at the back of the outpost. Fresh straw's over there."

It took Riam the rest of the afternoon to clean out the stall. It should've taken less than a glass, but the regular decided that since there was only one wheelbarrow and dumping it was the easy part, Riam should be the one to take care of that.

Every time he returned through the small rear gate, the regular was waiting, smile on his face, with a pile ready to be shoveled into the wheelbarrow. Riam was only able to get a few shovelfuls out of his stall before it was time to dump it again. He gave the soldier angry stares whenever the man wasn't looking.

With each trip, the regular's smile got larger, exposing the long, yellow teeth he kept sucking at. Somehow, the rest of the stalls were complete by the time Riam finished the single stall he'd been told to clean.

"Thanks for the help, boy," the regular said. He hung up his shovel and left the stable whistling a tune.

This wasn't the first time the regular had pulled the trick. It was too smooth and practiced. Riam picked up a dried horse dropping and started to throw it at the soldier, then thought better of it. The man had seemed pleasant and friendly, but like as not, he would cuff Riam upside the head if he threw it. With a sigh he tossed it away and went back to work.

He laid new straw in the stall and brushed the horse down with a hard-bristled comb he found hanging on the wall. There was no stool, so after wiping the wheelbarrow out with straw to keep his new sandals clean—or at least as clean as they could be after all the work he'd already done—he stood on top of it to reach the horse's back. Last, he brought the grain like he'd been told and used a small pick to clean out each of the horse's hooves. It wasn't difficult. He'd done it hundreds of times back home. When he finished, he put everything back and went to eat after washing his hands and face in a water trough.

The hall was nearly full when Riam arrived, and there were two tables filled with children his age dressed in the same gray shirts and breeches. Riam looked for Gairen, but the warden wasn't among the crowd. He closed his eyes. The blade was to his right; he could feel it in the direction Gairen had gone after sending him to the stable. He'd hoped to ask more questions.

He thought about waiting, but his stomach growled and made the decision for him. He went and stood in the line of people waiting to be served. The two cooks were busy, with no time for the morning's banter, although Jon gave him a wink when he dumped two ribs from the morning's pig on his plate and handed him a chunk of bread.

Riam didn't want to sit with the other children. The truth was, he didn't have much experience with others his own age except for Nola, and that hadn't turned out so well. Plus, he honestly didn't know what to say. He took his plate and sat alone at an empty bench in the corner with his back to the wall. The food was as good as it'd been earlier that morning. He tore the bread partway through, opened it, and placed chunks of rib meat inside to make a crude meat roll.

A girl with red hair dark enough that it could be mistaken for brown came in. Her lips were narrow, and her mouth was so straight and thin the feature stood out, neither turning up nor down at the edges. She wore the same gray outfit he and the other children wore, and judging by the Thaen Regulars around her, she was taller than he was. She turned in his direction, and he pretended to watch the cooks.

When she received her food, she moved in a straight line for his table. He looked left then right. *She's going to sit with me.* He groaned. *What do I say?* He looked down at his plate to avoid eye contact in the hope she would move on and sit somewhere else.

Her plate clacked down across from him.

He tore off a piece of bread from the meat roll and chewed slowly, giving him a reason not to speak.

After he'd taken two long, slow bites, the girl spoke up. "I'm Loral." She looked at him questioningly.

"Riam," he mumbled with his mouth full.

"I'm from Galtare."

He had no idea where that was. It must have been obvious.

"It's a port city on the Neshian side of the river from Thae. What about you?"

"I'm . . ." He searched his memory but came up blank. He didn't know the name of the town he was from. Grandfather and Lemual had always just said they were going to town, never a name. Surely somebody must have mentioned it, but if they had, he couldn't remember it to save his life. His mind was blank. He chuckled.

"Are you laughing at me?" Loral's mouth pressed into an even narrower line. She started to stand.

"No. Wait," he said. "I don't know the name of the town I'm from. I thought it was funny that until a few days ago, the world was so small that there was no need for it to have a name. I know it's somewhere near Cove, but more inland, on the edge of the plains."

"That's a lot farther north than where I'm from, but I think we might have traveled through the area on the way here. It's so flat and empty. All that emptiness scares me. It's too quiet. I like the noise of the city."

"I've never been to a city. Hath is the largest place I've ever seen."

The ends of her mouth turned upward for the first time, and she giggled. "Hath is tiny. Wait till we get to a real city."

Her laugh grated along Riam's back. It wasn't his fault he'd been born on a farm and never gone anywhere. "I don't know. I like the open land. I like the farms." He didn't know why he said that. It certainly wasn't true.

"Is that what your family does? Farm?"

"They did. They're all dead," he blurted out, wanting her to feel bad for laughing.

Her mouth went back to a narrow line. "I'm sorry."

They were both quiet after that. She looked uncomfortable and wouldn't look at him as they ate. The silence was awkward and heavy.

I shouldn't have said it that way. He'd been unfair to Nola at the stream, and she was gone before he could apologize. He took a deep breath. "Me, too. I shouldn't have put it like that."

Her mouth remained flat.

"How many of us are there?" He knew the answer from the money Gairen paid the tailor, but it was all he could think to ask. *I wish she'd smile again. She looks far too serious when she's not smiling.* He waited anxiously while she finished chewing.

"You make ten. I heard there was supposed to be one more, but something happened to her. They don't tell us much." She looked at him, expecting him to fill her in on the story.

Riam didn't say anything. He didn't want to talk about losing Nola to the Esharii. He shrugged his shoulders instead, hoping it was enough of a response.

"Anyway, we're all supposed to leave in the morning. You're lucky you arrived when you did. They've had us working around the outpost, cleaning the plates and pots, pulling weeds, mucking out the stable for that idiot, Maber . . . whatever the soldiers can think of to keep us busy. The old Draegoran is the worst. If he sees you doing nothing, he snaps his fingers and a regular comes running to put you to work."

"You mean Master Iwynd? He's the only Draegoran here, right? I mean besides Warden Gairen."

"Warden Gairen?"

"That's the Draegoran who brought me here. His rank is warden. The older one is Master Iwynd. At least that's what Gairen calls him. Anyway, just be glad he's an Owl."

"An owl?"

"Yes, but not the bird. That's the name of their regiment. It's like a clan or a school. There are six of them, and we will all be placed in one for training eventually. Anyway, if he were from the Wolf Regiment, it would have been much worse from what Gairen says."

Loral's brow furrowed and her narrow mouth formed a quiet "Oh." She looked at him as if he were an Esharii. "How do you know all this?"

"From Warden Gairen. Didn't the Draegoran who brought you here tell you anything?"

"It was a group of six that brought me, Tannon, and the twins." She pointed at a pair of boys at one of the tables that were obviously twins—they both had the same flat nose and wavy brown hair—though one seemed twice the size of the other. Between them sat a blond-haired boy with his arm in a sling. "The twins are Karyl and Marcus. The smaller one is Marcus. That is Vashi with the sling between them. He's nice, but he talks a lot. They're from small towns like you, but Tannon," she pointed to a boy who sat at another table with several other children, "is from Galtare like I am."

"If it was a group of six that brought you here, then it was a taulin—five armsmen and a taulin leader. That's what they call their patrols."

She held her palms up. "Now I'm the one who feels like she's from a farm and doesn't know anything." The corners of her mouth turned up again. "Guess we're even."

"Sure." He hadn't been trying to show her up. By the Fallen, he hadn't even told her all the ranks he'd learned, or about how every Draegoran was linked with the crystal in their sword. She'd probably think he was crazy if he told her they all carried the Fallen's blood. She was smiling, however, and for some strange reason, that was suddenly all that mattered.

"Anyway, the Draegorans . . . the taulin," she paused, and he nodded, confirming she'd said the name right, "left the next morning after bringing us here. That was more than a tenday ago." She took another bite of food, then spoke while chewing, "I was glad to get away from them. They let Tannon do what he wanted so long as we were ready each morning. Stay away from him as much as you can, by the way. He's dangerous. I've known lots of boys like him in Galtare—ones who like hurting people. He and I were the only two taken from the entire city, and I had to put up with him by myself until they found the twins up the coast. Thank Sollus that Karyl is bigger than Tannon."

Riam almost laughed at that. If he could survive his grandfather, the Esharii, and the wasps, he was fairly certain that there wasn't much worse the other boy could do to him.

"There are a couple of other 'young landowners' among us," she said sarcastically.

Riam knew she didn't mean that literally. Even where he was from, it was a common description for children who threw fits when things didn't go their way.

"Sitting with Tannon are Dunval, Ania, Sabat, and Jerald. Ania, she's their harmless pet, so don't worry about her. Sabat and Jerald aren't so bad one-on-one, but they follow Tannon's lead whenever they are with him." Loral hunched closer and lowered her voice. "Dunval, that's the one with short, dark hair and the narrow nose, he likes to fight, but only if the odds are two or three to one. He and Tannon caught Vashi in the dark one night near the privy. They beat him up pretty bad because he wouldn't trade work details with Tannon. That's why his arm is in a sling. One of the regulars questioned us about it, but no one said anything."

Riam looked again at the tables where the others sat as Loral continued to give him a rundown of the children. He could see the split between the groups now that she pointed it out. Tannon's group was loud and boisterous while the other table was subdued, as if they didn't want to be noticed.

Tannon caught Riam's attention. The boy was staring at him, a thoughtful look on his face behind eyes that were too narrow. Riam returned the stare and held it, refusing to look away. Tannon smiled, a big wide grin like he'd been given a new toy to play with.

On the other side of the outpost, Gairen sat staring at his sword.

It was a simple piece, with only the slightest curvature to it, but there was a grace to the modest, slow curve and to the faint scrollwork that turned with it below the narrow groove of the fuller. The guard was a single oval disk with smooth, rounded edges that was wide enough to prevent another weapon from sliding into the wielder's hand, but not so large as to impair movement. The blade collar was the color of soft gold and rose no more than a thumb's width from the guard, enfolding the blue-steel blade with only the slightest hint of a seam. A hilt of polished iron-wood encapsulated the tang, and the mastonhide-wrapped grip was stained dark with years of use. The pommel that held the crystal balanced the weapon perfectly.

The blade at his side was the sword's twin. They were a flawless matched set and irreplaceable, made by the best swordsmith the island of Draegora had known in the last five hundred years, Master Sorrant, the former kyden of Ironstriker Regiment. These were the last blades the master-swordsmith completed before dying, and they were one of only two matching sets he'd ever made. The other set was at the bottom of the ocean with Jonim, Gairen's brother.

Gairen looked at his reflection in the blade. His eyes were drawn and red, and the skin around them dark. Losing the link to the sword on the table had torn away half of the connection he held to his brother, not to mention giving him a pounding headache that wouldn't subside.

He ran a finger along the back of the blade. It was almost painful as the power of the weapon pulled at him, and he was forced to shield himself. The crystal had tasted his blood many times when he was wounded over the years, and now that it was no longer linked with him, it tried to steal away his life whenever he touched it. The weapon was foreign to him now, even though he'd carried it for years, and he didn't understand how the boy was able to take it. The crystals could be bonded to another if the owner was killed, but it was difficult and required several masters to accomplish. As far as he knew, what the boy had done was impossible.

Pulling his hand away from the blade, he leaned back in the chair. He was in Master Iwynd's quarters. The same room he'd been in the evening prior. Beside the sword, his report and a letter lay on the table. The letter explained who the boy was and what he'd done to the sword. It was sealed with wax and addressed to his father, Kyden Thalle, commander of Owl Regiment. The official report next to it detailed the attack in the timber yard. It left out the part about the sword.

There was no doubt that Jonim's boy had potential, even if what he'd done was a fluke. He might carry six, maybe even seven of the bloodlines if his grandmother had Esharii blood like her name implied. Maybe it was the Esharii blood that allowed him to take the sword. He didn't know of any other Draegoran who carried it. It might make him stronger than even Kyden Verros one day, the commander of Wolf Regiment. Verros wouldn't like that at all. *If he finds out, will he try and recruit him or kill him?* Neither answer would be good for the Owls, which explained why he'd left it out of the official report.

Gairen could imagine the infighting and maneuvering among the kydens to add the boy to their regiments if word got out about what he'd done. He could also imagine the boy living a very short life, killed by one of the other regiments who didn't get him. Add to this the knowledge of the boy's lineage, and the items in front of Gairen might very well be a death sentence, even if Father decided to train him.

No. He could send Riam to the island with the report, but if he sent the letter to his father, he doubted the boy had much of a chance.

Gairen stood up to get the bottle of brandy from the cupboard. For the first time since he'd come up with his plan of finding one of Jonim's children, he was no longer certain about what he should do. It was early in the day for it, but he needed a drink. At least it would help with the headache.

When the dark ones attacked, the Gods of Light opened themselves wide, embracing their timeless enemies instead of defending themselves. They wrapped their essence around their counterparts, binding and holding them fast. Then, as one, they gave up their immortality and power, dragging the profane dark ones with them down to the worlds of man.

While most of their power and memories were lost, they retained enough knowledge to continue their struggle and enough strength to reshape the worlds upon which they now lived.

Only a single pair remained in the heavens, Sollus and Faen, each the weakest of their kind.

—Edyin's *Complete Chronicle of the Fallen*

CHAPTER 11

The Esharii attacked the outpost in the deep of night, long after the moon fell beyond the horizon and well before it would rise again for its second journey among the stars. They didn't charge the damaged front gate Harol's men reinforced. They didn't come in through the small, well-lit rear gate either, not at first, and they didn't climb the walls in darkness between the sentry's rounds or ride in hidden under the hay of a wagon as the storymen romanticize it. Instead, they came in on their hands and knees through the shit and piss of the privy.

Four of the most experienced tribesmen, led by the scarred warrior, Ky'lem, crawled through the foul covered trench that would lead them to a drainage outlet under the wall. The stench was abhorrent, especially after taking the water from the lake of life that heightened the tribesmen's senses and abilities. Touching the water of the Najalii was forbidden to all but the okulu'tan, with one exception. Esharii warriors carried a paste made with the water and plants of the lake. It made the warriors stronger and faster, almost the equal of the gray demons when it was fresh. The paste they'd consumed this night was many days old, but still potent enough to make them more than a match for the

Thaens at the outpost. For the gray demons, they would need to work together.

To Ky'lem, this was cause for concern. Pai'le was like a brother to him—they'd both been named spears of the tribe on the same day and fought side by side against man and beast—but leadership had given the big tribesman a false pride Ky'lem could not break through. In past days, there had been a balance between Pai'le's bullheadedness and Ky'lem's thoughtfulness that had made them stronger together than apart. Since being named warleader of this raid, however, Pai'le refused to listen, even when given sound advice. He kept splitting the warband up when the best way to kill the gray demons was to overwhelm them with numbers. Fighting them piecemeal was a quick way to reach the great beyond, and while Ky'lem did not fear death, he had no desire to hasten the day of his journey.

My thoughts are too kind because we are like brothers. Pai'le was willfully leading with his heart instead of his head, acting on impulse and desire instead of strategy and sound thinking. He was far too worried about displaying his honor and prowess to the young spears, setting an example that would get them killed. It was maddening, but all Ky'lem could do was obey. At least Pai'le had listened this time and let Ky'lem lead the attack through the privy. As revolting as the trench was, Ky'lem's honor gave him no choice but to volunteer. He would never send men to do what he would not, and this way he could ensure it succeeded without wasting lives.

He slid forward and his hand sunk into the slime of human waste. *One day I will fill his blankets with screet shit as payment for this night.*

He forced himself to calm down, to hold his frustration in check. Emotion led to the rash mistakes he abhorred. Besides, even if Pai'le was acting like a man kicked in the head by a horse, it was better to fight under the man's command than miss the opportunity to gain honor and status in the tribe. There'd been few raids into the northern lands over the last ten years, and he would not allow Pai'le to fight while he sat at home with his wives in his longhut. Ky'lem would match him honor for honor, death for death. If Pai'le were ever elevated to the council, Ky'lem would need to remain right beside him for balance. He wanted to kill the oath-breaking gray demons as much as anyone, but he wanted to unite the tribes and wipe them out forever, not recklessly waste lives to kill only a few.

Then there was the okulu'tan, the true leader of this warband. The old spirit-walker's magic was strong, and he'd pulled the council's strings like a puppeteer, offering them the secret of soulfire to get their support for the raid. The council had lapped up his words like starving ga'ginga pups at a bowl of milk. The council didn't completely trust the okulu'tan—no one who truly valued his soul trusted a spirit-walker—but the secret to soulfire was far too much to ignore.

In truth, it wasn't just his honor and matching Pai'le's deeds that had Ky'lem crawling through the filth. Few okulu'tan joined the raids in the north like they had during his father's time, and a true spirit-walker, one who'd walked the paths of all life, hadn't been over the mountains in more than a generation. Ky'lem hadn't wanted to miss the chance of earning favor with the old one. To unite the tribes, he would need a powerful okulu'tan behind him.

Now one had offered him the chance, but at a price he didn't know if he was willing to pay—or if he could even trust the deal the okulu'tan had offered after the others left the tent. A spirit-walker's motives were never clear, and while they spoke truth, it was always their own version.

Ky'lem mopped sweat from his forehead with the back of his forearm, careful not to spread the filth of the trench onto his face or smear the stripes of his green-and-black face paint. *I need to worry about the offer later.* Worrying about tomorrow's fight in the heat of battle was another way to hasten the journey to the great beyond.

He resumed his slow, blind crawl through the muck and piss. Ahead of him, large grubs and beetles controlled by the spirit-walker had bored into the wood and packed earth that held the metal grate under the wall and barred access to the outpost. It broke away easily when he reached it, and his warriors climbed with determined sureness through the tunnel that led to the cesspit below the privy. Here the smell was worse, and breathing was difficult. He was proud that none of his warriors gave them away by retching or turning their stomachs out before they climbed up through one of the small chutes and into the outpost from below a waste hole.

Faint light filtered into the privy from a window. Ky'lem motioned three of the tribesmen up toward the top of the wall and the fourth toward the small rear gate. The warriors acknowledged the command with curt nods, and five Ti'yak longknives slid quietly from their sheaths. The reverse curve of the knives made shadows like fangs on the wall. Their swords had been left behind in favor of the longknives and the clay-encased balls of soulfire they carried. Ky'lem had tested the self-igniting weapons the spiritwalker offered before coming over the mountains, and they'd worked well on the gates and walls of the outpost two days earlier. The pig fat, pitch, and other mysterious ingredients burned so hot that water was little use putting out the flames. With it, the Ti'yak would gain a huge advantage over the other tribes.

His part in this raid was simple. Kill the sentries, open the rear gate, and fire the barracks, then help capture the children. Pai'le and the others were beyond the tree line, waiting for the sentries to be cleared and the rear gate to open. Ky'lem and his men would need to move fast once they left the privy. Their smell alone might alert the Thaens, although he doubted it. The ones who served the gray demons were little more than children playing with sharpened sticks when it came to fighting.

Ky'lem signed the command to move, and the five tribesmen fanned out toward their targets.

The first to die was a young Thaen Regular who stood no more than a pace from a ladder near the rear gate. He was bored, his eyes half closed, fighting sleep. He leaned on his spear and stared off at nothing. The Thaen had a quick moment to lift his head and sniff at the air questioningly before a hand clamped over his mouth. Ky'lem drove his knife into the man's neck until the tip protruded from the opposite side. The Thaen's eyes bulged, but he could make no sound.

Pulling back on the jaw, Ky'lem pushed outward with the knife. With his enhanced strength, the blade cut through cartilage, muscle, and tendons with ease, severing everything forward of the spine. Blood sprayed into the night.

Ky'lem took no pleasure in killing a warrior who was so

weak, but he didn't disdain it either. Like his frustration, he kept the rest of his emotions in check, saving his real fury for the gray demons.

He eased the body to the ground. Two of his tribesmen were already scrambling up the ladder while another removed the heavy crossbeams on the small gate. Soon he could let his anger at Pai'le and his hatred of the gray demons go, and if Sollus were with him, his knife would taste the blood of the true enemy, the servants of the dark one—unless, of course, Pai'le got them all killed first.

The small rear gate swung open with only the slightest creak. With luck, the whole of the warband would be inside the walls before an alarm sounded. Ky'lem and the warrior who'd opened the gate both pulled balls of soulfire from their waist and ran for the barracks.

The dying soldier on the ground's last vision was of Ky'lem's striped and scarred face, and his last thought was that the very apparition of death had arrived at the outpost to claim them all.

Gairen opened his eyes and listened. He heard nothing, but something was wrong—he could feel it. Survival as a scout depended on instincts, and he hadn't survived this long by ignoring his. He leaped up from his sleeping mat and grabbed both the blades that lay next to him. The sheaths made muted thumps as they fell to the floor. The sword linked to Jonim's boy rattled on the floor when he dropped it an instant later. "Faen's balls," he cursed. He shook his hand, trying to get the feeling back. He'd drawn both swords out of habit, forgetting that the second blade was no longer his to control.

Forgetting the weapon on the floor, he closed his eyes and pulled from the reservoir of energy stored in the crystal of the sword that remained to him. The soft orange glow of life should have surrounded him. Walls and lifeless objects should have melted into translucent glass. The guards who walked the walls and the horizontal forms of men sleeping should have radiated around him. Instead, a dark haze he could not penetrate blanketed his inner sight. He saw nothing—which meant something was very wrong. The Esharii were here, and with them, the okulu'tan and his magic.

Blind panic would solve nothing, so he took the time to don his shirt and boots before stepping warily out of the small building where he slept. Even without his inner sight, his vision should have been good enough to pick out the sentries who manned the walls. Their posts were empty— another bad sign. The lights from the oil pots scattered around the outpost revealed no movement, but if the sentries were missing, then the Esharii were already inside the walls. He needed to alert the regulars before it was too late.

Opening his link to the crystal wider, he drew in power and dashed toward the barracks, hoping to get there before there was an alarm. As a scout, he'd returned with news of an impending attack more than once. A hundred men awakened in the middle of the night by an attack created a lot of confusion. It would be better if he were there to get them organized first.

He rounded the last building in time to see two objects hurtling through the air toward the barracks. They hit the wooden building and exploded, splattering orange flames that clung to the door and wall. The whoosh of the fire filled the silence of the night as the flames gained air. Gairen could feel the wave of heat. Whatever had been thrown burned unnaturally hot. *So much for containing the chaos.*

There was another crash, and flames shot up from the opposite side of the barracks, exactly where the second door was located. He glimpsed an Esharii running between the buildings but resisted the urge to pursue. He needed to get the regulars moving.

The door to the barracks swung open, but the men would not be using it. The fire was already at eye level and far too hot to pass. Shutters on the first floor banged open, followed by two more on the second floor. Men and women began tumbling out through the narrow windows. He heard another crash in the distance.

Gairen grabbed the first man out. "The Esharii are inside the walls. Get the men armed and organized. Contain the fire, secure the gates, and protect the warehouse. Get men on the walls with bows if you can." If they didn't hurry, there'd be nothing left of the outpost by dawn but ash and cinders.

The soldier held his empty hands up in frustration. Most of the regulars coming out the windows were unarmed and half dressed. The man turned back to the window and yelled at his comrades to get weapons and armor before fleeing. Flames already licked the sky above the second-story roof.

Word of the attack spread, and men began to move with a purpose instead of blindly fleeing.

That was all Gairen needed to accomplish. He charged off in the direction the tribesmen had run. Even though he'd told the men to guard the warehouse, he didn't think the Esharii were here to simply destroy supplies. At least that wasn't their primary target. If it were, the warehouse would have been the first building to burn. He needed a moment to think. Clearing his mind, he used the energy of the blade to slip into the mahl-shae, the mental state used for fighting.

The world around him slowed, although that was a backward way of looking at it. More accurately, his mind sped up until the world around him moved in slow motion relative to his thoughts. The state also calmed the nerves and tempered the surge of energy the body created when faced with danger. He didn't have a lot of power left in the crystal—they drained quickly over a short time—so he wouldn't be able to stay in it for long. A moment in the mahl-shae, however, was all he needed to organize his thoughts.

The Esharii were not burning the warehouse, and they didn't have enough men inside the walls to pin the regulars inside the burning building. This meant that the fire would only slow the regulars down. The tribesmen had another objective, something that could be accomplished quickly. This was not an attack to destroy the outpost or weaken the keep it supplied. This was a targeted raid after something specific. The Esharii had come in by stealth and removed the sentries, but they hadn't come directly for him. That left only one other possibility—the children. Gairen released himself from the trancelike state and ran for the building where the children slept.

Heart racing, Riam bolted up from sleep. Somewhere on the other side of the outpost someone had touched the sword. His mind tingled, and he had the overwhelming urge to find the weapon.

Whoever it was hadn't touched it for long. *It had to be Gairen, but why would the warden be touching the blade in the middle of the night?* He lay back down, only to realize that he needed to relieve himself now that he was awake or he would never get back to sleep.

With a grunt, he reached for the new boots next to him. One of the boys from the tailor's shop had delivered them before sundown. He felt sorry for the tailor's boy and hadn't spoken to him much. The boots, though, were magnificent. They were simple and unadorned, but they fit well and were even lined with soft wool. He slipped them on, marveling again at how good they felt. They were by far the most expensive things he'd ever owned.

The room around him was crowded with the sleeping forms of the other children, not to mention the small packs they'd all been given for tomorrow's trip downriver. Riam couldn't believe he would be traveling by boat in the morning and that he wouldn't see Gairen again for years. It'd only been a few tendays, but Gairen was the only connection he held with his old life besides Lemual. He pushed the thought out of his mind. *I need to forget about Lemual and the past.*

A board creaked loudly when he stepped on it. Loral sat up, her hair poking in all directions.

"Where are you going?" she whispered.

"To the privy."

"I need to go, too. You can watch the door while I'm inside." She slid into her boots and rose beside him before he could think of a reason to say no. He doubted she needed him there. No one else would be using the privy at this time of night.

When they arrived, he let her go in first.

"Disgusting!" she shouted from inside. "Someone wiped shit around the holes and on the wall. I hope we leave before anyone notices or we'll be on a detail cleaning it up."

Riam was more shocked at Loral's cursing than he was at the mess she'd discovered.

Several loud crashes broke the night's silence, as if someone were smashing crockery, followed by bright flashes.

"What was that?" Loral asked.

"I don't know."

She was back in the doorway, looking over Riam's shoulder in the direction of the light. "The barracks are that way. On the other side of the mess hall," she said.

Now that she pointed it out, Riam could see the mess hall silhouetted by the glow of the oil pots. As he watched, the light flared brighter. He began to get a bad feeling in his stomach. If Gairen had touched the sword and there was a fire inside the outpost, the two events were connected.

In the distance, a man screamed.

"Come on!" Riam grabbed Loral and pulled her toward the glow.

"Shouldn't we go back?" she said but followed.

They rounded the mess hall to find the Thaen Regulars scrambling to form ranks.

"Get a weapon and form up. Doesn't matter if it's yours. The swaugs are inside the walls." They formed rows in four groups. Some held weapons, others did not. A few strapped on leather vests or pulled on boots.

Riam and Loral moved closer to the man shouting orders.

"Section leaders to me," the man yelled, and four regulars ran to him.

"Rollen, take your men and protect the warehouse. Once you have it secure, take half your section and clear the walls. Dorel, take your section to the rear gate. Errin, take yours to the front. And be ready. We don't know how many there are or what they're up to.

"Once the gates are secure, each of you work back toward the middle and clear out any swaugs you find. If you're engaged by a large force, don't be a hero. Form a line and defend until one of the other sections works their way to you and flanks them." Three of the soldiers nodded, and the man in charge turned to the fourth, a female with cropped hair. "Valora, get the closest water barrels and blankets for the fire. There's no saving the barracks, but you have to stop it from spreading, or we'll lose the whole outpost."

The four saluted and ran to their sections where they formed. Men and women still climbed out of the windows, and the section leaders called to them.

"First section, here!"

"Second! Let's go! Form up!"

"On me, third. Time to make the swaugs pay."

The man in charge saw Riam and Loral. "What are you two doing here?"

"Sir, we were going to the privy when we saw the fire."

"By the Fallen, I forgot the children. Valora!" The female section leader turned back toward the leader. "Take half your people and protect the children as soon as you have them ready, I'll get the remainder working on the fire."

"Yes, sir."

There was another scream in the distance. The voice sounded young, and Riam had the sinking feeling that it came from where he and Loral had been sleeping.

"Errin, hurry up and get a half-section moving to the front gate! You two," he pointed at Riam and Loral, "stay out of the way."

Someone on the top floor began throwing weapons and armor out the window, and men scrambled for the equipment. Judging by what could only be deemed organized chaos, it would take some time before any of the sections moved out.

Gairen's heightened senses saved his life. Two knives flew toward him through the darkness, thrown by unseen hands. He slipped into the mahl-shae, and the knives slowed until they floated leisurely through the air. He avoided them both easily. The mahl-shae didn't allow him to move any faster—momentum, speed, and strength remained unchanged—but it significantly improved his reaction and decision time.

His could slip in and out of this state at will, as long as his weapon contained the energy it required. As if on cue, the last of the power faded, and the knives flashed past him.

Four stripe-faced Esharii followed the knives. Two of the tribesmen held heavy, sweptback Arillian swords out in front of them. The other two carried the long, curved fighting knives the Esharii favored. One of the swordsmen came at him high, while the other came in low. They were young, but they worked like veterans who'd fought together for years. Gairen wished he still had both of his swords. He'd carried two for the majority of his life; fighting with only one felt awkward and clumsy.

He leaped forward and to the left, angling to prevent both of the tribesmen from bringing their swords to bear at the same time. Gairen's main advantage was in his speed and freedom, while the tribesmen were limited in the way they attacked by their numbers. The tribesman with his blade held high swung in a downward arc meant to split Gairen in half diagonally.

Gairen sidestepped and deflected the blade. He used his momentum to spin and swing his trailing foot toward the tribesman's front leg. He put all his strength behind the blow. The top of his foot smashed into the tribesman's kneecap—the force shattering bone—and the Esharii pitched forward.

Coming out of the spin, Gairen stood up straight and arched his body sideways just in time to avoid a thrust by one of the knifemen. He used his free hand to grab the tribesman's wrist and pull him forward, then struck with his other hand. The tribesman leaned away from the blow.

With a quick pivot, Gairen threw the tribesman face-first to the ground. He slid his sword along the man's neck, cutting into the throat and severing the artery. Stepping backward, he brought up his sword, ready to defend or attack.

Energy coursed through his weapon as the tribesman's life bled out, letting him slip back into the mahl-shae. The world froze. The second swordsman was only a long-step away, coming in over the top of the Esharii with the broken knee. The remaining tribesman prepared to throw his knife. Gairen pressed his attack.

He lowered his center and drove his sword toward the Esharii. The attack was a lightning strike, driving the blade toward the tribesman's face in a committed thrust.

To his credit, the warrior was quicker than Gairen expected, but with his blade too wide, he was unable to block the attack. The Esharii jerked his head back, attempting to keep his face out of reach. It did no good. The point of Gairen's blade drove like a needle up into the soft tissue beneath the jaw until a full hand of steel passed through the roof of his mouth and into his brain.

Before he could fall, Gairen was past the dying warrior, propelling himself at the remaining tribesman. Unfortunately, he was forced to leave his sword lodged in the previous attacker's face. It was a maneuver he'd used many times, and if he'd been carrying two blades, it would have worked perfectly.

Luck was with him, though. The knifeman misjudged his throw. The blade swept past Gairen's shoulder. The two men crashed together, both weaponless.

CHAPTER 12

Gairen tried to get his weight onto his shoulder and into the Esharii's midsection, attempting to knock the air from the warrior's lungs when they hit the ground. The tribesman shifted his body to prevent it. The two fighters hit the ground and rolled in a cloud of dust, each fighting for a position to dominate the other. This fight wouldn't be won with technique or finesse. This was a brawl in the dirt that would end with one of them ruined or dead. They rolled several times, coming to a stop with the tribesman on top.

Under different circumstances Gairen might have laughed at the irony. Master Iwynd had insisted that every one of his students carry a knife at all times throughout their training, even when they bathed and slept. For six years the unforgiving master had berated them all endlessly on the importance of carrying a small blade where it was easy to reach. Gairen's knife was back in his quarters, under his pallet.

Without a weapon, Gairen attacked the man's snarling face, digging and tearing at his brow and cheek and leaving long lines of torn skin and blood where his nails scraped away the green-and-black paint. His fingers sought the tribesman's eyes. The tribesman punched wildly at Gairen's head and neck. He blocked as many of the blows as he could, but several slipped by. He'd pay for those later.

An Esharii curse came from somewhere nearby—the tribesman with the broken knee. On your back, weaponless and pinned next to a building was not the ideal technique for fighting two enemies at once. He fought harder to get at the tribesman's eyes, to end the struggle before the other could join the fight. His efforts were rewarded. There was a pop, and fluid splashed down his wrist and arm when he forced his thumb deep into the man's eye socket.

The Esharii reared back, screaming. The point of a narrow blade emerged from his chest. The tribesman's cry dwindled to silence, and he crumpled. Master Iwynd stood behind him.

"You know," his old instructor said in the same irritating voice of Gairen's youth, "it's a lot easier if you keep your sword in your hand."

Gairen shoved the dying tribesman to the side. "I vaguely remember something like that in your lessons."

Master Iwynd helped Gairen up. After retrieving his blade from where it was lodged in the skull of his last kill, Gairen moved to dispatch the tribesman with the damaged knee. It turned out there was no need—Master Iwynd had already finished him.

"They have the children and are headed toward the front of the outpost," Master Iwynd said.

"Well, now we know why they burned the front wall. The new defenses are designed to keep them out, not in."

Master Iwynd nodded. "Four more like these ambushed me as I left my quarters. They meant to delay or kill us while the others escaped, and they knew exactly where we were."

"The spirit-taker?" Gairen asked.

"He's a strong one. Maybe even a spirit-walker, though I've never seen one on this side of the mountains. Before now, I'd have said that what he's doing to block our sight was impossible—it's incredibly dangerous."

"Maybe together, we can break through."

"Not a chance. All that power in the air has to go somewhere. It'd be like stabbing your sword into a thunderstorm. I'd rather not be around when that happens. The okulu'tan is close, though. Even if it is a spirit-walker, he can't project that much power without being at the heart of it."

"I'll stop the Esharii with the children. You find the spirit-walker." Even in his haste, Gairen framed it as a suggestion. A warden did not order a master.

Iwynd made a quick survey around them. "Agreed."

Gairen sprinted for the front gate.

Flames from the burning barracks raged against the night sky, casting an orange glow over the half-section of regulars who fought to prevent the fire from spreading. The timbers of the burning barracks cracked and popped, throwing sparks high into the air where they boiled and churned in the smoke. Ash floated around Riam like snowflakes. The troops threw water on the rooftops of the closest buildings to prevent the sparks from catching. Others used blankets to keep the flames from spreading. Their faces shone with a thick film of sweat.

The smoke burned Riam's eyes and the heat pressed at his lungs, but he didn't want to get too far from the soldiers for fear of the Esharii. As the flames grew hotter, he and Loral were forced to move farther away. There were only two regulars near them, and Riam began to think that maybe they should've followed one of the other sections instead of remaining behind. With only two soldiers close, Riam didn't feel very safe.

Something was in the air. The world felt foggy, and his head felt pressed as if he had the sweats or a clogged nose and ears from being ill, but he wasn't sick. It was more than the stinging smoke and heat. He squeezed his nose and blew, trying to get his ears to pop. It didn't help.

"You feel it, too, don't you?" Loral asked.

"Yeah." He made an effort to swallow and clear his throat. It was difficult. The air was so dry and smoky. "It's like something is trying to smother us. I can feel it."

"Me, too," Loral said. She kept checking around them, trying to peer into the shadows beyond the fire's light. "We need to get out of here."

"Maybe we should move to where there are more soldiers?"

The regular closest to them heard Riam. "Don't go runnin' off. Plenty of us around within earshot." The words weren't very convincing.

Loral rolled her eyes. The man's words held as little comfort for her as they did for Riam.

A large spark landed on the roof of the building nearest them. It brightened instead of dying out, and the two soldiers ran to smother it. It was too high to reach from the ground, so one of the men lifted the other to the roof.

There was no one else in sight. The pressure increased. "Come on," he told Loral. He eased back away from the light. They continued moving until the flames and the soldiers were out of sight.

Away from the fire, he could hear men yelling and fighting. The sound of metal striking metal came from all around them.

"Now what?" Loral asked.

"Well, one section was headed to the warehouse and another to the front gate. We could go to one of those two places." Although he spoke of the troops, he was more concerned with finding Gairen or Master Iwynd.

"What about going back to where we slept?"

He shook his head. "I think that would be a bad idea. The Esharii are here for us."

"How do you know?"

"Because I was attacked by the Esharii on the way here, and they took Nola. She's the missing one you asked about. They tried to capture both of us, but Gairen saved me."

He heard footsteps. "Shhh."

They crouched in the darkness against a wall. The crunch of the steps grew louder before fading away.

Riam felt more helpless than he had with the wasps. At least then he'd had the sword. At the thought of the blade, he used his senses to feel for it. This time he didn't even need to close his eyes to know it was lying exactly where Gairen had touched it earlier. Either he'd left it behind, or he wasn't moving. Riam hoped it was the first. Gairen wouldn't be sitting in one place during an attack unless something very bad had happened.

He didn't know if the sword would help or not—it wasn't like he knew how to use it—but it was better than nothing, and Gairen might still be near the weapon.

"I know where to go." Riam turned and ran, heading toward Gairen's quarters. There was fighting on the wall closest to them, men yelled and swore in the darkness, and twice he and Loral were startled by regulars. One yelled at them to find a room and lock themselves inside until the attack was over.

They reached the small building where Gairen slept. It sat in an open area, or at least as open as you could get inside a walled outpost. Riam's heart raced. He grasped the door's handle but hesitated before opening it. He hoped Gairen was inside, but he dreaded that something might have happened to him, that he would open the door and find the man injured or dead.

"What are you waiting for?" Loral whispered. She was pressed close behind him. Her breath on the back of his neck sent a chill down his spine.

I am being silly. Gairen won't be inside. He's fighting the Esharii. Riam pushed on the door, and it swung open. There was no one in the room. He sagged in relief. *Why am I so worried about Gairen? The man can take care of himself.*

On the floor next to a pallet was the sword. Riam ran to it and scooped it up.

"What are you doing? Everyone knows you'll die if you try to hold a Draegoran's sword."

He ignored her and held the blade up in front of him. The handle grew warm. The crystal in the hilt glowed with a soft white hue at his touch. His link to the blade opened wide, and energy coursed into him, filling him with strength. The room flared and brightened. He could see everything clearly, although it wasn't exactly like seeing in daylight. More like early morning before the sun rose. He stared at the naked blade in the light. It sent tingles through his body. The pressure he felt earlier subsided.

"Are you crazy?"

Her words sounded distorted, and the room darkened and faded and then brightened again. His link to the sword swelled and ebbed. He didn't know how to control it.

"Put it down before it kills you!" Loral was almost frantic. She tried to knock the weapon from his hand.

Energy rushed into him. Her hand came at him so slowly it seemed he had all the time in the world to move. He reached out with his left hand to catch her by the wrist. It seemed to take forever until he held her arm in his hand.

"You moved so fast!" Loral said, still trying to reach for the blade with her other hand.

"It's all right. This sword is mine."

She looked from his face to the blade and back. "I don't understand. How can you already have a sword like the Draegorans?"

"Long story." The world brightened and dimmed, then sped up and slowed down. Loral said something else, but he couldn't understand it. He shook his head and concentrated on slowing the flow of energy.

"Are you sure it's safe?" Loral asked.

Riam stared at her and almost dropped the sword in fear. Loral was a faceless shell of energy. He opened and closed his eyes several times and shook his head. A cloud hovered in the air around him, blocking his newfound vision. Reaching out, he pushed at the cloud with his mind, imagining a giant hand waving it out of the way like smoke. It swirled and lifted until suddenly he could see through the walls and buildings around him. He looked toward the front of the outpost. The faint, glowing forms of men fought near the gates and the damaged walls. A small group was trying to fight its way into the outpost against a much larger group.

"One of the sections is fighting to hold the front," he told her.

"How do you—"

"Wait." He cut her off. There were smaller forms—the other children. They glowed more brightly, and they were being carried toward the gate. It wasn't a small group of Esharii fighting to get in, it was a large group of Esharii fighting to get out, and they had the other children.

He turned the other way. "Aghhh . . ." The glow from the burning barracks blinded him. He moved his hand in front of his face, but it didn't do any good. He wasn't looking through his eyes. A flare of light in another direction caught his attention. That had to be Gairen or Master Iwynd, near the stables fighting against men on both sides of him.

"The Esharii have the other children and—" The darkness returned and slammed into Riam's mind like a fist. His vision turned black, and he dropped to one knee. The pressure and fog returned. The cloud thickened around him until it held his head in a vise.

Loral was at his side, holding his shoulder. "What happened? Is it the sword? I told you the sword was dangerous."

"It's not the sword. Something . . . someone hit me." He

pushed back as best he could and struggled to his feet. He fought to regain his balance.

It came from the other side of the outpost like an arrow and slammed into him again. Without Loral's support, he would have fallen. He tried to block the attack, but he didn't know what to do. The fog continued to thicken around him. He tried to push back. The nameless power punched through his feeble efforts and hit him a third time. Loral's support wasn't enough to hold him. He slipped from her grasp and fell to the floor, his head bouncing painfully on the wood. Above him, Loral screamed.

Riam came up onto his hands and knees and spat blood. *This would be a whole lot easier if I knew what I was doing.* He reached deep down the link and pulled from the sword with everything he could, filling himself with energy. When the next attack came, he was ready for it and threw the power he'd gathered back against it.

The two forces met somewhere above him and exploded. A blinding flash filled the room, burning the sight of Loral standing in open-mouthed terror into Riam's eyes. The explosion bloomed outward, and the blast threw both of them across the room. Instinctively, Riam used the last of the energy in the sword to push back at the expanding ball of fire and debris.

He felt the power surge back down the channel toward where it had come from, exploding on the other side of the outpost. Riam felt the other's surprise and pain just before he was slammed against the wall.

CHAPTER 13

Ky'lem dodged a spear thrust to the stomach, barely escaping the agonizing wound warriors lingered with for days before dying. A warrior should not have to die a long painful death from a battle that accomplished nothing. He and his fellow tribesmen fought in the shadowy firelight to break through the troops who blocked their escape. He'd been wrong about the soldiers. These were not the weak men he'd fought on previous raids. One on one, they were no match for a Ti'yak warrior, that was a given, but working together, arrayed in a line two deep, they were a formidable adversary. They fought staggered, so that both ranks could bring their spears to bear at the same time if needed, but their tactics went beyond that.

The front rank stabbed with their spears as one, thrusting twenty of the deadly weapons forward with the intent of punching holes through Ky'lem and his fellow tribesmen. The first rank pulled back and allowed the second rank to do the same as the first readied to thrust again. They were every bit as well drilled as the troops the gray demons used to defend the mountain passes. The tribesmen were repeatedly forced back.

With the length of the spears, it was difficult to get close enough to strike, and if they did, it left them exposed and

vulnerable to the next attack. There were not enough tribesmen to penetrate the line with a column or a wedge, or to
overwhelm spearmen with numbers. To make things worse,
the gray demon from the plains had arrived to direct their
movements. With the demon commanding them, there was
no way to slip by and escape.

To his right, Pai'le brushed aside the spear of a tall soldier in the front rank and darted forward to strike with his
sword. The enemy's second rank was slower this time, either by chance or because they were getting tired, and it
gave the big leader the opportunity to get close. Even then,
he was nearly impaled by three different spears before he
could leap back, grinning from ear to ear like a young boy,
out of the enemy's reach. Pai'le might have wounded his
foe, but Ky'lem hadn't seen the weapon bite. If it had, it
didn't bring the spearman down.

The tribesman to his left tried the same tactic, imitating
Pai'le, but the enemy was ready. A spear took the warrior
in the throat, its silver tip glistening in the orange firelight
where it protruded from the back of his neck. Small wings
at the base of the spearhead kept the weapon from pene-
trating too far and getting trapped. Blood sprayed across
Ky'lem when the long weapon was torn free. The warrior
fell gagging and choking. It was Nal'tae.

Nal'tae's lone wife was one of the most beautiful women
in the tribe, with long, dark hair that flowed like silk around
perfect upturned breasts. Ky'lem smiled as he dodged a
spear thrust. She'd need a new husband when the raid was
over. He already had two wives, but he was permitted to
take a third, as long as she was a widow.

The thought of the woman, naked and writhing beneath
him with his first and second wives to either side nearly
made up for the trouble they were in. He hadn't liked
Nal'tae much. The man had always been too eager to side
against him—as he had this time when Pai'le laid out the
details for the raid. Taking the warrior's wife seemed a fitting way to pay him back for years of opposition. Of course,
if he took the spirit-walker's offer, he wouldn't be taking
any new wives.

Ky'lem dodged another thrust and cursed himself for
letting his mind get distracted. He needed to find a way
past the enemy.

The plan had been to escape with the children through the damaged front of the stronghold once the soldiers were disorganized. After opening the lightly guarded rear gate and firing the enemy barracks, Ky'lem had followed Pai'le, along with over half of the warband, to the building that housed the children. They'd been able to snatch them easily enough, knocking them out by rubbing deathroot on their tongues. Four of their warriors had then carried the unconscious children, one over each shoulder, like sacks of linpana grain. They'd all but broken through the soldiers and escaped when reinforcements arrived, followed shortly after by the gray demon.

Now, the children were scattered on the ground behind them like the dead, the four warriors carrying them needed to hold off the enemy. Even with their addition, they were still outnumbered. Pai'le's plan had split them into too many pieces. Seven warriors had remained with the spirit-walker's pachna to keep up the pretense of attacking from the rear, six were fighting on the walls, if they were still alive, and two groups of four had been sent to delay the gray demons. Those eight had obviously been less than successful, just as he'd told Pai'le they would be.

Ky'lem had wanted to go after the gray men first, with all their forces, and kill them quickly. Pai'le had refused his advice and sent the youngest warriors. Those eight had known that few, if any, of them would survive, but they were young and eager to prove themselves. A young warrior returning from a raid with a gray demon's skin would be raised above his peers. To Ky'lem, the plan took too many risks and wasted men they could have used to fight their way clear and escape with the children. As it stood, they'd be lucky to break free at all. He wished he had more of the spirit-walker's soulfire. One or two thrown into the ranks in front of them would have scattered the enemy.

Catching Pai'le's attention, Ky'lem motioned behind them before backing away from the enemy line. Pai'le, and soon the rest of the warriors, followed suit, breaking off the attack. The enemy remained where they were, content to hold them inside the fort and wait for reinforcements. The two groups stood apart, watching each other for any sign of attack. Mangled and bleeding bodies from both sides lay between them, most of them tribesmen.

"It's no use," Ky'lem told Pai'le. "We need to find another way out before reinforcements arrive and flank us."

Pai'le waved his heavy blade in the direction of the enemy. "We'd be long gone if it were not for that one." The gray demon moved down the line, patting each of the soldiers on the back and speaking to them as he went. Those he spoke to stood up taller and squared their shoulders. "Faen take all the gray demons and their island. This should've worked."

Ky'lem wanted to tell Pai'le that he'd underestimated the enemy. He wanted to tell him that he shouldn't have split the warband into so many pieces. But doing so would only start them arguing again, so he bit his tongue.

"He escaped us on the plains, and he escaped the oku-lu'tan's magic. He has the favor of the Dark Gods, that one." Pai'le spat on the ground.

Ky'lem was growing more and more troubled with Pai'le. He wanted the man in gray to die, but right now the demon was not their first concern. Pai'le was wasting time worrying about the wrong thing. As the leader, he needed to decide what to do next to save the rest of his tribesmen. Dead warriors could not return to fight another day.

He tried to prod Pai'le into abandoning the children. "We can get around them, but not with the children. If we move to pick them up again, they'll attack, and we don't have enough warriors left to hold them off and skirt their flank. We're in a stalemate that has but one outcome, and time is not on our side."

"You're right, Ky'lem." Pai'le nodded slowly to himself, as if coming to some profound decision. "Very well. The spirit-walker has failed us. We attack again, but this time we will hold nothing back. We will break through their line and kill this gray man or die with honor trying."

Ky'lem's face flushed, the scars on his cheek going white beneath his face paint. It was the exact opposite of what he'd meant. *Where is the brother I know? The man before me is blind to his ego, and he will sacrifice us all before changing his plan.*

Pai'le spoke loudly, so that the remaining tribesmen could hear him. "We will attack the enemy with all the strength we possess. We are Ti'yak warriors. None can stand before us," he said boisterously. "These honorless men will know true fear in the moments before our swords tear the life from their flesh. We will leave their bodies upon the ground they defend, so that when they are found, their companions will know the horror of facing the Esharii."

The warriors around them cheered and yelled, readying to attack.

"No!" Ky'lem shouted, but the cheers drowned out his plea.

Ky'lem squeezed his sword hard enough he thought his hand would break. He wanted to swing the weapon at Pai'le, and if the warriors around him would not have hacked him down for doing so, he just might have done it. Pai'le was proof that the elders' system for choosing a popular warrior to serve as warleader was foolish. They thought nothing of the future, only of their pride and the old days. This was why their tribe was weak—the elders promoted those who thought as Pai'le did, not the ones who used their heads instead of their hands. *What good will come from impaling ourselves on our enemies' spears with honor if the gray demons win?*

Pai'le stepped out in front of Ky'lem and the others and turned his back to the enemy. His gaze slid from warrior to warrior, meeting each of their eyes. Behind him, more than forty spears leveled in a precise line. Pai'le and Ky'lem's eyes met, and Pai'le lifted his sword, preparing to give the command to attack. Ky'lem shook his head no, but his leader only grinned.

There was no stopping it. Ky'lem took a deep breath and prepared himself to enter the great beyond with his fellow tribesmen. While this was not the best way, he was Esharii, and he would follow his warleader into death despite his misgivings. Ky'lem's skin tingled and the hair on his arms stood out. The air around him felt charged with anticipation.

Pai'le still hadn't brought his sword down to give the command to attack when a bolt of lightning fractured its way across the sky and struck a building behind them. A flare like the sun lit up the enemy, and a clap of thunder tore through the outpost. The building exploded, and fighters on both sides were hurled from their feet.

The spears in front of Ky'lem tangled. Several dropped to the ground. The location of the explosion blinded the enemy and not the Esharii. Even the gray man was disoriented, stumbling backward and holding his head. This had to be the efforts of the okulu'tan. He had not failed them. Now was the time to break free, but Pai'le had been facing the blast and was as blind as the enemy.

Ky'lem raised his Arillian blade high, waving it at the spearmen. "Now! Kill them all!" he screamed and led the charge forward. He batted away a weak spear thrust but ignored the man behind it. Barreling through the first line of soldiers, he had only one target in mind. Behind him, the Esharii formed a short wedge with him at the tip.

A soldier from the second rank stepped before him with no weapon in his hands.

Ky'lem took part of the man's arm and head off in a single swing.

Another ran at him, wielding a broken spear like a club.

He deflected the blow and kicked the man beneath the chin, knocking him to the ground and leaving his death to the warriors who followed.

Only one soldier remained between him and the blind and disoriented gray demon—a stone-faced soldier with blond curls and a sword instead of a spear. Ky'lem grinned and launched himself at the swordsman. Nothing would stop him from taking the gray demon's skin.

The world was burning and green-and-black–faced Esharii were all around him. It was still night, but bursts of light exploded in Riam's eyes, stabbing painfully at his mind. His head throbbed and his body hurt. For the second time today, he thought he might die. He tried to sit up but couldn't move. He couldn't even turn his head to get a better look at the tribesmen who moved around him, but he could see them out of the corners of his eyes and feel their rough hands pinning him down. He was being held flat on his back. The Esharii spoke in a harsh, guttural language that made no sense. They danced and laughed.

Celebrating their victory, no doubt.

Riam struggled to twist and turn his body, attempting to escape from their grasp, but it was useless. He was no match for the hard, unyielding hands that held him, and the more he resisted, the more their hands pressed and dug painfully into his legs and chest. One was holding his leg in an excruciating grip that made him suck in his breath whenever he pulled against it.

An Esharii moved close. He could feel the man's hot breath. Through his distorted vision, the tribesman's mouth was the only thing he could see clearly. The lips moved.

"Riam," they said in a muffled voice.

How do the Esharii know my name?

"Can you hear me?"

The tribesman's mouth was oddly small, with thin, flat lips.

"I'm gonna get you out."

"That's good. It hurts," he mumbled. "You're a good Esharii." He closed his eyes. That seemed to help. At least it made the pain behind his eyes lessen. He wanted to drift away. Sinking into the numbness of sleep would be so much better than this.

A torturous pain shot up Riam's leg as the Esharii that held him pressed harder. "Faen's balls, stop!" he yelled. The pain brought the world into focus.

Loral stood before him, her face outlined by stars that shimmered in the open sky. A cut ran along her neck, though not deep, and there was either a bruise or a large smudge that spanned the length of her face. It was hard to tell in the flickering light.

Around them, most of Gairen's quarters were missing. Well, not exactly missing. It was more like a giant club had smashed away the top of the building, scattering logs and rubble. On this side of the room, the remainder of the roof protruded upward from the wall like large fingers reaching up to the heavens. Riam lay under a pile of debris. To make matters worse, the building was on fire. By the amount of destruction, he didn't have a clue how they were still alive or how Loral was walking.

"I can barely move the piece on your leg. You'll have to drag your foot out when I lift it." Loral strained against the beam. "Now," she groaned.

Riam tried to pull his leg free. It scraped along the wood painfully. It moved about a hand's length before it was wedged tight again. At least the weight no longer rested on the same spot. "You have to lift it higher."

"I'm lifting it as high as I can." She struggled a moment longer before throwing her hands up. "It's no use. I can't move it any more than that."

"Get something to pry it up. Something long and sturdy. We need to get out of here and find Gairen."

She dug through the rubble. What was left of the roof creaked and sagged. Flames licked up along the broken logs. "You might want to hurry," he told her.

"I am." She picked up a long, thin piece of wood. Twisting it in her hand, she stared at it, gauging it, before deciding it wasn't right and throwing it aside. She bent over again, shuffling through more pieces.

He watched the heavy beams above him. "Just grab something."

"Everything is either too big or too small," she said defensively.

He worked at freeing himself from the jumble of broken wood around him. Painful splinters stabbed at his fingers, but he ignored them. They needed to get out before what was left of the roof fell on top of them. That would be something, surviving the explosion only to be crushed by a log. With a combination of pulling and pushing, he was able to worm his way out from under everything but the heavy beam on his leg.

He put his hand down and felt cold metal—the sword. Riam felt along the back of the blade, careful not to slice himself, until he found the hilt. This time nothing happened when he held it. The weapon was cold and empty. Whatever power was in the sword before, it was gone now.

Loral returned, proudly brandishing a piece of wood that was taller than she was. "I think this one will work."

"I found something, too," Riam said, holding up the sword.

Her smile vanished. "Are you insane? That thing almost killed us."

"It wasn't the sword's fault. I think it saved us."

"Yeah, I'm not ready to believe that."

The remains of the roof above them shifted and screeched.

"We have something more important to worry about at the moment," Riam said, eyeing the heavy timbers. "Hurry up."

Working together, they were able to raise the beam high enough for him to free his leg. They'd no sooner crossed the threshold of the broken doorway than the remnants of the roof came crashing down.

Riam giggled softly—a low, almost manic sound.

"How can you laugh at a time like this?" Loral asked.

"I'm not."

"Yes, you are."

"It's not laughter. I've almost died three times in the last two days. I've been chased through the fields by the Esharii and stung by giant wasps. The whole outpost is under attack, and I think we were just hit by lightning that was thrown at us by an okulu'tan." He held up his hand as she opened her mouth. "Before you ask, I don't even know who or what that is."

He pointed at the remains of the building. His hand was shaking as he held it out. "Even the buildings are trying to kill us—all because we have some kind of special blood." His voice became more frantic. "I'm tired and exhausted, and we haven't even made it to the island yet." Everything he'd felt previously, about being meant for something more, could go jump in a river. He made a strangled sound.

Loral stared at him like he'd lost his mind.

"I never asked for this," he said.

She didn't reply.

His eyes watered. This was not the time or place to cry, but he couldn't help it. A tear slid down his cheek, hotter than any of the fires that burned around them. *That is all I need— to cry in front of her. I'm acting like a baby.* It made him angry with himself. He turned his face toward the ground.

He felt her hand on his arm and flinched.

"Nobody gave us a choice," she said softly.

He started to pull away and say something mean, as he'd done with Nola. Then he remembered how terrible he'd felt after losing her and how ashamed he'd felt for being mean during their last conversation. He didn't want to bear that again. He took a deep breath and lifted his head to face her. That simple motion was far harder than fighting the wasps or facing the Esharii.

Loral's red hair was matted to her head, half her face was covered in soot, and her clothes were dirty and stained, but she looked so strong. Then, he met her eyes and saw the same fear and frustration. Like him, she was scared, and behind that, her concern was real.

He took another deep breath, getting control of himself. "Thank you," he said. He forced himself to say the next words. "Everything will be fine."

"I know," she said and smiled weakly at him.

"We need to go."

She nodded, but neither of them moved. Her hand was still on his arm, and their gazes remained locked on each other. Something in Riam's chest began to tighten. This time, it wasn't anger, nor was it anything he'd ever felt. He reached out awkwardly, unsure of what he was doing.

Suddenly, they were holding each other. He'd never been embraced like this by anyone else in his life that he remembered, not even Lemual. It was the most wonderful, yet most foreign, thing he'd ever felt. She was warm and soft and firm and safe at the same time. Her hair smelled like smoke, and her cheek rubbed soot on his face as they held each other, but he didn't mind these things at all.

"Thank you," Riam said.

"There's nothing—"

Riam didn't hear the rest. A sudden pulse from the sword shot through his body. It was like a cry in the night, or a scream, and it tore out everything he had left. His eyes glazed over, and he dropped the weapon. He took a single step backward before his legs gave out. He knew exactly what the pulse meant. It was a message of sorts, and it left him aching through his core.

"Riam, what is it?"

He looked up at her helplessly with tears running down his face. He didn't care if she saw them this time. "It's Gairen. He is dead."

CHAPTER 14

"Are you sure he's dead?" Loral asked. "Maybe he's injured or unconscious."

The ground felt cold beneath Riam. He still shook, but the tears had stopped. Loral stood before him with her body half in shadow, the only light around them coming from the burning rubble they'd escaped. The flickering images created by the flames matched his heart—half lost, half hidden, half dark. The explosion would bring others, Harol's spearmen or the Esharii, but to be honest, Riam didn't care who arrived. Gairen was dead, and he knew it.

Riam's only connection to his family was lost. He might never know the truth about his father. He pulled his knees in close.

"No," he said after a time. "He's dead. I felt it through the sword. It used to be his, before I took control of it. Maybe it was still connected to him somehow, or maybe they're all connected, like a giant web. I don't know." When the wasps were close to killing him, he'd dived down into the power of the sword. There'd been a second channel of energy leading away into the distance beyond his awareness. Maybe that had something to do with it.

He explained it all to Loral—about how he'd broken Gairen's link and forged his own to keep from dying. "I only took control of one. The other is still his. Maybe the two swords are connected, or maybe they all are somehow. I don't know how any of this works, but I know what I felt. I felt him die."

The sword lay on the ground next to him. The fire's reflection danced on the flat of the blade. The once-white crystal was solid and clear, like a diamond. Where the weapon had excited him before, it now looked cold and treacherous. He didn't want to touch it.

"I could feel his life . . ." he struggled with the words, ". . . scatter and disappear, like mine before I used the sword to save myself." Riam's hand hovered over the hilt. He recognized the truth of what he'd sensed through his connection to the sword, but he wanted to see Gairen's body to confirm it; sitting here would do them no good.

He inhaled deeply through his nostrils. Wincing slightly, unsure of what would happen, he closed his hand over the hilt of the weapon. The leather-wrapped handle was cool and damp with sweat, but other than that, he didn't feel anything different. The crystal remained solid and empty. His feelings hovered between disappointment and relief. He climbed to his feet. "We need to find him."

Loral nodded once before the sound of rough footsteps pulled her attention away. Her eyes widened in horror, and she took a step backward.

Riam spun. It wasn't the Thaen Regulars who'd found them.

Two Esharii approached, their expressions grim behind their green-and-black face paint. The tribesmen had known they were here somehow, and by the way they held their swords, they brought only death with them.

Riam put his arm out in front of Loral protectively and pushed her behind him. "Run when I tell you," he said through the side of his mouth. He brought the sword up in front of him.

The tribesmen stopped, unsure of what to make of a young boy armed with a Draegoran sword. One looked to his left, at the destroyed building, then back at Riam. His expression was muted, but his eyes scanned the area rapidly, trying to put it all together and make a decision. The other warrior didn't mirror the same uncertainty. He stepped forward, his heavy sword gleaming in the light.

Riam held the Draegoran sword higher.

The Esharii swung, smashing Riam's weapon from his hands so hard he thought his arms were being torn from his shoulders. The blow numbed his fingers and yanked him off-balance.

The Esharii chuckled. "Good joke," he said in a thick accent. The tribesman grinned, revealing large, stained, square teeth, and raised the blade to swing again.

Riam should have been telling Loral to run, but he couldn't speak. Everything he'd endured for the past few days had been for nothing. It was all about to end.

A blur flew through the air and smashed into the Esharii's face, caving in the tribesman's cheek and shattering his jaw. Teeth scattered through the air like seeds from a batted melon. The tribesman flopped to the ground. A heavy cast-iron skillet, now smeared with green paint, landed with a dull thump.

Two men came racing into the light. One, with thin white hair standing out in all directions, wore a dirty apron and carried a long, wide cleaver. The other was missing a hand, but that didn't stop him from trying to outrace his disheveled coworker to get at the remaining tribesman with a second heavy iron skillet.

The cooks. Riam never would have imagined the cooks coming to their rescue.

The Esharii glanced at his companion on the ground, back up at Riam, and then at the charging cooks. Whatever he debated, he made up his mind and lunged forward, intent on killing Riam before the cooks could interfere.

The move surprised Riam. He stood frozen as the point of the blade drove toward him.

Loral saved him. She yanked him backward by the shirt far enough to avoid being impaled by less than a hand's length. The two of them tumbled backward, and there was no time for the Esharii to strike again before Brin was on him, wielding the iron skillet like an ax designed for battle.

If Brin were alone, it would have been a short fight, with Riam and Loral faring no better than before he arrived, but with Jon beside him, it was an even match. Obviously, the two men hadn't always been simple cooks. They fought well, and the sound of the Esharii blade ringing off the skillet and the cleaver showed the true measure of Brin and

Jon's abilities. After several attacks and counters, neither side had the advantage.

Riam scrambled for his sword.

"Don't!" Loral yelled at him.

Loral's yell tipped the balance. Her shout distracted the tribesman. Jon and Brin took advantage and attacked from both sides. Brin's swing was deflected, but Jon's caught the Esharii across the wrist with a full swing of the cleaver. There was a loud snap, and the Arillian blade slipped from the tribesman's half-severed hand.

Brin's next swing connected with the side of the tribesman's skull, felling the warrior and ending the fight.

"We need to find Gairen," Riam told the cooks.

"What we need is to get you two out of harm's way until this is over," Brin said.

Jon spoke rapidly after the other cook, "Lucky for you we were awake, getting ready to start roasting the morning meat, when the attack started. We locked ourselves in the mess hall until we heard the explosion. Felt like lightning hit right outside the hall. That was Sollus's own racket, wasn't it?"

"Sure was. I told Brin, 'Nothing good can come from that. The regulars might need us.' That's when we opened the door and saw these two," Jon waved his cleaver at the two fallen tribesmen, "ready to skewer you both."

"Speaking of skewering, no need to be standing out here gobbing. Let's go," Brin said.

"I told you. We're not going with you. We need to find Gairen."

"The warden can look after himself, boy."

"You don't understand . . ." Riam trailed off helplessly. He didn't want to say the words again. Every time he said them, it made them more real.

Brin tilted his head, waiting for more, but Riam didn't say anything. "Well? Spit it out. Why do we need to risk gettin' killed to find him?"

Loral rescued him. "Because he's dead."

"What? How do you know? What happened?"

"It was the sword." Riam held it up. "It told me."

The cooks looked closely at the weapon in his hand for the first time. Jon looked from the sword to the destroyed building and back. "I think there's a whole heap of story we're missing," he said.

"A whole heap," Brin echoed.

"We don't have time—" Riam started.

"We're not doing anything until you explain, so let's have it."

One of the Esharii groaned.

"Best we move back to the mess hall first," Jon said.

Riam started to protest, but Jon shushed him with a hand.

"After you tell us what you know, we'll go looking if it's the right thing to do."

"He's right," Brin said. He knelt next to the tribesman who'd stirred. He raised the skillet high into the air and brought it down, edge first, with all his strength. It was a smooth, well-practiced motion from years of butchering. There was a muted thunk, like a hatchet sinking into the end of a wet log.

Loral let out a yelp and turned away. Brin rose, moved to the other tribesman, and repeated the swing. There was another sickening thunk. Loral jumped at the sound of the second blow. Riam would never look at the cooks quite the same way again.

"Let's go," Brin said, wiping a blood spatter from his face.

Riam didn't argue.

They hurried to the mess hall. Brin unshuttered a lamp that hung in the center of the room while Jon barred the door.

Riam sat at one of the tables, tapping the knuckles of his fist against the surface. Loral pushed down on his hand to stop him. He tapped his heel instead. He didn't want to be here. He wanted to find Gairen, and the calm way that the cooks were taking everything frustrated him to no end. They should be out looking for Gairen, not sitting here. He kept picturing Gairen lying pale and dead, like one of the bodies lined up in the timber yard.

"Water for you young ones." Jon set a jug with cups stacked upside down on top of it in front of them. Then he pulled a bottle out from under his arm and put it next to the water. "Something a little more potent for Brin and me."

Once they were all seated, Brin told Riam that he wanted the whole story, "right from the beginning," so Riam began with the day Gairen arrived at the farmstead. He hurried through the death of his grandfather. The two cooks kept getting confused as to whether or not he lived with his father or his grandfather. He had to jump forward and explain about how he'd thought it was his father, but it was really his grandfather. Once that was sorted out, he told them about Nola and how the Esharii had taken her. Ashamed of how he'd acted, he left out the part about being mean to her.

When he told them about the wasps and how he'd come to be linked to the sword, they made him repeat the part where he broke Gairen's link, and they asked numerous questions about how he'd used the power in the sword before the explosion.

As if to prove it was real, Jon rubbed at the scar on Riam's nose where Gairen had cut him. "I think the boy is telling the truth, Brin. It feels like it's years old, but I know it wasn't there yesterday morning."

The other man rubbed at the stump of his missing hand and nodded in agreement.

Riam went on, telling them about waking up when Gairen touched the sword and the events up through the attack and the explosion. Loral gave them her view, adding in details that he missed.

He choked back tears when he told them about feeling Gairen's death.

Brin was thoughtful, continuing to rub at his stump a time before speaking. "First, are you sure it's Warden Gairen who's dead?"

"It had to be him. I felt it through the sword."

"I don't doubt what you felt, but how do you know that it was him? How do you know it wasn't Master Iwynd—not that it would make things any better? You're not exactly trained to use that thing, and I want to make sure."

"I . . ." Riam hadn't thought of that. *Is it possible?* Because the weapon had belonged to Gairen, he'd immediately assumed that it was Gairen who'd died. *Could it have been Master Iwynd?* He began to doubt the surety of what he'd felt. "I don't know. I hadn't thought of that, but it felt like Gairen. I can't explain why." He was almost whispering, but there was a spark of hope in his voice. Maybe it had been the older Draegoran. He felt a little guilt. He didn't want the old Draegoran to be dead either.

Sitting and doing nothing wouldn't help them figure out the answer. Riam stood. "We need to find out the truth."

"Sit back down. Running into the thick of it and dyin' isn't going to do any good. We'll sit right here and wait," Jon said. "I know it's hard, but we'll know the truth of things 'fore long."

"It's a poor thing losing either of them," Brin said. "As for your story, best you never repeat it again—ever—to anyone. At least not until you complete your training on the island and you're strong enough to defend yourself, and, even then, not to anyone you don't trust. There are those who'd see you dead because of what you've done. I can't put it more plain than that." He turned his attention on Loral. "That goes for you, too. They might kill you for knowing about it."

"Why?" she asked.

"The Draegorans, they may fight on the same side against the Esharii, but that doesn't mean they get along among themselves. I've served them for years, and it's come close to open war between the regiments more often than anyone would like. Now is one of those times when things aren't sittin' so well. The Wolves are getting a little too strong for the others' liking. A lot of people will want young Riam here in their regiment, or they'll see him as a threat and try to get rid of him."

"But I'm only a boy. I don't even know how to use the sword. I just didn't want to die." Riam laid the sword on the table. "I don't even want it. I'll give it away."

"It's too late for that. The only way to break the link is to die. Long ago the swords could be passed on to a descendant with the owner still living, but that ability was lost generations ago."

Jon snapped his fingers. "I'm betting that's how he could do it. Him being young and related to Gairen, they'd have nearly the same bloodlines. Maybe the crystal recognized him."

"What?" Riam asked.

"I hadn't thought of that," Brin said. He tapped his stump on the table.

Riam's knuckles were white where he gripped the table. "Are you saying that Gairen and I are related?"

"You mean you don't know? Gairen's your uncle. He's been out looking for you for two years, though none of us are supposed to know that. I thought that's why you're so upset," Jon said.

It all made sense. *That's how Gairen knew I had the blood before the test. That's why he knew my father so well. Why didn't he tell me?*

Riam hoped with all his heart that it was Master Iwynd who was dead. He knew it wasn't right to wish harm on another, but he couldn't help the way he felt. He put his forehead down on his arm and closed his eyes.

Please, Sollus, let it be Master Iwynd. Please, don't let it be Gairen.

Riam jumped at the sound of someone banging on the door. He scanned the room in confusion. Loral was still next to him, though the cooks were no longer seated across from them. The sword lay on the table where he'd left it.

Jon unlocked the door.

"Get them inside," a voice said. "On the tables."

"Watch that one's arm."

Piling into the room were a dozen or so of the Thaen Regulars carrying the other children who lay limp in their arms. There was blood everywhere.

"Faen take me. Have they killed them all?" Brin said as he hurried to help.

"The blood isn't theirs. We fought a nasty bunch of swaugs who were trying to carry them off. It was a near thing, especially after the lightning blinded us, but we were able to save the children."

Riam and Loral both scrambled out of the way as the regulars carefully laid out the children on the tables around them. He almost forgot the sword and snatched it away before one was placed in front of him. It was Tannon, the city boy who'd given Riam the intimidating look. He didn't look so intimidating now.

"Don't know what's wrong with them," the Thaen said. "Thought they were dead at first, but they're still breathing.

Might be swaug magic. Our mediker is busy with Commander Harol—he took a nasty blow to the head—so we
brought them here."

Brin used his thumb to push up on Tannon's eyebrow,
stretching an eye open. "Hmmm." He bent down to peer
at it closely, then moved his hand to Tannon's jaw and
pulled the boy's mouth open. He stuck his finger inside and
did something Riam couldn't see. "Yep. What I thought."

"Deathroot?" Jon asked, coming up beside Brin.

"Yep."

"Deathroot?" Loral said. "Are they dying?"

Brin chuckled. "No. They'll be out for a bit, but they're
not dying. Looks like they rubbed it in their mouths." He
held his finger up. It was smeared with a dark streak. "It's
purple when it's raw. Good for numbing and treating wounds
when it's mixed with honey, marigold, and yarrow. They'll
be fine, though. You have to really boil the stuff down to
make it deadly, but then it would be black like tar." Brin
reached over and wiped his finger on Jon's apron, leaving a
purple smudge, before putting his hand on the regular's
shoulder and walking him toward the door. "They'll be fine
after a time."

The regular whistled and made a circle in the air with
his hand. The soldiers began filing out of the room at the
signal.

Brin leaned in close to the leader of the Thaens and
spoke, but they were too far away, and the departing soldiers made too much noise for Riam to make out the words.

Yet he knew the cook had asked about Gairen. Riam
brought a hand up to push his hair out of his eyes. The scar
on his palm caught his eye. He'd never be able to look at
the thin white line without remembering his poor treat-
ment of Nola. *Is that all scars really are? Reminders of our
failures?* He knew the one on his nose would never let him
forget about the wasps and Gairen.

He slipped around a table and made his way toward the
door, trying to listen in on the conversation.

". . . at least ten of them escaped. Led by a big bastard-
of-a-swaug and another with a scarred face and torn
ear. They're the ones that got him when the lightning
blinded us."

Got who? Were they talking about Gairen?

"Make a hole!" the regular at the door yelled, and men sprang to either side to make way.

"All the children are accounted for?" a strong voice said from outside, growing louder as it spoke.

"Yes, sir," another responded.

A Draegoran stepped inside. His face was hidden from view by one of the regulars for an instant. Then the soldier moved.

Riam's sword dropped to the floor with a clang, and his heart dropped with it. Master Iwynd scanned the room. Their eyes met, but neither of them spoke.

He'd been right all along, but the cooks had given him hope. Not caring if it was safe, he walked out of the mess hall to find somewhere to be alone. He left the sword behind.

CHAPTER 15

The fire spread despite the best efforts of the Thaen Regulars. While they protected the buildings immediately surrounding the barracks, the billowing clouds of smoke threw sparks across the outpost, burning the line of cells Riam had stayed in the first night and another building used to store dry goods. It was a close thing for Master Iwynd's headquarters, with only the grit and bravery of the Thaens saving it from the flames. There were many heroes in the night, even Maber of all people, who saved the stables and the horses but suffered terrible burns to his face and hands. Between the night's attack and previous damage, more than half the outpost lay in ruins and more than thirty men were dead or wounded.

With so much needing to be done, the children didn't start downriver in the morning. Instead, they pitched in to clear debris, douse embers, and carry water to the soldiers and townsfolk who labored in the heat. The sounds of hammers and saws, of horses and wagons, and of chopping and digging filled the air, but everyone strove to say as little as possible while they worked to put the outpost to rights. Even the meals were subdued, with only the hurried sounds of scraping plates and creaking benches filling the room. When people did speak, they spoke in hushed tones and hesitant whispers. Riam kept to himself and refused to speak to anyone, even Loral. He would always remember this as one of the darkest days of his life.

All work ceased for a time that evening as the nineteen Thaen Regulars who succumbed to their wounds were given a short ceremony in a burial field near the outpost. The surviving soldiers stood straight in formation. The wounded who could walk were among them. Maber stood with his face and hands wrapped. Valora, the section leader who'd been sent to save the children, wore a sling, but she stood rigid and straight in front of the troops—she was now second-in-command behind Harol after the death of her half-troop leader. Riam and the other children were gathered in two ranks off to the side. Their first formation as soon-to-be recruits was a somber one. Harol, his head in a bloodstained dressing, stood before the formation a pace beyond the freshly turned soil of the mass grave. His hand rested on a single spear posted as a marker for the men and women buried beneath it.

"All things fall," Harol told them. "The strongest gods, Parron and Tomu, fell. Draegora and its cities fell. And one day this land, and even this world, will fall. It's the nature of things.

"Look around you. The trees that surround this field and the animals and birds that feed from it will also fall. Even the sun and moon fall from the heights above us. But when we fall as soldiers, it means something more."

How? Riam thought. *How does life mean anything if everything dies anyway?* He was in a foul mood, and the man's words made it worse.

"We Thaens do not believe in the Church of Man or its arrogance that states the Fallen were never truly gods above us. We know the truth of the last remaining god, Sollus, and we respect the Fallen Gods for their sacrifice. Like the Gods of Light, our men gave their lives in the defense of others. There is no greater achievement in the eyes of Sollus than this."

Yet Sollus is too weak to help. So why do we pray to him if it does no good?

"I hope that one day, when I fall, it will be the same, that it is to protect others. I hope that one of you will stand here in my place, reminding all of the honor in matching the

Fallen's sacrifice." Harol leaned forward and kissed the spear. He then stepped backward and saluted. "Honor to the fallen," he said and dropped the salute.

"Honor to the fallen," the regulars echoed and saluted in unison.

Riam watched the men and women move one by one to the spear and repeat Harol's gesture. *Honor? Is that really all there is?* It was not a satisfying answer. Honor didn't stop others from doing bad things. He wanted to hate the Esharii. He wanted to hate his grandfather. He wanted to hate Gairen and Lemual for lying to him. But he couldn't. He really didn't know whom to blame or why the world was the way that it was. *Is it Sollus's fault? The Fallen's? The dark ones'?*

His grandfather never spoke much about the Fallen, but then most people didn't unless it was the first days of high spring—the one time each year that everyone made a sacrifice of food or goods to the Fallen before the winter's end festival. The sacrifice itself was a personal matter, not discussed openly. Only those who followed the Church of Man worshipped together, but everyone back home said that only two types of people joined the Church of Man, the crazy and the foolish.

What little Riam knew about the gods came from Lemual—how the Gods of Light had fallen and how Sollus remained behind to watch over them with almost no power to intervene on their behalf. That was the point of the fall, so that the struggle between the Gods of Light and Dark would not destroy the worlds of man. *But what is the point if everyone still fights and dies anyway? Why save us?* He'd never thought about it before, and certainly no one had ever explained it to him.

Why had the gods created them and then died to protect them? What was so noble about giving up your life to help others? He thought about Gairen and that very question long into the night.

There was no ceremony for Gairen. Riam wanted to pay his respects and say good-bye, but when he asked Brin, he was told that Draegorans didn't have a ceremony other than entering the death glyph in the rolls of their regimental hall. Master Iwynd had already buried the body, alone.

Riam hadn't seen Master Iwynd since the attack. The old Draegoran seemed to be avoiding him, which didn't bother Riam one bit. Whenever Master Iwynd looked at him, he had the sense the man blamed him for Gairen's death.

That night Riam returned to the burial field. Since he didn't know exactly where Gairen was buried, he stood alone in the moonlight before the spear that marked the grave of Harol's regulars. The rich, damp smell of fresh-turned soil filled his nose.

"Gairen—" he began and stopped short. *No, not just Gairen. Uncle Gairen.* It was like Lemual's betrayal all over again, but worse. It hurt so much. *Why does everyone have to lie to me? Why can't they tell the truth?*

He took a deep breath and began again. "I don't know why you didn't tell me, but I wish you would have. And I wish you would have told me more about my father." Riam closed his eyes a moment and took another deep breath, trying to keep control of his emotions. "I don't think you would lie to me without a good reason, and you never tried to hurt me like my grandfather, but it still hurts.

"I've been doing a lot of thinking. You told me to forget my family and the past. You told me to commit everything I have to becoming a Draegoran, and that I would never become a Draegoran if I didn't want it, but you never told me why I should become one. No one ever tells me why. . . ." He trailed off.

A sound in the distance made Riam pause. The Esharii were long gone; at least he hoped they were. He listened for a moment while scanning the darkness. All he heard were crickets. He turned back to the grave.

"You saved me twice when you didn't have to. Three times if you count saving me from my grandfather, which I suppose counts as much as the other two. I also know from Brin that you spent two years looking for me and that you died preventing the other children from being taken.

"It's funny. Lemual used to scare me to death with his stories about Draegorans. I thought I was going to die right then when you walked into the farmhouse, but you turned out to be the one who kept saving me. You treated me fairly, and you were better to me than anyone I've ever known." He lifted his shoulders and drew himself up, ready to come to the point of what he wanted to say.

"You told me to become a Draegoran. So I will. I'll do it for you. I'll dedicate myself to becoming a Draegoran. I'll be like you and stop people like my grandfather and the Esharii from hurting others, and I'll make you proud, but I won't quit trying to find out the truth about my father and our family. That's my deal with you. I think it's fair." Riam listened to the night, as if his uncle might agree or object, or there might be a sign from Sollus. Aside from the crickets, the night remained silent. He took that for assent.

"We're leaving for the island soon, and I wanted to say thank you before I go. I never said thank you, but I should have."

He wanted to leave something as a sacrifice to Gairen and the Fallen, so he placed his new boots on the ground in front of the spear. It wasn't much of a sacrifice, but the boots were the most expensive thing he owned. In a sense, it was his uncle who'd given them to him in the first place.

He held his hand up in a half salute before making his way back to the outpost. The world around him seemed heavier and darker, but he had a purpose, and he would not fail his uncle. For Gairen, he would become the greatest Draegoran who ever lived—if it was within his ability.

By the morning of the third day, the outpost had returned to a more organized, albeit temporary, state. Riam and the others had spent the previous day hauling debris to a pile some distance from the walls. It was dull and monotonous work, but it had given him something to do. The remains of the barracks had been replaced by three lines of tents, and a short rain during the night cleared the smoke from the air and washed away some of the signs of battle.

In another twist of events, the taulin that had been guarding the supply run returned. It didn't remain long before setting out in pursuit of the Esharii. Riam still hadn't seen Master Iwynd, so he assumed the old Draegoran went with them. That was fine with Riam. He didn't have anything to say to Master Iwynd.

Riam and the other children left the outpost, escorted

by a full section of regulars—they were taking no chances with the children on the final day under their care. As they headed toward Hath, they walked through the timber yard, but unlike the last time, it was quiet, with only a few workers and a single maston. There was no sign of the teamsters or the timberwains. Sabat and Jerald, who walked in front of Riam, were pushing each other and shouting about the maston, having never seen one before, but Riam ignored them. He wasn't ready to be a part of the group yet, and he did his best to stay as far back as he could. Loral remained close, and she kept dropping back to speak to him, but he wasn't ready for that either. He was thankful she didn't push.

They were all filthy from their work, so they marched straight to the baths once they made it to Hath. The morning was like a repeat of his trip with Gairen. Even the tailor and his boys were at the baths, giving each of the children a new set of clothes to replace the torn and soot-stained ones they wore. It made Riam sink further into himself. He couldn't wait to get on the boat and leave Hath behind.

At last they were all dressed and moving to the docks. People lined their doorways to watch the procession make its way through the small town, many of them calling out.

"Luck to ya, boys!" an old man with a half dozen grandchildren around his legs yelled.

"Hey, we're not all boys!" Loral yelled back at him. Ania, the girl from Tannon's table in the mess hall, also waved at the man.

The whole family laughed at this. The man made a half bow in apology. "Sorry, missies, luck to you girls, too."

Others yelled their best wishes or thanked the regulars for their protection from the Esharii. All in all, the people of Hath seemed far kinder than back home. Riam guessed that if you lived your life next door to the Draegorans, you understood them. It was easier to blame someone far away for your troubles than your neighbors. That had to be what Gairen meant when he was complaining about the people of Nesh.

They arrived at the docks, where two barges were tied off to the small pier. They were roughly the same, both around forty Arillian rods long with raised decks on either end, and there were large, square holes in the lower, middle deck for taking in cargo. Big canvas covers stretched over the top of some of them. Above one of the barges, a wooden crane lowered a net filled with bales of dark wool into one of the holes while workers rolled a few final barrels up the ramp. The other barge sat empty except for a lone watchman sitting on the front deck whittling at a piece of wood.

A chubby-faced man with large, woolly sideburns and a thick mustache approached the section leader.

"Captain Karlet?" the section leader asked. Her name was Valora, if Riam remembered it right from the fire.

"That I am," said the man. He wore a yellow silk shirt and brown billowy pants that were tucked into hose just below the knee. None of the crew dressed as extravagantly. Most wore only pants with no shirt or shoes.

"Loading some last additions. The extra two days gave me time to fill another contract. This, added to the sum you paid me to wait, will make for a profitable turn back down the river. You have my thanks."

"Where do you want the children?"

The barge captain looked down the line, rubbing at one of his sideburns as if he were doing the math on where to stow cargo.

Riam and the other children watched him expectantly, their small bags of personal belongings and clothes clutched in their hands or slung over their shoulders. Many of them were eager to ride in a boat for the first time, and even Riam in his stupor felt a tug of excitement.

Judging by the wrinkles on Captain Karlet's forehead and his pursed lips, he didn't share the same eagerness. He spoke to the section leader, but he made sure all the children heard him. "As soon as the barrels are lashed down out of the way and the last of the cargo loaded, which will be any moment, they can come aboard, and we'll shove off. There's a bin under the lee of the forward deck they can put their bags in, and they can sit out of the way on the cargo covers while we push out into the current. The boatswain will come and explain the rules of my barge." He narrowed his eyes and gave the children a fierce look. "Nobody does anything but sit there quietly until he does."

Riam almost laughed at the obviousness of the feigned anger and barely kept his face straight. Compared to Gairen or the Esharii, the man was like a baby marcat growling.

"Riam, a word if you please," the voice of Master Iwynd called from behind him, wiping the moment of lightheartedness from his thoughts.

Loral raised her eyebrows at Riam questioningly.

He shrugged. "Yes, sir," he said and turned to face the old Draegoran.

Master Iwynd looked to have aged years in the past few days. The sags below his eyes hung lower, his glyphs appeared more faded, and his hair seemed a bit whiter. Even the owl on his neck looked tired instead of menacing, as if reflecting the old Draegoran's state.

"This way." Master Iwynd led him away from the dock until they were a good distance from anyone else. He removed a long, tubular, leather case that hung over his shoulder and held it out. The end of the tube was capped and wired shut. A wax seal dangled where the ends of the wire met, preventing anyone from opening the case without breaking the seal.

It didn't matter. Riam could feel what was inside. It was the sword. He reached forward hesitantly and took it from the old Draegoran. He frowned. It was heavier than he expected, and he had to use both hands to hold it. The mastonhide case was thick and strong.

"It holds both of *Gairen's* swords," Master Iwynd said, emphasizing his uncle's name. "There are also several reports and a letter. You are to deliver this case to the master of Owl Regiment, Kyden Thalle."

Master Iwynd's eyes still seemed to accuse him of something, but he wasn't sure what. Riam hung the case over his shoulder with mixed feelings. In some ways, he wanted nothing to do with the swords, especially the one linked to him, but it was the only connection he would ever have with Gairen. The strap on the case was wide, but it dug at his shoulder. It was like the whole world was inside, weighing it down. He wanted to say something to Master Iwynd, but he didn't know what to say.

"Nobody else touches the case," Master Iwynd said. "You will place it in Kyden Thalle's hands and no other's. If anyone tries to take it, you are to say that you are under orders from me and show them the seal on the case. You will not open it under any circumstances. Understood?"

"Yes, sir."

"Brin told me that he warned you not to tell anyone about your bond and the events in the timber yard. Let me make it even more clear. If anyone other than Kyden Thalle finds out about the sword or opens that case, you won't leave the island alive. Tell no one that Gairen was your uncle."

"I understand, sir."

"I hope you do. It's your life you're protecting. Now go and get on the barge. The others have already started boarding."

With a sigh, Riam walked away. Like everyone else, there were things that Master Iwynd wasn't telling him. *No one ever trusts me with the truth.*

"One more thing," Master Iwynd called.

Riam looked back over his shoulder at the old Draegoran.

"I'm sorry about Gairen. He was a good man, and one of my best students. The only one better was your father. Get through your training and return here as a Draegoran, and I'll tell you about both of them."

Riam stared defiantly at the old Draegoran. "But—" he began.

"I said when you return. Until then, you won't know enough to understand."

There was no arguing with his tone of voice. Riam met the man's eyes. "Yes, sir," he said. "When I return, but I won't forgive you for keeping it from me."

Riam jogged to the barge before Master Iwynd could reply. It was a small thing, but—in a way—he'd stood up for himself. They could withhold the truth from him, but they couldn't control him unless he let them. He would become a Draegoran, but it would be on his terms, not theirs.

Riam was the last one to board, and Captain Karlet gave the order to shove off as soon as he cleared the plank. After he put his bag of clothes in the bin with the others, he seated himself cross-legged next to Loral with the case across his lap. Some of the other children gave him curious looks, but he said nothing.

The men cast off unceremoniously, and the boat slid slowly away from the dock as the men pushed it out toward the center of the river with long poles. Soon the barge caught the current and started downriver. Looking back at the town of Hath, Riam could see Master Iwynd still standing where he'd left him, watching.

It might be years before he returned to get any answers from the old Draegoran. He hoped they both lived that long.

After the Fall, few understood why the gods abandoned them. Most knew only that the gods were gone, and that the one god who remained was powerless to help them, but the priests of Sollus knew the truth.

The priests trained the Naleer, the nameless ones, and sent them searching Draegora for the God of Light who'd been reborn. For the child of the darkness, they sent a hundred more as assassins.

Both groups failed, and a demon rose up from the land. His name was Tomu, strongest of the dark ones, and the land burned while the Naleer searched for the Fallen God of Light destined to oppose him.

—Edyin's *Complete Chronicle of the Fallen*

CHAPTER 16

Nola rubbed at the pink lines and puckered skin that circled her wrists after Scrape untied her. She opened and closed her hands. Imaginary needles jabbed at her fingers and palms. Usually, the tribesmen didn't tie the thin leather straps used to bind her wrists to the saddle so tightly, but it'd been the big Esharii, the one in charge with a fat black line painted across his eyes, who'd done it this time. He always tied her wrists that way, and if she made a noise or complained, he would cinch the leather down even harder. It was one of the few times the big man looked happy, and he knew exactly how to make her the most uncomfortable without causing any lasting damage. Her hands never turned white or blue, but the feeling came and went depending on how she held them in her lap. There was never a position that didn't make one or the other go numb.

Scrape examined her skin and grunted in disapproval. Like most of the Esharii, Scrape's head was shaved except for a small topknot, and the skin around his face paint was paler than the moon. He wore a narrow beard, wound into a single braid with gold-and-silver rings wrapped into the weave. He, too, was big although not nearly as big as the one in charge, but still larger than the rest and more muscled. She called him Scrape because of the scars on the side of his face and his torn ear. They reminded her of the way her knee or her elbow looked right after a bad fall, with deep gouges and rough, pitted skin that even his thick face paint couldn't hide. Whatever created them must have been painful. Maybe he'd fallen on his face after being thrown from a horse the same as her. No matter how it happened, Scrape's face reminded her of how lucky she was. She'd landed in soft dirt, not rock, and only suffered a single cut near her hairline, although she hadn't felt lucky at the time.

Nola ran her fingers along the scab on her forehead, feeling the thick stitches that jutted out. She'd screamed when the old Esharii cleaned the wound, and she'd screamed even louder when he used the bone needle to tie the wound closed. That was the only time the tribesmen had allowed her to cry without punishing her. The wound still hurt and itched. She tried not to scratch or pick at it, but touching the wound reminded her of Riam.

At first, she'd been angry with him and the Draegoran for abandoning her, angrier than she'd been when Riam yelled at her. Later, she'd calmed down. There was nothing they could have done. One man and a boy were not going to rescue her from these savages—even if that one man was a Draegoran. She truly hoped that they'd made it to the safety of the outpost. In her dreams it was her capture that had allowed them to escape. That dream comforted her and let her believe they were alive and free because of her.

Scrape shook the leather straps in the direction of the big Esharii. "Nune'ta en ha'ikana tol," he mumbled.

"I agree. He's a screet," Nola said.

He cocked his head to the right, looking at her with his eyebrows raised. The gesture stretched his scars and pulled the lines on his face into a grotesque expression. A tenday ago, it would have horrified her, but not after what she'd been through. Scrape was gentler than the first Esharii who'd been assigned to watch over her captivity. It wasn't that Scrape was kind. He wasn't. He'd been hard on her over the last four days, but he wasn't cruel. Thank the Fallen the cruel one had been killed three days ago.

Has it really been three days since the battle? Three days since they left me tied to a tree for an entire night.

It'd been terrifying. At the time, she wasn't sure they

were coming back, and she'd feared they'd left her to die—
to be eaten by wild animals. The evening had been over-
cast. So when the moon went down the first time, the night
turned black without the light of a single star. She'd heard
the grunts of an animal and the shuffle of its footsteps.
Something came close enough to sniff at her leg. She'd
peed herself in fear when she smelled its rotting breath and
it touched her leg with a claw. She'd kicked and yelled at it
to leave her alone before tearing at the ropes until she was
exhausted. In the end, all she could do was sit in the dark
and cry for her father to come and rescue her. She imagined
him rushing out of the darkness, brandishing a torch to
scare the beast away and save her, but that didn't happen.
There was no way for him to know she was in trouble. He'd
sold her to the Draegoran, just like the goods he traded,
and she would never see him or her mother again.

Near dawn of that terrible night, the tribesmen had returned, but with far fewer men. The fight hadn't gone their
way, and there were several wounded with two unable to
ride. Those two were left behind when the rest took her and
rode south, straight toward the mountains and toward the
Esharii lands beyond. They rarely stopped while there was
light enough to travel. The only good thing that had come
from that horrible night, besides not being eaten, was the
loss of the tribesman who'd originally had charge of her.
He'd been one of the two left behind. Nola hoped he'd
survived long enough to fear the darkness, and she hoped
that something large and scary had done more than sniff at
his leg.

Her mind drifted back to her father. *How could he let
the Draegoran take me away?* It wasn't the first time she'd
asked herself the question. Her mother had screamed at
Father after they returned home—something she'd never
heard her mother do—but Father had remained a stone
through it all, sitting in his rocking chair and staring at the
hearth until her mother gave up and took Nola to bed with
her. Even their house servant, Lemara, had dared to berate
him for doing nothing. Mother held her the entire night,
and when Nola woke the next morning, Father was still in
the chair, still staring at the fire with her unwrapped birthday present in his hand. He rose quietly when it was time
to meet the Draegoran and drove her on one of the wagons

into town alone. His only words were to tell her that he
loved her before hugging her one final time. Then he pried
her arms from around his neck, slid the birthday present
into her small bag, and passed her to Gairen. She'd watched
him climb back into the wagon and snap the reins, heading
for home, and she'd continued to watch him until he made
the turn by the cemetery. He never looked back. As much
as she wished he'd been there to rescue her, she would
never forgive him.

Satisfied that her hands were not damaged, Scrape fell
into his usual camp routine, starting with his horse. He
mostly left her alone for the evening, as long as she obeyed
and didn't try to run. In the morning he would tie her hands
again—at least she hoped it would be him tying her hands
and not the big Esharii—and they would continue toward the
mountains.

Nola couldn't see them now, but the mountains were
there somewhere, hidden by the surrounding hills. Over
the past few days, the band of Esharii had climbed steadily
higher. The forest had given way to rough hill country filled
with shrubs and small, twisted trees, and the nights were
getting colder. It wouldn't be long before they were over
those mountains. She wasn't sure what would happen then,
but she would soon find out. Nobody would be coming to
save her.

The growl from her stomach roused her from her thoughts.
She was starving, but there were things that needed to be
done before she would be allowed to eat. First, the horse had
to be unsaddled and hobbled, and like everything else, she
was expected to do it herself. It wasn't fair. She'd grown up
with servants doing these things for her, but the Esharii
didn't treat her like the landowner she'd been raised to become. The first tribesman who'd been in charge of her had
made that clear between shoves and backhands that made
her ears ring. He wouldn't give her any food or water until
her horse and bedding were taken care of, and if she cried, he
wouldn't give her any food at all. Nola didn't think Scrape
would treat her as badly, but she wasn't going to take the
chance. Caring for the animal wasn't hard, and it was far
better than going hungry.

Esharii saddles were simple and light without a horn—
just cut leather hide with a single cinch, a chest strap, and

rope stirrups. Folded underneath the saddle was a thick blanket that served as padding. The same blanket was used for sleeping at night, and it made everyone smell like horse sweat. She didn't think she'd ever get the sweet, musky smell out of her nose.

After watering and leading the horse to a nearby knoll where the other horses grazed, Nola pulled the saddle and blanket off and worked to disconnect the stirrups from the saddle. Once she worked both knots through the holes in the leather, they came free. They were cleverly made so that they could also be used to hobble the horse at night. She fumbled with the ropes and then stood back to be sure they wouldn't come off—she'd been punished for that once already and wasn't going to let it happen again. In the fading light she could just make out the other group of Esharii, the plain-faced ones, setting up camp nearby.

The two groups were complete opposites. Where the stripe-faced tribesmen simply found a place on the ground and threw down their blankets before eating, practicing with blades or speaking together before sleep, the ones with unpainted faces were orderly and silent. Every night they set up a small tent and spaced their blankets evenly around it, pointing out like the spokes on a wagon wheel. She counted six of the plain-faced tribesmen—there'd been ten before the battle. They never joked or laughed, and aside from going to relieve themselves, taking care of the horses, or eating, they stood guard around the tent while taking turns sleeping. Nola was reminded of a pack of guard dogs, like the ones Father used to guard the wagon trains. Only, instead of goods, the plain-faced tribesmen guarded the old spirit-walker.

She'd had glimpses of him over the past few days, riding a pure black horse that stood out among the sorrels and paints. He always seemed to be staring right at her. Well, not exactly at her. It was more like he was looking through her, as if his unnatural red eyes saw something behind her. She could never keep from checking over her shoulder whenever he looked in her direction.

The two groups seldom mingled or spoke to one another, but it was the lack of interaction between the groups that shouted louder than words. It reminded Nola of when Mother and Father argued. They never spoke to one another when they were angry, unless they were really angry, but the silence between them was as chilling and tense as any argument. The tension between the camps felt the same.

Convinced the hobbles would stay on, Nola grabbed the horse blanket and saddle. She found a level spot a few paces from Scrape's blanket and, after sweeping away the rocks with her hands and smoothing the ground as best she could, laid the blanket out flat. She pulled several handfuls of rough grass from nearby and rolled the leather saddle around the tufts to form a pillow. Then she sat down and waited for Scrape to notice she was finished.

Her stomach growled again. She'd never been so hungry. The Esharii carried little with them, which meant that they didn't eat much, although they did eat more now that their numbers were smaller. She'd never gone hungry at home.

Home . . .

All she wanted was to go home. The days were becoming hazy and blending together. She was tired all the time, and she wished that they would get to wherever they were going. She wanted to sleep inside, and she wanted to talk to someone who understood her words . . . and a bath. At least when she was with the Draegoran, she had Riam to talk with. At the thought of Riam, she touched her forehead reflexively, feeling at the stitches.

"Durak!" Scrape yelled at her. He shook his head no while pointing to his forehead.

"I wasn't going to pick at it," she said. "I was thinking." She pointed at the saddlebags near his feet and brought her hand to her mouth several times. "I'm hungry, by the way." Despite the boldness of her words she was careful to make sure her tone was submissive. They might not understand what she said, but they definitely understood how she said it.

Scrape threw the bag toward her. She knew what was inside. The same thing they ate every day—cold mush. At least that's what it looked like when water was added to it. It might be ground oats or wheat, but the taste was off. There were traces of color that brightened when the water was added. The reds and greens were some kind of vegetable, but she couldn't imagine what the crunchy black-and-brown flakes were. It didn't taste bad, a little chalky and gritty, but she'd eaten it twice a day since her capture, and she was tired of it.

Even weary of it, however, she would eat the whole bag if they let her. She was tempted to mix a second bowl, but she knew better. No one seemed to be watching, but they were, and they would catch her if she ate a single bite more than the portion allowed. She finished the meager bowl and cleaned it out before putting it back in the bag and carrying it to Scrape.

The moon was up, and Scrape was by himself, practicing with his weapons. He held his sword in one hand and a wicked knife that curved like a talon in the other as he twisted and turned, fighting invisible opponents. He was more agile than his size suggested. He would spin and jump, launching kicks and punches between thrusts and slashes of the sword. The knife he held reversed, running along the side of his forearm, and he used it to block imaginary blows. He was covered in sweat by the time he stopped and waved at his bedding with the sword.

Nola placed the bag next to his blanket and moved back to her own. She'd slept soundly the first few nights with the Esharii, worn out from the long rides, but as she adapted to the routine, she found it difficult to sleep. Soon they would be over the mountains, and then she'd never get to go home. She would spend the rest of her life with these people. It wasn't right. She didn't want to go with them. She wished they'd taken Riam instead of her. She knew that wasn't true, but it didn't matter. Nothing mattered. She flopped down on the blanket.

Much later, Nola lay awake, staring at the stars. She wanted to cry. She was scared and alone, but she kept her jaw locked and breathed deeply, fighting it. Only the occasional tear escaped, sliding from the corner of her eye down to the leather of the makeshift pillow.

She heard soft footsteps and quickly wiped the tears away. Closing her eyes, she pretended to sleep, hoping the tribesman hadn't spied her crying. *I didn't make any noise. Please let him keep walking.*

The footsteps stopped next to her, then a hand touched her shoulder. Nola covered her face and curled into a ball. Any moment and the blow would come. She held her breath.

Nothing happened. She peered between her fingers and saw a plain-faced tribesman kneeling over her. The tribesman put a finger to his lips, motioning for her to keep silent, before beckoning her to follow. Nola was confused. Nearby, Scrape's blankets were empty. No one else was awake that she could see, but that didn't mean much in the dim moonlight—there were never fewer than three or four sentries around the camp.

She wasn't sure what to do. Scrape always stood his watch early in the morning, never in the middle of the night. If he'd gone to relieve himself and returned to find her missing, she didn't know what he would do, but it wouldn't be good.

The plain-faced Esharii beckoned her a second time. "Asha, come," he whispered just loud enough for her to hear. He scanned around the camp quickly and waved at her again. "Must hurry. They come." His accent was thick.

Who is Asha? Who is coming? Nola looked at Scrape's empty blanket again. Her mouth was dry, and she licked her lips. She didn't know what to do.

The plain-faced tribesman grunted softly in frustration and strode back toward her. He was angry. This was the Esharii she'd come to know. She closed her eyes tight, bracing for the blow. She should have followed his orders the moment he spoke them. You did what the tribesmen wanted, and you did it without hesitating. He'd tricked her with his polite manner.

But he didn't hit her. Instead, she felt him next to her, his hot breath on her ear. "You want life, you come now. Soon too late."

Too late for what?

The plain-faced tribesman didn't give her any more time to think about it. He pulled her up, and she stumbled to her feet. She tried to jerk away, but he held her firmly by the arm and marched her beside him. She thought briefly of yelling out to wake the tribesmen around her but decided against it.

The man led her to the second camp, but he sped up instead of stopping. They moved past the small tent. The Esharii who normally guarded it were missing. The tent door flapped in the breeze.

He led her down a small hill until they reached the bottom of a dry wash. It was darker here. The hills and shrubs created long shadows that hid more than she could see, and it was difficult for her to keep pace. The tribesman followed the wadi, his steps crunching on the small stones of the wash bed. Soon they would be out of earshot of the camp.

Nola stopped. Her heart thumped hard in her chest. *What if he wants me for something else . . . something bad?* She should've stayed in the camp. Her mother had warned her about men—how some might try and "take her" if they got her alone. She didn't want to go any farther with the plain-faced tribesman.

As if sensing her fear, the man spoke. "Not long, asha," he called over his shoulder. "Okulu'tan waits." He didn't stop. Soon she would lose him in the darkness.

Why is the okulu'tan waiting for me? Nola touched the stitches on her forehead again. The old Esharii had sewn the wound shut. *He wouldn't do that if he was going to hurt me—would he?* She looked back up the hill and then down the wadi once more. Scrape would have returned to camp by now. She couldn't return alone without getting punished.

"Fallen's mercy," she whispered and hurried after the tribesman.

CHAPTER 17

Nola fell twice trying to catch up with the plain-faced warrior, jarring her wrists and banging her side painfully against the rocks. Nothing felt broken, but her hip hurt and would be bruised. In a short time, the wash bed widened and leveled off; while it was still dark, it was easier going. Then, with a splash, she stepped in a puddle of water that was hidden in a shadow. It was muddy and cold.

She was so preoccupied with shaking the mud from her sandal that she almost didn't notice the firelight flickering on the embankment ahead of her. Whatever they were doing out here in the middle of the night, she was about to find out. Her steps were hesitant as she walked around the final bend.

It wasn't firelight. She stood before a glowing pool of water. Kneeling in the shallow water with his bare, wrinkled torso above the surface was the okulu'tan. Next to the water, sitting cross-legged in the sand, sat Scrape. Nola's heart fluttered in panic.

Scrape looked at her quizzically a moment before jumping to his feet and shouting in the rough Esharii language. Nola attempted to back up, but another plain-faced Esharii was behind her. His hands clamped down on her shoulders, preventing her from escaping.

She'd never seen Scrape truly angry before, and she was glad. He drew his sword and waved it in the air, accenting his words with thrusts that matched each yell. Five plain-faced Esharii scurried into the light, surrounding Scrape, swords also drawn. There was no fear on the scarred warrior's face. If anything, he looked prepared to kill all five.

The okulu'tan put a hand out and spoke. "Hosla'an durak," he said calmly. "Kallum en braun'eum," he added, and the plain-faced tribesmen reluctantly backed away. They didn't go far. Remaining at the edge of the water's light, they kept their weapons drawn.

The old Esharii turned his attention to Scrape. "Mish ta'al durak!" he commanded sharply.

The harsh words ended Scrape's rant in an instant. He threw his sword to the sand in disgust and sat back down. His eyes burned in the glow of the light.

The okulu'tan waved Nola forward. "There's nothing to fear. Come."

The scratchy voice gave her no comfort, but there was no sense in disobeying. She tried to convince herself of this as she pushed herself a step at a time closer to the water. Scrape's hands were clenched into fists on his lap, and the muscles of his jaw stood out below his scars. She was careful to move to a spot outside his reach.

"Ky'lem is surprised to see you here. It's not . . . what he expected, and he is not pleased. He is a smart man, though, and he will soon realize that it is a foolish thing to not accept a path that is already beneath your feet."

Nola swallowed. Saying Scrape wasn't pleased was an understatement. She was pretty sure he wanted to hack someone to death with his sword, and she didn't think he'd be very particular about who it was.

"Sit," the okulu'tan said and motioned to the sand next to Scrape.

Nola looked at the spot, but she didn't move. She didn't want to get within reach of Scrape, or Ky'lem as the okulu'tan had named him, or whatever he was called.

"Sit, asha. He will never be able to harm you."

She wasn't sure she believed him. Keeping her eyes on Scrape, Nola slid closer and sat down.

The okulu'tan smiled at her, but it was a sad smile—the

kind Lemara, her family's house servant, sometimes gave her when she thought no one was looking. At least the old okulu'tan still had all his teeth. Many of the old men back in Steading Rock had none, and the pink, toothless gums made her queasy whenever they spoke to her.

The okulu'tan reached out toward her. Nola's instincts were to pull away, but she held herself firm. A wet, wrinkled hand brushed her cheek.

"A dark-skinned asha—young and fragile and not of the people. Sollus has played a good joke on me . . . but he asks even more of Ky'lem." He chuckled.

Nola had no idea what the old man was talking about.

"I have traveled the ways for the final time. Farther than I have ever gone before. Too far, actually, but I had no choice." The words were wistful and far away. "Everything I've worked toward may come to nothing—all because of two ga'ginga pups, you and the boy we did not take." He sighed. "So much wasted because I could not see far enough ahead. But not all paths are closed. Only mine." The old okulu'tan stared off into the darkness. "But the child sings with Parron's light. Do you see him? He blazes like the sun. He will serve the people."

His words made no sense. *Is the old man insane?*

"Jalla estana asha'inda em hara, Ky'lem. Asha'inda em karii. Pim'ta dem'coranta," the okulu'tan said softly.

Scrape stiffened.

The okulu'tan cocked his head to the side, listening. "The gray demons come. I can hear them on the wind, like the rush of a fire, consuming everything in its path. They will kill most of the warriors, but a few will escape through the pass. They will see Esharii lands once more. I had hoped it would be more."

The Draegorans were coming! A flicker of hope gathered in Nola's chest. They would rescue her.

The old okulu'tan grabbed her chin and brought his face to hers. His red eyes bored into her. "If I warn the warriors, they will break camp and ride, but they will all die trapped in a canyon not far from here. It is a terrible burden to walk the ways. Who do you save? Who do you let die? Which memories are true, and which follow a path that has already failed?"

Suddenly it dawned on her. He was talking about seeing the future. If she'd known the future, she never would have been captured. She wouldn't even be here.

"Scrape, as you call him in your thoughts, he will survive. That's what he's so angry about. He would rather die than face the task I have set before him." The okulu'tan laughed again in a mad chuckle. "You don't see the humor in this, but you will."

There was no doubt in Nola's mind now. The okulu'tan was crazy.

The old man pulled her face closer. He spoke rapidly, almost too fast for her to follow. "The big man, Pai'le, the one who leads the warriors, if his first action during the attack is to run to the horses, he will die. If he attacks the first gray demon he sees, he will live, but another will die in his place. Should I tell him and spare his life in favor of the other warrior?"

Nola didn't like this conversation. *Why can't they let me go and let everyone live in peace?*

The okulu'tan shook her painfully. "Answer me, asha. Should I tell him?"

Fine. The big man was cruel. "No. Let him die," she said.

"Ah, good. A choice." He let go of her chin. "But what if I tell you that should the big man die, your father will also die, and if the other lives, he will cause the deaths of hundreds of your people, many of them children like you? Now what would you do?"

Nola was horrified. She didn't want her father to die, but she didn't want hundreds of others to die either. Her eyes watered. "How can I make a choice like that?"

"But you must choose, because now you know the two possibilities. Simply doing nothing is a choice in itself. There is no running away from it once you have seen a path among the ways." He shook her head by the chin. "Now choose! Do you let him live to save your father, or do you let him die to save hundreds of others?

"I'll make it easy for you. What if all the people in your tribe will die? What if all the people north of the mountains will die? Do you save your father anyway, or do you let him perish?"

Tears ran down Nola's face. *Why is he asking this?* She

didn't want her father to die. His red eyes held her, waiting. Finally, Nola shook her head no.

"So, you are not so weak. Be still. The big man's death has nothing to do with your father, but do you see the difficulty?"

Nola nodded. Seeing the future had become much less appealing. She didn't want to make choices like that.

"Your future is much like the big man's. If you return to the camp, the gray demons will rescue you and take you to their island, but you will die within three years of this night. There is a small chance you will live beyond that time, but no matter the course, if you are rescued, you will not survive to leave their cursed island."

"I don't understand," Nola said. She looked to Scrape and back at the okulu'tan.

"The gray men take the grandchildren of Parron and train them in their ways before linking them to Tomu," the okulu'tan explained, "but the link requires much blood and death, and not all survive. Should they rescue you, you will die, drained like a fly in the web of their deceit." The okulu'tan paused to let the words sink in. "But there is a choice for you, asha. I can break the gray demons' net and send you away with Ky'lem. You will become an okulu'tan like me—the first asha'han to be trained as one. It will be a great honor.

"Yet it will also be a painful life, filled with losses you cannot imagine, but it is life nonetheless, and it will have a purpose. What more can anyone, even an asha, ask for than this? The decision, however, is up to you. I cannot force you. I can only place the path beneath your feet." The old man's eyes shone brighter than the pool he knelt in.

What choice has he given me? Live a few years with the Draegorans or become some kind of crazy Esharii witch-woman. *That isn't much of a choice, and neither is very appealing. Why can't things go back to the way they were? I'm only twelve, for Fallen's sake!*

The okulu'tan leaned forward, the muscles of his face tense in the soft light.

It was important to him that she said yes. *Why? What did he gain from it?*

"Why do you want me to do it?" she asked.

At the question, he relaxed and let go of her. "Good,

asha. Hold on to that desire for the truth, and we may fix the world yet."

The okulu'tan yelled a command to one of the plain-faced bodyguards, then turned and spoke to Scrape in the strange Esharii language.

She hadn't said yes, but he seemed to know she would agree before she knew the answer herself.

Scrape stiffened. He jumped to his feet and looked around, as if he could see beyond the walls of the wadi and through the darkness. In the distance, there was a faint yell. The okulu'tan hadn't told Scrape about the Draegorans until now.

"It is time. I must bond the two of you."

The okulu'tan spoke to Scrape once more, and the scar-faced tribesman came and took her hand, palm to palm, his rough hand dwarfing hers. It was an unexpected gesture. The Esharii didn't seem the type to hold hands. The okulu'tan motioned them closer to the water and pushed their hands beneath the surface.

Nola felt a slight tingle.

Scrape drew the knife from his belt with his other hand and passed it to the okulu'tan.

What is happening?

Scrape squeezed her hand so hard she thought it would break. She tried to jerk her hand away, but it was like pulling against iron.

The okulu'tan placed the tip of the knife on the back of Scrape's hand.

"I am sorry for this pain," the okulu'tan said and drove the narrow blade down through the back of Scrape's hand. The point continued down, stabbing through skin and sliding between bones. Nola felt the skin on the back of her hand stretch, then pop as the blade pushed the final distance through both of their hands. Blood swirled in the water. Searing pain flared through her palm, and she screamed.

The scream tapered off as the pain dulled to a throbbing agony. Nola sucked in her breath and whimpered. *Sollus, it hurt.* Then, beneath the agony, she felt something else. *Rage. Humiliation. Anger at being bonded to an asha—a female child. Something worthless. Fit only for breeding when it grew older. Not Esharii. Not even the proper color. Pathetic.*

Nola gasped. Scrape's feelings threatened to overwhelm her. He hadn't been nice to her because he was a better person than the big Esharii. He'd only *appeared* to be nicer because she was beneath him—less than chattel. It wouldn't make sense to be mean to her any more than it made sense to be mean to a cow or a goat that provided milk. Nola had never felt so worthless in her life. The revulsion made her look down in shame, but there was no retreating from it. It was inside her. She could feel it in her mind and in her heart—crushing her in pounding waves that washed over her body—and it was a hundred times worse than seeing it on his face.

What have I agreed to? If all the Esharii will think so little of me ... She couldn't continue the thought. It was too terrible to contemplate. *How will I survive among a people who think of me this way?*

Head down in shame, not wanting to live another moment, Nola grasped for anything that would give her the strength. That's when she felt Scrape's heart. It had a strong, steady beat. She drew on his strength, and it filled her. Her mind swelled. She no longer cared what he or any of the other Esharii thought. Her head snapped up. She wanted more. Scrape seemed to deflate in front of her. She was stronger than him.

"Careful, asha. The bond is new. You will kill your pachna if you draw out too much of his life." The okulu'tan held up the knife he'd used. He pressed the flat of the blade to his forearms, one at a time, one side on each. Their blood sank beneath the skin, absorbed as if the old okulu'tan were a sponge. He handed the knife, now clean, back to Scrape.

Nola looked down. She hadn't felt the blade being removed or Scrape letting go. There was a cloud of blood in the water, but there was no wound upon her skin, only a faint white line on both the palm and back of her hand.

She could feel Scrape's frustration, and underneath it, she could feel his memories. They were there for her to swim among as she desired. She saw his daughters and his wives. She saw the longhut where he lived. She knew his favorite meal of tiger liver and how it was prepared, knew his pride, knew the way he felt in battle, and to her embarrassment, knew the way it felt as he thrust into his wives. His thoughts and feelings threatened to crush her, but she did not want to stop. It was like living another's life, and deep down, it fascinated her. She knew him for his true name, Ky'lem, and she heard the way his daughter said it with excitement whenever he returned from a hunt or a battle.

"Stop!" Ky'lem yelled at her, and his rebuff slapped at her mind. He didn't want her inside his head. He wanted only to be free to fight the Draegorans who were attacking the camp.

"You may not go, Ky'lem," the okulu'tan told him. "You are chae'lon. You have no tribe now. Besides, it will do no good. The gray demons have already surrounded the camp. You must escape with Ni'ola and make your way to the Najalii. She will not survive the journey without you, and the other okulu'tan will kill her if you are not there as her pachna even if she did. You must be with her. It is the only way they will train her. By Sollus and the lives of the people, I swear to you, if you or she dies, the tribes will never be united again."

"I have served my tribe with honor my whole life. How can you do this to me? How can you make me her pachna? The shame is too much," Ky'lem said.

It hit Nola. They were speaking the Esharii language, yet she could understand every word. *What has the okulu'tan done to me?*

"You see?" Ky'lem said. "Her thoughts are simple and foreign. They are the thoughts of a lamb. She is not of the people. They will never accept her."

"The Najalii, Ky'lem, before Faen next swallows Sollus in the sky. I have placed a shield around her, but as time passes, it will fade, and Parron's light will reach for her. You must be at the lake soon after—before the power consumes both of you. Your fate is bonded with hers. Do not fail her or our people."

"I should never have listened to you." Ky'lem snatched up his sword and tore away into the darkness. His presence inside her faded, yet it did not go away completely. He was running back toward the camp. She could feel his footsteps as he ran. She could feel his anger.

"Do not fear, Ni'ola, he will return for you. I have seen to this. His anger will fade, and he cannot return to his tribe." The okulu'tan pointed at one of the plain-faced guards. "Bring my horse," he commanded.

"Ni'ola?" she asked, but already knew the answer. *It is the Esharii word for the purple flower that grows in the crevices of rocks and trees.*

"It is the closest word to your name in our tongue. It is how you will be known among the people. It is a good name."

The plain-faced warrior returned, leading the old man's stallion. She'd viewed it from a distance. Up close, it was the most beautiful horse Nola had ever seen—sleek and black like the night except for a single white mark on its forehead. It was easily fifteen hands tall. A horse like that would be worth more than Father made on a journey to Arillia. The warrior led the stallion into the water.

The okulu'tan addressed the guards. "I must release the spell that hides us from the gray demons. You will hold them at bay until Ky'lem returns for Ni'ola. You may return to your tribes, redeemed as new men, your debt paid and no longer chae'lon after he returns if you survive. Do not attempt to use Weeping Pass as planned, but instead make for the High Sun Path and the Notch. Now, move away from the water lest you be drained."

"Into the water," he told Nola. "I must do all I can, or none will escape this night. Try and follow what I do with your mind. It is, unfortunately, the only lesson I will ever be able to share with you."

Reluctantly, she stepped forward into the glowing water. The okulu'tan led her to the center of the waist-deep pool.

"Just a nick. The magic requires only a few drops, and we don't want to spook him." The okulu'tan spoke his intentions slowly, as if there was no hurry for the battle that would soon rage around him.

The okulu'tan rubbed the mount on the forehead and whispered to it, keeping it calm. He slid his hands to each side of the horse's head. Gazing into the horse's eyes, he mumbled something, and the horse froze. "Now," he whispered.

With a quick slice, one of his pachna made a small cut on the horse's shoulder. Not even its tail twitched. The warrior backed away quickly.

The old Esharii slid his hands along the horse's neck and down to the wound that glistened in the dim light. Thunder rattled, and a gust of wind hit them when he touched the horse's blood. The light from the pool grew brighter.

"It saddens me to take his spirit for this, but what I must do requires more strength than my pachna can provide."

Nola could feel the power building in the air around them. The wind sped up, and for a moment, she thought she could see a faint glow emanate from beneath the horse's hide.

"Before I begin, asha, you must promise me one thing," the okulu'tan said.

Lightning smashed a hilltop nearby, blinding her, and the wind howled. "One day there will come a choice for you," he shouted over the wind. "A gray demon will be lying near a pool much like this." The wind whipped harder and harder as he spoke. "You must not kill him, no matter the cost, no matter the pain it will bring you. The lives of all hang in the balance." The wind howled around them and lightning crashed with his final words.

Nola nodded.

The okulu'tan accepted her nod as agreement. "I will now take the horse's spirit. It will be strong within me, and I will want more. You must always fight the desire for more than you need." He turned back to the horse. Stroking the beast's neck, he touched his lips to the blood of the wound.

The horse jerked its head up and whickered. Its whole body shivered. In flashes of lightning, she saw the horse wither before her until it was scrawny and feeble, like a starved animal near the end of its days.

The wind howled around them now, carrying dirt and debris that stung Nola's face and arms. She huddled down, close to the water, trying to protect herself. Blood from the horse swirled in the water around her. The crazy old okulu'tan was going to kill them both.

He loomed over her, his red eyes burning into hers. "All waters are connected to each other. Water can shield you from the power or enhance it, depending on how it is used. Remember this." He placed a hand on her head but paused in whatever he was about to do. "Do not forget, asha—you must make him yours, no matter the cost."

Before she had time to nod or draw a breath, the okulu'tan pushed her down beneath the surface of the water.

Nola sucked in bloody water and panicked. Choking, she flailed and kicked to get away, but he was too strong. She had a moment of clarity, as if the water were suddenly clear as glass. She could see the okulu'tan standing over her, one hand in the water holding her under, the other reaching for the heavens.

Lightning struck his outstretched palm, turning the world into a blaze of light. The surface of the water above her sizzled with energy. For a bizarre instant, Nola saw Riam struggling in the water next to her. A moment later, he was gone, replaced by Ky'lem charging into camp, sword drawn. The okulu'tan pulled her up, shattering the visions.

Power coursed through the okulu'tan. Nola could feel it writhing beneath his skin. While his outward appearance remained unchanged to her eyes, in her mind, he was a shell that was filled with liquid fire. Where his hand touched her, he overloaded the senses of her skin—burning, freezing, tingling, wet, soft—every sensation that existed all at once. Nola shrank away, attempting to cower back under the water, but the old man's grasp would not release her.

Blackened glass surrounded the pool. The grass and shrubs beyond were charred lumps. She could smell smoke on the wind.

The okulu'tan let go of her arm and wound his hands in the air above his head. His forearms glowed in the night. The energy manifested itself there, in two blazing points that made Nola's eyes tear when she looked at them.

His hands continued their mysterious weave. Nola could vaguely sense a pattern to the movement, but she could not follow it.

"Kalin Ani'emor!" the okulu'tan yelled and brought his hands down sharply. The night sky lit with a dozen bolts of lightning in the direction of the camp.

The thunder that followed was deafening. It shook Nola's bones and rattled her teeth, and all she wanted to do was run. Run and get away from the madness and chaos the okulu'tan was creating with his magic. The storm spun around the pool. It tore the charred shrubs from the ground and shattered the few twisted trees that hung over the edge of the wadi, whipping them around the pool at lethal speed.

"Do you feel it, asha? Do you hear it call?" The okulu'tan yelled.

Nola didn't know what she was supposed to feel or hear. The okulu'tan's face held the smile of a madman, grinning from ear to ear. He terrified her.

"I will miss this world." The okulu'tan swung his arms as if hurling a massive rock or bale of hay.

The storm around them followed his movement. No longer anchored to the pond, the swirling wind sped away. Nola could see the whole of it now, and her mouth dropped open. A great funnel of wind stretched from the ground to the heavens, and where it touched the earth, it tore the land apart. In moments, it faded away into the darkness in the direction of the camp.

Nothing could survive in the path of that storm. *If I'd fled into that . . .*

Around Nola, the wind was eerily still and quiet. She swallowed hard and turned to face the man who would create something so deadly.

The water's surface was flat and empty. Both the okulu'tan and the horse were gone. All that remained were two glowing lights at the bottom of the pool.

There was something important about them—something important for her and her alone. There was no danger. Her heart told her this while her mind screamed for her to run away as fast as her feet could carry her. The pull of the lights won out over her fear. Hesitantly, Nola waded toward them. She cocked her head this way and that, trying to puzzle out the source. Making up her mind at last, she ducked beneath the surface long enough to grasp the lights, one in each hand.

She felt the hardness of them, like stone, with sharp edges that dug into her palms. They were warm as well, but not hot. She brought them above the surface and gasped. On each of her palms lay a crystal that glowed softly with the power the okulu'tan had wielded. They were hers. A final gift from a madman.

These are what he'd used to call the magic—these and blood. She shivered and almost dropped them.

She tucked the crystals into her clothing and climbed from the water. The fired sand crunched beneath her feet.

CHAPTER 18

K y'lem ran as fast as he could through the darkness of the night, following the twists and turns of the wadi. He ran hard, his blood pounding in his ears. He held his sword in one hand and his knife in the other, just as he trained each night, and he ran without regard for the danger of the crevices and rocks of the wash bed that waited to snap a bone and leave him broken and useless in enemy lands. At the very least, a misstep might turn an ankle or trip him, but even then, unless he was lucky, the rocks would be unforgiving when he fell. A broken arm or shoulder would be as fatal as a broken leg this side of the mountains. Fortunately, he had help.

The spirit paste improved his vision, but there had to be some light for it to work. In the deepest shadows of the wadi, there was none. This, however, did not slow him down. His kinsmen were dying, and even though he was now chae'lon and owed them nothing, he could not bring himself to abandon them. He'd been made a plain-faced pachna only moments earlier, but he'd fought as a Ti'yak his entire life.

"Stupid," he mumbled, but he wasn't talking about the dangers of running in the dark or helping his former kinsmen fight the gray demons. *Stupid to make a deal with the crazy old spirit-walker.* Look where it'd gotten him.

Bonded to an asha. It was unheard of for a tribesman of his stature, second to the warleader and one day a member of the tribe's council, to become one of the tribeless, plain-faced warriors. The thought of going without his paint, like an unproven boy or a slave, was shameful. It was for the young or the unwanted—those who had no honor—no other choice save death.

Worse, he would have to give up his two wives. *Faen take all the okulu'tan!* They were good women, and they'd given him fine children. They weren't going to be happy when they found out, especially his firstwife, Tsi'shan, wedded to secure peace with the Arpatha tribe. He'd given both wives a good life, and they'd risen in status with him as he'd risen in the tribe. Now, they would need to wed other warriors, likely far below his rank, and many of the younger warriors were not as kind to their women as he was. There would also be consequences for the Ti'yak as a whole. If Tsi'shan did not take a new husband of sufficient rank in the tribe, the peace between Ti'yak and Arpatha would falter. No, it was not going to be easy for either of his wives, and he didn't like abandoning them.

All because he'd been stupid enough to make a deal with an okulu'tan. The spirit-walkers never gave exactly as they promised, but after the failed battle at the outpost, Ky'lem had been angry with Pai'le—so angry that he'd been ready to challenge him for his position as warleader. He would have done so if the okulu'tan hadn't brought him to his tent a second time and offered him something else, something Ky'lem wanted even more.

"Challenge Pai'le and you will die," the okulu'tan told him in his cracked and wheezy voice, "but serve me and you'll have a chance to unite the tribes as warleader of all the Esharii, not just a Ti'yak warband. You could become the Sko'dran, the Destroyer of the Night, the one who will lead our people to defeat the gray demons. If you accomplish this, the tribes will sing songs of you until the Esharii are no more."

The okulu'tan hadn't mentioned anything about being bonded to an asha when he'd made his glorious offer. *How can I unite the tribes and defeat the Draegorans as pachna to a foreign asha?* It was impossible. His desire for great-

ness had made him a fool, and he'd thrown everything away
for an insane man's vision.

The last was certainly true. The old okulu'tan really was
crazy. Ky'lem had paid attention to the old stories when he
was young. Few spirit-takers were strong enough to travel
the ways and become a spirit-walker, less than one in a
generation, and every one of them went insane. All knew
it, and this okulu'tan had done it three times—three times!

What most seemed to forget, and what he'd foolishly
paid attention to, was that behind every great leader who'd
united the tribes, a powerful spirit-walker who'd traveled
the ways guided him. This was why he'd listened, even
when he knew better. In his desire to conquer the gray demons, he'd underestimated the spirit-walker's madness.

*And the last commands, the ones he'd shouted just be-
fore bonding him to the asha. I don't even want to think of
the consequences.*

*There has to be a way out of this. Think . . . use your
head. Isn't that what I always tell Pai'le?*

He could pretend none of it ever happened. The okulu'tan would be dead soon, his life used up fighting the gray
demons. The asha would never make it to the Najalii alone.
Even if, by the mercy of Sollus, she did reach the Najalii,
the okulu'tan who guarded the lake of life would not train
her, and they would kill her if she had no pachna. They
might kill them both anyway, even if he did guide her.

*Has the bond grown strong enough to consume us both
if she dies now? Perhaps not, if she dies quickly with no
warning before the bond is truly set.*

A shiver of revulsion passed through him at the thought
of the asha coming to harm. Already, the link would not let
him hurt her. *But someone else could.* A spasm clenched
his heart, and he almost fell. Even the thought of allowing
her to die by another's hand brought him pain. Soon the
bond would grow until he protected her to his dying breath.

If only she died this night. He could remain with his
tribe as if he'd never agreed to anything. His face was still
painted. As long as none of the spirit-walker's pachna survived, no one would ever know. That was easy enough to
ensure with a blade if he reached Weeping Pass before they
did. He felt no compulsion to protect them, and he was a

far better swordsman than any of the plain-faced warriors. *It isn't as if I would need to kill them all. I need only make sure none of the survivors of this night make it back across the mountains.*

Ky'lem was tempted to break his word, to find some way around the bond, but the spirit-walker's impending sacrifice gave him something to cling to—a reason to hope—that somewhere in this foolishness lay a way to unite the tribes and destroy the gray demons. *Would the old man really drain himself to save the asha if she were not important? The okulu'tan wouldn't have bound me to her if she weren't meant for something great.*

A spirit-walker might mislead with half-truths and possibilities, but they rarely lied. Somehow, serving this asha would lead to a chance of uniting the tribes and defeating the Draegorans. That chance, no matter how small, stoked a burning ember in Ky'lem's heart that he would never be able to smother. He had no choice. For a single chance in a thousand he would serve this asha to his death. The tribes were more important than his honor . . . more important than the truth of his life.

The clangor of battle reached Ky'lem as he left the wadi and scrambled up the loose shale slope that led back to camp. He nearly tripped on the body of a sentry, seeing the dark unmoving form at the last moment and leaping at an odd angle to keep from stepping on an outstretched arm. A sudden unnatural wind buffeted him when he crested the rise. A fire had blazed at the center of the camp when he'd left, but the heavy wind quashed the flames, reducing it like a fluttering candle. It did little to improve his vision, even with the spirit paste flowing through his veins. Vague silhouettes fought and yelled, and blades clashed, but it was difficult to distinguish Esharii from Draegoran.

Lightning flashed, exposing the camp, and Ky'lem's hopes were scattered like the flames of the fire. At least three of the enemy's taulins, maybe more, fought in and around the camp—some on foot, some still mounted. Several of his tribesmen were already down. Against one taulin, the warriors had a chance. Against the number of gray men before him, they would be slaughtered. Only the spirit-walker's magic could save them.

Darkness returned, making it even more difficult to see

after the bright flash. The wind grew stronger, churning up sand and dirt that stung Ky'lem's face as he waited for his sight to readjust to the dim light. The okulu'tan had to be creating the wind. If it grew any worse, there would be a sandstorm equal to those of the Great Keln in the far south, but it gave Ky'lem hope. Some of his tribesmen might escape under the cover of the gale to reach the Weeping Pass. The spirit-walker's parting gift.

Lightning struck again, and this time, Ky'lem saw Pai'le. The big war leader had chosen his spot to sleep well away from the others, and he fought alone against a single gray demon. His back was to a twisted tree barely large enough to shield him. Behind the tree, a single gray demon approached unseen.

It hit Ky'lem as suddenly as the lightning around them. He'd been with the asha at the start of the attack. There was no need for the storm to let him and the girl escape. *So why the storm? Why let me return?* There was someone else the okulu'tan needed to survive, and Ky'lem knew who it must be—Pai'le. *That is why the okulu'tan prevented me from challenging him.* The okulu'tan had only said that he would die if he challenged Pai'le, not that he would lose the fight. All men died eventually. *Half-truths and madness. It all made sense.* He could have spirited the girl away in the night if that was all the okulu'tan wanted. They would have been halfway to the mountains before the attack had come.

"Faen's ass. Why not just tell me the truth, old man?"

Ky'lem raised his sword and sprinted to Pai'le's aid.

The gray demons were inhumanly fast, but they still had to know the weapon was coming to dodge it. Whether it was because of the wind and sand or because the gray man was too intent on killing Pai'le, it didn't matter. He never saw Ky'lem. Ky'lem's blade bit into the side of the gray man's neck, nearly taking the head off, and the swirling wind flung a spray of blood in all directions that spattered them both in a hard rain. He knelt, and in one quick slice, removed the wolf from the gray man's neck—proof of his kill.

Pai'le was suddenly next to him. The big warrior looked from the tree to the body to Ky'lem, nodding his acknowledgment of what had just occurred. On the other side of the tree, the gray demon Pai'le had been fighting lay on the ground unmoving.

"Wh . . . t . . . horse . . . ry!" The wind tore Pai'le's words
to fragments, but Ky'lem understood and obeyed, running
toward where the horses were hobbled. Halfway there, he
slid to a stop. Two gray men rode toward him. He could not
defeat both at once, and without the horses there was no
escape.

"Faen take the gray demons," Ky'lem cursed.

Pai'le came rushing to his side just as the two Draegorans closed. Pai'le dove to the left, and a blade swung
through the air where his head had been an instant earlier.
The second horseman intended to trample Ky'lem. Ky'lem
threw his knife with all the force he could get behind it and
dove to the side. There was a loud clang when the rider
deflected it with his sword. He hadn't really expected the
knife to do any damage; he'd only needed to distract the
rider long enough to get out of the horse's way.

Lightning flashed a third time, and—by the grace of
Sollus—his knife had landed nearby. He dove to retrieve it.

The gray demons leaped from their saddles and ad-
vanced toward him and Pai'le. Ky'lem took a deep breath
to calm his heart. The gray men were incredibly fast, but
he'd fought them before and lived. If he defeated this one,
he'd claim a third skin on this raid, and he wanted a third
badly. No living Esharii could claim three skins on a single
raid. What a story this would make—killing the third Draegoran while the spirit-walker's great windstorm swelled
around him.

He dashed forward, swinging his sword in a downward
slash aimed at the first gray man. Pai'le attacked the other.
The first gray demon met Ky'lem's blade, letting the heavy
Arillian sword slide down the curve of his saber and away
from him before countering. Ky'lem brought his sword
back in low, toward the man's legs. The swing carried little
strength, and the gray man blocked it with ease. The weapons rang out when they met. The two stepped apart, circling one another.

Ky'lem searched for an opening to attack. With speed
on the Draegoran's side, it was best to stay on the offensive.

A gust of wind from behind Ky'lem threw sand and
brush at the gray man, and Ky'lem used the opening to
make a thrust at his face. The gray man avoided it and
jabbed his sword toward Ky'lem's stomach. Ky'lem brought

the knife down to deflect the blow, but not fast enough. The saber grazed along the side of his waist. Ky'lem ignored the line of fire and stepped in close, bringing his knee up toward the man's groin. The gray man twisted and Ky'lem's knee slammed into his hip, knocking him off-balance.

Ky'lem pressed the attack. He had little time. A gray demon could leach away his spirit from even the smallest of wounds. He dropped to one knee and used his sword to brush away a weak attack, then hooked his knife around the inside of the Draegoran's thigh. The Draegoran tried to kick his leg up and out of the way, but he was still off-balance. Ky'lem tightened the grip on his knife and pulled. He felt the blade scrape along bone.

By the time the gray man broke free, there was a deep gash below his groin from the back to the front of his inner thigh. Blood poured down his leg. The gray man wobbled unsteadily and fell.

Ky'lem kicked the sword away from his opponent's hand and turned to aid Pai'le. It was unnecessary. The other gray demon lay on the ground at Pai'le's feet holding his stomach with his entrails spilled next to him. Ky'lem looked around for the next opponent, but they were left alone momentarily—a pocket of calmness around which the fighting turned with the storm.

It would not be for long. Three gray men rode through the horses, scattering them. One of his former kinsmen was halfway into the saddle when a blade slashed down his back. The tribesman pitched forward, out of the saddle, and the horse bolted. The dying tribesman was dragged away, his foot caught in the stirrup.

Three Esharii fought near the fire, but they were outnumbered. They wouldn't be able to hold off the attack much longer. On the other side of the camp, another tribesman fought to escape two Draegorans. Ky'lem moved to help.

"No, Ky'lem!" Pai'le's words stopped him. "It is not your fight."

One of the three Esharii by the fire went down, and the remaining two fought back-to-back. They were outnumbered five to two. He started forward.

Pai'le grabbed Ky'lem by the arm and spun him around. "I will help them. I am their warleader," he brought his sword up between them, "and you are no longer a member of this tribe."

Ky'lem drew back.

"You think I don't know when one of my own warriors has betrayed me? You think I don't know that you planned to challenge me and take my place? The okulu'tan told me everything, right after you groveled at his feet, begging for him to take my spirit. You think I'm stupid?" Pai'le waved his sword back and forth with his words. "If you had not saved my life, I would kill you. Consider the debt paid."

Ky'lem's head spun faster than the wind. *What is Pai'le talking about?* While he'd thought of challenging Pai'le, he hadn't gone to the okulu'tan for help. The okulu'tan had asked to speak to him.

"It wasn't . . . I . . ." Ky'lem stopped. He almost laughed at the absurdity of the world. The crazy old spirit-walker's half-truths went deeper and farther than he could fathom. He'd played on Pai'le's fears and made it so Ky'lem could never return to his tribe. There was no other choice than to become the asha's protector. No matter what he did now, he was chae'lon, and a chae'lon who did not serve an okulu'tan was as good as dead or, worse, a slave.

"Go. You are not wanted here." Pai'le raised the sword threateningly, like a man scaring away a dog. "Go. Hide behind your spirit-walker while you can. If I ever find you with the paint of a true warrior on your face again, I will kill you for the honorless coward you are."

Ky'lem's blood pounded in outrage, but he backed away. *The tribes are more important than the truth.* He told himself those words again and again, using them as a shield against the shame.

Pai'le spat on the ground between them and turned his back to Ky'lem.

Feeling like the coward Pai'le named him, Ky'lem moved away. He nearly tripped over the body of the gray demon he'd killed. He would still take his skin for the kill. Pai'le could not take away that honor.

He half sliced, half ripped the square symbol from the dead man's neck. He tucked the bloody skin into a pouch. With the wolf he'd taken and the dried-up owl he'd carved off the Draegoran at the outpost, he had his three.

After a last look at his kinsmen, Ky'lem ran to catch one

of the mounts that had scattered. He was running away
now because he had no choice, but if he ever united the
tribes, he wouldn't rest until he'd carved the skin off the
neck of every living gray demon in payment for the shame
of today.

He did not see the great vortex of wind strike the camp
behind him or hear the screams of the men it lifted into the
air and dashed against the rocks. Nor did he see Pai'le leading the last of the Esharii in a desperate charge to escape.
He had only one thing left to him—the asha.

She'd better be worth the price of my honor.

CHAPTER 19

Riam and the other children changed boats when they reached the city of Ibbal, arriving in the morning and leaving the same day. The river they traveled joined the Layren a few steads above the city, more than doubling its size and speeding up, just as Gairen said it would. No chain could ever be stretched across it like the one at the timber yard. A half dozen barges lined end to end would not span the river's murky depths.

"Ibb is the Draegoran word for stone," a thin, wiry-haired boatman said. "So Ibbal means 'place of stone.'"

It was an accurate description. High rock walls protected the city and the crowded docks that jutted from the iron gates along their base. Riam and the others never saw behind those gates. It took no more than a sandglass to march to another boat and for Captain Karlet's personal gear to be transferred before shoving off again. They now rode a much larger barge used to carry grain downriver.

Captain Karlet, it seemed, owned a fleet of barges that transported everything from wood and grain to livestock downriver. The barges would then be towed back upriver filled with finished goods and other "rare materials," as he put it. Normally, Captain Karlet remained in Parthusal with his warehouses, but every now and then he ventured out on the river to "regain the feel of his operations and get the measure of his crews." None of the men on the barge seemed to enjoy his presence. They all looked nervously over their shoulders as they worked, and there seemed to be some confusion between the usual captain and Captain Karlet's orders.

Riam and the children spent the day the same as they'd spent their previous days on the smaller vessel, trying to stay out from under the feet of the boatmen and the two captains. They'd all learned the hard way that getting in the way was a fast method for learning how to properly scrub a deck.

The small crew cabin at the rear of the barge and the areas where the crew worked the sweeps were forbidden, which pretty much meant that the whole rear and the majority of the sides of the barge were off limits. The only places left were either along the front or on one of the heavy scantlings that ran the width of the ship and separated the grain into multiple open holds. Thick tarpaulins stretched over the mounds of grain to protect them and were battened to the scantlings. The mounds looked like they would be comfortable to sit on. Instead, they were scorching hot from the afternoon sun. There was no rail on the barge, only a short, raised coaming that ran the perimeter of the nearly rectangular hull. The front was the better of the two spots. It had the best view and was the coolest place to ride, and because the barge was what the boatmen called a "rake," the front curved back underneath and allowed a person to sit with their legs dangling over the water. Unfortunately, Tannon and his gang had laid claim to the front, leaving the scantlings to Riam and the other outcasts—the name Vashi had given to those who didn't do what Tannon ordered. The sandy-haired boy's arm was out of the sling now, and he never sat in one place for long—and always bouncing and fidgeting when he did. Right now he was walking back and forth across a tarpaulin, heel-to-toe with his arms out wide, counting his steps.

Riam and Loral sat together on one of the scantlings, watching a long, slender ship lined with oars tow another barge upstream. The oars were mesmerizing—up, forward, down and into the water, all in perfect time, like a giant caterpillar crawling on glass. The barge behind the oared ship rode high in the water, its bright red loadline a rod above the water's surface, which meant a light cargo. Marcus and Karyl were currently playing a slap game with their hands on the other side of Loral from Riam.

"The one in front is a prison ship," Marcus said without looking up from his brother's hands. He squinted his eyes in concentration, watching his big brother's hands and trying not to blink.

Karyl nodded, affirming the smaller brother's words. Marcus did most of the speaking for the larger brother who tended to hover on the fringe of conversations without saying much. Karyl flipped his hand over and smacked the back of Marcus's hand before the smaller boy could pull it away.

"Ouch!"

"What?" Loral asked.

"I said, 'ouch.'"

Loral rolled her eyes. "I know that. I meant about the boats."

"The ship pulling the barge. Prisoners row it. Free men don't row on ships, at least not the ones on rivers."

"Oh."

"It's a life sentence," Marcus added, "so they're really just slaves."

"But only the Arillians have slaves. The Covenant forbids slavery," Loral said.

"Exactly—that's why they're called *prisoners*," Marcus said.

"That doesn't seem right. They're still slaves, even if you don't call them that," Loral said before pressing her lips into a flat line—the way she did whenever thinking deeply about something she didn't like.

After several days together, Riam knew that look. In the mess hall he'd wanted to change it into a smile, but over the last few days he'd learned it was better to get out of her way than to attempt to change it. He'd also come to the conclusion, after being yelled at twice, that it wasn't his responsibility to change it. Riam slid a few hands away from her.

"I wonder what they did," she said.

"Thieves maybe, or beggars. It's a crime to beg," Marcus

said. "Their crimes can't be too bad, though, or they would've been executed by their district wardens."

"Well, that's a great choice; be a slave or starve with no money," Loral said.

Riam didn't say what they were all thinking. Someday it might be them who enforced the law. He thought of his grandfather. That helped put it into perspective. "They broke the law. People who break the law deserve to be punished." He said the words to himself, but the others heard him.

Loral gave him an exasperated look.

"It's not evil to protect others by stopping those who are bad," he explained.

"It's horrible, spending your life rowing a boat because you don't have any money," she replied.

"I'm sure they are all criminals and deserve it," Marcus said, giving her a big smile.

Smack!

"Ow!" A wince replaced Marcus's smile. His brother had used the opportunity to put more effort into his swing. "That wasn't fair. I was talking," he said, shaking his fingers out to try and ease the pain.

"Serves you right," Loral said. "You wouldn't think you deserved it if you were forced to spend your life as a slave and your only crime was being poor and hungry." She made a big deal of jumping down from the scantling and stomping across the tarpaulin cover, forcing Vashi to lose count of his steps as he jumped out of her way. The grain shifted beneath her, and she nearly lost her balance. She glanced back at Riam and the others, but they were smart enough not to laugh.

Marcus and Karyl both looked to Riam; their hands were back together between them.

Riam shrugged. "I think it has something to do with someone in her family. She'll be back when she cools down."

The twins nodded.

Smack!

"Would you stop doing that when I am not looking, you stupid screet!"

Riam chuckled at the twins' bickering. Other than a slight similarity in looks, they were really nothing alike, except that they were both getting their adult teeth later than the others. Marcus, the small one, was always wiggling a loose tooth, while Karyl's two eyeteeth were coming in at different angles. The crooked teeth, combined with his size and how little he spoke, made many of the boatmen take Karyl for a simpleton, but he was far smarter than his over-talkative brother. Like most of the children, all except for Loral, Tannon, Dunval, and Vashi, the twins were from a small town—somewhere on the coast where they'd worked their father's fishing boat. Karyl was the one who'd taught Riam the words for the different parts of the barge and what a loadline was. Riam understood why you said port and starboard, but why you couldn't just say front and back instead of fore and aft was a question neither of the twins could answer.

The five of them, when he added himself, Loral, and Vashi to the twins, had formed a loose friendship. At night they slept under tarps that were stretched overhead to keep the rain off. Marcus and Tannon had argued about who slept where the first night out of Hath. Tannon had forgotten about the larger twin when he insulted Marcus, calling him a "stupid, little, village bastard." Tannon never saw the fist that knocked him to the deck, but he was lucky. Before Karyl could do more, Dunval and Sabat tackled him. That's when Vashi joined in to even things up. The last two members of Tannon's group, Jerald and Ania quickly followed.

Riam hadn't meant to get involved. After his conversation with Master Iwynd, he'd wanted to keep apart from the other children—well, all of them except for Loral—but the sight of her leaping wildly onto Ania and pulling her long black hair like it was the bridle for steering a horse changed his mind. Unwilling to be outdone by her, Riam had added himself to the chaos of children wrestling on the deck. The boatmen broke up the fight before any of them were injured, although several had bloody noses and a few wore black eyes like medals. The battle was over, but the war was not. Captain Karlet finally separated the two groups after the third fight—once there'd been nothing left for them to scrub.

The children now did everything exclusively in two groups—Riam's and Tannon's. How the outcasts had become his group Riam didn't know. He suspected it had to do with Loral telling everyone some of what had happened during the attack on the outpost—most everything besides the sword and the explosion—or because carrying a sealed case that he never let out of his sight somehow made him look important. Whatever their reasons, the outcasts went with whatever he decided, even Loral, unless she was angry.

He liked his new friends, especially Karyl and Loral. For Riam, who hadn't grown up around other children his age, the big quiet twin made a good companion when separated from his brother Marcus. Both Marcus and Vashi reminded him too much of Nola with their constant chatter.

Riam usually spent the long, boring mornings talking to Loral. She had a quiet seriousness that the others lacked, and he guessed she came from a home that wasn't a normal family—similar to him. That was something he'd picked up on, that his grandfather, besides being a criminal, hadn't been normal. Riam hadn't told anyone about him, but he'd listened to enough of the others' stories to figure it out.

"Come on," Marcus said, tugging on Riam's arm. Vashi stood behind him. "We're going to go to the front scantling and make faces at Tannon." Marcus and Vashi's eyes sparkled mischievously.

"You'll start another fight, and we'll all end up scrubbing again," Riam said.

"As long as we all have to do it, I don't mind," Marcus said. "I never could stay out of trouble on my dad's boat, so it doesn't bother me. I grew up spending my free time scrubbing and sanding."

Karyl nodded in affirmation.

"Beats sittin' and bakin' in the sun," Vashi added.

Riam stood to go with them but then saw Loral staring and sat back down. He didn't want to look childish in front of her. "You go. I'm . . . I'm not feeling up to it."

"Thinking about your brother back home again?" Marcus asked.

Karyl hit his brother on the arm.

"Wha . . . oh. Sorry, Riam. I didn't mean to bring it up."

"It's fine. You go ahead. Don't throw the first punch if it comes to that. The captains will be harsher with whichever side lays the first blow."

Having gained Riam's approval, Marcus and Vashi scurried off down the beam. Karyl gave Riam a helpless look that said, "Sorry."

"I know. Try and keep them from getting us all into

trouble," Riam told Karyl. The big twin shrugged and hurried off after the first three.

Riam didn't have to sit alone for long. Loral made her way back to the beam where he sat.

"Mind if I sit with you?" she asked, standing above him. The sun highlighted her dark red hair. Her soft green eyes were as serious as ever, but her mouth was no longer pressed into a thin line.

Riam's heart sped up. He tried to answer her, but he couldn't get his throat to make the right sounds. His answer turned into an embarrassing screech.

Loral smiled at his awkwardness, making it impossible for him to recover his voice. All he could do was slide over.

Captain Karlet's mood went from tense to foul over the next few days. They were behind schedule, and the barge's hired captain, a short man named Stovall who walked with a limp and whose right eye never opened as far as his left, couldn't do anything to gain Captain Karlet's approval. It was morning, and the cool water created a rising mist in the fast-warming air that made things damp and uncomfortable. By the conversations of the boatmen, they were five days out from their destination, the city of Parthusal.

Riam and the other outcasts sat on their usual scantling midship, eating smoked fish and biscuits while the crew untangled a mess of chain and rope along the narrow deck that ran half the perimeter of the barge. Above them, the morning sun hid behind boiling clouds that promised rain.

"The captain woke with a viper in his trousers today," one of the crewmen said. "Wasn't anyone's fault the anchor got fouled. Just bad luck."

"Captain Karlet don't believe in luck."

"Captain Stovall's worried that Karlet will toss the lot of us off the boat when we make it to Parthusal and hire a new crew if we're late."

"Forget bein' late. I need the bonus we get for being early. I've got debts to pay. I'll not end up like my brother, rowing a boat till it kills me."

"Relax, Raulf. We'll make it up. We're always behind till we come to the buoys that mark the deeper channel. Once we're there, we can run both day and night to make up the time. Even if we're late, it'll only be the second time."

"That's if we don't run aground on a sandbar. We've made bad time ever since Dathen came aboard, both on our last run and this one. Lots of bad luck since he signed on." The anchor chain made a clunk as Raulf threw the section he held to the deck and made the sign of the Fallen in the air. "It's not normal, catchin' a rope from a sunk boat when we dropped anchor. What are the odds on a river this size? I tell ya, we need old Pallan and his brother back on the sweeps. Never had these problems when they was here."

"It's not the new man's fault. Strange things happen on the river all the time. It goes in cycles. Why, once, when I was young, we were snared on a bone half as long as this barge. Never seen anything in the river big enough to have a bone that big. Even the great gnurls of the deep don't get big enough to have bones that size. Kept me afraid of the water for months."

"You're full of screet shit, Tem. Ain't nothin' on the river that big. Probably old, bleached ironwood."

"Calling me a liar? It was bone. I know bone from ironwood." Tem stood up straighter, arching his back to push his chest out, and his mustache flared out like the hair on the back of an angry marcat.

The man's posture reminded Riam of Tannon before the last fight. *Do people change so little when they grow older?*

"Calm down. No one's calling you a liar. We're only talking 'bout our luck," Raulf said.

Tem's chest deflated some, but his back remained stiff. "It's not Dathen's fault," he mumbled.

"Well, someone's draggin' Faen's luck along with them, whether it's him or one of those Fallen-cursed children."

"It's not our fault," Vashi said from behind Riam. "We weren't on board for the last run, so it can't be us."

"Hmmf. Come help untangle this chain instead of sitting useless."

Riam and the other outcasts gave Vashi dark looks.

"It's not my fault," Vashi said as they moved to help.

Lightning cracked, burning the sky for an instant.

"See. It is your fault. Everyone knows lightning strikes right after you speak false," Marcus told Vashi.

"That's a tale made up by old fishermen." Thunder rumbled around Vashi's words, and as if Sollus was trying to prove him wrong, a second flash of lightning flared across the sky.

"Like I said, Sollus always speaks out against an untruth." Marcus made the sign of the Fallen.

Riam didn't believe that Sollus had anything to do with the lightning. Sollus never made lightning strike when his grandfather lied about his mother, or when anyone else lied to him for that matter, and those were big lies. If Sollus really cared about something like lying, then surely he would have riddled the sky with lightning wherever his grandfather went. Maybe before the gods fell, when there were hundreds of them watching from across the heavens, they might have cared about such small things, but not now when only one remained. Riam doubted the last God of Light had time for anything so small.

It began to rain before they finished with the anchor chain, and it continued all day, stopping just long enough for the air to become hot and damp again before drenching them all in a fresh downpour. When evening came, two canopies were erected to shelter them while they slept, one on each side of the crew cabin. As usual, the children split into two groups—Tannon's on one side and Riam's on the other—but unlike the previous nights, the barge wasn't stopped and anchored. True to the crewman's word, once they reached a point on the river where a large red buoy floated on the water, Captain Stovall announced that the crew would split into two watches and would no longer stop at night.

Riam slept fitfully. There was too much thunder, and the rain on the canvas above them was nearly as loud. Vashi shook him from his half-sleep, and Riam sat up, rubbing his eyes. A fine mist of water sprayed his face from the rain.

"What is it?" he asked.

Vashi put his finger to his lips. "Shhh. Come with me," he said, not providing any explanation.

Puzzled, and not at all happy about getting soaked again, Riam shrugged off the damp blanket and followed Vashi. Whatever the boy was up to, Riam was sure it would end with trouble. There were few things Vashi did that didn't end without someone running afoul of the crew.

Vashi led him out into the rain. The only boatmen in sight were the ones manning the sweeps and the pilot up front with the lamp who shouted occasional commands back to them. One of the men watched Riam and Vashi for a moment, but judging from the man's posture, he didn't care what they did.

"Stay here and keep watch for me," Vashi said.

Riam nodded. He wasn't exactly sure what to watch for, but Vashi left him standing in the rain without explanation and moved to a ladder on the side of the crew cabin.

The rain grew stronger while Riam waited, turning into large, cold drops. Riam wished he'd hurry.

Vashi appeared at the top of the ladder. He moved slowly, his wet and matted blond hair hanging down into his eyes. He stretched toward the corner of the building and fumbled with something.

What is Vashi doing? At any moment one of the crew would see him.

Whether Vashi was sneakier than Riam realized or lucky, he finished whatever he was doing and began creeping back down the ladder without anyone noticing.

"What are you doing?" The voice behind Riam made him jump. Vashi had been spotted.

"I said, 'What are you doing?'"

The voice was speaking to him, not Vashi. Riam turned around to see Tem, the mustached crewman who'd been working on the anchor chain, squinting at him.

"Sir, I was going . . . going to go pee." After the scare, he really did have to go. The man gave him a sharp look. Riam slipped past him and moved to the side of the boat.

"Me, too, sir." Vashi came sliding up beside Riam.

"Floggin' children," the man mumbled. "Stand out in the rain in the middle of the night woolgathering. Hurry up and get back with the others." Tem moved off toward the front of the barge.

"What were you doing?" Riam asked, keeping his voice low.

Vashi had a wide, stupid grin on his face below his fading black eye. "I loosened the ropes on the canvas above Tannon so that it sags and catches the rain. The weight of the water should pull the ropes free when it fills up."

Riam closed his eyes. He wanted to be mad at Vashi for the prank, but the thought of Tannon and his friends getting soaked made him giggle. Soon both boys were trying to keep from laughing in fits and starts. They were still giggling when they went back to where the others slept. Their noise woke Loral and Marcus.

"What's going on?" Marcus asked. "Are we in Parthusal?"

"Shhh!" Riam said, trying to keep him from waking everyone. "Vashi loosened the ropes of the canvas over Tannon's group so that the rain will collapse it on their heads."

Vashi giggled again. Marcus began to giggle as well.

Loral looked at each of them in turn. "You're all childish," she said.

The three boys looked at each other and burst out laughing. Loral gave them a disgusted look and lay back down.

"Quiet down over there!" the man at the port sweep said in a firm but hushed tone.

"Let's wake Karyl and tell him," Marcus whispered. The other two nodded and Loral groaned.

They woke Karyl and explained what Vashi had done. This prompted another round of fits.

"Wish I could see Tannon and the others get soaked," Marcus said.

"Me, too," Vashi added.

They waited in silence, listening to the rain for some time before one of them spoke again.

"Think we'll end up training together, once we get to the island?" Karyl said.

They hadn't spoken much about what lay ahead, not out of a desire to keep it to themselves, but because none of them knew much.

Marcus wiggled at his front tooth. "I doubt it. There'll be a lot more of us, and we'll be separated into different regiments."

"Too bad," said Vashi.

"It'll be a while before we join any of the regiments. At least we have until then."

"Yeah, but how long will that last?"

"Too long, with all of you," Loral said.

"Quiet down! Last warning I'm gonna give you," the crewman on the swoop said.

His words were useless, though, for suddenly there were shouts from the other side of the cabin. Riam and the others began laughing.

"What's going on over there!" the crewman yelled.

The commotion increased and several of the crew appeared, looking for the emergency. Riam heard Captain Stovall's voice. "Pipe down! What's going on?" Tannon and the others quieted. "What's all the shouting about?" the captain's voice bellowed. Riam couldn't hear the rest of the conversation over the rain.

After a time, Captain Stovall came into view. He stopped, surveying Riam and the rest of the outcasts.

"What happened?" Vashi asked, giving his best puzzled-but-curious expression. Riam looked down to keep from laughing.

"Fallen strange. Rope on their canvas came untied. Actually, two of them." He eyed Riam and the others. "A little unusual, wouldn't you say?"

"Yes, sir," Vashi said.

"None of you been messing around with the ropes, have you?"

"No, sir," they answered together.

The captain stared at Vashi a moment longer. "Pain-in-the-ass children," he muttered as he turned and left.

Once the captain was safely out of earshot, Riam let out a sigh of relief. Tem stepped out of the shadows. "Captain would've strapped your hides for that. Now get to sleep or I'll do it myself."

Riam and the others lay down quickly and pulled their blankets up around them. None of them spoke again, but occasionally one of them would giggle and start the others going. As the night grew cooler, Loral moved closer and closer to Riam until they were pressed next to each other for warmth. Her hand somehow found its way into his, and it became impossible to sleep. All he could think about was

her hand and how soft it was, but he didn't pull away. He
lay motionless in the moonlight, breathing hard and sweating, Loral on one side and the sealed case with the sword
on the other. He was nervous and scared, but for once,
things seemed to be going well. Riam placed his free hand
on the leather case.

CHAPTER 20

The sharp pain of a knee pressing down on his chest woke Riam from sleep. He tried to call out into the darkness, but a hand clamped over his mouth. He struggled, but found his wrists pinned to the deck. Someone else had a handful of his hair.

Tannon's face slid into view. "Shhhh . . ." he said, his teeth white against the night. He smiled in the same malicious way he had back in the mess hall—the same way Riam imagined a wolf would smile, right before it locked its jaws around another animal's throat. Tannon's matted hair gave him a crazed look that matched his smile, and the whites of his eyes stood out brighter than his teeth.

Tannon leaned in close, until Riam felt the other boy's breath against his ear. "It's time we talked, crofter boy." He said the last words as if there were bitters in his mouth.

Riam struggled against the hands and lost a chunk of hair for the effort, but it wasn't in vain, he'd been able to get a good look to both his left and right before his head was wrenched back down. There was no sign of Loral, and he'd seen the shapes of the other children, still sleeping. The sound of the rain drumming on the deck hid the sounds of the scuffle.

Tannon pressed harder on his chest, making it impossible to breathe. Riam thought his ribs would break.

"I just want to talk, but if you struggle like that again and wake the others, you'll regret it. I'll break Vashi's arm this time. I promise. Dunval was gentle with him compared to what I'll do. You can't stay together every moment."

Riam continued to struggle, hoping that one of the boatmen would see the commotion and help, but no one came.

"If you insist on waking the others, I'll start with Loral instead of Vashi," Tannon whispered. "Notice she isn't here? Where do you think she might be?"

Riam froze.

Tannon patted Riam on the cheek. "I thought that might settle you down."

Riam nodded as much as his captors would allow.

"It's too bad. She's not worth your loyalty," Tannon said.

The pressure lifted from Riam's chest. Tannon stood up, and the hand came away from Riam's mouth. He sucked in air, and Jared and Sabat lifted him to his feet.

With one boy on either side, they steered him to the railing. Although the moon created a light haze in the sky above them, the clouds kept the night dark. From where they stopped, he couldn't see any of the crew.

"Right by the edge," Tannon told the others.

The coaming came to right above the knees, and they'd all been warned to be careful when walking close to it. The two boys turned Riam so that the backs of his legs pressed against it. That's when he saw Loral slip out of the darkness and join them. She wasn't alone. Dunval held her by the shirt and walked her to the rail next to Riam. Dunval pushed her back, leaned out over the side enough to keep her off-balance, and she gripped his arm tightly to keep from falling overboard. *They wouldn't really let her fall, would they?*

"Twice you've made a fool out of me," Tannon said. "You think you're special because you had an uncle who was a Draegoran, and because you have this?" He held up the case Master Iwynd had given him. "You think this makes you better than us?" He ran his hand down the side. The seal was still intact. "I know what's in here, crofter boy. It's one of your uncle's swords."

How did Tannon know? Master Iwynd had told him to

keep the knowledge to himself, and he had. The only other people who knew about the sword and his uncle were still at the outpost.

It suddenly dawned on Riam. *Everyone but Loral.*

He looked toward her, but she didn't look at him. Instead she stared at Tannon, her lips snarling.

As if to confirm his thoughts, Tannon spoke. "Oh, yes. She told me. Didn't I say that she wasn't worth your loyalty? She told me all your secrets."

Loral tried to jerk away from Dunval's grip. "It wasn't like that. I was trying to help." She gave up struggling and looked back and forth from Tannon to Riam. "He's twisting it all around. I . . . I . . ."

Tannon chuckled.

"Oh, never mind. You won't believe me now."

Maybe she'd told Tannon, but at that moment, Riam didn't care. It must have been for a good reason. He couldn't bring himself to think she'd betray him like everyone else. He could learn why later. Right now, he needed to find a way to get the case away from Tannon. He could feel the sword. If he could get the case back, maybe he could put a stop to all this before it went too far.

Riam looked toward the rear of the barge, hoping one of the crewmen would see them, or that he would spy something that would help.

"Captain's asleep. No one awake will help. A little of my father's silver has deafened their ears and dimmed their vision.

"I've been watching you," Tannon said, "and thinking about what I should do to you for leading the others against me. At first, I was prepared to let it go. After all, you did help save us from the Esharii at the outpost, and I'm not unreasonable." He turned to Loral. "See, I can be practical, like you asked."

"You're an ass," Loral told him. "I should've known better. You haven't changed one bit."

Dunval pushed her out over the water.

"Stop!" Riam said.

"Quiet, or I swear by the Fallen I'll push you both overboard." He put the end of the case against Riam's chest and gave him a small shove. Jared's and Sabat's tight holds were the only things keeping him from falling.

"What's wrong with you? He hasn't done anything to you," Loral said.

"Hasn't done anything? You mean, hasn't done anything except get the rabble to band against me, start fights, and soak us all with rainwater while we slept. Seems to me he's done a lot of things, and it seems to me that he needs to learn who the real leader will be." He pushed Riam a little farther out over the water.

"Leave him alone."

Tannon swung the case around, pointing it at Loral and allowing Riam to get his balance back. "I don't understand you. We grew up together. Why do you side with them? You know I was born for this, not him."

Riam put it together. *Loral is a landowner's daughter?* That wasn't what she'd told him. She'd said she was from a poor city family. Telling Tannon about the sword and his uncle hadn't bothered Riam a moment ago, but suddenly, coupled with another lie, it suddenly did. *Is there anyone who doesn't lie to me?* "I thought you were my friend," he said softly.

"Your friend?" Tannon laughed. "That is funny." He stepped closer to Loral. "Did she tell you we were supposed to be married one day? That our families had an agreement?" He touched Loral's face, and she flinched away. "After I was tested, I thought it no longer mattered. How ironic that in all of Galtare she was the only other one who carried the blood. It seems Sollus means for us to be together forever."

Even in the darkness, the hurt Riam felt must have been visible on his face.

"You don't understand. It's not like that. I hate my father. He's a monster. I wasn't lying. I just didn't tell you everything."

"Well, the whole marriage thing doesn't really matter anymore," Tannon said. He looked down at the case in his hand. "I am still curious, though. Why do you choose to follow crofter boy? What makes him so special? Is it this?" He rubbed his thumb along the seal.

"He doesn't hurt people because they don't do what he says," Loral answered. "He isn't cruel like you or my father."

"He will be if he wants to survive the training."

"What are you talking about?" Riam asked.

"You don't know, none of you do, but we have to kill to complete our training—twice. It's how we bond with our sword. They bring in criminals for us to fight.

"You think he's special because of this," he held it up in front of Loral, "but he's not. We'll all have one eventually, as long as we pass the test to get our crystals."

"He's better than you," Loral hissed.

Tannon stared at Loral for a moment, and then threw the case out over the rail.

"No," Riam called, but it was too late. The case flew out into the darkness. Riam yanked and pulled at his captors frantically, but the boys held him. The case hung in the air for one frozen moment and was gone. There was a quiet splash when it hit the water. Riam could feel the distance between him and the sword widen as it sank and the barge moved on.

"Why would you do that?"

"Because you're not special. You are nothing but a weak little crofter boy who doesn't know his place. You've been playing at being a leader, but that's all you've been doing, playing. I've been trained for this, and it isn't a game." He turned back to Loral. "You really like him, don't you?"

She dropped her gaze to the deck. "Yes."

Tannon shook his head. "It's sad. Everything your father did for you, and you're willing to give yourself to a farmhand. No . . . I take that back, it's not sad . . . it's pathetic."

"There's nothing you can do about it, Tannon."

"Oh, there is. I can save you from yourself."

"What?" Loral's head came up.

"Don't hurt her. If you hurt her, I'll—" Riam started.

"You'll what?" Tannon held up his hands and cocked his head questioningly. "That's right, you'll do nothing."

What is Tannon going to do, throw her in? He would go after her if Tannon did. He wasn't a very good swimmer, but he'd do it if he had to. "I'll save her," he said.

"I'm not going to push her overboard, you idiot." Tannon stepped closer. "I'm going to get rid of you." He punched Riam in the stomach.

Riam doubled over, gasping.

"Good-bye, crofter boy." Tannon shoved Riam. Jared

and Sabat let go, and—like the case a moment earlier—
Riam toppled out over the water.

The world spun round and round before the water smacked
him in the face. Disoriented and stunned, he plummeted beneath the surface of the river. He tried to keep from breathing
in water, but his body betrayed him, and he sucked it in. His
lungs burned as they filled. He gagged and choked uncontrol-
lably. He couldn't tell down from up. It was all the same. He
breathed in more water. He flailed for the surface, desperate,
but couldn't reach it.

He was going to drown, just like his father. Riam stopped
flailing and a calm settled over him. *Where is the justice in
this?* He'd come all this way, seen everyone around him lie
and betray him, only to drown. It all flashed before him
again—his grandfather being stabbed, his uncle Gairen
torn away, every lie they told him, from Lemual to Loral.
An uneasy peace came over him, and he floated along with
the current.

Now that he no longer flailed, he rose to the surface. He
could feel the air on the back of his head. All he had to do
was turn his head and start breathing, but he couldn't do it.
It seemed too difficult, and he felt so weak, like his body
weighed a thousand stones. *Why should I? Who would
care?* He gave himself over to the water's murky depths and
drifted.

Something nagged at the back of his mind—a promise
he'd made. A promise over a grave, that he would become
a Draegoran and find out the truth about his family. He
needed to survive. He made a futile attempt to lift his head,
but his muscles didn't work right. He could no longer save
himself. He gave up and drifted.

Out of the water's murky depths he saw Nola staring back
at him. *Have I died? Is she dead, too? Is she coming for me?*
If she was, she hadn't expected to see him either because her
face held a look of surprise that twisted the stitches on her
forehead. *Stitches?* The last time he'd seen her, they'd both
been thrown from the horse. He'd grabbed her hand and
pulled her up to run. There'd been blood on her face that
he'd wiped away. *How is this happening? Why is she in the
water, too?*

"You will survive this! You cannot drown."

The words resonated inside Riam's head. It wasn't

Nola's voice. They were the words of an older man with a thick accent. There was a sudden, blinding flash of light, and Nola was gone.

The sword pulsed, off to his right, upriver. The link was thin, like a spiderweb floating on the wind, but it was there. With everything he had, he pulled from the sword. Nothing happened. He pulled again, this time more desperate, and was rewarded with a small surge of energy. It wasn't much, but it was enough. It gave him the strength to get his head out of the water. He hacked and coughed, slowly emptying the water from his lungs. Even with the pain in his chest, the air tasted sweet.

Treading water, he continued to hack and cough until he could breathe well enough to get his bearings. Nothing was in sight—no barge, no bank, only darkness and the dim glow of the moon behind the clouds—and strangest of all, it no longer rained. The current of the river pulled him along. *Where is the barge? It couldn't have drifted away so quickly.*

Paddling like a dog, he swam across the flow, hoping that he'd chosen the closest bank. For an instant, he saw a flicker of light and made his way toward it. He was a terrible swimmer, but he kept at it and didn't give up, even when his arms burned.

Finally, he felt reeds brush his hands and face. Thank the Fallen. The bank was close. He didn't know how much longer he could keep swimming. He felt mushy soil. Too tired to stand, he moved on all fours until he reached land. Hand-over-hand, he pulled at the reeds until the upper half of his body lay on the solid ground. Mud and slime caked his face and body, but he didn't care. He'd made it.

"Who's there?" a gruff voice asked.

Riam didn't reply. His head rang like a worked anvil, and all he could do was lie there panting, trying to catch his breath.

"Be careful, Warril. It could have been a river dragon." A woman's voice, farther off.

"It isn't a river dragon, woman. The big lizards don't like the deep channels, only the swamps. It was a person I heard splashing around down here. I know the sound of someone swimming when I hear it."

The crack of brush breaking came from nearby. Riam

saw a light, and it grew brighter, flickering and casting shadows around a man searching along the riverbank.

"Of course. You're always right, like when you said it was too cold for snakes when we crossed the Horn."

"That was an honest mistake, woman. How was I supposed to know there was such a thing as an ice snake?" the man yelled back. "By the Fallen," the man mumbled, "one snake in the tent and the woman won't ever let me live it down. Wasn't like it was poisonous enough to kill her. Only made her sick—quietest week of my life."

The man came closer.

"Sollus's mercy! There's a child down here."

Riam heard the squish of footsteps as the man came to his side on the muddy riverbank.

"A what?"

Hands grabbed Riam and flipped him over. He blinked away tears from the bright light.

"A boy!" the man yelled over his shoulder.

"What's a boy doing out here in the middle of the night? We're at least twenty steads from Parthusal."

"Now, how would I know that?" The man felt Riam's neck.

"I'm alive," Riam croaked.

"Couldn't tell it by lookin' at you. You're as pale as a wax candle. Nothin' broke, is there?"

"No, sir."

"Can you walk?"

Riam struggled to rise.

"Let me help."

A rough hand grabbed Riam by the arm and helped him to his feet. He tried to take a step and nearly pitched forward onto his face.

"Easy there. I'll carry you. You can't weigh much more than a sack of grain by the size of you. I think I can manage." The man leaned down and pulled Riam up over his shoulder.

Judging by the way he tossed Riam around, the man was strong. His clothes were plain and cared for, or at least they had been. The mud and water would stain them.

"I'm ruining your shirt. You should let me walk," Riam croaked.

"No worries, son. It's not the first shirt I've dirtied, and

I'm not so poor that it's my only one. Here we go, then."
The man made his way up the bank, holding Riam over one
shoulder and the lantern out before him with his other
hand.

Riam felt like the sack of grain the man mentioned—a
sack of grain that'd been thrown off a cliff and dunked in
a pond. An invisible giant squeezed his head. Everything
seemed to be happening from far away. His vision blurred,
and that didn't make it any better. He hoped that he didn't
throw up on the man.

It suddenly hit him—Loral and the barge were gone.
*How long will it be before they realize I'm missing? Will
they stop? Will they look for me, or will they continue on?
Had Tannon thrown Loral in behind me? Could she swim?*

"Loral," Riam said between the man's jarring steps.
"We need to look for Loral." His words slurred.

"There's no one else out here. There's only Polla and the
wagons. She'll take care of you."

"Put him down here," a woman's voice said. "What was
he doing in the river?"

The man plopped Riam down on a blanket. "Again, how
would I know that? The boy's delirious."

"Poor thing is shivering. He needs a fire."

"Can't risk a fire—lantern's more light than I like."

"Well, dig one of the furs out."

Riam didn't feel cold, but then he didn't feel much of
anything. He was numb except for the pounding in his
head, and his eyesight continued to dim and brighten with
the pulse of his heartbeat. He could just make out three
large covered wagons around them.

"Get the wet clothes off him. I'll get one of the furs out
of the winter box."

Riam's head hurt too much to be embarrassed when the
woman pulled off his clothes. Once they were off, she
rubbed his legs and arms between her hands.

"Have to get your blood flowing."

As she rubbed, his skin began to tingle, and soon after
he felt the cool air of the night, making him shiver.

"Such pretty young skin," the woman cooed. "I loved
my boys when they were your age." Her hands slid close
enough to his groin to make Riam uncomfortable, even in
his current state. He tried to push her hands away.

"Here. I've got a heavy fur."

The woman's hands withdrew, and a weight blanketed him. The woman tucked it around him.

Riam closed his eyes. The fur was comforting and warm. There was the clink of glass and the smell of mint filled the air. A damp cloth pressed over Riam's face. The fumes burned his lungs. He shook his head, trying to get it away from his mouth.

"Breathe it in, boy. It'll help get the water out of your lungs."

He didn't believe the man. There was something wrong with these two people, but he couldn't figure out what. His head was too muddled from the river.

"Where do you suppose he came from?"

"Either off a boat or swam across. I suspect he's running from something," the man said.

The fumes continued to burn Riam's lungs. He tried to pull away again and found that he couldn't move. He couldn't even blink.

"That ought to do it, Warril. Don't want him damaged."

"His clothes . . ."

"What about them?"

"They were gray," the woman said. "You know what that means."

"I saw 'em. If he's running, I can't say I blame him."

"What if they're searching for him? If they find us with the wagons full like they are, it won't be the ships for us. They'll kill us."

"They won't. Think I'd risk it if I thought they were coming?"

"We could leave him here, just in case."

"No. He's worth a gold dreg in Parthusal. They always need new boys for the streets. We'll put him with the others after he warms up a bit and then move on. It's almost morning anyway. You get rid of his clothes. Throw them in the river. Get rid of the sandals while you're at it. We don't want anything that might draw attention to him."

"Seems a shame to waste him on the churps." The woman's hand stroked Riam's chest.

"None of that. We need to get moving. I'll wake Nem. After he marks the boy, we'll hitch the horses. If the boy is running from the Draegorans, we don't want to be here when they come looking . . . and, Polla," the man's tone became more stern, "he goes to the churps as soon as we make it to the city. No argument."

It seemed as if the whole conversation were occurring in a dream—a dream from which he couldn't wake. Riam wanted to cry, but he couldn't even do that.

The two remaining gods, Sollus and Faen, are like twin boys who hate each other steering the same boat down a river. One wants to stop, and the other wants to know where the river ends, and neither of them holds a paddle.

—*Okulu'tan proverb*

CHAPTER 21

Despite the bitter chill and weariness in his bones, Ky'lem continued to move, each step a battle between willpower and frozen death. While it was summer in the lands below, he'd climbed high enough to reach the frozen snow that never melted. He wasn't dressed for the cold, and the icy wind burned his exposed skin. Over his shoulders, he carried the asha, wrapped in the wool saddle blanket he'd taken from the horse when it collapsed. His shoulders and legs burned, and his breath was short, but he kept moving. Ahead of him, the last rise taunted his tired body. At the top of the rise sat the Notch. From this close, he could see the line marking the narrow fissure in the rock that served as a passage over the spine of the mountains. A passage that would offer him and the asha shelter for a time and lead him into Esharii lands once more. To either side, snow-encrusted cliffs rose up toward clouded peaks.

Taking the High Sun Path through the Notch was always a gamble, even in summer, but the gray demons hadn't ceased in their pursuit and had cut them off from Weeping Pass. They'd lost the horse escaping the gray men's grasp, making any other route impossible. If he was going to make it to the Najalii as the okulu'tan commanded, this was his only option with her slowing him down. Before him, footsteps in the snow led toward the Notch. At least one of his desperate kinsmen had escaped and come this way.

Former kinsman. Now that he was chae'lon, he had no tribe. Regardless, he hoped it was a tribesman who'd made the tracks. There were dangers that walked on two legs in the mountains. More than one warrior had become a meal for a hungry merdon in these mountains. The snow beasts were a twisted blend of ape and pig that were far too humanlike in appearance for comfort and far too beastlike to ever garner sympathy. As good as he was with a sword, he didn't want to face one of the great, lumbering beasts alone, especially when he'd already used up the last of his spirit paste.

Ky'lem paused long enough to kneel and brush at the edges of a footprint. There were no short scratches at the front to mark the tips of clawed toes, and the prints were soft, caving in at the slightest touch. *Human . . . and recent.* He checked a second print. It was slightly longer than the first. He rocked back on his heels and looked down the line of footsteps, taking in everything without concentrating on a single print. More than one was off size. *Two men, then, with one following in the first man's tracks.* He rose to his feet, groaning with the asha's weight on his shoulders. Whether two men or one had lived to escape this way, it didn't matter. They had to go through the Notch.

Thunder rumbled to the south. It was distant, but not so far away that it kept him from worrying. Getting to the Najalii wasn't the only reason he needed to keep moving. So far, the weather had been his ally, but even a mild storm at this height would delay them into death. If Sollus was with them, however, they'd be down the other side of the mountains and far enough to be safe before the storm reached them.

He almost laughed at the thought of dying here, frozen, for a warband to find on their way to kill the very gray demons who'd forced him to use the pass. They would certainly laugh at his weakness. A true Esharii warrior turned on his pursuers and died in battle; he did not collapse in the snow and die like a feeble old man. The thought burned more than the wind—more so because it had nearly happened the previous night. He'd fallen, and it had taken every bit of his strength and the asha pounding on his back to keep from surrendering to the cold. The shame of her coaxing him up still stung at his pride.

Angry at his own weakness, Ky'lem charged up the steep incline. The crunch of snow and ice echoed off the cliffs as he pounded his way upward. The asha grunted with each jarring step and the rough blanket rubbed painfully against his torn ear. It was stained with green-and-black smears from his face paint. In truth, he should have removed what remained of the paint before now, but he was loath to cut away the last link to his tribe. He must if he was going to embrace the future the okulu'tan had forced him into. It was too late to worry about it, though—there was nothing to wash his face and arms with. He'd given the asha the last of the water this morning.

Ky'lem's legs burned, but he pushed himself harder when he reached the narrow entrance to the Notch. At its center, the fissure would widen, creating a large shelf with a deep crevice to one side. Warbands used the spot to camp and rest. With luck, there would be wood left behind to make a fire and sleep. They couldn't afford to rest for long with the storm coming, but even a short sleep near the warmth of the flames would do wonders for his spirit. The mixture of ice and rock beneath his feet became slick and treacherous, but he did not slow. At least there was no more snow, and the narrow, winding fissure protected him from the bite of the wind.

He rounded the final bend. A plain-faced warrior sat with his back to the wall in the dim light that filtered down from the narrow crack above. His sword lay across his lap, a hand resting on the hilt. The remains of a fire sat next to him. Ky'lem shook his head in disappointment. What scraps of wood had been left behind were now useless ash, but at least he was no longer alone.

"Ho, brother. It is good to see someone other than the gray demons," Ky'lem called.

The pachna was silent.

Ky'lem's eyes adjusted to the dim light. There would never be a response. The man was frozen dead.

Ky'lem slid the asha from his shoulders. She readjusted the blanket so that her face peered out between a fold. Her dark skin had a waxy cast to it, and her lips held a bluish tint around the edges. By the numbness of his face, he was sure he appeared much worse.

Motioning for her to keep silent, he drew his sword and, keeping a shoulder to the rock wall, moved closer to the body. The warrior may have simply wanted to die with his sword in his hand, but by the way he sat facing the entrance, he'd either been waiting for other survivors from the warband or preparing to defend against something else. Most likely the warrior had succumbed to the cold, but until he was sure, he would take no chances. He stopped and closed his eyes for several breaths, listening. He heard the wind on the rocks above and the asha's breathing, but nothing else.

"Pah," he said, "letting my fears get to me." He moved to the dead warrior's side and combed his hand through the ashes. *Cool, but not frozen—one, maybe two days old at most.*

The dizziness of fatigue hit him when he tried to stand, and he nearly toppled over. He placed his hand on the body's shoulder to steady himself.

"So, how did you die, my friend?" he asked after the dizziness passed. He searched the man's clothing. No coin, no food, and no water—not a single item beyond his sword and his clothing. Either he'd lost everything getting to the Notch, or someone had already been here and taken his belongings. *The second set of prints?* There were no wounds on the body.

The asha moved to his side. "What happened to him?"

"The cold. He slept too long, most likely."

Deeming they were safe enough for the moment, Ky'lem stumbled back to a wall for support. His eyes burned, and his eyelids felt as if there were stones woven into his lashes like the rings in his beard. He needed to rest, and the chamber was his only chance before returning to the snow-packed surface. A short rest only, and then they would move on. It would have to be enough.

He slid down the wall and placed his sword across his thighs. Another day to reach the tree line where he would find wood enough to make a fire, another six to cross Ti'yak lands and reach the river, and then another eight by raft to the Najalii. Sixteen total, and that was without the need to hunt for food. Altogether, they had eighteen days left in the okulu'tan's warning if he counted right since the last light-less night. It would be close—very close.

If he were any other warrior, he'd say it couldn't be done, but he was Ky'lem—the only warrior alive to slay three gray men in a single raid, the warrior who would one day unite the tribes. He would get the asha to the lake in time to save them both.

The asha flung her blanket over them both. He was thankful for the sudden warmth. Wordlessly, she squeezed in close. He put an arm around her though he kept his other arm free with his sword ready.

Through half-closed eyes, Ky'lem stared at the top of the asha's head. The girl had changed since the pool. She was still simple in the way most children were, but she was stronger, with little thought to herself. She had not complained over the last few days, nor had she made any outlandish requests, and she did not quit. If anything, she was driving them harder than he was. He'd seen the crystals she carried—the parting gift of the old okulu'tan. Perhaps those were what pushed her. He had little understanding of how the spirit-walker's magic worked aside from the bond.

No, she was not the weak asha he'd originally thought. He didn't know exactly what she was or what she would become, but there was something powerful within her waiting to come to the surface. Perhaps one day she would be worthy of his service.

Is this the truth? Or is it the bond growing stronger that makes me feel this way? It was hard to know what his true feelings were, especially when he was so tired. The mind played tricks on a man when he became delirious with exhaustion.

He looked sleepily at the body of the plain-faced warrior. He recognized the man—one of the spirit-walker's pachna. The dead warrior had failed to make it home, just as he'd failed to protect the okulu'tan from himself in the end. He tightened his grip on the hilt of his sword. "Unlike you, I will not falter."

They mirrored one another—backs to the wall, no supplies, and a weapon held upon their laps. He threw the blanket off and scrambled to his feet.

"What is it?" The asha looked around warily, startled by his sudden movement.

"I will not die here like you. I am stronger. I am Ky'lem!" he raved at the corpse.

The asha rubbed his arm. "Of course, you will not fail." Her face had a determined set to it, and she looked at him with a seriousness far beyond her age. "And I will not fail you."

Their eyes locked together, and a rush of emotions passed between them: wariness, cold, fear, fatigue, and—beneath those—an iron bond of loyalty neither could break, even if they wanted to.

"You will both fail," the dead pachna rasped.

Ky'lem spun at the words. He raised his sword and moved to shield the asha. "What is this?" He wasn't delirious. The corpse *had* spoken.

The dead pachna rose to its feet in stiff, jerky movements, its joints cracking as they broke free from their frozen positions. It rolled its shoulders, like a living man working the kinks out upon waking from a hard sleep. Then it raised its sword and slashed back and forth, testing the blade in the air. The halting movements became smoother. While it acted like a man, its eyes remained glassy and its expression slack and empty.

"I do not desire to kill you, but the asha may not return with you," the corpse said.

"Who speaks to me? What demon fouls this man's skin?"

"I would tell you to forget the girl and return to your tribe, but it's too late for that. The two of you are nearly one." The corpse stepped in front of the opening that led to Esharii lands.

The asha hit him on his back. "Don't talk to it, kill it!"

Ky'lem had fought against the gray demons, he'd fought for his place among the Ti'yak, and against creatures large and small, but never had he faced the dead. Against the living, he was fearless. Against a possessed corpse, he was a young boy fighting to earn his face paint. His heart raced. His sword felt awkward and clumsy in his hands. "I will take her to the Najalii. I will save her," he said, more to regain his confidence than to argue with whatever controlled the dead man's body.

The corpse lunged toward Ky'lem, and the asha shrieked behind him.

Ky'lem was as slow and stiff as the corpse, too much walking and too much cold, but he managed to block the attack.

"Back the way we came!" he yelled at the asha.

The next thrust against him came faster.

Ky'lem blocked the attack and stepped out of reach, drawing a deep breath to calm himself. He was close to the narrow point where they'd entered the chamber. The asha was behind him, safe for the moment. He placed himself in front of her. Any farther back, and he'd no longer have room to swing his sword. They could retreat the way they'd come if they had to, but it would only work to the corpse's advantage. To retreat was to die in the coming storm.

Ky'lem roared and charged. The clash of their swords rang out deafeningly in the enclosed chamber. Twice Ky'lem wounded the dead warrior, but it did not bleed. One left a gaping wound across the corpse's shoulder—a wound that would have dropped a mortal man. So large was the cut that Ky'lem could see bone.

The dead warrior simply passed its weapon to its other hand and attacked again, all the while its face remaining slack and empty.

Ky'lem blocked a vicious cut toward his legs and ran the dead warrior through. This, too, had no effect. The creature, for that's what it was—not a dead man, not a corpse—grabbed Ky'lem's blade with its free hand and swung its sword at Ky'lem's neck.

Ky'lem released his blade to keep from being decapitated.

The creature pressed the advantage, and Ky'lem dodged and ducked his way around the room in a maneuver that became part dance, part mad scramble. His only hope lay in using his speed to escape with the asha back the way they had come, to take their chances in the storm while they searched for some unknown way over the mountains.

Unfortunately, whatever possessed the corpse knew his intent. Each time Ky'lem worked his way close to the exit, the creature cut off his escape. It was a stalemate. The creature could not turn its back on Ky'lem to pursue the asha, and Ky'lem could not reach her.

As Ky'lem tired, each of the creature's swings came closer to finding its mark. He steered it close to the chasm, and after a wild swing that nearly split his head, he darted in and threw his shoulder into the creature's side.

It stumbled backward and tilted out over the edge, but it did not fall. Ky'lem pushed with all his strength. Still the creature held.

In a blur, the asha was there, throwing her weight with his. Her slight form didn't add much, but it was enough.

Farther and farther the creature leaned out over the edge, until at last it began to tumble away. In a reckless move, Ky'lem lunged and snatched the handle of his sword before it was out of arm's reach. The sword did not come free at first, and Ky'lem nearly followed the creature into the chasm. With a popping sound the sword came loose, and the creature tumbled away, bouncing between the walls and smashing to the bottom. After a brief silence, the sound of the creature scratching at the rocks rose from the deep.

The asha peered down into the darkness.

Ky'lem doubled over, putting a hand on his knee. His arms shook. Never in his life had he seen such a thing. "It should be trapped. The walls are steep and smooth. Come away from the edge," he said between gasping breaths.

"That was well fought, *pachna*." The word *pachna* was drawn out and derisive.

Ky'lem spun about.

Pai'le stood at the entrance to the chamber, his sword out and ready.

Ky'lem looked warily at the weapon in the big warrior's hand. He bent his knees slightly, preparing for an attack if it came, although in his weakened condition, he doubted he would have much chance against the big man.

"I said I'd kill you if I ever found you with paint on your face, didn't I?" He turned the weapon in his hand, appearing to mull the idea over, and then sheathed it in a quick, fluid motion. "But not today. Today I am curious why one of the spirit-takers wants you dead."

"An okulu'tan did this?"

"Who else has the power to command such a thing?"

Ky'lem opened his mouth to rebut the explanation but had no words. There was no other answer. While he'd heard that the spirit-takers could possess a man, he'd never heard of any that could raise the dead to fight. And this was certainly no trick of the gray demons. Their arts lay in different areas.

"Curious that you are made a pachna by a spirit-walker, yet a lesser okulu'tan wants you to die. Clearly, they are as scattered as the tribes. Yet you choose to serve the old one anyway."

Ky'lem hadn't considered that there would be factions among the okulu'tan. What had he expected—that they would open their ways to a female from another land? Even with the loyalty of the bond, the idea sounded foolish.

"So, where is your new master? Did he escape beyond the mountains and leave you to bring the asha back on your own?"

"I didn't bond with the old one. He's dead, sacrificing himself to create the storm that saved you." He let Pai'le make the connection between the storm and his escape.

Pai'le scrunched his eyes in confusion. "So you are free? Then why are they trying to kill you?"

Ky'lem looked to the asha and back to Pai'le. "Because I am bonded to the girl." He expected anger or rage. Instead, laughter filled the chamber.

"Oh, Ky'lem. All your strategy and logic, yet you are an even greater fool than I am."

Ky'lem's ears blazed at the insult. "The old one understood more than you think. The Fallen grow stronger, yet we destroy ourselves with our incessant tribal wars. Already, Tomu stirs. If the Esharii do not destroy the gray demons soon, it will be too late. The old spirit-walker believed she is the key to uniting the tribes again."

"He was mad," Pai'le said flatly, not budging a finger's width. "If they train one, then soon others will want to be trained. What's next? Train our women to fight such as the gray demons do? Asha'han as pachna—as council members?" Pai'le shook his head. "The path he placed you on will not work."

As always, Pai'le remained in the present and was blind to the future. "It will take all our people to defeat the gray men, asha'han included."

"And you abandoned me, the man you'd sworn on your sword and your blood to follow on this raid, for an asha that will not be trained?" Pai'le grabbed the hilt of his sword, as if he'd changed his mind.

I didn't abandon you, you idiot. I'm trying to save us all.
The man was so thickheaded.

"I would kill you, but I find that the okulu'tan has played me for as big a fool as you." Pai'le let his hand fall away from the sword's hilt. "I choose not to believe you wanted me dead in order to take my place, else why risk yourself to save me in the storm? I have racked my thoughts for another reason and can find none. Therefore, the okulu'tan must have lied to me."

"That is the truth," Ky'lem said. "While I have been frustrated with you, maybe even angry, I would not challenge you."

"But surely you see that if the okulu'tan lied to me, he also lied to you?"

There was a strong possibility Pai'le was right. Perhaps the spirit-walker had been completely insane. *Perhaps I am a fool. Just as Pai'le let emotion and pride get in the way, perhaps I let the spirit-walker blind me with my own cold logic.* Ky'lem looked over at the asha. She glared at both of them and seemed ready to bolt if she must. He could not bear the thought of her facing the world alone. Part of him knew it was the bond that spoke. *Did it matter? Despite his doubts and his foolishness, it was far too late to go back now. He must embrace his path and hope it one day led to his desires.*

Ky'lem faced Pai'le and drew himself up to his full height. "She will be trained, and I'm afraid there's one more edict I've been commanded to break."

"Oh? And what is that? Will you kill a spirit-taker or swim in the water of the sacred lake?"

Ky'lem ignored the sarcasm. "After Ni'ola completes her training and is made an okulu'tan, she will become my wife."

Ni'ola's shock traveling across the bond nearly knocked Ky'lem from his feet, and it wasn't because he'd used her name for the first time.

Ky'lem staggered to one knee near the edge of the chasm. He peered down into darkness. He'd only spoken half of the spirit-walker's deranged command. If he'd have told all, he might have found himself joining the creature at the bottom.

CHAPTER 22

How the two warriors could rest with the clawing below, Nola didn't understand. Every time she grew
close to sleep, the horrid scratching on the rocks
brought her wide-awake. Whenever she closed her eyes,
she imagined its nails snapping and tearing on the stone
and pictured the fingers, pale and bloodless, meat torn
away from the tips, clawing until bone scraped rock. She
expected it to climb over the lip at any moment, its mangled
hands reaching for her throat and the two warriors sleeping
soundly through her death.

She grunted and flipped over, putting a hand over her ear.
The two warriors must be exhausted, especially Ky'lem. He'd
carried her up the last of the climb without a complaint—
neither in words, nor through the bond.

The bond.

She could not stop thinking about what the okulu'tan
had done and the link between her and Ky'lem. It was all
she could think about, all she could feel, besides the bite of
the cold and the nagging fear that death would come for her.

For the hundredth time since the night of the storm, she
withdrew the two red crystals from the pocket at her waist-
line. They were small but heavy in her hand, and they
glowed with a light of their own, reminding her of the way

the spirit-walker's eyes had gleamed red in the night. The two crystals were all that was left of the crazy old man. The storm he'd called had consumed him. But before he'd died, the okulu'tan had done more than bond her to Ky'lem. She could feel it. With each passing day, the glow in the gems grew brighter and the strength of the connection grew stronger, pushing at the threshold of her awareness. She felt them always. When she slept, she dreamed of them, and when she woke, they were in her hand. She knew with certainty that there was something she needed to do before they overwhelmed her. She just didn't know what.

Why hadn't the okulu'tan explained more? There'd been plenty of time during the days leading up to the attack. It was a mystery she couldn't solve, and the only person who could explain it to her had left this world. The okulu'tan of the lake would know what to do, but she feared them as much as she feared the creature clawing below.

By the Fallen, what have I agreed to? But she knew the answer—a chance at survival and, maybe, something more. It was the only decision she'd been given since the Draegoran had placed his sword against her forehead to test her—survive with the Esharii or die on the island of the Draegorans. When put in those terms, there'd really been no decision at all.

Ky'lem's snores pulled her from her thoughts and brought memories of her home. If her face were not so frozen with the cold, she would have laughed. In all their time together, the scar-faced warrior had never made a sound while sleeping, and now his snores rumbled through the chamber and echoed from the walls.

Pai'le woke with a start from one of Ky'lem's loud snorts. His sleep-filled eyes searching for danger before he shook his head in disgust. He clopped Ky'lem on the shoulder and rolled back over. The snoring stopped, and it was Ky'lem's turn to sit up bleary-eyed and confused.

Nola giggled. Her father snored when he was very tired or very drunk—which wasn't often—during festival or on special occasions. Her mother had been far less gentle than Pai'le when the snoring woke her. For all Ky'lem's gruff tone and prowess, hearing him snore made him seem . . . well . . . like any other man. He was not any other man, though. She knew that from the bond.

The bond again. Always the bond. I need to stop thinking about it. Thinking about it only led to the one thing she truly wanted to avoid—his statement that they would one day marry. The mirth drained from her cheeks and they tingled in anger at the thought. *He had no right to say those words without my agreement. I'm far too young to marry, and marriage is the woman's choice, not the man's. Everyone knows that. How could the man expect me to marry him one day? He's at least twice my age. Would he force himself on me?*

She shuddered, surprised she would think of such a thing. She wouldn't have before the bond, but his experiences had exposed her to thoughts and knowledge that took her far beyond the world she'd known only days ago. The world was a darker and more dangerous place than she'd ever imagined.

She didn't think Ky'lem would hurt her, but the Esharii were different than the people back home. Some of the things she knew about Ky'lem made her sick. He was ruthless and hard, without a shred of guilt or remorse for those he killed, whether it was her people or his own. He'd stolen wives and horses, and the things he'd done to a captured Draegoran in his youth made her want to vomit. He'd treated her fairly before the bond, but that was because she was little more than property. Now, however, his thoughts confused her. One moment he was angry with her and the next he was making sure she was uninjured and wrapping her in a blanket with the deepest concern, as if she were his own daughter.

Or future wife . . .

For Fallen's sake. Stop it! She didn't know what to think. She wasn't supposed to be crossing the world, escaping living corpses, and becoming some sort of witch-woman-bride for the Esharii. She wasn't supposed to know the things that filled her with horror. She was supposed to be home, playing with her dolls and helping her mother cook. *It wasn't fair. Not at all.* The bond had taken something from her, and she could never get it back.

Fair or not, though, nothing could be done, but if she ever became a powerful okulu'tan, things would change. *I'll decide whom I marry and what I do.*

The crystals in her hand flared with her sudden confidence, acknowledging her will. They pressed against her head, threatening to burst through. They wanted to be used.

"I don't know what to do!" she hissed at the crystals.

There was no response—only the continued desperate push at the edge of her thoughts.

She jammed them back into her pocket, pulled the horse blanket tight around her, and tried to sleep. It never came, and before she knew it, they were heading down the Esharii side of the pass.

For two days they traveled, following a thin, winding trail with sheer drop-offs to one side and steep walls on the other. They spent the first night huddled between rock outcroppings, and the next saw them making camp in a large stone bowl with water flowing through its center. The flow was too large to be called a stream and too small to be called a river, and the end of the bowl formed a narrow channel that drained the water over a cliff so high Ky'lem said the water never reached the rocks at the bottom. Nola slid forward on her belly and peered over the edge to see if it were true, but she could not see through the mist.

Ky'lem knelt at the water's edge and washed away the remainder of his face paint. When he was done, he seemed a new person. Neither of the tribesmen had been much for conversation, but the lack of face paint made Ky'lem even more withdrawn and sullen. He threw one of the waterskins to the stone. It skittered and tumbled to a stop, but thankfully did not tear. Nola felt his irritation. He was frustrated with Pai'le—frustrated because he worried the big man was right and he'd been played for a fool. The unpainted face marked him so in his mind.

Well, she'd agreed with the okulu'tan's offer the same as he had, making her no less of a fool. They must go to the Najalii as commanded to find out the true results of their decisions.

Ky'lem picked the waterskin back up and faced her. The clean face highlighted his scars, making them more pronounced and his face more menacing.

We are fools together. The thought came to her clearly across the bond. He looked up at the crescent of Sollus hanging low in the sky. *Two fools who will likely die when Faen swallows the moon.*

Eight days from the cold of the mountain pass saw them building a raft on the bank of the great river. Ky'lem's anger bled across the bond. The use of his sword to cut down trees, even those that were young and soft, brought curses to his lips about the nights it would take to resharpen the blade. He became angrier with every swing. Nola felt the rhythm of that anger. It pitched toward her in time with the chunk of the blade striking wood. Any other blade than the heavy Arillian style he and Pai'le carried would have been useless for the task, but between the weight of the sword and Ky'lem's powerful swings, there were a dozen small logs lying near the bank.

The logs were long and straight, with few limbs and a thin bark that looked more like skin than wood. Where the bark was cut, the pale white wood matched the tribesmen's skin. Pai'le worked at stripping away the limbs.

The two tribesmen wore little more than loincloths in the sweltering, damp heat. Sweat coated the muscles of their chests and backs, dripping from faces and arms while they worked. It was an odd sight, and not because of the bare skin. Just days ago, freezing to death had been a close thing. Now they roasted in a steaming forest so thick Nola couldn't see more than twenty paces in any direction. Above them, a canopy of broad leaves blocked out all trace of the sun.

The discordant calls of birds and animals never ceased in the thick, lush forest. Strange animals, like the small, brown furry creatures called tit'tai for the sounds they made. They looked like squirrels, but they were not like any of the friendly chattering squirrels Nola knew from home. The tit'tai scurried up the trees till they were lost from sight and then descended on the wind in winding circles to attack birds that were just as peculiar—bright with an infinite variety of blues and greens and yellows, odd-shaped beaks, and piercing calls. Worse than the noise and heat of the forest were the insects. Great swarms floated in the air.

Nola worked her way along the bank doing her best to avoid those swarms while cutting creepers with a knife and dragging them back to be woven into rope to hold the raft together. It was slow and difficult work, made worse by the clothes she wore. Her shirt and breeches clung wetly to her skin. Ky'lem told her to remove her shirt, that all Esharii women went topless like the men. "It is the way of the People. There is no shame in it," he'd told her. She knew the words were true, but she'd lashed out at him anyway, telling him she was not Esharii and that it wasn't proper. She'd buttoned her shirt higher to prove her point. She hadn't let the heat slow her down either, and a sizable pile of creepers sat ready for use.

They would ride the raft down the great river that marked the border between Ti'yak and Arpatha lands. For generations, the two tribes had fought over everything, from the fish taken from the water to the rights of use for travel. Luckily for them, the two tribes were now at peace. Ky'lem was the reason for that peace. His firstwife was an Arpatha warleader's only daughter. Without his negotiations and their marriage, the two tribes would still be at war. Nola knew this because Ky'lem knew it, and his anger opened his thoughts so that they flowed like the water down the river. It was another of his contradictions. He'd taken pleasure in fighting the Arpatha, but he'd taken more from the peace he'd brokered between them. It made no sense.

How can he savor fighting and peace at the same time?

She took hold of another creeper and a long, narrow thorn stabbed into her thumb. Ky'lem ceased mid-chop and stood up straight, his eyes scanning the forest around her. The creepers themselves held no thorns, but they tended to be found among others vines that did, making a thick bramble that had to be untangled.

I'm fine. A thorn.

She dropped the knife and sat down to rest. Pressing her thumb to her lips, she tasted the metallic tang of blood on her tongue. The thorn had gone in deep.

Bless Sollus. The blood would attract more bugs, as if they weren't thick enough already.

Kachunk . . . kachunk . . . kachunk.

The sound of Ky'lem's chopping returned to its rhythmic beat behind her. His anger appeared to be subsiding. That was good. Despite the fact that he was filled with irritation and was far more quick to anger since Pai'le had arrived, Nola found traveling with the two men less unpleasant than she'd first feared.

Ky'lem seemed to be coming to accept her. Whether it was the bond or on his own, Nola wasn't sure. She'd behaved as the Esharii expected a young girl should, except for the clothes, and she'd done her best to help where she could, gathering firewood and such, and staying quiet and out of the way when the two warriors were talking or hunting. Ky'lem had responded by teaching her how to set a fire and which spiders and plants were poisonous and which were not.

Pai'le, on the other hand, never spoke to her. Instead, he relayed his commands through Ky'lem as if she were his property. She knew what the big Esharii thought of her. She was beneath him. So far beneath she barely existed in his eyes, although she'd noticed him staring at her several times like he was trying to decide what to make of her. His silence was fine with her.

She glanced back at the big warrior. He made his way down a log, stripping away branches. He stopped, sensing her eyes on him, and she turned away quickly.

"Tell your asha she should be working, not resting."

She rolled her eyes. *I'm almost done.*

"Let her rest. She is not used to such labor. We are not ready for the vines yet, and she is nearly finished." There was no disappointment in his thoughts—the opposite. He seemed to be pleased she'd done so much so quickly.

Pai'le grunted but did not object. She felt him staring at her as he worked, but she would not give him the satisfaction of looking back or acknowledging his words.

Let him continue to puzzle over me. She withdrew the crystals and tumbled them absently in her hand, one over the other. *One day, I will show him that I am beneath no one.*

Blood from the thorn prick welled on her thumb and smeared across her forefinger. Each turn of the crystals brought them closer. Focused on Pai'le, she didn't notice them grow warmer in her hand. Blood smeared the inside of her middle finger. Soon after, it trickled to her palm—blood and crystal met.

A deafening pop reverberated in Nola's ears, and she gasped. The pressure was gone, replaced by a rush of fire that slammed into the very core of her being. It coursed through her chest and lungs, running down her legs until she felt its burn from the hair on her head to the tips of her toes. The muscles of her body contracted, and she arched backward to the ground, arms pulled in with her hands locked into fists above her. Her jaw clenched so tightly she thought her teeth would break. Her legs remained bent, as they had been when she'd sat down, so that she now lay frozen on her back, limbs seized in the air above her, like an upside-down beetle. The vines and trees above her flickered with mesmerizing speed between the world she knew and one of radiant light.

She could not move, could not speak, could not draw breath—so strong were the energies that filled her—and she could not call to Ky'lem. The bond with him remained, but the power swept it to the farthest edge of her awareness. She fought against the onrush, trying to reach him, mentally screaming for help. It was as useless as trying to swim upstream in the great river. She could not feel anything beyond the flow of energy that threatened to drown her.

The crystals in her fist shone with power, like a full moon on a cloudless night—power left by the okulu'tan for her and her alone. It wanted her, and to her amazement, she wanted it. Hesitantly, instead of fighting it, she opened herself to the crystals. Energy came pouring into her in a torrential flood, warm and soothing, as if the initial shock and pain had been from her resistance alone.

The crystals had wanted this all along—to be connected to her, to be a part of her, to be used. It felt magnificent. She swallowed it in until she thought she would explode into a million pieces, and still she wanted more. All the fear she'd felt since leaving her home was replaced with the glorious strength of the energy that suffused her. If she could have moved, she would have danced with joy.

She pulled at the energy, trying to get more of it inside her. The world dimmed. The sound of trees cracking and falling reached her. Around her the tall grass withered and died. Her hunger for more killed every living thing around her. A gust of wind swept over her, whipping at the dead grass before moving off in a whirlwind over the river.

Stop, asha. You will kill us both!

She didn't care if the power washed her away or burned her from the world as it had the old okulu'tan. It felt magnificent. She pulled in more.

Ky'lem appeared beside her, and his left hand locked around her wrist. He pried at her fingers, trying to get at the crystals.

No! These are mine! She shoved the energy toward him. It roared through the bond.

Ky'lem staggered backward, holding his head.

You must let go! He moved toward her once more.

No! Her mental scream buffeted him, but he kept on moving.

She would not allow him to come between her and the power that bathed her. Nola pushed more energy into her second shove. It was easier this time—like learning to exhale in a different way. Ky'lem flew backward through the air. He landed awkwardly on one shoulder among the reeds of the bank and tumbled into the river.

He would not stop her. She pulled more of the energy into herself. It was all she ever needed. *It's his fault if he's hurt. I told him no.*

A thick tree limb struck her hand. She heard the crack of bones and was vaguely aware of the pain, but it was like recalling a faint memory with little meaning. The power knitted the bones back together. Her fist remained locked around the crystals.

Pai'le raised the limb for another blow.

I will show him that I am more than a simple asha. Not holding back, she threw twice the energy at the big warrior as she'd done with Ky'lem. Energy crackled around her, but to her disbelief, nothing happened. The energy puffed out like a cloud and dissipated between them. She would not stop Pai'le's next swing.

Time stretched. The limb swung toward her at a snail's pace. Pai'le hadn't aimed the blow at her hand this time, but at her head. She tried to move but could not.

She willed herself out of the way—anywhere to escape the blow. She groped at the energy, pushing and pulling without knowing what to do.

She tore frantically at the air in desperation, tearing holes in the fabric of the world around her. Light blinded her from beyond the damage. Picking a tear at random, she dove into the blinding light, leaving her body just before the tree limb struck her temple.

CHAPTER 23

Riam's arm itched, although "itched" did not describe the sensation very well. The feeling was more of a tingle that no amount of rubbing or scratching would satisfy. Standing in the center of a crowded city street, he rubbed the glyph on his forearm for the hundredth time, even though it was a useless gesture. He'd rubbed at it all morning, and all he'd succeeded in doing was making the skin red and irritated. The swirling black lines that wrapped around his forearm meant nothing to him, and the mere fact that a glyph marked his arm made no sense at all. *By Gairen's words, it had to have been placed there by a Draegoran, but when, and why for that matter, had it been done?* There hadn't been a Draegoran on the barge, and the last thing he remembered was the warmth of a campfire and the odd couple wrapping him in a blanket. Everything since then, right up until this morning, was a contorted blur of lights and sounds that made his head hurt. He was in Parthusal, he knew that much—to either side of him, two- and three-story buildings lined the street as far as he could see—but that knowledge didn't clear up any of his confusion. It only made it worse.

"Get that mess, boy," Pekol told him, the man's deep, hoarse voice a mismatch to his thin, wiry frame. His small size, however, did nothing to make the command less fear-some. Although small for an adult, there was an air of dis-passionate viciousness to his calm orders. It reminded Riam of his grandfather's quiet voice. The dangerous one he used when he'd gone beyond rage.

Mistaking Riam's lack of response for confusion, Pekol pointed a callused hand toward a small pile of refuse pushed against the wall on the far side of the cobblestone street. "A good churp doesn't wait for his raker to point things out for him."

Riam had been with Pekol for most of the morning, cleaning the city streets and dumping chamber pots down holes that were spaced irregularly along the narrow lanes. He'd thought of running away, but fear and confusion kept him from bolting—for now anyway. He was biding his time, looking for the right moment and sorting things out.

He didn't know the city, and the endless crowds of peo-ple and stone buildings terrified him nearly as much as Pe-kol. Even now, as he stood lost in thought, people flowed around him, as if he were no more than a stone in the road or a post that had been there forever. Nobody paid atten-tion to him unless he bumped into them. Even then, they only moved around him or told him to mind his way. He had the feeling that if he collapsed on the street, he'd starve to death long before anyone would help, and that included Pekol.

He'd only been in the sprawling madness for a single morning, but already he felt more alone than he'd ever been. Even after Gairen killed his grandfather and dragged him from his home, he hadn't felt like this. The feeling was almost as bad as losing his uncle, and the worst part about it all was Loral's betrayal.

He balled his hands into fists. What a fool she'd made of him, pretending to like him, making him think she cared. He tried to tell himself it didn't matter, but deep down, in the marrow of his bones, it hurt. With Nola, there'd been no choice, he'd been stuck with her, but Loral was different. They'd gone through the Esharii attack together, and she'd been there for him when Gairen died.

And then there was Tannon. He didn't know if Tannon was involved with this mix-up, but Riam would make him pay for throwing the swords into the river . . . and for taking Loral away from him.

"Stop woolgathering and get moving." Pekol cuffed the side of Riam's head with the back of his hand. "I want to be done with my lanes 'fore dark."

Riam worked his way through the crowd, rubbing the side of his head and doing his best to stay out of people's way. Behind him, Pekol grunted as he lifted the arms of the cart. The metal-shod wheels creaked and bumped over the stones, following him toward the refuse.

When Pekol made it across the street, Riam loaded the rubbish—mostly rotten food and a torn, greasy blanket that smelled like a dead screet left in the sun. Riam coughed and would have vomited from the smell if there'd been anything in his stomach. Instead he dry-heaved painfully. His eyes watered. Flies buzzed around him. He swatted one away that landed on his lip and threatened to crawl into his mouth. Sweat ran down his back where he knelt, doubled over against a rough wall trying to catch his breath.

"Horrid stuff, but you'll get used to it."

Riam tilted his head enough to glare at the man.

Pekol let out a cackle that turned into a cough. "People are vile, boy, and rich or poor, their throwings stink the same. Get that stuff in the cart and be done with it."

Riam lifted the blanket gingerly and animal shit fell out, landing on his foot. At least, he hoped it came from an animal. He kicked it away into the street with disgust.

"Going to have to pick that up. District warden sees we left it and it won't go well for either of us, and I can guarantee you'll get twice the thumping I do."

If I see this district warden and explain things, you'll be the only one getting thumped!

Despite his brave thoughts, Riam did as told and used a corner of the blanket to pick up the feces and carry it at arm's length to the nearest piss hole on the street.

"Good boy," Pekol said with satisfaction. "We're going to do fine. Not like Doby. Kept trying to run away. Had to keep him chained to the cart. Then he plain gave up and refused to work. Finally, had to have a warden spike him. You do as I say, though, and you'll make it through your punishment—they only gave you two years."

Riam spun around at the words. "Two years? Punishment?"

"That's what the glyph on your arm says. Two years for stealing. Been a raker long enough to know how to read the symbols. Once your time is up, it'll come off and you're free to do as you like."

Riam stood up straight. "Steal? I didn't steal anything!"

Pekol cackled again. The sound was as disturbing as his voice—a grating, painful sound that hurt the listener as much as it hurt the little man. Riam imagined something tearing loose inside Pekol's throat whenever he heard it. The cackle faded to its usual sickly cough.

"You all say that at first," Pekol said when the coughing subsided, "but there's no use denying it. Only a Draegoran can put that mark on your arm, and they don't do it without reading your thoughts. You're lucky I needed a new churp today. You'd have ended up rowing a boat or laying stone, or worse, if I'd left you in the cage."

Looking at Pekol, Riam didn't think anything could be worse. *How did I end up here for stealing? Tannon couldn't have arranged all this from the barge.* Although his memories were missing, he knew he hadn't stolen anything—he'd never taken anything that didn't belong to him in his entire life. He concentrated, trying to remember more. He caught a sliver of a memory, the old woman rubbing his thigh. The image made him shiver and didn't help. There was simply nothing there to explain waking up at sunrise, half delirious and starving, in a cell full of dirty faces.

When he'd regained enough of his wits to focus on the world around him at dawn, a threadbare shirt and a worn-out pair of breeches had replaced his gray clothing. The first boy he'd spoken to, one older than him with a broken, jagged tooth, had knocked him to the ground and split his lip.

"Your food is mine, understand?" the boy told him.

The others in the cage were even less friendly, so Riam crawled to a corner and kept to himself until Pekol arrived with a pock-faced man holding a ring of keys. Both men stood at the door to the cell until everyone lined up facing them.

Pekol had walked down the row, looking them up and down, and paused when he'd come to Riam. Even though Pekol's scraggly haired face and protruding underbite reminded Riam of an angry dog, at the time, he'd seemed like Sollus himself come down to save him.

"What happened to your lip?" Pekol had asked.

Riam had glanced toward the large boy who'd hit him. He wasn't stupid. "I fell," he said, loud enough for all to hear.

That was the first time he'd heard the cackle. "He'll do," Pekol told the pock-faced man after regaining his breath.

He'd been with Pekol cleaning filth off the streets the remainder of the morning.

"The cart's nearly full. We'll finish Grantor's Street and head to the Raker's Square before going to the pit."

"Peke!" a soot-stained boy no older than Riam called. "Got a barrel of ash in back of the shop. I'll give you a fresh loaf of bread if you'll get it, so I don't have to drag it around to the street."

"Your master will take a switch to you if he knows you're giving away bread to save you on your chores."

"He won't find out. He's at the market and won't be back for at least a glass."

"Sorry, Jami, load's almost full. You'll have to wait till tomorrow." There was satisfaction in Pekol's voice. He enjoyed telling the boy no.

"Aw, come on, Peke. Supposed to have it out before you came. I'll get switched for sure if it's still here when he gets back."

Pekol rubbed at the motley stubble of his chin, making the boy wait, and then smiled good-naturedly.

Jami's shoulders sagged in relief.

"No," Pekol said. "I'll not do it."

"Come on," Jami pleaded, his whole body jerking with a small tantrum. "Two loaves, then—the ones with olives baked inside and a cup of cider." He glanced down the street nervously. His voice went up an octave. "It has to be gone before Master Silva gets back."

Pekol made a show of looking at the cart, as if weighing whether or not he had room. "Don't think—"

"Please!" There was real fear behind the boy's desperation.

Riam watched Pekol through the exchange. This wasn't playful banter. The spark in Pekol's eyes hadn't been there before. He enjoyed making Jami squirm.

"Please, Peke," Jami begged.

"All right." Pekol leaned forward, his underbite pushing the jagged row of bottom teeth out in front of his top lip. "But you'll owe me a favor when I need one."

"Thanks, Peke."

"Say it."

"Say what?"

"Say that you'll owe me a favor." He said the words slowly, savoring them.

Jami licked his lips. He glanced down the street again.

Pekol folded his arms and stood firm. He knew he had the boy right where he wanted him.

There was a long, silent moment. Jami clearly didn't like the idea of owing Pekol anything. Riam didn't blame him.

"Right. You're on your own." Pekol lifted the handles on the cart.

"Fine. Fine. I'll owe you a favor."

The front of the cart came back down with a thump. "No complaints and no questions."

"No complaints, but you have to hurry."

"Make some room," he told Riam. "We'll load the barrel and bring it back empty."

The three of them struggled with the heavy barrel, but they managed to get it into the cart without spilling too much ash. Pekol made Riam use his hands to collect what spilled on the street. When they were done, Pekol withdrew a wooden-handled knife from his belt. He used it to cut one of the loaves Jami brought in half. He kept the larger half for himself, along with the other full loaf and the cider, and gave Riam the smaller end.

Riam devoured it so fast he didn't taste it. He hadn't realized how hungry he was. His stomach growled at him, wanting more. *How long has it been since I ate?* That was another problem with running away—no food and no money. Finding this district warden seemed like the best way to straighten things out.

"Thought you could use that," Pekol said after finishing off the cider.

"Thank you," Riam said.

"Save your thanks. You can't work if you're too weak to move, but understand this, I'll beat you as soon as feed you if it means getting my streets done faster. Best you keep that in mind." He grabbed the handles again. "Get behind and push. It'll be heavy with the ash loaded. We'll go straight to the square and then to the pit. Have to make two runs today."

Raker's Square turned out to be a large, open lot surrounded by crumbling half-walls that were a patchwork of brick and mortar from repairs over the years. Entire sections were missing or lying in heaps. Tall weeds grew among the scattered bricks. Inside, the square was anything but abandoned. Carts, some two-wheeled like Pekol's, and some four, the size of small wagons, were arranged haphazardly wherever there was an open spot. Smoke rose from several small fires where pots and kettles hung over open flames. Men and women gathered around the pots, and the sounds of their conversations filled the air.

"Anything worth trading?" a dark-skinned man wearing a robe asked Pekol. Of all the people in the square, the man stood out like a maston in a garden. Besides his dark skin and long robe, he was clean and walked as if he owned everything in sight.

"Nothing you'd be interested in. Picked up a barrel of ash, worth a few dregs to the soap makers, couple of unbroken bottles, and there's a left boot in good shape."

The robed man waved a hand in the air, uninterested, and walked away.

"Who's that?" Riam asked.

"Sadal. He owns the yard and gets first trade rights to anything we bring in. Arillian bastard." Pekol spat on the ground.

Pekol bartered the left boot for a cup of tea and the ash and bottles for three copper dregs as he made his way around to the other carts. At each, there was at least one boy or girl like Riam. Some of the rakers had two or three children working for them. Many had lengths of chain that led from the carts to either a collar or a clamp around an ankle, and more than one showed the results of being whipped or beaten. All had a glyph on their left arm. Pekol waved Riam back to the cart before collecting his tea with a group of rakers squatting around one of the fires.

Riam sat and rubbed at his feet while he waited. He'd gone barefoot for most of his childhood, but he'd never spent a day on the hard stones of the streets. Around him, carts and men came and went, each a repeat of what Pekol had done—a brief question or two from Sadal and then a walk around to the other carts to sell or trade. He contemplated slipping away until another boy approached.

"Stick," the boy said and leaned on the cart as if he didn't have a care in the world. He was older than Riam by three or four years, was dressed in rags more threadbare than Riam's own clothes, and his long, brown hair was ratty and greasy. His nose was flatter than it should have been, with an unnatural turn near the bridge. Around his neck lay a leather thong with a charm dangling from it—a small, flat rock with an eye painted inside a blue circle. The center of the pupil held a sliver of yellow, making the eye look feline.

There was something familiar about it. He'd seen it before but couldn't remember where. Riam watched the other boy warily. He didn't want a repeat of the events in the cage. "What do you mean, stick?"

"Stick. As in, that's what they call me 'cause it took a stick to get me to work when I first got here."

"Oh." Riam relaxed. The boy didn't appear to be a threat.

"Guess Peke finally had enough of Doby. Too bad." Stick reached into the cart and dug through the refuse. "Anything good today?" He found a half-rotten apple and smeared away the soft, brown side against a wooden slat before biting into the firmer portion that remained.

It was disgusting. Without thinking, Riam tried to knock the apple away.

"Oomph," Stick said through a mouthful, mistaking the gesture for a grab at the food. "Sorry. Didn't know you were saving it. Most of us carry a sack for the things we want to keep." He shook a small cloth bag tied to his waist.

Riam ignored the apple. "No, I don't want it. I was . . . won't it make you sick?"

Stick shrugged. "Better than starving or giving it to the pigs." He took another bite. "You'll get used to it."

Riam looked back at Pekol. The man squatted beyond the fire, drinking his tea. "I've heard those words more than once today."

Stick pointed at Riam's glyph. "So, what'd you do to end up as a churp?"

Riam scratched at his forearm. "Pekol told me two years for stealing."

Stick held up his arm so that the sleeve of his shirt fell down around his elbow, revealing a different mark, more intricate with tighter spirals. "Five years for me, but it wasn't for stealing." He took another bite. "Burned down my master's shop." His eyes glazed over, and his chewing slowed down until it stopped. He stared off at nothing. "I had no idea he was inside when I did it. Nearly roasted the bastard." He smiled, as if recalling a fond memory. "Lost all his hair, he did. Worth every day of my sentence."

"But I didn't steal anything," Riam said. "I was pushed off a barge, almost drowned and woke up in a cell with the glyph on my arm."

"Sure. Whatever you say." Stick took another bite. "You're new, so people will understand you not wanting to admit your crimes, but if I were you, I'd keep the whole 'I'm innocent' thing to myself, especially since you're churping for Peke. He was a churp once himself. He's been a raker since he finished his time, and he doesn't like seeing anyone else go free, especially if he feels they haven't learned their lesson."

"What do you mean?"

"That mark don't come off by itself, despite whatever he told you. You have to go before the district warden and at least two rakers have to vouch for you. The sooner you show 'em you've learned your lesson, the more likely the rakers are to vouch for you, but I wouldn't count on Peke. He never vouches for anyone. That's why Doby gave up. He was a good kid, even after Peke told the warden he wasn't ready to be released after his first sentence was up. It was the second time that broke him. Peke had as good as told Doby he'd go free, even trusted him with bringing the cart back from the pit by himself, so Doby only found one other raker to go with them to see the warden. Then Peke stood right in front of him and did the opposite."

"Why'd he do that?"

"Like I said, he was a hard worker." Stick finished off the apple and tossed the core into the cart. "Be careful. Pekol is as dangerous as they come."

Riam didn't need the warning. He already feared the man enough to know not to cross him.

"If I were you, I'd figure out a way to get him to trade you for another churp." Stick held up the charm he wore.

"Pekol doesn't like the Church of Man, so I prattled on day after day about it. Took a few beatings, but eventually he gave up and traded me for Doby. Don't think that'll work for you, but you need to find something he doesn't like. Not bad enough that he hurts you, but annoying enough that he doesn't want you around."

"I won't be here long enough to worry about it. First chance I get, I'm gone," Riam said.

"You can try running if you want, but there's nowhere to go. No one will speak to you or help you with that glyph on your arm. You can't hide it, and they won't let you out of the gate without your raker. Worse, anyone figures out you're running, and they'll drag you right back to the square for a reward. Warden will make an example out of you by adding more time to your sentence in front of everyone."

No wonder Pekol was so lax. There's nowhere to run. He certainly wasn't going to be a churp for the next two years. He was going to the island to become a Draegoran. He needed to find this district warden and explain what had happened. Soon, before Pekol could hurt him.

"Stick, don't you have something better to do than pester my new churp?" Pekol's voice said from behind Riam.

"Just killing time and giving . . ." He looked questioningly at Riam.

"Riam."

"Giving Riam some advice."

"Be sure and ignore any advice Stick gives you. He'll never make it through his time."

"Too late for that, Peke. Another tenday, and I'll be free. You'll never see me again."

"You don't deserve it." Pekol's voice was sharp. "You were a criminal the day they put that glyph on you, and you're as much a criminal today as you were then, but you're right on one good count. Once your sentence is up, I'll never have to look at you again."

There was something eerie about the way Pekol said the last words. It made the hair on Riam's arms stand up.

Stick didn't notice. "Well, there are at least two other rakers who disagree. I'm getting out of here and there's not a Fallen thing you can do about it."

"I should have broken more than your nose before I traded you for Doby, but who would have thought there were two rakers dumb enough to believe you are worth anything more than a churp. You won't last two days if they release you 'fore you're back here . . . or worse."

"We'll see about that."

"Mark my words, two days."

Told you, Stick mouthed to Riam before strolling away.

Pekol stared at the back of Stick's head, his fingers rubbing at the hilt of his knife, until the young man had returned to his cart. "No one gets away," he mumbled. He moved to the cart and lifted the handles with an already too familiar grunt. "Come on, boy. We've a long walk ahead of us, but at least the ash is gone."

CHAPTER 24

The pit was more than a simple hole in the ground. It was a canyon bordered by pig farms far outside the city walls. Riam and Pekol made their way down from the city proper, past tall, well-kept buildings that gave way to short, squat brick-and-rock homes, then to log homes and finally to rapidly thrown-together buildings that were little more than hovels interspersed among large shops and storehouses. In the lower city, the harsh clank of hammers pounding on iron rang out from every direction, men yelled, and wagons rolled noisily down streets more dirt than stone and littered with waste. Exotic smokes and smells drifted on the wind, some acrid and some sweet. Some made Riam's eyes sting, and still others were so putrid they made him choke. Such a mass of people and activity was beyond Riam's comprehension before today. Parthusal was an immense city, the biggest under the Draegoran Covenant, and he hadn't even seen the market or riverside sections. It reminded Riam of a giant beehive after striking it with a rock or, worse, the flood of wasps in the timber yard.

He still had trouble comprehending the true magnitude

of it all when they suddenly passed beyond the second wall and moved outside the city proper. But even here there were "outbuildings," as Pekol called them—holding pens, farmhouses, and barns that dotted the landscape. He'd never seen so many animals, but he imagined they were needed to feed all the people crammed inside the city. For every animal he recognized, two more he didn't grazed in the fields or paced back and forth in pens or cages. There were mastons and glints, the small wild, black-horned goats from the plains, cattle and oxen, and even a cage full of something resembling marcats, only larger with spots. There were birds, bigger than a man, with legs a rod long and razor-sharp spurs, though steel caps covered most of the spurs to protect the handlers. Something like a bear, but smaller and striped, with long toenails, climbed trees to get at the leaves. In one cage a massive beast with long tusks and a body like a man but covered in thick hair thumped its chest and roared behind the thick iron bars. The sound sent every animal in the area scurrying for the far corners of their pens.

Along a parallel road, wagons lined up, waiting for entrance to a gate farther down the wall. *How do they sort it all out*? He wanted to keep moving down the road until it was all behind him and never return.

After another stead of pushing, Riam could see why Pekol didn't like making more than one trip a day down the long, dirt road. It helped that the ashes had been sold off and the barrel was empty, making the cart lighter, but it'd still taken nearly a full glass to get this far. Luckily, they traveled downhill for most of the journey.

He smelled the pit before they arrived. The stench of a thousand pigs, of refuse, and of rot and decay assailed Riam—so heavy and strong he felt it in his nostrils and tasted it on his tongue like the film of dust deposited by windstorm. It made his saliva thick, and no matter how much he spat, he tasted the smell. Whenever he thought it could get no worse, the warm breeze would hit them, raising the repulsive odor to a new level.

"I'm not going to lie, you never get used to the pit or the piggeries in high summer," Pekol told him when at last they came to a spot near the canyon's edge and stopped. He

handed Riam a thin scarf and wrapped another around his
face, covering his nose and mouth.

Riam took the scarf thankfully. It didn't help with the
smell, but it took some of the thickness out of the air.

Filth-stained children carrying woven reed baskets set
upon the cart like locusts and pulled out anything that
could be fed to the pigs. They were younger than Riam. He
tried speaking to one, but the child growled like an animal
and bared his teeth. When the children were done, Pekol
backed the cart close to the edge of the canyon. Ropes with
hooks on one end lay scattered near large wooden stakes.
Riam wondered what they were used for. He didn't have to
wonder long.

"Grab a rope, crawl under, and hook the axle. Sometimes the edge gets soft. Don't want to lose the cart when
we dump it."

Riam grabbed a metal hook. It was hot from sitting in
the sun, so he tossed it from hand to hand to keep it from
burning his palms while he scurried underneath and fastened it to the axle.

"Come here and watch me." Pekol lifted the rope, gauging the slack for the right length. "Make a loop this way,
then another that way, about a hand apart. Cross them over
to make a hitch and drop them over the stake. Last, tug the
slack out. Got it?" He demonstrated the hitch.

Riam nodded.

Pekol untied the rope and handed it to him. "You do it.
There should be enough rope so that the wheels stop at the
edge. You'll do it from now on, and if the cart goes over,
you'll follow before it hits the bottom."

Riam eyed Pekol's face for traces of humor, but Pekol
wasn't joking. He tied the simple hitch with ease but gave
it several yanks to make doubly sure it would hold before
they dumped the cart.

They made the trek back to the city. Riam thought
about running out here in the open where no one watched.
He was pretty sure he could outrun Pekol. *But outrun him
to where—back to the gates of the city, to men who will return me for a reward? What can I tell them when I don't
even know how I arrived here myself?* No, going to the city
guards wasn't going to help, nor would fleeing into the

countryside dressed in rags. The only safe bet lay in proving he wasn't supposed to be here.

When they returned to the outer wall, Riam expected them to have to wait in line like the rest of the wagons on the road to gain entrance, but instead they returned by the same gate they'd come out.

"Need to see your chit," said the guard at the gate around the wad of torgana leaves in his mouth, "and to check the cart." The guard's beard was stained black at the edges of his lips from the leaves, and his leather vest was wet with sweat.

"You let the other rakers go through without all the fuss."

"Most of them have never been caught smuggling, have they?"

"That was years ago."

"Three years to be exact, and it still bothers me that you didn't go to the mines or the ships. The Draegorans don't give second chances, but for some reason, you're still here."

"I haven't smuggled a Fallen thing since, and you've seen the chit enough times to know I don't need a new stamp until winter."

The guard spat out juice from the torgana leaves in a brown stream that splattered on the ground near Pekol's feet. "Have to check the cart every time and make sure your stamp's current. Otherwise, you go to the trade gate and pay the entry tax."

Pekol pulled out a stiff square of parchment and shoved it toward the guard. "There!" He put his hands on his hips. "Half the time you don't even look at it, and I'm fairly certain you're not smart enough to read it. Can we go now?"

The guard stared at the chit for a time. "Jans, can you come read this?" he called to a female guard examining another cart. She arched an eyebrow. "'Cause you know, I'm not smart enough to read the thing."

"Come on. You saw it yesterday. I've another street to clean." Pekol held his hand out for the chit.

The guard ignored Pekol, making them wait until Jans finished the other cart. Both guards looked at it quizzically, turning it this way and that.

Pekol's face reddened. He opened his mouth several times to say something, but each time thought better of it and clamped it shut. Riam coughed into his shirt to keep from smiling. He didn't want Pekol's anger directed toward him.

Finally, the guard handed it back. "Mind your tongue next time, or you'll pay at the trade gate, stamp or no stamp."

Pekol stuffed the parchment back into his shirt. "Come on, boy." He grabbed the handles of the cart with a jerk. They moved through the gate while the guards chuckled behind them.

"Oh, and Pekol," the guard called. "I was smart enough to catch you."

"About time somebody did something about that bastard," Pekol grumbled, his voice barely loud enough to hear over the rattle of the wheels.

Riam figured he'd better watch what he did until Pekol's mood changed. He knew how to be invisible when a man's temper was foul. He'd had lots of practice with his grandfather.

"You stay with the cart at night," Pekol told Riam, "and you don't stray farther than the nearest hole to piss in except for Bortha's place."

They'd returned from a second run to the pit, and the cart was tucked away in an alley. Riam thought they were somewhere near where they'd first started that morning, but he couldn't be sure, too many of the buildings looked the same.

"Bortha's inn is a few buildings down from here on the left. Get a few armloads of straw from his stables and line the bottom of the cart 'fore you go to sleep."

Riam was so tired he didn't care if there was straw to sleep on. He could climb in and sleep right now.

"It's not for you," Pekol said, reading his expression. "It keeps the cart from smelling so bad. Tell Bortha you're my new churp, and he'll let you get the straw and give you some scraps to eat if he has them. Don't ever take anything else, even if he offers. He'll charge me for anything you get from him 'sides the straw and scraps. You'll have a worse nick-name than Stick if that happens."

"Yes, sir."

"Good. Let's see, there was something else . . . oh, you'll scrub the cart with sand once every tenday. It's too late tonight, but you'll do it tomorrow."

"Yes, sir."

He grabbed Riam's shirt and pulled him up onto his toes so that their faces were only a hand apart. "Don't even think of running or going anywhere else. With that glyph on your arm, no one will help you. They won't even let you buy anything if you have the dregs to pay for it—not even food—and when I find you, you'll spend the next month chained to the cart."

Riam nodded.

"Well, what are you waiting for? Get the straw." Pekol shoved him away and pointed down the lane. "I'll be back at sunrise," he called over his shoulder as he headed the opposite way.

Riam watched Pekol until he disappeared—likely going home or to a tavern to drink. Pekol reminded Riam of his grandfather in that regard. He seemed the type to spend his nights in a cup.

Once he was gone, Riam headed toward the inn—only he didn't stop when he came to it. Instead, he walked down the lane for a time, taking in the shops and homes. The lane was lit here and there by lamps, and a few men and women were out in the early night. They didn't move in fear of the darkness, but they didn't dally along either. A few glanced his direction apprehensively, but as soon as they spotted the glyph on his arm, he became invisible to them.

A short man with a head-wrap came out of a nearby shop. He struggled one by one with the rolled-up rugs that leaned against the wall, bringing them in for the night.

"Would you like some help?" Riam asked when the man came out for the third one.

The man took one look at Riam's arm and turned away. "Get away from my shop, or I'll call the guard," he said. "Filthy little criminal."

The man didn't seem in a hurry to do it, but Riam moved

quickly down the lane just the same. It probably wouldn't go well if the guards found him out wandering.

The lane met a wide street, double the width of the one he walked. In the center of the intersection stood a statue depicting Parron, the Fallen God of Light. The god held a sword at the ready and long wings protruded from its back, coming down so far they nearly touched the cobblestones of the street. He'd never heard of the Fallen having wings. He supposed it was possible since they'd come from the heavens, but he doubted it. Gairen said that Draegorans were descended from Parron, and none of them had wings— nor did he for that matter. He ran a hand over the smooth stone. He couldn't imagine how it was made or what tools were used to make something so exquisite with rock. Magic maybe. The details of the face captivated Riam. The Fallen God appeared vengeful and sorrowful at the same time, depending on where Riam stood. It seemed to mirror his own feelings. *Crazy to think I'm somehow related to this thing.* They would stone him for blasphemy for thinking such a thing back home.

A woman walked by and scrunched her eyes in suspicion at seeing him touching the statue, but she didn't say anything. It was odd to be so free and yet not free at the same time. *I could walk this street all the way to the docks, but then what?* There was no guarantee he'd find a Draegoran, and if Pekol found him missing, the man would keep him locked to the cart once the guard caught him.

It was hunger that finally brought him back to the inn. He would worry about finding the docks and a Draegoran tomorrow. He poked his head through the gate. In the darkness he could make out the stables and a pile of hay against the far wall. He grabbed an armload and moved back toward the gate.

"You must be Doby's replacement," a voice said.

Riam dropped the hay and spun around. The silhouette of a man stood in the shadows next to the back door of the inn. Something small and red glowed in his hand.

"I suppose I am," Riam said.

The man put the glow to his lips. It brightened as he inhaled and his face lit up, revealing a thick mustache and dark eyes. Exhaling loudly, he stepped out of the shadows.

The smell of burning torgana leaves filled the air. "I saw you on the street. You were smart to come back. Most new churps try to run at first. It never ends well for them, and I'm sure Pekol's hoping you try so he can give you a lesson for it. He likes to start off new churps that way."

Riam swallowed. "He told me to get straw from here," Riam said defensively. "Are you Bortha? He said you two have an arrangement."

"I am, and we do." The man inhaled from the rolled torgana a final time and dropped it to the ground. "Once you get the straw you need, come by the kitchen." He stepped on the burning ember, twisting his foot back and forth to make sure it was out.

It took three trips, and Riam's stomach growled by the time he had the straw spread evenly in the bed of the cart. Three armloads didn't look like much, but he measured it would be enough to satisfy Pekol. It certainly wouldn't make it any softer for sleeping, but it wouldn't be much different than the deck of the barge. It was certainly better than the cage.

Riam knocked on the side door of the inn. No one answered, so he opened it, revealing a small but organized kitchen with an oven, a few cupboards, and a table. Pots hung from hooks and two washtubs were poked in the corner. A large block in the center of the room held several knives and a small cleaver.

For a brief moment Riam thought of taking one of the knives. *For Fallen's sake, what do I need a knife for?* The answer came quickly—nothing. There wouldn't be any Esharii in the city, and there was no one he could trade or sell it to with the glyph on his arm. Plus, it was stealing. He couldn't see himself stealing anything without it being a matter of life and death. In truth, he felt a little guilty for having thought about taking it at all. And besides, he still had Gairen's sword. It'd been thrown in the river, but he could still feel it whenever he thought about it. It was simply a matter of retrieving it somehow.

He closed his eyes. It was definitely the sword he felt in the distance—like a beacon, somewhere far and faint, off to his left. With his eyes closed, he could see the thin line that connected him to the weapon. He reached toward it, his arm out like a compass needle, and his eyes came open in surprise. The glyph glowed. He opened and closed his eyes, comparing the tattoo-like lines on his skin to what he saw in his mind when his eyes were closed. With them open, the lines were black and flat, like a drawing, but with them closed, the lines went deeper and wove in and out, like a rope. No, a rope was too large—more of a thread, or several threads, winding their way in and out of his skin. He followed the lines with his senses. The threads formed a complicated knot centered in his forearm.

He touched one of the threads where it came to the surface of the skin with his other hand and pushed gently. Nothing happened. He continued to examine the lines. They reminded him a bit of the line connecting him to Gairen's sword. He'd used his mind, not his hands to save himself from being drained by the sword. *Would that work again here?* He concentrated on one of the strands and tried to push it to the side with his thoughts.

The line quivered and pain shot up his arm and into his chest. He sucked in his breath between his teeth as the pain faded. He tried again.

The knot moved once more, pulling the strands around his arm tighter. The pain returned, but this time he was prepared for it. He tugged harder and the pain increased.

"What are you doing?"

Riam let go and opened his eyes to find Bortha watching him curiously.

"Nothing," Riam answered. "I'm tired. I almost fell asleep standing here."

"With your arm sticking out?"

Riam shrugged.

"It looked like the glyph on your arm moved. Must be the light playing tricks on me. Guess we're both tired." Bortha moved to the table that held the knives. "Are you hungry? You look like you haven't eaten in days."

"Starving."

"I'll make you a plate."

Riam started to protest, "Pekol said nothing but scraps—"

"Pekol can go pound sand up his ass. If I want to give you a plate of food, I'll give you a plate of food." He grabbed a knife and a tin plate and opened the large, wood-burning oven to reveal the remains of a large bird.

Riam's mouth hung open. He'd never heard anyone use words quite like that. It was worse than Gairen's talk at the baths.

Bortha dug around the carcass and cut away some of the remaining meat. He tossed it on a tin and added something like a tuber back home, only orange with yellow skin, and a scoop of beans from a pot. He slapped the tin onto the table and set a knife next to it. "Go ahead. I'm sorry I've no bread left tonight."

Riam looked from the tin to Bortha. *Is the man trying to trick me?* He didn't want to be in trouble with Pekol. He scratched at the glyph on his arm. The tingling had returned.

"If you don't eat it, I'll throw it out. It's late enough that no one's ordering anything but ale or wine in the main room."

Riam stepped forward hesitantly.

"Doby and I had an arrangement, and I'm hoping to continue it." Bortha took off his apron and hung it on a peg. He placed his palms on the table and nodded for Riam to eat.

Riam couldn't resist any longer. He slid forward and grabbed the knife. He wanted to fall on the food and devour it in big, heaping bites, but he didn't want to appear as desperate as he felt. He forced himself to cut off a small piece of meat and used the knife to skewer it.

"Well, you've more manners than Doby."

Riam cut a second piece and ate it slowly. The dark, almost black meat melted in his mouth. It had to be one of the large birds with sharp spurs he'd seen outside the wall. It had a gamy flavor, but it beat eating sage hens flat out. No wonder they went to the trouble of keeping the dangerous birds.

"I've no stable boy, so I'll make you the same deal as Doby. A plate like this every night, and in return you'll muck out the stables and brush down any of the animals I tell you need it."

Riam didn't think he'd be around long enough to keep his end of the arrangement, but it didn't hurt to agree. It might take longer than a day to find a Draegoran. Besides, Pekol wasn't going to feed him any more than it took to keep him alive. "I'll do it, but I'm afraid Pekol won't like it."

"As long as you do your work and I'm paying the cost of feeding you, he'll be content. Besides, he doesn't have to know a thing about it. In fact, no one needs to know anything about it. I'm bending the rules a bit feeding you. Don't let it bite me in the ass."

Riam choked on his food. City folk were certainly more direct with their words.

CHAPTER 25

A body lay at the mouth of an alley on Painter's Street on the morning of Tenth Day. Riam found it face-down with its arms bound behind its back. At first, he feared it might be Stick because it sat right at the border between Pekol's lanes and where the older churp worked with his raker, but when they flipped it over, a woolly beard adorned the face. Whoever the man was, he'd had the life sucked out of him until all that remained was a withered corpse—the work of a Draegoran. The body had darkened and shrunk, leaving the face stretched tight over the skull. It looked familiar, but it could have been anyone.

The grotesqueness of it gave Riam the shivers, and he watched his hands to keep from staring. He counted the days on grimy fingers. *How had a tenday passed so quickly?* It didn't seem possible. He hadn't intended to remain with Pekol so long, no more than a day or two at most, but he'd not seen a single Draegoran—or anyone else who looked like they could help for that matter—on their rounds or during his short walks while exploring at night. The Drae-gorans, it seemed, were like the rabbits he'd hunted back home. If you were short on food, you never saw one, but if you left your sling at home, you'd see a dozen.

The days with Pekol were hard and long, partially explaining why he hadn't found a Draegoran to hear his case. Picking up refuse from sunrise to sundown, interspersed with trips to the pit, and then cleaning Bortha's stalls to earn enough food to keep from starving didn't give him much time for anything else. Every day lasted an eternity, with the same mindless routine, and he was so tired that he kept putting off his escape. Yet the tenday had flown by like the wind. He hadn't even had a chance to do more with the glyph on his arm than to take a few halfhearted looks at it with his inner sight before falling asleep.

If he could figure out how to remove the glyph, he would be free to do whatever he wanted. No one would question him searching out a way to the island. The idea had come to him last night before falling asleep in the back of the cart. If he didn't find a Draegoran soon, he would need to find a way to untangle the glyph.

"Quit dallying and grab the legs."

Riam did as Pekol said, and they carried the dead man to the cart. The skin around the man's ankles crumbled and flaked away in Riam's hands, brittle as rotten wood, exposing the dried veins and sinews beneath. The muscles felt like weathered strips of leather beneath Riam's fingers. Even the exposed bone was sun-white and porous. The corpse mirrored the last image he held of his grandfather. He tried not to look at the face, but he found himself drawn to the way the lips pulled back into a morbid smile, as if the man died happy instead of in the agonizing pain of being drained—a pain Riam remembered from the timber yard.

Pekol let out one of his usual cackles, tearing Riam away from his thoughts. "Reminds me of Doby," he said when he stopped laughing.

How could the man laugh while they were carrying a body, and especially about the death of a churp who'd served him for years? Stick was right. There was something very wrong with Pekol. The raker would never let him go, even if he served the full time—which he would not. He needed to get away, and he needed to get to the island to begin his training as a Draegoran.

"We'll go straight to the pit. District wardens don't like us parading their handiwork around the city for all to see."

They rolled the body over the sidewall and dropped it into the back of the cart with a thump. The dead man's purse fell from beneath his vest and lay exposed on the floorboard of the wagon. Pekol ignored it, which was puzzling. The man never let a thing go into the cart without checking and rechecking it for anything he could sell or trade. He knew Pekol saw it fall. *Why ignore the pouch?* There was something going on here he didn't understand.

Pekol moved to take the handles of the cart. Without thinking, Riam reached for the pouch. He closed his hand around it and yanked, but the cord fixing it to the corpse's belt held. He expected the pouch to be hard with coin, but instead it felt soft.

Pekol stepped around the arm of the cart. Riam pulled again, harder this time. The cord snapped, and he hit the sidewall with a loud thwack. With nowhere to hide the pouch, Riam dropped it to the ground right as Pekol looked back.

Pekol tilted his head quizzically. "What are you doing?"

Riam rubbed at his hand. "Splinter," he said. His heartbeat pounded in his ears. The pouch by his feet seemed larger than the cart. He forced himself to stare at his hand and did his best to look uncaring about anything else. *Please, don't let him look down.*

Pekol rubbed his bottom teeth back and forth against his upper lip.

Riam pretended to bite at a splinter. He felt a flake of skin on his tongue and jerked his hand away, spitting until he was sure it was gone.

"Let's get going," Pekol said. He took up his position.

Riam started to grab the pouch before the cart rolled past and froze. The pouch had come open when it landed, spilling a dark wad of torgana leaves. With a sinking feeling, he knew whose body lay in the cart, and he knew that somehow Pekol was responsible. He didn't know how Pekol had arranged for a Draegoran to kill the guard from the gate, but that meant there was at least one Draegoran around. *Do I really want to find one who is killing guards for Pekol?*

Pekol whistled and hummed for the rest of the morning. He didn't yell at Riam once to hurry or scold him for missing

something that he hadn't had time to collect. He even paid
for a small meat pie that they split after finishing their first
two lanes and returning from the pit. Riam sat on the back
of the cart, eating the pie. Pekol stood next to him. Around
the square, rakers haggled over their finds. From a simple
sandal lace to a cracked tankard, everything usable held
value to someone in the square.

"Beautiful day to be alive," Pekol said between mouthfuls.

Riam didn't know how to answer. The sun burned down
from above, making the air hot and sticky.

"Easy runs, a fine spiced pie, what more can you ask for,
eh, Doby?"

"I'm not Doby," Riam said. The pie tasted bland and the
crust soggy. Between that and thoughts of the dead guard,
he'd only been able to eat a few bites.

"What's that?"

"You called me Doby. Doby's dead."

"I did not. The heat's rattled you. You're hearing things."

"You did." Riam knew better than to press, but he
couldn't help himself. Pekol's smug happiness made something inside Riam burn. Pekol had been a part of the
guard's death and he'd had Doby killed. *And those things
made him happy?* Riam wished he still had Gairen's
sword with him. If he did, he'd do his best to run Pekol
through.

"I know Doby's dead. Shut up and eat your pie."

"No, he's right. You called him Doby," Stick said from
behind them.

"Butt out, Stick."

"Why? Today's the day, Peke," Stick said, walking confidently up to them. "I'll be free as soon as the district warden arrives, and he's on his way."

Riam sat up straight, his grim mood forgotten. He would
finally get his chance to talk to a Draegoran and be free of
Pekol. Somehow, he would get the warden's attention without Pekol stopping him.

"Is it, now?" Pekol said. He tossed the remainder of his
pie into the cart.

Riam added his own behind Pekol's and slid from his
seat on the sidewall to the ground.

"I'll soon be free and with a few dregs to boot," Stick

said. He turned to Riam, exposing the cat-eye charm that hung around his neck.

Pekol scowled at Stick.

Stick was oblivious to Pekol's look. "They give you ten dregs for each year you served. That way you have enough coin to start out and don't go straight to begging. That's fifty copper dregs for my five years—almost a full gold—and enough to buy some decent clothing and maybe start an apprenticeship somewhere."

"Like anyone will take you."

The words were too calm and controlled. Riam could tell Pekol wanted to say more, but he was clearly holding back.

"Well, it won't be nothing too fine, but honest work learning a trade's better than this, even if it's only hammering nails. But first, I'm going to celebrate. Get a bath and a real meal. No more rotten fruit and soured meat. What do you think, Peke, the Blue Duck on Linvar for my first meal? Bet you've never eaten there. Bet they wouldn't let you in. They don't serve rakers."

"If I were you, I wouldn't taunt me, Stick." Pekol pulled the knife from his belt and scraped it sideways against his thumb, testing the edge. "Your first night free wouldn't be very pleasant with a hole in your stomach."

"You wouldn't." Stick swallowed and looked left and right, unsure if Pekol would really use the knife right here in front of everyone. "I'm going to be free. Assaulting me would send you to the mines."

Pekol pointed the knife at Stick's arm. "Not until he removes that glyph, it won't."

"You're bluffing." Stick took a step back out of reach despite his words.

"Ever known me to make an empty threat?" Pekol grinned with his lower jaw jutting out so far that his bottom lip covered part of the top one. "Say one more word to me . . . just one."

Stick took a deep breath, preparing to say something stupid, no doubt. *Why couldn't Stick walk away and leave Peke alone?*

A commotion at the entrance to the yard came just in time to save Stick from himself. People hurried out of the way to clear a path for a tall man in gray.

Stick grinned ear to ear. "Too late, Peke. You lost," he said out the side of his mouth.

Pekol's eyes narrowed and his bottom jaw trembled. His hand tensed on the knife, and Riam knew Pekol was going to use it while he had the chance, before Stick was free. Stick was an idiot. He wasn't paying attention to the danger next to him anymore, as if merely seeing the Draegoran protected him.

Pekol lunged with the knife.

No! Riam's mind screamed. He couldn't let Pekol kill the older boy like this—not when he had the chance to save him. He threw himself forward and the world slowed around him. Without thinking about what he was doing, Riam punched at Pekol's knife hand. It moved so slowly it was easy. His fist connected with the back of Pekol's hand and the blade went flying. The world returned to normal speed. Riam felt drained, as if he'd run a long distance.

Pekol's eyes went wide in surprise. Then they narrowed as he realized what had happened. He backhanded Riam with all his adult strength, holding nothing back.

Riam hit the ground hard, the side of his face burning from the impact. He put a hand to his cheek and rubbed. He felt blood on his fingers. It hurt like the Fallen. He smiled up at Pekol. "Guess you'll just beat me like Doby." Riam knew he shouldn't have said it as soon as the words left his mouth. It was dumb, inciting Pekol to hit him again, but he'd only meant to keep the man's attention away from Stick and maybe attract the warden.

Murderous rage flashed across Pekol's face. "If that's what you want, you little shit." Pekol charged toward him.

Riam tried to scramble away, but this time he was too slow. Pekol's foot slammed into his side with a loud crack, lifting him into the air. He tumbled and sprawled in the dirt. It felt like a horse kicked him.

"How's that?" Pekol asked. "Got anything more you want to say?"

Riam climbed to all fours. He tried to gasp out a reply. "You're—"

This time Pekol kicked him in the belly. It was worse than the first blow. Riam clawed at the dirt but couldn't get any air.

"I've been looking forward to this. Most churps need to learn their place sooner or later. Today's as good as any for you to learn yours." He stepped on Riam's arm above the wrist and ground his heel down.

Riam thought the bones of his arm would break. He tried to scream, but he couldn't draw a breath.

"Look at the glyph on your arm." He put more weight down. "Look at it!"

Riam's eyes watered and his mouth opened and closed as he fought for air, but he tried his best to look at his arm. He'd do whatever the man said to get him to stop. *Gods, it hurt!*

"Get a good look. As long as you wear that mark, I can do whatever I want with you. You're nothing. Understand? Nothing. I paid good money for you. You'll keep your mouth shut and never interfere again, or by the Fallen I'll make this feel like paradise in comparison." Spittle dripped from Pekol's mouth and splattered on Riam's face.

"I think he gets it," a voice said.

"Who the fuck—" Pekol turned to the newcomer. The pressure left Riam's arm.

Riam collapsed, putting his face in the dirt and sucking in air. It felt like drowning in the river all over again.

"Deepest apologies, Warden. Didn't realize it was you."

Riam's eyes cleared enough to see the man who'd saved him. He was one of the ugliest people he'd ever seen, even uglier than Pekol, with eyes that were too small for his wide face, but right now Riam wanted to hug the Draegoran. He was dressed the same as Gairen, but with a single sword hanging from his belt. On the side of his neck, the face of a wolf stood out against his pasty-white skin. *Finally, I will be out of this mess. All I need to do is explain things and let the Draegoran read the truth.*

"Trouble with your churp?"

"No. No trouble. Teaching him a lesson."

"Well, it seems he has it now."

"Not a churp . . . didn't steal anything," Riam said.

"I guess he doesn't," the Draegoran said. "By all means, continue."

Pekol didn't need any more prompting. He moved toward Riam.

"No," Riam protested. "I'm not supposed to be here. I have the—"

Pekol kicked him in the face this time. He didn't put as much force behind it as the other blows, but it was hard enough. Whimpering, Riam curled into a ball and held his face in his hands. Blood poured freely from his nose.

Pekol cackled above him.

"Bastard!" Riam said.

Pekol raised his foot above Riam's head.

"Wait," the Draegoran said. "Let me help." He stepped forward and took Riam's wrist in his hands.

Relief flooded through Riam. *Now the man will see the truth.* He would be saved.

Agonizing pain shot down Riam's arm. The Draegoran manipulated the glyph somehow. The lines burned through muscle and bone as they changed into a new pattern. A loud, painful whistle tore at Riam's ears.

"There." The Draegoran released his hold. "That's a half-year added to his sentence for disobedience."

Riam lay in the dirt in tears, his ears ringing and his nose throbbing. *This isn't fair. All the Draegoran has to do is read my thoughts.*

Pekol cackled louder as he and the Draegoran moved to the cart. Riam missed most of their conversation, but he caught a few words over the ringing in his ears.

". . . questions?"

"No . . . was there early."

". . . doubling the price . . ."

Riam couldn't be sure who said what, his thoughts were too muddled by the pain, but Pekol must be paying the Draegoran for killing the guard and now the Draegoran wanted more money. But that didn't make sense. *Draegorans are supposed to be the ones who enforce the laws, not break them . . . and they don't need money.*

He looked at the glyph on his arm. A Draegoran had placed it there, and he'd done nothing wrong. Now he had another half-year added to his time for keeping Stick alive. Things didn't make sense—not with everything he'd learned from Gairen. Otherwise, the Draegorans were no better than anybody else, simply more powerful. Between sips of air, Riam wondered if he really wanted to be a Draegoran after all.

———

Riam stumbled through the gate of the inn and collapsed. Pekol had dumped him in the alley where they kept the cart and left him there while he went to finish his lanes. He'd tried to get up but blacked out. When he awoke, it was dark; the cart was back in its usual place for the night. He wasn't sure if Pekol expected him to get straw, but the truth was, he didn't really care. All the man could do was beat him again. He'd lived through worse with his grandfather. Bortha, however, was expecting him to clean two of the stables tonight, and he didn't want to let the innkeeper down. He also needed the food he would earn. With a groan, he pushed himself to his feet.

It was slow work, and he had to do most of the shoveling with only one arm, but he managed to get the first stall clean. He would get the other one done. He only needed to rest a moment first. He slid down the wall and sat on the ground, still holding the rake. His ribs throbbed.

"What in Sollus's name?"

Bortha stood over him, a lantern in his hand.

"I'll get the other stall done. I didn't mean to fall asleep." Riam started to get up, but pain ripped through his chest. He fell back against the wall and slid back to the ground.

"Fool boy. I wasn't talking about that. You look as if you've been trampled. Did one of the horses get you?"

Riam put his hand on his ribs, bracing them, and took shallow sips of air. "Pekol was teaching me a lesson by kicking me in the ribs."

"You've blood all over your face."

"Apparently, I'm not a very good student." He would have laughed if it didn't hurt so much.

"Faen take that man." Bortha lifted Riam and carried him into the inn.

Instead of the kitchen, he continued on to a storage room. A small pallet sat in the corner. Bortha placed him on it and hung the lamp on a nail before rushing out.

He returned with a young woman. Her dark, curly hair came down below her shoulders, and she wore a tight-fitting blue dress that left enough of her chest exposed to make Riam look in the other direction despite the pain the sudden movement caused. He continued to watch the two from the corner of his eye.

"What happened to him?"

"What does it look like? His raker beat him."

"He's a churp?" She shrank back and wrinkled her nose.

"Get water and a towel to clean him up."

"We're caring for churps again?"

"No. We're caring for a boy who needs help."

"It's a crime to aid anyone with a glyph. Feeding them is bad enough. The warden warned you about this with Doby."

"I don't give a screet's ass what he said. Shut up and get something to clean him up, or you can find another inn to work."

The woman stomped her foot down. "Bortha—"

"I'm not joking, Serina. I'm going to go find a mediker. I expect him to be cleaned up by the time I return."

Serina's eyes shone with anger in the lantern light.

"And be gentle. I think his ribs are broken," Bortha called on the way out the door.

Serina looked Riam up and down. She frowned. "Well, I suppose I've cleaned up worse."

"Don't worry," Riam said. "It looks worse than it is."

"Somehow, little man, I doubt that."

The old mediker finished prodding at Riam's side. "Well, his ribs are where they should be, and I can't feel a break."

"That's good."

"That doesn't mean one or two aren't cracked or that something inside isn't damaged, but if he isn't dead by morning, I suspect he'll be fine within a tenday or two. The young heal fast."

"Reminds me of my first month with Pekol," a familiar voice said.

Stick stood in the doorway, leaning against the frame. Riam almost didn't recognize him. He looked nothing like the churp from the square. For one, he was clean, and that alone would have made it difficult to spot him in a crowd. Second, he wore new clothing and a green hat cocked to one side. He looked fine enough to be mistaken for a young landowner. The shirt was black and laced around the collar, except where it was notched open in the front, exposing the charm he always wore. A small pack hung over his shoulder.

"What are you doing here?"

"Came by to say farewell to you and Bortha. You're not the first churp he's helped survive Pekol's temper." The words were meant to be light, but a look of guilt flashed across Stick's face for an instant before his goofy smile returned.

"You're leaving the city?"

"Going home. I don't know that anyone will be happy to see me, but I need to check on Ma and let her know I'm alive. I owe her that at least, even if she doesn't want me to stay."

"You're leaving right now?" Riam asked.

"In the morning. It's a long way to the Green Isles."

"If you're done with the social call, I need to bind his chest," the mediker said before turning to Bortha. "He'll need it wrapped tight for a few days. Have him drink as much milk as he can. It'll help strengthen the bones."

"Thank you, I will," Bortha said.

"No thanks needed. You're paying for this, though for the life of me, I don't know why. Waste of money. Most churps don't make it through their sentence these days." The mediker pulled a rolled-up bandage from his bag. "The boy related to you or something?"

"No," Bortha replied curtly.

"Well, it's none of my business. Hold this here a moment," he told Riam, placing the end of the bandage on his uninjured side.

Riam put his hand on the end, and the mediker wrapped it around his chest several times. It hurt like the Fallen, but when the mediker finished and tied it off, he could breathe a little easier.

The man eased him down onto his back. "Course, if anyone asks, I wasn't here."

"Of course not," Bortha said, dropping a small pouch into the mediker's leather bag. There was a distinct clank when the pouch landed.

The mediker gave Riam an apologetic smile and a pat on the arm. He reached into the bag.

Riam thought the man was reaching for the coin. Instead he withdrew a short, smooth rod. *What is that for?*

He turned to Bortha and Stick. "I'll need both of you to hold him."

Bortha's hands clamped down on Riam's shoulders. Stick clasped his forehead and Serina turned away.

"You'll want to bite down on this while I set that nose." The rod was shoved roughly into his mouth.

Fight. Challenge one another. Let no tribe grow weak or lazy. War will keep our blades strong and our people hard. Only then will they be prepared to fight the gray demons north of the mountains.

But remember, the battle between Parron and Tomu has not ended, and while we fight among ourselves to stay strong, we must put away our squabbles when the Fallen Gods prepare to walk again. If any among us forget and lose their way, or worse, lose themselves to the Dark One, they must be cut away.

Nothing can be allowed to stop the tribes from gathering when the Destroyer of the Night comes to lead us in the final battle against Tomu.

—King Eisha Ryn at the First Gathering
of the People

CHAPTER 26

Ky'lem jumped from the raft and sank into ankle-deep mud. The blue-green water came to his waist, with clouds of silt swirling around his body. Thin yellow reeds climbed to heights that towered over him. He held his boots and the rest of his possessions over his head in one hand and the crude rope that led to the raft in the other. A thick swarm of river flies engulfed him, landing on his face and arms. He shook his head like a dog, trying to drive them away.

The flies were not so easily dissuaded. They buzzed past his ears and landed on his skin, biting at his scalp. Trying to dislodge them did little good. Not for the first time he wished he still wore the face paint of the Ti'yak. Besides providing concealment in the lush forest, the paint kept the flies away.

A loud splash came from behind him, and a wave slapped his back—Pai'le getting off the raft where Ni'ola lay. He gritted his teeth at the thought of her, and the muscles along his jaw flared out.

For half a moon he and the girl had traveled together, through deadly snows along the High Sun Path, down the jagged slopes of the mountains, through the rain forests of Ti'yak lands and finally south, carried by the great river.

They had faced death at the hands of the gray demons and a living corpse. They might face it again against the okulu'tan. What he hadn't counted on was facing death at the girl's hands, and him helpless to do anything.

The old spirit-walker had warned him, but his protection should've lasted until they made it to the Najalii. It had not. If it were not for her inexperience and Pai'le's assistance when the barrier to her magic collapsed, he would likely be dead and in a grave.

He looked up. The sun hung low in the east. The thin sliver of the moon floated in the sky near it. Tomorrow, Sollus would be completely eaten by Faen and the night cast into darkness. For tonight, they would camp here—their last night along the river—and in the morning Pai'le would return to Ti'yak lands while Ky'lem would take Ni'ola on to the okulu'tan village. If they left at sunrise, they would be there by late afternoon. It might not be soon enough.

He could feel her fading away. Her spirit surged and dimmed, like the waves of the deep water, sometimes pushing, sometimes calm. He did not know what the magic was doing to her mind, but it was taking a toll on her body. She did not speak, and her skin felt dry and hot. Her narrow face had lost much of its child fat, as if whatever magic held her in its grasp aged her, and unless he was as crazy as the old spirit-walker, she was now taller and more gaunt. They had separated her from the crystals, but it'd done little good. She remained in a trance. He feared for her—feared for both of them—for what would be lost if it was already too late.

There had been more to the spirit-walker's command than to marry the asha. He'd kept it out of his thoughts so that he would not reveal it across the bond. It was only now, when he was sure she could not hear him, that he dared let it come to mind. "Marry her after she is okulu'tan" had been the old one's words. "Marry her and raise the child as Ti'yak." A puzzling command. Any child of their marriage would be raised in a longhut. *So why give it? Did the okulu'tan think her bronze skin or her ancestors would make a difference?* It would not. The girl was obviously part Arillian with her dark coloring, but his people had traded with Arillians his whole life, and mixed-bloods were not shunned.

*Is it because I am chae'lon? A way of saying that I should
be released from the bond once we are married?* He hoped
this was the true reason. *How else am I to raise the child as
Ti'yak?* He would keep this part of the command to himself until he sniffed out the answer. It would not matter for
years—and might not matter at all if things went poorly
with the okulu'tan of the lake.

Ky'lem knew nothing of what would happen when they
reached the village. The old okulu'tan had only told him that
if they did not make it in time, prior to the night Faen swallowed the moon, the magic would consume both of them.
The old spirit-walker, however, could not have known the
barrier he'd placed over her would be broken prior to their
arrival.

Or had he? It was impossible to know what the old
spirit-walker planned.

In either case, the okulu'tan would help Ni'ola control the
magic—if they would help at all. He wasn't convinced they
would. If they did not, the chance of anyone uniting the
tribes would die with her, and so, too, might the world.

Behind him, he could feel Ni'ola's mind stir faintly. The
bond had changed after the barrier collapsed. Where before her thoughts and feelings came through clear and direct, now they hovered like ghosts or shouts in the distance
carried on the wind, too faint to be understood.

"Fallen's blood," Pai'le cursed from behind him. "What
are you waiting for? Hurry up before the flies take all my
blood."

Ky'lem pushed his way through the reeds toward the
shore, the mud sucking at his bare feet. Something large
slithered across his shin and he froze.

"What do you keep stopping for?"

"Hold." Careful not to move his legs, Ky'lem handed his
bundle and the rope back to Pai'le. He felt rough scales
slide over his skin.

After a bit of fumbling, Pai'le held both of their possessions awkwardly above his head.

Making no sudden moves, Ky'lem pulled his knife from
the bundle.

Fearing betrayal, Pai'le sloshed backward, out of reach,
and sank to his neck in a hole. He struggled to keep his
balance and their possessions out of the river.

Ky'lem ignored him and dropped down into the now murky water. The snake tried to strike when he grabbed it, but he yanked it away before its fangs could reach him. He stood and pulled it from the water, swinging it by the middle in a wide arc. The head swept by Pai'le, who was forced to step back into the hole he'd just climbed out of. His face sank beneath the surface.

Bringing the green-and-yellow snake around and over his head, Ky'lem slapped it onto the surface of the water, stunning the creature long enough to slip his grip forward and grasp it behind its head. It twisted and turned, wrapping its long body around his arm. He pinched at the back of the snake's head and the mouth opened, exposing long pale fangs that dripped thick, milky venom. He shoved the knife, point first, into the snake's mouth.

Pai'le came up sputtering and cursing. "Faen take you, Ky'lem!"

Ky'lem ignored him and ground the knife around in a tight circle, severing the snake's throat and spine. It was the easiest way to kill a water viper without an ax or a sword— their skins were as tough as mastonhide. He left the knife in the snake's mouth and held the long body up as explanation. "Dinner," he said.

With a great amount of splashing and cursing, Pai'le stormed past him toward the bank, pulling the raft behind him.

A short time later a small fire crackled in front of them. Pai'le knelt across from Ky'lem, scraping the inside of the snake's skin with a knife. Ni'ola sat on a log nearby, staring off into the distance. She had not moved since he placed her there. *Is it a trick of the light from the fire, or is there a red tint to her eyes?* He imagined the old spirit-walker's red, piercing eyes surrounded by Ni'ola's face.

Ky'lem shivered and turned back to the snake roasting over the fire. It looked cooked enough. He leaned forward and tore free a strand of meat. It was greasy and tasteless, but it was hot. They'd need their strength for the final leg of the journey. He placed a morsel of the meat in Ni'ola's mouth, and she chewed.

She'd been like this since Pai'le hit her over the head with the tree limb. After he'd done it, she'd remained unconscious for some time. When Ky'lem had thrown water on her to wake her, she'd opened her eyes in a vacant stare. He'd tried everything to rouse her from the trance—more water, yelling her name, prodding, and even a few hard slaps across her cheeks. Nothing worked. She would eat if you put food in her mouth and walk if you pulled her along by the hand, but other than following simple prompts, her condition hadn't changed since starting down the river.

Across from him, Pai'le stopped scraping and peered into the flames, a grim expression on his face.

"You should eat, too," Ky'lem said to Pai'le. "It is a long journey back to the longhuts."

The big warrior didn't reach for the meat. Instead, he stared at Ky'lem over the flames. They cracked and popped, sending sparks into the air. "I no longer see you without your face paint—only a pachna who frets over an asha who will soon be dead. She will die, you know."

"Perhaps it is your fault. Perhaps you hit her too hard."

"For the last time. I did not. I know my own strength and how much of it to use. Whatever ails her, it is from the spirit-walker's magic, not the blow to her head."

Ky'lem grunted. He believed the big warrior, but it didn't make things any better between them. He knew the blow had been necessary, but it still angered him that the big man had struck her. Ni'ola might be an asha, but her heart and mind were as strong as any child of the people. She did not deserve the big man's scorn.

"I could kill her for you," Pai'le said. "Perhaps while she is like this, she will not pull you into the great beyond with her."

A low growl came from Ky'lem's throat—a primal response. *I will never allow anyone to harm her—not you, not the okulu'tan.*

"Easy." Pai'le held up his hands. "It was only an offer of mercy. I simply do not want you to die when the magic takes her. What will I do with no Ky'lem to argue with me before the council?"

"You will do as you always do, lead Ti'yak warbands head-on against the gray demons. Someone else will take my place to argue the stupidity of butting heads with a ram."

Pai'le tilted his head. The quizzical arch of his eyebrows told Ky'lem the big warrior was trying to decide if he'd just been called stupid.

"I have the strength in my arms and the desire in my heart to fight the gray bastards, but I don't have your patience," Pai'le said at last. His voice was quiet, lacking its usual boisterous tone. He threw a small twig onto the flames and stood. "Look at the results of this raid." He began to pace. "You and I are all that is left. I always figured you thought too much about the future and not enough about the present—but perhaps you are right. Meeting the demons head-on may not always be the best method."

Ky'lem nearly dropped the meat he held. All these years of bickering and the man chose now, when Ky'lem could do nothing and would likely die, to finally make sense. "Make Tal'nar your new second. He uses his head more than the others. If you can control your desire to smash at the gray demons with a club long enough to listen to him, you will become a great warleader."

Pai'le stopped and squared himself to Ky'lem, a hand on his sword hilt. "I am already a great leader."

There was some truth to the statement, and Ky'lem wished he'd been more careful with his words. Pai'le was a good leader when it came to getting men to follow him and to fight beyond the moments they would surrender to their fears. Where he had trouble was keeping warriors alive beyond the first fight. "I meant no offense, brother. You *are* a good warleader, but a great warleader worries at the loss of a single warrior because he plans for the next fight . . . and the one after that."

"Bah. Let the old men on the council worry about the future. I am the tip of their blade. Made only to be thrust at the demons."

"You could be more."

For a moment, the big warrior was silent, his mind churning on the idea. Then he laughed. "You are a dangerous man, Ky'lem. I've known this since you forced peace with the Arpatha. As much as it saddens me, perhaps it is good you will not live more than a day or two longer."

"Just because she is ill does not mean I will die, and I will still be Ti'yak in my heart, even though I am her pachna."

"If you live, you will serve an okulu'tan. There will come a time when . . ." He looked at Ni'ola, pausing while he chose his words. ". . . your spirit-taker's needs will come before the tribe. You will have no choice but to side against us."

Ky'lem had nothing to say in response. They both knew the truth of the statement and which side Ky'lem must take.

Pai'le watched the flames dance. He did not look up toward Ky'lem, and when the big man spoke again, the words were soft. "The okulu'tan lied to us both, Ky'lem. I hope your sacrifice is worth it, and that you find a way to unite us all somehow."

The words were as much support to Ky'lem's decision as the big man was capable of making. In all the years they'd fought side by side, neither had ever told the other their true thoughts. "While I may be a fool, if bonding with an asha is the risk I must take to save our people, then I would do it a thousand—" A wave of dizziness swept over him, cutting off his words. He put a hand down to keep from falling over.

"What is it?" Pai'le asked. He moved to Ky'lem's side, helping to steady him. "Are you ill?" There was true concern in his voice.

"No . . . it is Ni'ola," he managed between deep breaths. He hated showing weakness in front of the big warrior, but there was nothing he could do. Without Pai'le's support, he would have tumbled forward into the fire. The world bucked around him, as if he rode a wild, crazed horse—one that had jumped off a cliff. When he thought it could get no worse, it did.

Ni'ola tore at his spirit. He could feel the life flowing out of his body—could feel her drinking it in greedily. Whatever was happening to her, she needed his strength, and he had no choice but to give it. That is what a pachna was made for, to protect the okulu'tan and to provide the life they needed for the magic when there was nowhere else to draw from. He feared that in her condition, she would not limit how much she took.

Careful, asha, you will kill us both. He doubted she could hear the thought, but he threw it toward her on the chance she might.

Pai'le's eyebrows rose. "Should I hit her again?" His voice came to Ky'lem in warbled loud and soft tones.

"No!" he snapped back. He hoped it wouldn't come to that. He would not see her hurt any more than she'd already been injured. Besides, he was not sure that it would do any good.

In the pouch at Ky'lem's side, the crystals flared hot, burning him through the leather. *Should I return them to her?* Without them, he was the only reservoir she could draw from, but her inability to control the gems had nearly killed her the last time she held them. It hadn't done much good for him either. His shoulder still throbbed from where he'd landed on it.

Faen's ass! There was too much he didn't know, and with no okulu'tan here to help, all he could do was guess. Giving her the crystals felt like the right thing to do. If they were responsible for her going into this trance, perhaps they were necessary to get her out.

More energy was torn from him, and he wilted to the ground in Pai'le's hands.

"Give . . . crystals," he mumbled. It took all his remaining strength to get the words out.

Pai'le drew back as if Ky'lem had swung another water viper in front of him. "She almost killed you with them the last time."

"She is . . . killing me . . . without them." Ky'lem's head fell back against the log, and he closed his eyes. "Do it."

"You are as insane as the old spirit-walker," Pai'le said.

Ky'lem felt Pai'le tear the pouch from his waist. Giving the asha the crystals would either save them or kill them. He wasn't sure which, but he could think of nothing else. Maybe Pai'le was right. Maybe he should have let the big man knock her unconscious one more time.

Pai'le upended the pouch into Ni'ola's hand. The plants around her began to wither and die. Ky'lem felt their strength flowing into her. It was too late to change his mind now.

"Must you leave now?" Pai'le asked. "Beasts hunt the land surrounding the lake at night. You couldn't fight off a ga'ginga pup, much less a mergol, in your condition."

While he wasn't as feeble as Pai'le suggested, it had taken more than a glass to regain the strength needed to set out for the lake. In that time, Ni'ola had aged at least a year. He was sure of it. Returning the crystals had worked, but whatever the magic was doing to her, the crystals were accelerating it. Ky'lem was right about one thing, though. Traveling at night held many dangers that could be avoided in daylight—especially this night when so little of Sollus was left in the sky—but he couldn't wait for morning. He had no choice.

I am the warrior who slew three gray demons in a single day. I am stronger than Faen's darkness. Some of the weakness slid away as he recited the mantra. He stood up straight. He would not fail.

"At least wait until the morning is closer and you are more rested. Who is acting like a charging bull now?"

"This is not the same, Pai'le. Look at her. If I wait until morning, she will be an old woman by the time we reach the Najalii."

"I admit she does look different, but it does not matter. As I told you before, she will die. If not from this, then from the okulu'tan who will kill you both. Take a chance and end it quickly now, brother, before she takes you with her to the beyond."

Ky'lem grunted in disgust. *Not this again.* He'd thought they had moved past it after their words over the fire. "I thought you understood. No matter how she dies, I will follow her. If we can get to the lake in time, the okulu'tan will save her. I will not let them harm her."

"Phaw. The Ky'lem I know would risk death to be free of the okulu'tan, not hide behind the skirt of a foreign asha. Even if they do accept her, what kind of survival is being her pachna? I see no way for you to reach your goal."

Ky'lem ignored Pai'le's goading and hung one of the two waterskins over his shoulder. It hung like a stone weight around his neck. He was strong enough to make the journey, but he wouldn't be much use in protecting her along the way.

"Sollus's blessings be with you during your journey home, Pai'le. I am leaving. See to my firstwife. If she is mistreated, the truce with the Arpatha will not hold."

Pai'le laughed. "All that is before you, and your first concern is another tribe's daughter. You are chae'lon. It's no longer your concern."

"Pai'le—"

The big warrior held up his hand. "Rest easy. She has the sharpest tongue in the village, but I will ensure she finds the appropriate husband to keep peace with the Arpatha."

Ky'lem watched Pai'le's face for signs he lied. The big warrior surprised him again. There were none. "Thank you."

"Go." Pai'le shooed him. "Take your asha and die in the darkness."

Ky'lem took Ni'ola's hand and pulled her up. She rose to her feet, unaware of the world around her. Stepping off, he pulled her with him into the blackness of the forest.

"Sollus's blessing be upon you, pachna," Pai'le called behind them.

Ky'lem steered Ni'ola around a patch of deep shadows. As if Pai'le's earlier use of the beast's name had summoned it, a mergol roared in the distance. A second, much farther away, bellowed in response. The forest beasts were larger and stronger than their mountain cousins, the merdon. He would need more than Sollus's blessing to get them through Faen's darkness this night.

CHAPTER 27

The night passed, with progress measured in the hesitant steps and stumbles of a blind man. The forest canopy above Ky'lem and Ni'ola blocked out all traces of the thin moon. Ky'lem could see no more than a rod in front of him, and that only by the faint glow of the crystals that escaped between Ni'ola's fingers. Ky'lem held her wrist, keeping her hand at shoulder level to get as much of the weak light in front of them as possible. Their movements were an awkward dance of tugs and turns that slowed them every bit as much as the darkness of the forest.

Any progress is better than none in this mess.

Ni'ola's trance and the absence of Sollus were not the only things slowing them down. Frequent pools of putrid marsh water blocked their way. It forced them into a winding course that more than doubled their travel time. The stale pools smelled of rotten eggs and rotting vegetation, and the soggy ground coated their feet with mud and slime, but it meant the lake was near. As long as Ky'lem kept the worst of the wetlands to his left, they would not get lost, and once they were through the marsh, the rocky shore would make for faster travel.

Ky'lem ducked under a web strung between two moss-covered trees. Ni'ola did not. Calm and impassive, she walked into the sticky threads. The web wrapped around her face, and a black-and-red spider, easily bigger than Ky'lem's thumb, scrambled down the side of her neck and disappeared under her shirt.

Seeing it made Ky'lem's skin go cold. His heart pounded while he lifted her shirt gently until he spotted movement beside one of her small breasts. He gently swept the spider away with the back of his hand. It fell to the ground and scrambled toward her feet.

Ky'lem jerked her out of the spider's path. Once the thing disappeared in the darkness, he yanked Ni'ola's shirt this way and that, checking her skin for bites. Finding nothing, he wrapped his arms around Ni'ola protectively and lifted her into the air in an embrace. "I am sorry, asha," he mumbled into her ear.

Stupid. He'd been careless for only an instant and nearly lost her to one of the smallest dangers in the forest—one easily avoided. If the spider had bitten her, she would be dead before sunrise.

What am I doing? He put Ni'ola down so quickly she nearly fell.

He was Ky'lem, a great warrior of the people, and she a foreigner. She might become his okulu'tan, and maybe even his wife someday, but she was . . . she was . . . He'd been about to use the word "nothing," that she was merely a tool—a means for him to unite the tribes—but that was no longer true. *Curse the old spirit-walker's magic. I will protect her, but I will never truly care for her. Never.*

He snatched her wrist and hauled her forward. Their awkward dance through the marsh continued.

Sometime between midnight and dawn, while stumbling along the rocky shore of the Najalii, Ky'lem heard the deep roar of a mergol behind them. A second answered, far too close for his liking. There was something different about these two. He could feel it in his bones. He'd heard them off and on as they moved through wetlands, but he'd never before heard two at once without them bellowing challenges at one another. The beasts were territorial and far

more likely to attack their own kind if one ventured into
another's hunting grounds.

Ky'lem moved closer to the shore. By the light of the
stars, the water sat black and impenetrable, with the barest
of waves lapping at the rocks. If it were any other lake, he
would take Ni'ola into the water and continue their journey
in the shallows along the water's edge. If one of the mergol
had their scent and decided they were prey, it would be
hunting them already and moving far faster than he could
travel with Ni'ola in tow. The beasts were smart, but they
couldn't follow a trail that wasn't there—especially with
the breeze carrying their scent out over the lake. The Najalii was sacred, though, and it was against the laws of Eisha
for all but the okulu'tan to break its surface.

A mergol roared, closer this time, and even with his
deep-seated obedience to the edicts, he still considered
stepping into the water. The okulu'tan might forgive the
asha if they accepted her, but a pachna they never would.
They would execute him for the transgression without
hesitation, and there would be no hiding it from them. He
picked up a rock and stopped himself short of throwing it
into the lake. Instead, he turned and threw it into the
forest.

*Sollus take me. Does everything have to be so cursed
difficult this night?* He had to save her . . . had to. Otherwise, his life and the life of the old okulu'tan had been for
nothing. He caught Ni'ola's blank stare in the corner of his
eye. *Her life as well. She might very well be more important
than either of us.* It was hard to admit that.

He looked at her more closely, as if her appearance
alone would answer the question of her importance. She
had continued to age through the night, growing taller and
more filled out. Her once baggy breeches and shirt were
now too tight for the body that wore them. No longer an
asha, she'd grown into an asha'han, a young woman. He
could still see the child in her eyes and cheekbones, and her
breasts were not as large as they could be, but she was not
unappealing. Her dark skin gave her an exotic look, and
the scar on her forehead had thinned to a barely visible
line. If they were back home in his village, many a young
warrior would seek to add her to his longhut. He'd never
allow it, of course. While he doubted he would ever see

anything other than the asha in her face, no matter how much she aged—even if she was made old and gray—he'd never let another have her.

He didn't understand this magic, and he didn't like things he didn't understand. *Where were her thoughts? Does she know what is happening to her, or will she wake in shock at the changes, an asha'han with the mind of a child?* He prayed to Sollus this was part of the old spirit-walker's plan and that his dreams were not lost like her youth.

The mergol behind them let out another roar. Ky'lem looked to the water longingly, but he couldn't bring himself to break the edict. They must take their chances along the shore and with the beasts.

They traveled faster, but it was not long before Ky'lem knew both of the mergols pursued them. The one to their rear was not moving fast, but it was getting closer by the sound of its frequent roars. The two were calling to each other, like a ga'ginga pack, boxing them in against the lake. Ky'lem had never heard of the beasts working together. Only one explanation made sense. *An okulu'tan is controlling them.* Whoever had attacked them in the pass worked to prevent them from reaching the village. *What better time than now, while I am weak and Ni'ola is helpless . . . and Pai'le gone?* That struck him as odd. No attempts had come while Pai'le traveled with them. It had to be a coincidence. Perhaps his unseen enemy had been unable to find them on the river.

Another roar sounded and was echoed by the second beast. Ky'lem quickened their pace as much as he dared, even though he knew it would do little good. It took all his will not to hurl Ni'ola and himself into the water. It might be all that could save them.

And then it was too late. To his right, not fifty paces away, one of the mergol broke from the forest and let out a triumphant roar. It ran in an apelike, loping gait toward them. It stood half again taller than a man, with hair of mottled brown and yellow and long arms that ended in talons as sharp as knives. Its face was hideous—a snout that was flat, exposing open nostrils, and flanked by dagger-length tusks that protruded to either side. Its eyes and ears were manlike, but its neck sat hidden behind a thick, coarse mane that made it difficult to strike at the beast's throat.

Ky'lem had fought only one in his lifetime, as part of a full warband armed with spears. They'd lost three men to the beast.

Ky'lem shoved Ni'ola to the ground and drew both his weapons to meet the attack. It would do little good. He had no chance alone against a mergol at his best. Now he faced two, and he was in little better shape than the asha'han he guarded. *Pai'le was right. I should have waited until morning.*

The mergol closed the distance. He would not be able to dodge the beast's charge as he had the Draegoran's horse on the other side of the mountains. At least this death would be an honorable one. That he was chae'lon did not matter. He would die in battle as a true warrior of the Esharii. No one would know here in this world, but he would take the honor with him to the great beyond.

He crouched, weapons ready. A calm came over him. He had no fear. He only wished that he'd had a chance to kill the spirit-taker who controlled the beast. The man was unworthy of the people and deserved a coward's death. Ky'lem had a sudden vision of the old spirit-taker sitting in his tent on the plains with the golden bowl in front of him. *". . . the trap failed. The Church of Man's agent stirred the creatures up . . . making them difficult to control."*

Ky'lem straightened from his crouch and lowered his sword and knife.

"You have returned again, spirit-taker," he called. "Why do you fear me so much that you desire my death?" His mind screamed at him to run or fight, but he held himself upright and calm as the beast barreled toward him. If he were wrong about the okulu'tan, he would die without striking a single blow against the beast. It risked his honor. *The tribe is more important than the truth . . . or my honor.* He hoped he was right.

The mergol slid to a stop less than a rod away, its massive claw raised with talons ready to tear Ky'lem in half with a single swing. Saliva dripped from its mouth. Its bloodshot eyes darted from Ky'lem to its own trembling arm, but it did not strike. It sniffed at the air in confusion.

"You are a fool, Ti'yak, but a brave fool," the mergol said in a guttural tongue over a mouth full of tusk and teeth never meant for human speech. "If you were not bonded to the asha, I would reward you by taking you as one of my pachna."

"I would not serve a spirit-taker who attacks behind the eyes of others while safe from harm."

The beast growled low in its throat, and its body shook in restrained eagerness. "I have faced dangers far greater than you could imagine. Not all dangers wear a sword or burnish claws. But I am not without honor. Step aside. She will feel nothing while trapped within the ways, and your death will be much less painful if the bond takes you instead of the mergol."

Ky'lem's eyes widened. *Ni'ola travels the paths of the future? How? Few spirit-takers had the power to become spirit-walkers, and she'd done it as soon as she'd come in contact with the crystals.* In the trees Ky'lem heard the second beast approaching. He must stall a bit longer. He needed both beasts here for what he had in mind.

"You say you have honor, yet you use the dead and a mergol to kill a helpless asha. If it is not me you fear, then you must be frightened of her. What makes you fear an asha so?"

The beast let out a roar that nearly knocked Ky'lem from his feet. For an instant, the mergol broke free of the okulu'tan's control. It swung one of its deadly claws toward Ky'lem.

Ky'lem didn't move, and the claw passed over his head, close enough to feel the wind.

The mergol wrestled with itself, twisting and shaking. Slowly, it calmed.

"I fear nothing, pachna," the okulu'tan said.

"Then why the attacks? Why the need to kill her?"

"It is a waste of time to tell secrets to a dead man. You cannot stop this, so why fight? Why feel these claws ripping your body apart? Your death will have no meaning. It is only the bond that compels you to save her."

The second mergol appeared while the okulu'tan spoke through the beast. It ran along the shoreline and roared its challenge. In front of him, the mergol fought to turn and face the newcomer, but the okulu'tan held it fast.

"I do not protect her because of the bond," Ky'lem said. "I protect her because she will help me unite our people."

The second mergol reached them and slid to a stop,

roaring in frustration. Fury boiled behind its eyes. Whether directed at him or the other mergol, Ky'lem could not tell. It swung its claws at the empty air and stomped in a circle.

"Ri'jarra was a fool. He traveled the ways one too many times and paid for it with his sanity. He wasted his life sending you back with this foreign asha. I am simply cleaning up the abomination his arrogance created."

"I think you are scared, okulu'tan. Scared the old spirit-walker was right. Scared because she is already more powerful than you." Both beasts roared at this, and their muscles rippled under the mottled hair. Ky'lem took a step back but did not let up. "I think you are not worthy of being called okulu'tan. Tomu stirs and it is time for change, time for the people to unite and destroy the gray demons. You will not be a part of that change. If the asha lives, she will know your true heart and cast you aside for your weakness." He put conviction into his words, and with a start, realized he believed what he was saying. They were not simple taunts. "You have the honor of a Draegoran whore and are unworthy to be called Esharii. I will see you stripped of everything you desire before you die."

Ky'lem flicked his hand up, hurling his knife toward the beast's face. The mergol brought its claws up to protect its eyes, but that wasn't Ky'lem's target. The knife buried itself in the beast's snout. A deafening roar of rage and pain split the air. The beast backed away, clawing at its face.

Ky'lem launched himself into the air at the second mergol. He slashed at the beast's head and ignored the talons that tore down his side and leg. He needed one good strike. The mergol ducked away from the swing, but Ky'lem's sword caught the side of the beast's head and slid downward, shaving an ear from the scalp.

The mergol roared in fury and batted Ky'lem away with one swing of its arm. The beast's claw tore across the skin and muscles of his back, and Ky'lem's sword flew from his hands. He landed in a heap on the rocks of the shore.

Fire burned across Ky'lem's back, down his side, and through his leg. He tried to stand but couldn't. He looked at his thigh and saw bone beneath the torn skin and muscle.

The two mergols circled and roared their challenges at each other. They moved in fits and jerks as the okulu'tan fought for control, but pain and the smell of blood pushed them beyond the spirit-taker's abilities. With a final roar, the two beasts closed on each other. It made a fearsome sight. Talon and tusk slashed at inhuman speed as the beasts collided and tore gaping wounds one upon the other.

Ky'lem tried to crawl to Ni'ola's side, but his arms and legs would not work. Too many muscles and tendons had been severed, and each attempt to move felt like his skin was being torn from his body all over again. *Return, Ni'ola! Wake and flee into the water. Do not let my death be for nothing!* Ky'lem screamed the words through the bond.

He put his head down on the blood-drenched rocks. His vision faded. He no longer saw the mergols, but he heard the snarls and roars of their conflict. *Wake for me, Ni'ola. Wake for me . . .*

CHAPTER 28

Blood pooled and seeped into the dark-stained sand. Nola's opponent lay before her, writhing on the ground. He arched his back one final time, heels digging in, and then collapsed. The boy still breathed, but gurgling and wheezing sounds accompanied the rise and fall of his chest. The boy was strong, but he'd relied too much on techniques designed to fight others who equaled him in strength—fire forms at first in the offense, then earth forms to defend when he'd realized she would not meet him blow for blow. Nola had spent most of her time training in the more precise forms of wind and water. Her attacks had flowed around his defenses with no more difficulty than a river flows around a rock. She had no remorse for killing the other boy. He would have killed her to gain his freedom, and fighting an opponent as they were, instead of how you expected them to be, was as good a lesson as any for him to take into death.

She knelt beside the boy, careful to stay away from his clenched hands—although she doubted he had any fight left—and used one of his baggy pant legs to wipe her blade free of blood. When it was clean to her satisfaction, she took a step back and sat down cross-legged in the sand to wait. She'd pierced a lung with her last thrust, effectively ending the match, but it would not be over until he died. She couldn't help him along on the journey now that he no longer fought. "An opponent must be allowed to experience their own death, just as they have their life," were the words of her kyden. It wasn't a quick death, but it wasn't a long one either. Half a sandglass later, the boy's breathing ceased.

Her shoulders sagged the barest fraction when the doors to the arena creaked opened. She would not be allowed to join with the crystal in her blade today. It was only mild disappointment, however. Most recruits were not given the honor of linking with their blades after their first match, and she would still receive her second glyph. She was proud of that—few of her fellow recruits had received their second glyph—especially since she'd started her training a year behind the others because of her time with the Esharii. It'd taken half a year to return from the lake of life after escaping, and then another half-year of frustration while she waited on the council to decide her fate.

Today, she'd proven their decision correct. She kept her face a blank mask, head up and back locked straight, devoid of any telling body language that would display her pride. The kydens in the seats around her did not approve of vanity in any form. She grabbed a handful of sand, rose to her feet, and held it over her opponent.

"Dalor salorea lon braeda!" She opened her hand, letting the dark grains pour through her fingers. *The death of one advances another.*

Nola moved toward the doorway. Instead of the hallway beyond, the doorway glowed with a surreal light that tugged at her mind. She stopped in front of it and tilted her head, studying it. The glow brought a tickle of familiarity, like she once knew its purpose but had forgotten. Her kyden had not mentioned this part of the match. *Am I supposed to go through or wait?* She glanced back over her shoulder at the kydens. None seemed to notice the glow, or if they did, they acted as if it was as natural as the air around them.

Taking a deep breath, she stepped through the light . . .

. . . and returned to her longhut after checking on Hop'san. The woman was bedridden with fever dreams and none of

Ni'ola's medicines made a difference. She would try adding deathroot to the palic tomorrow. It wouldn't help with the sickness, but a few drops might give the woman a night of true sleep. If she didn't get better soon, Ni'ola would be forced to try more dangerous herbs.

"Mother!" her daughter shouted and ran to her.

"My beautiful asha!" Ni'ola lifted Baht into the air and spun her in a circle before putting her down. "Where is your father?"

Baht pulled on her wrist, leading her toward the back door of the longhut. "He is with Wahn'le and Pan'le. They are training. Grandfather is with them."

Ni'ola frowned at the thought of her sons training for war, especially with their grandfather Pai'le. The boys revered him and loved to listen to his stories, but he was always too loud and boisterous, too full of pride. His stories would get the boys killed if they ever tried to live up to the feats he described.

She'd lived with the Ti'yak for two dozen years and had been married to Kahn'le, her second husband, for sixteen of them, but the Esharii's single-minded pursuit of fighting still made her recoil inside. She understood and followed the edicts of Eisha Ryn, and she believed with all her heart that they were necessary to prepare the people for what must one day come, yet she found it difficult to embrace the warfare and death that came with those edicts. It went beyond the fear all mothers have for their children, back to the small shards of her childhood memories that remained and to the loss of her first husband.

Always the sword and the spear. It would be so until the Sko'dran came and the Esharii defeated the gray demons.

Baht led her to the back door that opened to the practice yard. The doorway filled with a shimmering light she could not see through. She knew this light. It would take her away. She tried to stop, but Baht still held her wrist and pulled her forward into . . .

. . . battle.

Fire arced from the smoke in front of Ni'ola and splashed into the ranks of Esharii warriors to her right. She couldn't afford to spend the energy she held in her tan'tari to protect them, even though her forearms shone bright with power. Men and women shrieked their defiance at Tomu's army until they perished from the flames. Arrow, rock, and spear followed, and scores more fell crushed and pierced. Yet still her people held. They had no choice. There was nowhere left to go.

Around her, the once dense forests and fertile fields of the Esharii homelands were gone, replaced with ash and soot. Only the occasional blackened stump rose up in defiance to proclaim what had once thrived here, and the destruction stretched for a thousand steads north to the mountains—and beyond. For all Ni'ola knew, her former homeland lay just as desolate after the gray demons' defeat of the Church of Man. Wherever Tomu's army marched, no life remained. Behind her, the Najalii was a fetid quagmire of dead animals and rotting vegetation. Despite a thousand sacrifices, the Fallen God Parron did not have the power to wake and fight his ancient enemy.

A deafening thunder built up, shaking the ground beneath her. From the smoke a line of horsemen appeared, stretching farther than she could see to either direction. They charged with long, steel-tipped lances held out before them, and a sea of footmen followed behind. She recognized the red-caped spearmen of Thae, the black coats of the swordsmen of Mirlond, and so many others besides them. All the lands of the Covenant were represented in the horde that charged toward her people, and among them rode the gray demons, urging the army forward with blazing swords held high. The enemy held nothing back in the final attack against Parron's resting place. The lancers would shatter the Esharii, and the footmen who followed would cut the survivors of the charge to pieces.

But the Esharii were not done fighting.

Ni'ola raised her arms and pulled in the strength of the Ti'yak, adding it to the power she'd saved for this moment. All members of the Ti'yak tribe were her pachna now, and so it was for the other tribes. She was one of seven new enta'esk okulu, the spirit-warrior for her tribe.

Ni'ola released the torrent of power she held within her and sent it to the creatures below the earth—into the worms and ants, into boring beetles and larvae, into anything that

remained alive below the charred surface. The power she
forced into the creatures could not be contained by their
small forms. For a stretch two hundred paces wide, the
earth below the horsemen heaved upward and exploded.
Horses screamed and died with their riders. Down the line
of Esharii, the other spirit-warriors followed her example.
Six more explosions erupted below the riders, and hundreds more horsemen died.

It was not enough to stop the charge.

Ni'ola pulled in more power—so much she nearly lost
control. At the last instant before the power burned her
away, she lowered her hands. Howling winds screamed and
buffeted the riders. Men tumbled from saddles or were
blinded by the ash the wind carried.

The charge slowed but did not stop. For every rider that
fell, two more took their place. They were less than fifty
paces away—close enough to make out the determination
on their faces. Tomu lived behind their eyes, and they
would never break and run.

Ni'ola pointed at a rider before her, and a line of fire
burst from her fingertips. It burned through the rider's chest
and took another behind him. Both men toppled from their
saddles. She did it again and again. There was no shortage
of targets, but her strength dwindled. She could only pull so
much from her people, or they would be too weak to fight.
She had done as much as she could against the horsemen.
Now it was the people's turn to fight.

The charge slammed into the Esharii line, spears and
lances splintering in a staccato that was interspersed with
battle cries and screams. Where the horsemen held together, they bowled through the line, trampling all in their
path. In other places the Esharii warriors held, and the
horsemen were pulled from their mounts and hacked to
death by heavy Arillian blades.

In front of her, the gray demons swarmed toward her
and the other spirit-warriors like iron filings to lodestones.
At least ten angled toward her through the mass of footmen who came next. She could not stop so many. The Draegorans' powers had grown a hundredfold with Tomu's
awakening. One leveled his sword toward her, and fire shot
from the blade.

Ni'ola raised her hands defensively, and the flames hit a

wall of air in front of her. She felt a second attack join the first and then a third. Spirit-fire sprayed out around the wall and turned the tribesmen beside her to ash. The attack forced the wall back toward her, and Ni'ola's feet slid in the dirt, pushed back with it. She drew more power from around her, and for a moment, the wall held.

More Draegorans joined the attack. Her shield flickered, threatening to shatter. She glanced back, looking desperately for a place that might protect her. Instead of the low hills and lake that should have been behind her, she saw a glowing square of light, and the Draegorans pushed her toward it.

It must be a trap.

She redoubled her efforts. Her shield held, but she still slid hand-by-hand closer to the wall behind her. Her shoulder reached it. She felt nothing—no pain and no resistance. *It was not a Draegoran trap. It was—*

Her shield failed and she was thrown backward through the air, tumbling and landing . . .

. . . on her side in the grass next to Riam with her clothes strung over the nearby fountain in the courtyard. They lay side by side, and he drew her into an embrace and kissed her with the eagerness of too much wine and too little patience. The rough hair of his chest tickled her breasts, and the warmth of his skin in contrast to the cool, night air sent a shiver down her body. She pushed back one side of his long dark hair, revealing the wolf on his neck, and stroked the rough stubble along his jaw. His tongue teased along the edges of her lips while a hand roamed down her back till it cupped one of her bare cheeks. She responded by grinding her hips against him. His shaft swelled in response.

Riam groaned and withdrew from the kiss. His mouth slid along her jawline to her ear. "I'm so glad you came back," he whispered. "I blamed myself for years . . ."

She placed her hand over his mouth. "Shhh . . ."

He could not see the sneer that formed in response to his lies. All he cared for was her body. She was merely something new to him—something exotic he could possess as a toy for a time and discard. It had to be this way.

While his embrace had sent a shiver through her body, it was a purely physical response to the vileness of Tomu's spirit that suffused his touch and Tomu's foul scent that rose above the cinnamon oil he wore—or perhaps the shiver had come from her eagerness for her true task this night. It was not his touch, she told herself. It could not be.

After days of letting him defile her body and pretending to enjoy it, tonight his life, and the lives of all the Draegorans on this cursed island would be taken. While he seduced her, the Sko'dran and five hundred warriors, the strongest from across the tribes, swam for the island, smuggled north by Arillian ships and their Church of Man allies. Hers would be the first strike in the attack, killing the kyden of the Wolves.

Once Riam was dead, she would get her tan'tari back from Ky'lem. She felt far more vulnerable without the crystals than she did nude in the courtyard surrounded by her enemies, but the plan wouldn't have worked if she still carried them. The Draegorans would never have believed her story of escaping and returning if they knew she was linked to the tan'tari of an okulu'tan.

Ni'ola glanced up. The moon neared its summit.

She pushed Riam over to his back and straddled him. His hands moved to the outside of her thighs and then down to guide himself into her, but she brushed him away and did not let him enter. That time was behind her and she would not allow this final indignity on the night that would be her victory. Instead, she slid herself back and forth along his length. He would die wanting and panting like a dog, a slave to his passion just as all Draegorans were slaves to Tomu.

He squeezed at her breasts as she continued to work him beneath her. His breathing grew labored, and he moaned with the heat of desire to finish.

Ni'ola's breath grew ragged along with his. Warmth flowed up from where she ground along him, creating an ache within her. She wanted him inside her—wanted him.

I am not a slave to this. I will not betray my people.

She looked to the clothes nearby, where her knife lay hidden, but she did not reach for it or cease her movements upon him. If anything, they became more frantic.

Sweat glistened on the curves and ridges of Riam's body

below her. The smell of cinnamon drowned out her thoughts. His hands found the sides of her waist and she could hold back no longer.

Instead of the knife, she found herself reaching for him. She lifted herself and he slid into her, filling her, making them one. She closed her eyes, savoring the feel of him deep inside her.

An alarm bell rang out in the night and was quickly followed by the shouts of men.

Riam sat up, his head whipping left and right as he searched for danger. He twisted his body and pulled away from her.

"No!" Ni'ola shouted. She dove for the knife and fumbled with her clothes to retrieve it. Once she had it, she spun around toward Riam.

It was too late. He buttoned his breeches with one hand and shook the scabbard from his sword with the other.

He raised an eyebrow, yet he did not look angry—the opposite. "If whatever is out there gets this far, I doubt that knife will do you any good." He walked confidently to her, wrapped his free arm around her, and, pulling her up onto her toes, kissed her passionately. This time, there was nothing teasing about his tongue.

The smell of cinnamon filled Ni'ola's head once more. Her blood pounded. She still wanted him. *Strike now!*

Her knife hand dropped slowly to her side.

He withdrew from the kiss and sat her on the fountain. "I'll return from dealing with whatever this is before you have time to clothe yourself," he said and was gone.

Ni'ola put her hands to her face and wept for the first time since she'd met with the old spirit-walker in her youth. She had failed the people and herself. Shame filled her.

Beside her, the pool shimmered. She wiped the tears from her face. She remembered something about the light . . . something important.

She reached for it and snatched her hand back before touching it. There was great pain on the other side of the light. He was dying.

"Ky'lem." She said the name softly. *But how can that be? He is here with the other warriors, attacking the Draegorans.* She could feel his presence through the bond. His heart raced, but his thoughts were calm. It was as if there were two Ky'lems—one here in the world and another in the light.

The feeling came again—filled with desperate, agonizing pain, as if the skin of Ky'lem's body had been torn away. Ni'ola's fingers whitened where they gripped the fountain's edge.

She reached for the light again, but hesitated short of touching it. *What if this was a trap? Did Riam know her true plan this night? Had he only pretended and this was some game he played?*

A third cry of pain came, and it didn't matter. Ky'lem needed her. She had no choice but to go to his aid. She dove into the fountain, her mind reaching for him, and . . .

. . . sat up to blood and chaos on the shore of the Najalii. The world was hazy and dark, filled with snarls and howls. She didn't understand how she'd come to be at the sacred lake. Her body felt wrong and her mind jumbled, as if waking abruptly from a long night's sleep with tangled thoughts— only worse. Fragments from a hundred shattered dreams and lives spun through her mind, and she struggled to match this place to one of them. She groped for one to cling to, anything to anchor her to the world around her, but they all felt correct and wrong at the same time. She could not hold them all. There were too many. She lost herself among them, her mind scattering like the memories.

Then she found one—Ky'lem fighting a corpse in a cave. She clung to the memory like a lifeline until she found another—Ky'lem sitting next to her. A third came after— Ky'lem flying through the air by the bank of a river. One by one, she sorted the scattered pieces of herself, rebuilding her life. The memories that did not belong dissolved and faded. One came pressing over the others so strongly she nearly lost all she'd built.

Ky'lem needs me. He is dying.

She felt for him through the bond, but he wasn't there— replaced by a hollow void. She prayed to Sollus she hadn't arrived too late.

Wait . . . arrived from where? They'd been building a raft, days from the Najalii. She fastened herself to the memory and let it lead her along until she saw Pai'le swinging the tree limb for her head. Like turning on a lamp, the realization of who and where she was coalesced. *I am Nola.* All the other memories that threatened to overwhelm her faded, and the world fell into place around her.

Two mergols fought only paces away. The beasts roared and struck at one another—talons slashing and feet kicking. One with a missing ear pinned the other on its back and slashed furiously at its head. The one beneath barely kept the attacks away from its face. From somewhere, she had a faint memory of this—more of a feeling that she should remember it—as if she'd dreamed the scene in front of her but could not recall the details. *It makes no sense. I've never been to the lake of life, and I've never seen a mergol.*

She had no time to wonder at the strangeness of it all. The two beasts rolled toward her and stopped just short of crushing her beneath them. She dove away from the creatures and stumbled toward the water of the lake. Her body felt gangly and unbalanced. Mergols didn't swim, and if she could get out into the water far enough, she would be safe.

The stark white of bone caught her eye. A mangled body lay in a heap near the shoreline.

"No!" she screamed.

It was Ky'lem, or what was left of him. It was impossible for something so maimed to be alive. Deep gouges ran along his back, and the white lines of his exposed ribs were what had caught her attention. The damage did not stop there. Wide punctures wrapped around to his side, and a section of his insides hung out in a loop that glistened wet in the starlight. His leg was twisted to an impossible angle, with the muscles of his thigh torn worse than his back. And the blood . . . there was so much blood.

The sight of such vast injuries hit her in the stomach like a stone, taking the wind from her lungs. She dropped to her knees beside him, choking back a sob. *Don't be dead. You are not supposed to be dead.* Tears fell from her lashes and ran down her cheeks. *This is wrong.*

His chest moved.

He breathes!

Tears of despair became tears of hope. *I will save him. I treated worse holding the mountain passes against Tomu's army.*

She shook her head. *What mountain passes?*

The memory had come from those discarded and lost. *Am I going crazy?*

It did not matter. The knowledge of how to save him was there. She needed her tan'tari. She looked to her wrists for the slight bulges along the inside of her forearms and froze. *The okulu'tan hadn't set them. I have not been tested yet. I am still Nola.*

Behind her came a roar of triumph. One-ear stood above the still form of the other beast. It lifted its face to the stars and pounded its massive chest, announcing its victory to the forest.

Nola opened her hand. There were the crystals, glowing red in her palm. She hesitated. *If I embrace them now to save Ky'lem, there will be no going back. There will never be another chance to escape the Esharii. I will be Ni'ola.* The thought came from deep within her, and she knew the truth of it, although she could not have explained it. This was a central branch in the paths. She could save Ky'lem or run away and escape back to her homeland, but she could not do both.

". . . have to . . . leave me," Ky'lem mumbled.

He lay close to death, yet his final thoughts were of her. Nola nodded slowly to herself. She could not abandon him to die. She closed her hand into a tight fist around her tan'tari. She would need more than weeds and shrubs for the power required to save her pachna. She needed blood and a powerful spirit, and she knew where she must get it. She searched Ky'lem's uninjured side, but the sheath to his knife sat empty. It didn't matter. Ni'ola climbed to her feet and turned to face the mergol. A knife was not the only way to take the beast's soul.

CHAPTER 29

Loral and Tannon were led to the Wolves.

Before them, a giant wolf's head, cast in high relief, stretched across a set of bronze double doors that stood twice the height of a man and wide enough that both she and Tannon could lie down end to end between the jambs of the frame. Two large, tapered emeralds served as the wolf's eyes. They flickered with the light of the half dozen sconces that lined the walls of the hallway, giving the eyes the semblance of life. Its lips were pulled back in a hungry snarl, with enough of a gap between the fangs to make it appear Loral could look down the throat of the beast if the light were right. On the other side of the door was the true danger if what Riam had told her back at the outpost was correct. The doorway marked the entrance to the Wolf Regiment's training grounds.

The Draegoran escorting them pushed lightly on one side of the doorway and it swung open, splitting the wolf's face down the middle. "This way," he said.

The wolf grinned at Loral when she slipped past, and she shivered with a sudden chill.

She and Tannon were shuffled down hallways until they came to a small courtyard with archways surrounding it, all carved from the rock of the island.

"Kyden Verros is in the garden. Through there." The Draegoran pointed, obviously expecting them to go alone.

The arch he pointed to led to another courtyard unlike anything Loral had seen on the island. Except for a narrow gravel path that wound through the center, a neatly manicured lawn—as smooth as any rug she'd ever seen—replaced the rock floors she'd become accustomed to. Small, delicate trees and perfectly square shrubs lined the path. Moonlight streamed in through a domed glass ceiling, and the sounds of birds and running water echoed off the walls. In the center of the room, the path circled a large fountain before splitting off in new directions.

"What do you suppose they want with us?" Loral said.

"Probably something to do with your missing boyfriend," Tannon said. He lowered his voice to a whisper. "Remember what I said, 'He ran away.' Not a word otherwise, or I promise you the rest of the rabble you've sided with will never make it through training—starting with the big, stupid twin. I'll find a way to make sure they all fail." He left her standing at the entrance to the courtyard, heading to the fountain.

After a moment of hesitation, Loral followed. "You're not going to get away with what you did to Riam," she said after catching up to him. It sounded childish and empty, but it was the only response she could think of.

"I already have," he said. He leaned over the fountain and peered into the water. "You didn't say anything when I told them he'd jumped from the barge to escape. If you change your story now, you'll be as guilty as I am."

"I didn't say anything because you told me you would hurt Vashi and the others."

"I wasn't joking. I will."

"How? If I tell them everything, they'll read your mind and know the truth."

Tannon splashed at the water, and a school of orange-and-white fish converged on the disturbance.

"So what if they do? Do you think it'll change anything? It won't. I'm a landowner's son, and it's not like I hurt him—much." Tannon giggled. "Oh, they may have some small punishment for me, but in the end it won't matter. They need us. There are too few with the blood to worry about a petty quarrel between children. And besides, they'll find him and bring him here anyway. So in the end, it won't even matter." He smiled with mock sincerity. "Except that I will make life painful for everyone you care about if you betray me."

"They won't let that happen."

"Oh, they will. In fact, they'll encourage it. They're going to put swords in our hands and force us to spar with each other eventually. My father spent years training me. It wouldn't take much for an unchecked swing to slice an arm here or leg there—it might even be fatal. I'm sure Dunval would love to help."

"If that's true, you're going to try and hurt them anyway."

"Not true. As long as you don't betray me, I won't go out of my way to hurt them. There's a difference."

"You're such a bastard," Loral said, pushing him away. She hated Tannon. *Why did he have to carry the blood, too? It isn't fair.* Being selected by the Draegorans had been her escape from people like him. His presence ruined it.

He laughed at her. "Poor Loral," he chided. "Do you know what the best part is?" He gave her time to think about it before continuing. "If your boyfriend didn't drown, he probably hates you more than he does me. You're the one who betrayed him."

She let out a gurgling scream and lunged at him. He stepped smoothly to the side and tripped her. The gravel bit into her palms and knees.

Why did I tell him anything? Tears welled up in her eyes. *Because I'm stupid, that's why.* She'd thought being selected would make things different—that they would all be equals—but she'd been wrong. People like Tannon would always believe they were better than everyone else.

Tannon saw the tears in her eyes and laughed harder. He sat down on the stone rim of the fountain with his legs sprawled out in front of him.

I'm going to pay him back for this someday. I don't care how long it takes.

The crunch of footsteps sounded behind her. "Well, what is happening here? Hmm. A quarrel among new recruits?"

The newcomer's hair hung shoulder length, with streaks of gray, and his thick eyebrows sat over narrow eyes that sunk back in his head. He walked with his hands behind his back, and his long black robes skimmed the surface of the path. He was older than most of the Draegorans Loral had seen so far, except for maybe Master Iwynd at the outpost. To his left and right a pair of muscular young men flanked him.

He stopped in front of Loral. "You would be Loral," he said. He looked from her to Tannon. "And you Tannon." A smirk formed below his thin mustache, as if he found something amusing. "Both from minor landowning families in Galtare . . . interesting." He pinched softly at his bottom lip, contemplating his next words.

"I am Kyden Verros," he said. "Welcome to the Regiment of the Wolves." The tone was friendly, but there was nothing welcoming about the deadness of his eyes.

Tannon gave her a look that said she'd better keep her mouth shut.

She squinted back at him. *Go shit yourself.*

Kyden Verros scanned the garden slowly, taking in the trees and the birds in the moonlight. "This is my favorite place within the grounds. There was another garden here when I became kyden, but it wasn't mine, so I had it torn out and designed this one, all but the fountain. It is the only place on the island I find truly peaceful—where I can relax. It provides balance to the harshness of life. I especially love the fountain. My predecessor brought the stone all the way from the mountains in Thae."

Tannon stood up quickly and checked to make sure he hadn't disturbed anything that might offend the kyden.

"It occurs to me that you may be the first recruits to ever set foot within the garden's walls. That is quite an honor." He looked at Loral and lifted his chin, motioning her to get up.

She climbed to her feet and moved to a spot an arm's length from Tannon.

"So, what do you think of my work?"

"It's beautiful," Loral said in a guarded tone.

"It is. I'm not a patient man, and it was my thought that the tranquility of this place might help me keep my temper.

"You see, I am not a kind man either, and when I lose my temper, I am prone to making rash decisions. The kinds of decisions that cannot be undone." He brought his arm around from behind his back. In his hand he held Riam's case from the barge, the one containing Gairen's sword—the same one Tannon had thrown into the river. "I would very much like to know about the boy who carried this and where he is." He pinched at his lip again. "Yes, I would like that very much."

Loral turned her gaze to the water, afraid to meet the kyden's eyes.

"I can assure you he's not in the fountain," he said harshly. Gone was the wistful amusement his voice had carried a moment ago.

Loral swallowed. She didn't know what to say. She could tell the truth and risk Tannon's threats against the others or hold her tongue and risk Kyden Verros's anger. Neither was appealing.

"His name was Riam, and he ran away!" Tannon blurted out.

Loral's head whipped around. "Liar!"

"You see," Kyden Verros said, addressing Loral. "I was right to choose this room. It seems I will need patience. A short lesson, then, for both of you before I ask again."

The Draegorans flanking Kyden Verros stepped toward Tannon.

"What are you doing?" Tannon tried to dodge their hands, but they grabbed him by the arms and held him between them. "Don't touch me."

"Please be quiet," Kyden Verros said.

"When my father—"

One of the Draegorans clamped his hand roughly over Tannon's mouth.

Kyden Verros approached Loral and put his arm around her, turning her to face the fountain. "Do you like the fish?"

When you were raised in a port city, fish were food or a commodity, not pets. "They are very colorful," she answered.

"An accurate description, but not an answer. Your fellow Neshian would do well to learn the subtle diplomacy of your response." He pointed to the water. "The fish are called flayers. If your friend had disturbed the water a second time, it would've been very unpleasant for him. They are quite aggressive in the areas where they spawn. Although they are thick around the island this time of year, they are surprisingly rare in other parts of the world."

Loral looked at the fish more closely. They swam lazily through the water. Only about a hand long, they looked harmless.

The kyden read her expression. "Looks can be deceiving. For instance, see the two that are a shade darker than the others, almost red instead of orange?"

Loral wasn't sure she could, but she thought one near the edge might be a little darker. It was hard to tell in the shadows along the fountain's edge.

"Those two aren't flayers. They're sun drops. They imitate the flayers but are quite harmless. They lay their eggs in the same area and live and swim among them, using them for protection. Yet the whole time, they eat the eggs the flayers lay. Most of the flayers never know the difference, though occasionally one is discovered and devoured by the school."

He turned to Tannon. "You are right-handed, yes?"

There was a muffled response, and Tannon nodded.

"Start with the left hand, then—for a count of five."

The Draegoran uncovered Tannon's mouth and twisted the boy's right arm behind his back, forcing him to bend down close to the water. "Wait! I'll tell you everything!" Tannon said. "It was me. I threw him off the boat." The other Draegoran grabbed Tannon's other hand by the wrist and pushed it toward the water. "Please! For Fallen's sake, I'll tell you everything!"

Loral hated Tannon, but not enough to see him harmed. "Just read his thoughts!" she pleaded.

"Sadly, I cannot do that here on the island. The vault is too close. I suppose I could have you both taken back to the mainland and the truth read there, but as I said earlier, I'm not a patient man."

Kyden Verros nodded and the Draegoran holding Tannon's wrist pushed the boy's hand beneath the water's surface. For the first moments, nothing happened.

"One."

"You don't have to do this," Loral said. "We'll tell you what you want to know."

"Oh, I know you will," Kyden Verros said and patted her

on the shoulder. "But you would miss the most important part of the lesson if we stopped."

"Two."

The first of the flayers struck. Tannon screamed. A puff of red spread outward in the water. This sent the other fish darting about in a frenzy. Another struck, then another. Tannon struggled and jerked, but the two Draegorans held him tight, keeping him from pulling free. Tears streamed down Tannon's face while he continued to scream. The water churned and turned red.

It took a very long time to count to five.

Kyden Verros leaned against the fountain once the children were escorted from the garden. He faced the water, palms on the wide rim, and stared down into the pool's depths. The water cleared as the channel that ran beneath the island dispersed the boy's blood. The flayers drifted leisurely in the current as if nothing had ever disturbed their spawning area. A few of the fish darted this way and that, trying to entice a female to lay her eggs in one of the crevices of the rock. It amazed him. The fish swam hundreds of steads out into the deep of the ocean every winter and returned to spawn in the spring, never losing the memory of how to return from so far away, yet violence was forgotten in an instant. They were the complete opposite of people. People held tightly to their memories of violence, but easily lost their way. There were many truths a person—or a recruit—could learn from the fish.

The right side of Verros's mouth lifted into a lopsided grin. The boy's expression, right at the moment he realized they were, in fact, going to put his hand in the water was priceless. He was not a man who enjoyed torture, but this Tannon boy was an ass. The lesson would shorten the time it took to eliminate his self-centered nature. He had spirit, though, and that could be forged into a sharp weapon. The girl's expression was something else, full of fear and concern for a boy she appeared to hate. They would need to break her of that. He would keep a close eye on them both. He would never let either go to another regiment, not with what they knew. He would arrange for "training accidents" before he let that happen.

He ran his fingers through the blood on the fountain's rim, leaving crimson lines on the stone. He thought about ordering his men to bring the boy back to clean it before his hand was healed at the infirmary and then changed his mind. While it would certainly pound the lesson home, the blood made the garden more intimidating—that might be useful. Perhaps he would bring others here for mentoring.

While he'd lied to the girl about being short on patience—he was quite certain he was the most patient man on the island—he'd been honest about one thing. He did love this garden. When he'd become kyden of the regiment, he'd thought it served no purpose but to placate some small nostalgia for the forests of his predecessor's childhood, but after making it his own design, with the same meticulous attention to detail he gave to training and commanding the Wolf Regiment, he'd realized the garden mirrored his true desires. Like the recruits who joined his regiment's ranks each year, the garden took time to develop, with each plant requiring individual care. If you wanted a garden, it took time and dedication to grow it from seed to bloom, and it took patience—it also took removing a few weeds.

In the same way, he'd planted the seeds for a larger regiment years ago, sending his Wolves to every land of the Covenant to bed women in every village from Yaden to Mirlond—whether they liked it or not. Despite an alarming number of deaths in recruits inexplicably failing to retrieve a crystal these past years, there would soon be a crop the size of which had never been seen on the island . . . and they would all be his once the Owls and the Stonebreakers were out of the way. Neither the Hounds nor the Bloodhammers would stand against him, and the Ironstrikers would always remain neutral.

He slid his fingers farther along the fountain, admiring its simple beauty. He barely felt the tight seams between the blocks. The mason who'd built the fountain was a master of his craft. Verros appreciated a man who excelled in his position and took pride in his work. He also appreciated the kyden before him who'd ordered the fountain's construction.

It'd taken no small feat of engineering to break through

the rock floor and tap into the waterway, but this was how it was with all things worth obtaining. It took willpower and commitment to shape the world. He never questioned a decision once made—only the timing of things. Act too late, and the best-laid plans were destined to fail—spring a trap too soon, and the hunter exposed himself to the hunted before the killing blow.

The Owls would have fought tooth and nail to remove him from his position as kyden of the Wolf Regiment for his plan to expand the regiments, especially if they knew he intended to claim them all. He'd cut the head of the snake off long ago, attacking Kyden Barsol's ship without a trace of evidence pointing back to him or his regiment, but the body still thrashed.

His replacement, Kyden Thalle, was reclusive and short-sighted, failing to see what was necessary, but he wasn't weak or a fool. The old Owl thwarted him on the council whenever he could, but the idiot had ceased training replacements, making it easy for Verros to chip away at the Owl's ranks. One by one, his men had removed the Owls— a scout sent on a mission into an ambush, a warden disappearing in the night, an unlucky fall or accident. It was almost too easy.

Kyden Verros looked at the case sitting next to him on the lip of the fountain. *And now they've handed me the key to the final lock.* An armsman who could strip a crystal from a Draegoran at will would make a powerful weapon. Once he had that, the other kydens would have no choice but to obey him, or he would tear away their crystals and feed their souls to his blade. With his army of new recruits, he would crush the Church of Man in Mirlond, drive the Esharii into the sea, and add Arillia to the Covenant. *I will succeed where my predecessors failed.*

Perhaps the time was right to move against the Owls. The Stonebreakers would be easy once the last of the Owls were out of the way.

Footsteps behind Kyden Verros pulled him from his thoughts. Roshan, the regiment's arms-master, approached. He wore a sleeveless shirt and his arms were nearly black from the numerous glyphs that covered his biceps and forearms. He stopped a few paces short of the fountain and folded those arms over his chest, waiting to be acknowl-

edged. Roshan's discipline was unmatched. He would stand
there and remain still until the island sank before interrupting his kyden's thoughts.

Verros didn't make him wait. Not today. Today marked
the beginning of a new age. "Take the boy to the infirmary.
Heal his hand, but not completely. It wouldn't be much of
a lesson if he didn't carry a reminder with him."

"So we'll add him to our ranks?" The arms-master did
not seem pleased with the idea of training the boy.

"Oh, yes. I want as many of this year's recruits as you
can obtain. Trade in every favor we have with the other
regiments. Barter for them. Pay them gold. Promise them
anything. By next year it will not matter. All the regiments
will serve the Wolves in one way or another by then."

"I will do as you command."

Verros held up the case. "You read the letter?"

"Yes, my Kyden. When the taulin brought it in this morning."

"Do you believe Thalle's son, about the boy taking his
sword?"

"Warden Gairen had no reason to lie. He didn't know
the letter would end up in our hands. He certainly didn't
expect to die."

"We need this boy, Roshan. His ability will make it far
easier to subdue the Stonebreakers once the Owls are out
of the way."

The arms-master frowned. "We'll find him, but it may
be only his remains we find. There's no guarantee he made
it to shore."

"Oh, he's alive, Roshan. I know it." *Sollus would never
tease me with such a gift to merely snatch it away again. Not
when my plan to bring the known world under the Covenant is so close.*

"He could be anywhere, my Kyden."

"I don't think so. Where would you go if you were selected to be a Draegoran and then were thrown from a
barge by someone you hated? Someone you might want
revenge against?"

"I would be on my way to Parthusal and then here, but
he should have arrived already."

"Perhaps Roshan . . . or perhaps he was delayed."

"Or the Owls have him already," Roshan grumbled.

Verros didn't believe that. His spies couldn't be so inept as to miss the boy's arrival. "No. I have a hunch he is in the city somewhere. Send word to our district wardens—one of them may have already seen the boy without knowing it—and send a taulin to each of the other regiments' districts to search. Tell them to examine every boy who is new to the city," Kyden Verros said. "I want him found and on his way to the island yesterday. Keep a ship ready to sail from Parthusal within a glass upon his discovery. I don't care about the cost or who you have to kill to make it happen. He's that important."

"Yes, my Kyden." The arms-master saluted and hurried away.

Verros wanted to call him back, to add the order to move against the Owls—but not yet. It was too soon. Once he found this boy, Riam, however . . .

CHAPTER 30

"Where's he at! I know you have him!" Pekol yelled.

"He's in no shape to work today."

The voices came from the kitchen.

"Oh, he'll work today. I'll not have my churp lounging while I do his work. I'll have the warden slice his throat before that happens."

"Listen, you dumb bastard, he can't work. You've seen to that. What are you going to do, haul him around in your cart?"

"It's none of your business what I do with him, Bortha."

"First it was Nemon, then Stick and Doby, now this boy—what's happened to you, Peke?"

"You are full of screet shit—so high and mighty—ever since you married into the inn. I'm doing what I have to in order to survive. You're no different."

"That was years ago. Things have changed."

"Maybe for you—not for me."

"I never hurt children."

"Children? They're not children. They're criminals."

"So were we. I can't keep watching you mutilate them because you hate yourself and what you've become."

"So stop watching. Don't forget that I can end this little

illusion of yours in a glass. All I gotta do is tell the warden and you lose your wife, the inn—everything."

"You wouldn't do that. We'd both be wearing glyphs again—or dead."

"Don't be so sure about that. I've got a deal worked out with the district warden."

"You wouldn't—"

"We still owe each other, Bortha, but back off before I forget old times."

"I don't owe you anything."

"You gonna hand him over, or do I have to come back with the warden?"

"Two or three days. Give him the time to heal and I won't say another word. He'll be useless until then anyway."

"No."

Riam grabbed his shirt from where it hung on a peg. He couldn't let Bortha get into trouble for helping him.

"I'll do it."

It was Stick's voice. *What is he doing? My beating will be for nothing if Pekol gets his hands on Stick.*

"No!" Bortha said. "You can't."

"I've been doing it for five years. What are a few more days? Besides, I owe Riam, and he can't touch me now that I'm free."

"Deal," Pekol said.

The answer came too quickly. Pekol wanted to hurt Stick badly, if not outright kill him. It would not end well.

"Don't do it, Stick," Bortha said.

Riam climbed to his feet. It was harder than he thought, and he had to rest a moment before moving toward the kitchen. By the time he pushed the door open, Stick and Pekol were gone. Bortha scrubbed furiously at a table that didn't need cleaning, his face red. He didn't even look at Riam.

"You can't let Stick do this. Something bad is going to happen."

Bortha lifted his head and stopped scrubbing. "Stick knows what he's doing."

"You don't understand. Pekol hates him and doesn't want him to be free."

"I know."

"Then why'd you let him go?"

"Because Pekol is right. I owe him. If he goes to the warden, I'll lose everything."

"This is all my fault," Riam said.

"It's not your fault, boy. Pekol and I have a long history that isn't finished. If it wasn't you, it'd be something else setting it off."

But it is my fault. Stick is in danger because of me, and there's nothing I can do about it. Riam pounded on the wall with his fist.

Two and a half years—he'd be lucky to survive two and a half months. It didn't seem like finding a Draegoran was the answer when they all seemed to wear the wolf on their neck. He needed to get himself out of this.

Riam sat on the bunk in the storage room, scratching at the lines on his arm. He'd been there for two frustrating days. The glyph had to be the key. He had to get it off, recover Gairen's swords, and get to the island, and he had to get Stick out of the city before Pekol killed him. *How am I going to do that when I can barely walk?* He closed his eyes. The faint orange line was still there, leading off into the distance toward the sword. It wasn't where he remembered it—perhaps it'd floated downstream—but it didn't matter. What mattered was the link. The crystal in the pommel had healed him once, when he was desperate. Well . . . he was desperate now.

He pulled at the orange line, willing the sword to feed him with the same healing energy it had before. Nothing happened. He pounded his fist against the wall again. *I can't sit here doing nothing.*

"Right," he said out loud. "If the sword won't help me, I'll do it myself."

He held his arm up and closed his eyes. He took his time, studying the threads of energy that wove around and through his forearm. He had to unravel the knot where all the threads came together—that had to be the way to remove it—but it was so complex. He braced himself for the pain and pulled one by one at the threads, trying to understand how the glyph worked. With each tug, the nagging, dull pain that ran up his arm and into his chest increased.

After a half-glass, he hadn't accomplished anything. The knot sat as tight as when he'd begun. He stopped touching the threads and waited till the pain eased.

Can I just tear it out? The thought made him break into a cold sweat. *What other choice do I have? Slave away until Pekol kills me? There is no other choice.*

He took a deep breath and wrapped his thoughts around the whole knot, like grabbing the center of a spiderweb — only one made of steel. He could feel each of the threads that branched out tug at his body. He pictured the ends of those threads, sunk like fishhooks in the flesh and bones of his arm. The thought of them ripping out almost made him falter. He took several long breaths, trying to calm his racing heart. His mouth was dry. He licked his lips.

On three, then. "One . . . two . . . three!" With the final word he tore at the knot with all his strength, willing it to rip free.

Later, he would learn his scream was heard all the way at the market, four streets from the inn.

CHAPTER 31

"I believe she can hear us." Piercing light jabbed at Ni'ola's eyes and surrounded the washed-out form of the speaker hovering over her. Ni'ola heard other voices, but they were muffled, and she couldn't make out the words.

"Don't try and move, asha'han. You used far more oya'sha than is safe for one without the tan'tari set in their bones." The voice spoke in the thick Esharii tongue. "It's like staring at the sun for too long. You should have healed yourself when you were done saving your pachna, but it will pass on its own."

Oya'sha. "Oya" is life and "sha" is the spirit—the spirit of life that resides in all living things. The meaning came unbidden to her thoughts, and she could not explain the source.

Ni'ola's tongue felt wrapped in a blanket. "Ky'lem lives?" she croaked.

"His wounds are healed, to the extent he will survive, but he is weak. You must be careful not to draw from him until he has regained his strength."

Thank the Fallen. She'd known what to do to save him; knowing what to do and actually doing it, however, were two vastly different things. Taking the mergol's spirit had been the easy part. Putting Ky'lem's torn flesh back together had required a precise control that lay beyond her unpracticed abilities. There were moments when she was sure she was doing more harm than good, but eventually she'd stopped the worst of the bleeding and closed the wounds. He would add several ugly scars to those he already wore because of her inexperience.

As for the stranger's other words, she wasn't about to try and move. Her body felt as if it'd been pummeled by the mergol, and her ears rang. Even her hair hurt. In her thoughts, however, she was herself again. Well, not herself exactly. She was no longer the girl who'd been captured on the plains. She'd seen too much—remembered too many fragments of future lives—to ever be Nola again. The power of the crystals had taken what little remained of her youth and scattered it like the memories. As a result, she would forever be Ni'ola. *I can live with that. I made my choice.*

"Drink this."

Someone grabbed her shoulders and lifted her till she sat upright. A wooden cup was thrust into her hands. She fumbled at it with numb fingers and almost dropped it, but then the hands were there again, helping her until she held it on her own. She sniffed at the cup and wrinkled her nose. It smelled like a wet dog, just as she remembered.

"The palic smells terrible, and tastes worse, but it will help your body recover."

"I remember what it tastes like. I've made the tincture since . . ." She paused in confusion. She was about to say since she was an asha'han, but that was not right. She'd never made it before. The odd memories that bubbled up felt so real when they came, but they couldn't be real. *I'm going as crazy as the old spirit-walker.*

She braced herself and took a sip. The mixture tasted worse than she remembered—what she could only imagine as horse piss fermented in the sun. It burned her lips and mouth. Even prepared for the bitter taste, she still choked and sprayed the foul liquid out in front of her. "Give me a moment," she said through a mouthful of fire. She tried to hand the cup back to whoever had given it to her.

"No. You must drink," the voice said, mistaking her pause for refusal. The cup was pushed back toward her. "You are as weak as your pachna. There is a sickness that

comes with using too much of your own oya'sha. The palic
will save you from a slow and painful recovery."

The stranger knew everything. An okulu'tan, then. They
must have found her, with Ky'lem injured and the dead
mergols nearby. It would be obvious to them that she'd
taken one of the beast's oya'sha. Between that and the crystals in her hand, it wouldn't be hard to paint a picture of
last night's events. *The crystals! Where are my tan'tari?*

Ni'ola ignored the proffered cup and patted down her
clothing. They were not there, but they were close. She could
feel them nearby. Blindly, she ran her hands over the rocks
in front of her. She jerked her hands back when she felt the
stranger's legs in front of her. *Of course, the okulu'tan had
taken them.*

"Drink. It is much better if we do not have to force you,"
the voice said.

Ni'ola recognized the voice from a fleeting memory,
Li'sun, the leader of the village and a powerful okulu'tan,
but still only a spirit-taker. She couldn't see him, but she
knew the frown that would be on his face. He wore it whenever he mulled over a problem or dilemma. He would wear
that face many times during their lessons. *I've had no lessons! Or have I?* She was so confused. *What is happening
to me?* Maybe she needed the palic more than she thought.
She took the cup and brought it to her lips again, careful
not to smell the acrid odor. She took another sip and made
herself swallow.

"Good. Keep drinking until it is gone."

The pain behind her eyes and ringing in her ears eased
with each sip. It didn't taste as bad by the third and fourth—
her mouth becoming as numb as her fingers. That didn't
mean it tasted good. *Best not to prolong it.* She tilted her
head back, swallowing the last of the palic in large gulps.
She held the cup out in front of her when she was done.
"Thank you, Li'sun."

There was a gasp behind her, and several voices spoke
at once.

"She knows you, Li'sun," one said.

"You were right. She has traveled the ways," a deep
voice behind her said.

"Wait!" a new voice, young and nasal, shouted. "Just
because the asha'han speaks our tongue and knows Li'sun's

name doesn't mean anything. She likely heard it while pretending to be unconscious."

Ni'ola's lip curled into a sneer at the sound of the voice. *Jal'kun. She should have known he would be here.* She was startled at the hatred that came with the memory of the young spirit-taker's name.

"I am Ni'ola, Jal'kun, and I know the sacred lake, as all okulu'tan know it," she said in the Esharii tongue. "It sits beside us in the center of Esharii lands. It is chae'lon, of no tribe, and only the okulu'tan and their pachna may reside along its shores." The memories came unbidden and she responded to them without thought, her voice growing stronger and louder. "It is where the okulu'tan come to share knowledge and sing the songs of the Fallen, of Parron and his war against Tomu, and of the final war that will be. It is here the okulu'tan learn to use their gift and pay tribute to Sollus, and it is here that Li'sun will train me as Ri'jarra intended."

If there were shouts before, they were nothing compared to the response to her words. *I should not push them so—I need them—but hearing Jal'kun's voice set her on edge and filled her with anger.*

"She's an abomination!" one shouted.

"Ri'jarra was mad, bonding a pachna to an Arillian half-breed."

"If she has traveled the ways, it is too late. She must be tested."

"Look at her eyes. It is obvious she has traveled the ways."

Ni'ola swiveled her head back and forth slowly, letting them look at her eyes even though she could not see them. *The okulu'tan respect courage.* She was fairly certain they wouldn't kill her. In a blink the confidence melted away. *What am I doing?*

As if sensing her fear, Jal'kun spoke out, his voice louder than the others, "This is Draegoran magic—one of their tricks to spy on us. We must kill her before they learn anything more of the lake."

It is Jal'kun who fears me. He will never be strong enough to lead, and he knows it, yet he still tries to command.

"Yes! Kill her," another okulu'tan agreed. "Her presence defiles Parron's resting place."

Ni'ola's vision had improved, and she could make out the rough shape of Li'sun kneeling in front of her and a few of the others behind him. They wore robes of bright colors that came down to their calves. Several of the okulu'tan waved their hands frantically with their words in heated debate. Some looked angry, others curious, and too many agreed with the nasal-voiced okulu'tan.

"Silence!" Li'sun yelled.

Jal'kun ignored him. He held up something long and silver—a knife. "I will do it myself." He stepped forward.

Ky'lem was up and in front of her in an instant, although how he managed it was a miracle. His knees trembled, and he appeared ready to collapse at the merest breeze, but he was there, shielding her with his fragile body. He did not hold his sword—*thank the Fallen*— for to do so here would have meant death.

Ky'lem, no. He will not attempt to hurt me . . . yet. Jal'kun might be the one behind the attacks against them, but she could not be certain. There were many who looked as angry as the young okulu'tan. Either way, he would not attack her without Li'sun's permission.

"This discussion is not for your pachna," Li'sun said. "He will leave us now."

"Not while that one has the knife, I won't." Ky'lem pointed toward Jal'kun.

I told you. He will not harm me. "Go. Leave us!" she commanded Ky'lem.

Surprise and a trace of defiance came back to her along the bond and beneath that pain. Not from the wounds, but from her words. She'd hurt him with her sharp rebuke.

If they truly want me dead, you could not stop them. Your remaining will only serve against us in their eyes. They must believe I control my pachna. It will add weight to their decision. They were not exactly words that went across the bonds—closer to feelings—but he would understand them.

You will never control me! Ky'lem thought sharply. His response surprised her.

Ky'lem was as intolerant as the okulu'tan around her, even after their time bonded together. Taking a deep breath, she formed her thoughts and feelings carefully. *We will never be as other okulu'tan and their pachnas, Ky'lem.*

I do not seek to command you, but I ask that you leave. It will make our position stronger.

Grumbling to himself, he nodded.

"You may go, Ky'lem," she said loud enough for all to hear. "He will need assistance," she told Li'sun.

She cringed at the response that came from Ky'lem. There was no guarantee the okulu'tan would not kill them both, and if she must sacrifice Ky'lem's pride to prevent their deaths, so be it. She could pay for her words later.

"Of course." Li'sun's eyes glazed over for an instant.

Two plain-faced warriors arrived in moments and took Ky'lem by the arms. He tried to shake their hands away at first, but he couldn't have gone ten steps without their support. She felt his shame at needing their assistance. *Men . . . too proud for their own good.*

You fought two mergols, Draegorans, and a living corpse to get us here, Ky'lem. Wear your injuries with honor. None will doubt your strength.

Nothing came back to her along the bond, but he relaxed. Hopefully, it would temper his anger for the way she'd spoken, although she doubted it.

The okulu'tan milled angrily while they waited for the warriors to be gone, but as soon as the warriors were out of earshot, they began arguing among themselves once more.

Li'sun let them go for a time, giving them a chance to expend some of their anger. "Enough!" Li'sun called. "I would like to hear her story. The ga'ginga that attacks before it knows what it hunts dies young." He turned on Jal'kun. "You will put the knife away. If you cannot control yourself, I will send you away with the pachna."

Jal'kun's upper lip curled back as if he would defy Li'sun. Ni'ola smiled innocently at him. His fingers whitened on the handle, but he jammed it back into the sheath at his side and held up his palms. "Let the half-breed have her say before she dies. It will change nothing." His words were colder than the mountains. The man would attack her at the first opportunity that presented itself, even if they let her live. She must always be ready.

Li'sun glared at Jal'kun a moment before returning his attention to Ni'ola. "Like all spirit-walkers who've traveled the ways, Ri'jarra was unpredictable, and he lived a very solitary life. When he last spoke to us, he said he must go over the mountains. He said nothing about an asha'han or his death." He sat down, crossing his legs in front of her. "Tell us everything that has happened, beginning with how you came to be with Ri'jarra. Spare no detail."

It was hard to separate the Nola parts of her life from the influence of Ni'ola and the fragments of the futures she remembered. Her life prior to being captured was so trivial and distant, seemingly unimportant. She had no desire to speak of it, but she had no choice. Li'sun must know all, including the memories of her other lives. She took a deep breath. "I was called Nola, and I come from Nesh—the area you call Hansha'tal north of the mountains. My father was a landowner and a trader. My mother was the daughter of an Arillian merchant . . ."

Ni'ola told them of her journey, of being tested by the Draegoran and her days with Riam. She didn't like thinking about her time with Riam—she'd acted nervous and foolish—so she skipped that part and told them about the Draegoran killing the Esharii warriors under the moon's light and of being captured. She hated to speak of the attack. At the time, she'd wanted the Draegoran to kill them, but now it made her sad for the loss of the tribesmen. She told the truth of her feelings, though, and several of the okulu'tan gave her angry stares.

From there, she told them everything about her time with Ky'lem and Pai'le, and she told them of the final night with Ri'jarra, when he called her to the pool. They had her repeat the words the old spirit-walker had spoken to her before bonding her to Ky'lem. She did not tell them about the final orders to Ky'lem or the creature in the cave. No good would come from telling them about the first, and they would not believe one of their own had already attacked her and Ky'lem—not once, but twice.

When she talked of Pai'le hitting her and the light she'd escaped into, they asked her many questions. She remembered little from the dreams. She knew there had been hundreds—maybe even thousands—but she could not remember any one in particular. What memories she had came in random thoughts that seemed unrelated to the dreams, such as the knowledge of how to take the mergol's oya'sha and how to heal Ky'lem.

"She is lying!" Jal'kun shouted when she finished. He leaped to his feet, the knife back in his hand.

"She speaks the truth," Li'sun said. "I sense no deception in her words, although she hasn't told us everything."

"I agree," another okulu'tan said. His face bore the wrinkles of many years. "She has walked the ways and seen the paths of all life. We cannot kill her and waste Parron's gift, especially when Ri'jarra named her his ent'lai." There were several nods of agreement.

Ent'lai—successor or follower. Ni'ola wanted to laugh. *One lesson did not make for much of a successor.*

". . . but she is also an asha'han and a foreigner. To train her is forbidden by the edicts," the elderly okulu'tan added. There were far more who agreed with this last sentiment.

"I agree. An asha'han cannot be trained," one yelled.

"There is no place for her here!"

With the last, the arguments among them broke out again.

"There is only one solution," Li'sun said. He looked around deliberately at the other okulu'tan, waiting for them to quiet and listen. "The edicts are clear. She cannot be trained to become an okulu'tan, but they do not say an asha'han may not *be* an okulu'tan. She will be tested. Tonight. With no training. If it is Sollus's will, she will become one of us. If it is not his desire, her oya'sha will feed Parron's return."

Jal'kun pointed his knife threateningly at Li'sun. "You are twisting Eisha's words and defiling the edicts."

Li'sun looked pointedly at the knife. "You push too far, Jal'kun. Are you challenging me?" His eyebrows lifted with the question. "Will any second that challenge?" He turned slowly, staring the others down. None moved or said a word.

He returned his gaze to Jal'kun. "Why do you fear this asha'han, Jal'kun? Is there something you are not telling us?" He took a step forward. Ni'ola could feel the power building in Li'sun. "You mistake my open mind and trust in Sollus for weakness."

Sweat beaded on Jal'kun's forehead, but he made no move toward Li'sun, nor did he attempt to draw any power to himself.

The wrinkled okulu'tan moved between the two. "Many here agree with Jal'kun, Li'sun. Even I desire to spill the asha'han's blood into the lake, but Ri'jarra saw much that he did not tell us. If it is Sollus's will that this asha'han replace him, so be it. I will follow Parron's decision if she is tested and survives. Who are we to quibble over what the edicts mean?"

There were nods of assent around the group, but here and there Ni'ola saw those who bit their tongues despite the disagreement plain on their faces. Those she would need to mark and watch.

"I still say she is a spy." Jal'kun looked to the others for support, but none spoke up. "You are all weak old men!" he yelled in frustration. With an undulating cry the young okulu'tan pulled the knife back behind his ear, preparing to throw.

"Jal'kun, no!" Li'sun yelled.

Ni'ola tried to back away, but firm hands continued to hold her shoulders, preventing her from moving.

Jal'kun's hand snapped forward and the blade streaked through the air, burying itself in the ground between Ni'ola's legs with a loud thunk.

"Soon," the young okulu'tan said. He stalked away.

"Jal'kun is young, and his blood is hot," Li'sun said, as if this were the only explanation needed.

"What will happen to me at this test?" Ni'ola asked, staring at the blade still protruding from the ground between her thighs. None of the memories she could recall told her anything about the test.

"You will know Parron and fight for the privilege of your life and the honor of serving him," the wrinkled okulu'tan answered. "Many spend years training for this day and still fail, but if this is truly what Sollus desires, you will survive somehow." The old one followed the words with a crazed, toothless grin that did little to ease Nola's concerns over her fate with the spirit-takers.

The city of Mirl was breathtaking, with narrow spires that reached up to the heavens from a myriad of multicolored temples. Truly beloved by the gods, the city stood as the jewel of Draegora and its spires defied the laws of nature.

When the dark ones returned and the gods fell, the fragile towers could no longer stand without the power of their deities. In the dark hours of the morning, thousands perished when the city collapsed into ruin.

Only one tower remained. Built by man, it was a weak imitation of the others' greatness, but on that day, it became a symbol of man's ascension and a symbol of his true freedom.

—*The Prescripts of the Church of Man*

CHAPTER 32

Riam was back at the outpost. Around him, buildings burned, and in every direction Harol's regulars died. The Esharii outnumbered them, and their heavy Arillian blades cut the men down like defenseless children. With no resistance, they fell by the dozens—faces smashed, heads split, and bodies ripped open. Waves of blood soaked the soil. Harol died last. He stared at Riam with an idiot's grin while a sword severed his head from his shoulders. The head rolled along the ground, and when it came to rest in the dirt at Riam's feet, it held his grandfather's face.

The Esharii turned on Riam, forming a circle of painted faces around him that provided no path to safety. A fearsome tribesman with a scarred, unpainted face and part of his ear missing stepped forward, leaving a gap in the ring of tribesmen. He raised his sword. The flames of the burning buildings reflected off the blade, making it appear to glow with a light of its own. It was Riam's turn to die. By his feet, his grandfather's head laughed.

The unpainted Esharii held the blade high, prepared to strike, but waiting.

A woman stepped through the gap in the circle.

"Nola?" Riam said, recognizing her in the aged face of the woman.

"Kill him," she told the plain-faced Esharii.

The blade came down.

Riam threw his arm up to shield himself, useless though it would be against the two-handed sword. The blade smashed into his forearm, cutting through tendon and bone. Blood washed over his face—

He woke from the nightmare, sopping wet. Serina stood above him, wearing only a short silk robe and holding an empty pitcher in her hand. "You were thrashing and yelling. It disturbed my client."

Riam sputtered water from his mouth and wiped his eyes clear.

"Let me see your arm." She bent over him and a breast slipped partially free from the confines of her robe, the circle around the nipple pink against the smooth, white skin. She looked down at it and then back at Riam, but she didn't bother to cover it up.

He turned his face away.

"Oh, what's the matter, you don't like it?" She pulled the robe open, exposing the other breast.

Riam's face flushed with heat. He did his best not to look, but with her leaning over him, it was impossible not to see her exposed chest. He didn't think to close his eyes.

Serina giggled.

"Please," Riam croaked.

"Serina, leave the boy alone," Bortha said, coming into the room.

"What? I was only taking his mind off the injuries. It seems to have worked." She winked at Riam. "It's not like I would touch him. He's too young for that."

"Why don't you get him food? I'm sure he's hungry after sleeping so long."

"Get it yourself. I'm not one of your empty-headed serving girls, and I have a client waiting for me to return."

"Serina . . ."

"Fine." She stood up tall and pulled the robe closed with feigned regalness.

Riam watched the way her hips moved as she strode away. He was breathing harder than when he woke from the nightmare.

"That woman has a wicked sense of humor, but her voice is as pure as honey when she sings. Brings a crowd every night—well, her voice and the chance to sleep with her." There was a wistful hint to his voice. "My wife hates her." He turned back to Riam. "How's the arm doing?"

Riam held it out and found it wrapped in bandages from shoulder to wrist. Blood seeped through, and his hand was swollen and discolored. He opened and closed his fingers. There was no pain. In fact, he didn't feel anything. He touched the back of his bruised wrist. It was like touching someone else. He felt nothing.

"What happened?" Riam said.

"I was about to ask you the same question. I found you unconscious and bleeding from more than a dozen wounds."

Riam closed his eyes and used his strange inner sight to examine the arm. He couldn't see or feel anything with his mind either. The arm didn't exist. "It's gone!" he exclaimed.

"The glyph? Yes, it's gone. Your arm was sliced up pretty bad—used up all the gut I owned and had to buy more to finish stitching you up. At first, when I saw the blood, I thought you'd tried to cut it out. Saw a man try that once, but Draegorans aren't fools. It killed him before it was half done."

"I didn't cut it out."

"I know—which explains why you're still alive. I locked the door when I went to the market and there wasn't a knife in the room. I heard the screams all the way from there, by the way. Wouldn't be surprised if everyone in this section of the city heard them. Mind telling me what happened? For the life of me, I can't figure how you did it."

Riam remembered the warning from the cooks. He clamped his mouth shut.

"That's all I get for saving you and stitching you up, a closed mouth?"

Bortha was right. Riam owed him more. He chose his words carefully. "Thank you for all you've done, but I'm not sure myself." It wasn't much, but it wasn't a complete lie. He really didn't know what he'd done exactly, and although he trusted Bortha, he wasn't sure it was safe to tell him more.

"That's not much to guess on, but I suppose we all have secrets. Well, no matter how you did it, you'll have to leave the city. Pekol sees your arm like that and he'll drag you straight to the district warden. The Draegorans will rip out your memories to find the answer, right before they kill you. A secret like that is dangerous, and not only from them. I know more than a few men who'd pull out your fingernails to learn how you removed the glyph."

"What about Stick?"

"He can slip away a few days after you're gone. There's no law holding him here."

"I'm not leaving unless he leaves with me," Riam said.

"Don't be stupid. Best thing to do is to get you away from Pekol. Without the glyph, there's nothing to stop you from leaving, and there's no need to give Pekol an excuse to have you tortured and killed."

"Like the guard."

Bortha squinted and cocked his head. "The guard?"

"The guard at the gate—the one who caught Pekol smuggling years ago. He was killed by a Draegoran."

"What's that have to do with Pekol?"

"He gave Pekol a hard time at the gate, and I heard Pekol say it was about time 'somebody took care of him.' Before Pekol beat me, we picked up his body. He'd been drained by a Draegoran."

"You're sure it was him?"

Riam pictured the dried corpse on the street and the pouch of torgana leaves on the ground. "It was him."

Bortha pinched at his mustache. "That doesn't prove he had anything to do with it, and even if he did, it doesn't change things, except to make it more urgent for you to get out of the city. You have to leave, preferably tonight."

Riam wasn't going to run. He'd had a lot of time to think about what he was going to do before removing the glyph. Despite everything that had happened, he still wanted to be like his uncle Gairen. It wasn't to get revenge. It was to do what was right for others who couldn't do right for themselves. That was what he'd truly learned from his uncle.

In the square he'd learned something else, too, though it had been at a high cost. He should have known the warden wouldn't help as soon as he saw the wolf glyph. The cooks had as good as warned him about the Wolves, but what was behind the warning was the real truth. Draegorans were no different than normal people. Some were good, like the tailor or the cooks. Some were bad, like Pekol and the district warden.

If people behaved wrong or were evil, it was the duty of honest men to stop them—Draegoran, landowner, or low-born, male or female, young or old, it didn't matter. He would go to the island and become a Draegoran in order to help others who couldn't help themselves, but not before he knew Stick was safe. That was *his* duty to the former churp. He hoped Bortha would trust him and either help or at least leave him to his reasons.

Bracing himself for an argument, Riam spoke. "I'm not running away. All I've done since I left home is go where I'm told and run when I'm told. I'm done running. I'm not leaving the city that way. I'm going to the island, but not until I know Stick is safe."

Bortha rocked back on his heels, appraising Riam's words. "The island, huh? Well, that explains some of it. You've got their blood, don't you?"

Riam frowned. He hadn't meant to give that much away. He kept his lips closed.

"I don't know why I'm even thinking of listening to the decisions of a boy barely old enough to be off the tits he just saw," he ran a hand through his hair, "but I believe you know the risk involved, so I'll stay out of the way—especially if it means getting Stick out of Pekol's reach. Now, I know you're not telling me things."

"I—"

Bortha put a hand up. "Shut up and listen. I'm not a fool, and I'm not asking you to explain, but anyone who can re-move a glyph and see things that only Draegorans can see will attract the attention of dangerous men. If you are going to do this, you need to do it right, and you'd be wise to do a better job of hiding who you are. We'll begin by getting you a long shirt and a sling to cover your arm. Then I'll tell Pekol that the mediker says your arm is broken. That should buy enough time to get Stick out of the city, and then we'll get you out a few days later."

Riam was confused. "I don't understand."

"Pekol may be a bastard, but he's a smart bastard. If both you and Stick disappear at the same time, he'll have the Draegorans hunting you both, thinking Stick snuck you out of the city. You might get to the island and be safe, but Stick would pay for your escape. If you return to churping and don't disappear until a few days after Stick is gone, he might not connect the two. That is, if you think you can do it. He won't push you so hard with your injuries, but he won't make it easy for you either."

Riam's ribs still jabbed at him when he moved, and his nose ached. If the arm stayed numb, though, he could manage. He didn't have a choice, and he would do more than get Stick out of the city. He didn't know how, but he would make sure Pekol never hurt anyone again. Only one thing really worried him. "I heard Pekol threatening you. You don't have to get involved. You can't risk angering Pekol."

"I make my own decisions, and—like you—my reasons are my own. Let's just say that old wounds still bite. I've built a nice place for myself here, but life has a way of boiling over even the largest stoup when there's a fire put under it. Right now, Pekol is lighting that fire."

"What if Pekol's already harmed Stick?"

"Then you won't have to worry about Pekol at all. I'll kill him myself."

The look that crossed Bortha's face reminded Riam that the man hadn't always been an innkeeper.

Sure as the sun came up, Pekol walked into the inn the next morning.

"Where's he at? I've given you the days," Riam heard from the next room. He took as deep a breath as he could with the bandage around his chest and pushed himself to his feet. It hurt, but he could make it. He had to. He put on the sling and hobbled toward the kitchen.

"Where's Stick?" Riam asked, limping into the room.

Pekol whistled. "By the Fallen, I marked him up good, didn't I, Bortha?" His underbite stuck out farther than usual.

The innkeeper nodded at Riam from behind Pekol. A silent gesture that was all the encouragement the man could give him with Pekol in the room. It was enough. Riam straightened himself up. "No worse than the beatings my grandfather gave me back home."

Pekol let out his peculiar cackle. "By the Fallen, I like this boy. Eyes black as night and arm in a sling, and he's still got some fight left in him. Knew I chose right when I picked him."

"You've always had a good eye for fighters, Peke."

"That I have. Remember the half-blood? Made a fortune off him, and even more when he finally lost."

"Well, you also have the good sense to know when to bet on a man and when it's safe to go against him." Bortha placed his hand on the chopping block near the knives.

"That I have." Pekol rubbed his bottom teeth against his lip while he measured Bortha up and down. Whatever decision he came to made him smile. "They've some good fights lined up this Tenth Day. Been years since we went to the rings together."

"You know I can't."

"That pecking woman of yours . . ." Pekol trailed off.

Neither of the men spoke for several moments, but their eyes remained locked on one another. Riam remained still, trying not to disturb the awkward silence. There was definitely more going on here than two men reminiscing about old times—both were tensed-up, like loaded springs on a wain. Pekol's hand hovered over his belt, where he kept his knife. Bortha's hand didn't stray from the knives Riam had eyed on his first visit to the inn.

Finally, Bortha pulled his hand away from the block and grabbed a cleaning rag. "So where's Stick?" He asked the question offhandedly.

"How would I know? He did the work like he said he would and then disappeared as soon as we dumped the cart yesterday." He grinned at the last words. He let his hand fall away from his belt. "You've always let yourself be manipulated by the people you care for. It's your biggest flaw."

"Maybe, but I'm doing fine by it." Bortha spread his hands and waved them at the inn around them.

"For now, Bortha, for now. Come on, boy, we've work to do." He jerked his thumb toward the door before heading out.

"Mediker says his arm's broken and that it can't be used for at least a tenday."

"Well, he's got another to rake the streets with, don't he?" Bortha called over his shoulder.

It would be painful, but all Riam had to do was keep his arm out of sight and make it through a few days of churping while he figured out how to stop Pekol for good.

"Hold up. Your sling is coming loose," Bortha said far louder than necessary. He bent down and turned Riam so that his back was to the door. He glanced over Riam's shoulder to make sure Pekol wasn't looking, then pulled a long, narrow blade from his sleeve. It was thin and flat, made for throwing.

"Just in case," Bortha whispered. He slid the knife under Riam's bandage and tucked the edges of the wrap around it to prevent it from falling out. When he was satisfied it wouldn't be seen, he leaned in close and met Riam's eyes. "It comes to it, you drive that deep without a thought and run straight back here. Hide in the stables if I'm gone. I'll find Stick and get him out of the city."

Riam nodded.

"Hurry up, boy. We've streets to clean," Pekol yelled.

"Sollus's luck be with you," Bortha said, shooing him after Pekol.

Riam hoped he didn't need luck or the knife.

CHAPTER 33

For all his cruel traits, Pekol didn't go out of his way to be spiteful for the duration of the morning. He told Riam to "hurry up" numerous times and not to be "milking his injuries to make his lot easier," but the words were hollow and without real threat. Riam worried to no end, far worse than if Pekol acted angry or violent. To his mind, only two things put Pekol in good spirits—shoving dregs in his purse and making someone else suffer. Which of the two he enjoyed more could be debated. Only one thing fit with Pekol's current temperament, and it meant bad news for Stick.

Worry for the older boy gnawed at Riam up Tinkers' Street and down Maiden's Fare, almost enough to take his mind off the rotten and foul discardings of so many people crammed together—things that even the beggars avoided. With only one good arm, he fumbled a chamber pot and dumped it down his breeches. "For Fallen's sake . . ." he got out before the smell made him gag. He shook off what he could and dumped what didn't spill down one of the waste holes into the sewers. He slammed the brass pot back onto the doorstep with a clank.

The work hadn't bothered him so much prior to his injuries, but after being washed and treated like a free person again, the filth made him want to tear off his clothes and jump into the nearest fountain to scrub himself clean. *No one should be forced to do this*. If there were no churps, people would dump their own pots and get rid of their own filth.

He hid his disgust from Pekol and pretended to ignore his soiled clothing. He didn't want to hear that annoying cackle anymore. It was almost funny, really. He'd hated being forced to bathe by his uncle; now it sat second on his list of desires.

The thing he most wanted, even more than the bath, was to get Pekol talking, to try and tease out something that would let him know the truth of where Stick was and if he was alive. He couldn't think of a way to bring it up without it making Pekol angry. He might not survive another beating.

"It's a good day, boy," Pekol said, pulling the cart through the crowd where Maiden's Fare fed into the Walk.

The area where the two streets joined filled at sundown with grease-painted women selling their bodies. Riam knew about sex. His brother had explained it to him the first time he'd seen a pair of horses going at it. He just didn't understand what brought so many men down to this end of Maiden's Fare. The women here were not pretty, not like Serina. He reddened at the thought of her half-naked body.

A woman with smeared paint leaned out from a row of windows and threw a platter of bones and spoiled vegetables toward the cart. They thudded against the sidewall and scattered along the street. Her curly black hair stood matted to one side of her head, and she wore a dingy yellow shift that hung on the bones of her shoulders.

"I've warned you about that, you stupid whore!" Pekol called up to the window.

The woman laughed and flipped her hand under her chin toward them.

Pekol's lower jaw pushed out so far Riam thought it would cover his nose. He pulled his purse from beneath his shirt and shook it toward the woman. The fat purse jangled with the sound of coin, making more than one passerby stop and eye the raker. There were far more coins in the purse than when Pekol paid for the meat pies three days ago, and only one place Riam imagined it could have come from—Stick's payment for completing his time. The woman in the window stopped laughing.

Pekol looked up at her with his doglike underbite and narrow eyes. "You heard that, didn't you?"

An old man with drool on his chin stopped to watch the exchange.

Pekol spoke slow and clear, "Throw your rubbish one more time, and I'll come back and buy you for the night." He reached out and grabbed Riam by the hair, tilting his bruised face up toward the window. "See this? I like my whores the way I like my churps."

The tone of the words reminded Riam of his arm being crushed into the dirt in the Raker's Square.

"Not even the scum down dockside'll want you when I'm done, and I'll count it dregs well spent."

Even with the greasepaint, Riam could see the woman pale.

The threat lit a fire inside Riam—another person Pekol would hurt. The knife under his bandage felt heavy as an anvil. He could thrust it into Pekol's exposed side before the man ever knew what happened. Pekol wouldn't hurt anyone after that. He could picture Pekol's surprise when the blade drove in toward his heart, his mouth wide open while his blood spilled onto the very streets he'd spent his life cleaning. It would make a fitting end for the horrid man. It wasn't murder. A man didn't call it murder when he put down a rabid dog, and Pekol was far more dangerous than that. Riam's good hand moved under the wrap of the sling.

It would be the right thing to do. It was what his Uncle Gairen had called "honest anger." He'd said to "use that rage . . . that wrath, to get through doing what needs to be done." Riam's fingers closed around the warm steel handle. It felt good against his palm, like it was meant to be there, like it was meant for him to use. His hand started to tremble, but not from fear. He'd never stabbed a man before— only pretend thieves and robbers with his brother.

He looked at Pekol's face, at the glee in his eyes and his

wide grin. The man bounced with excitement. He would enjoy hurting the woman. *I stood my ground against the Esharii and the wasps. I can do what needs to be done.*

He tightened his grip on the knife and concentrated on calming his mind, driving himself to the same state he'd used to examine the glyphs, then he went farther. In his urgency, it came almost naturally, like he'd done it a thousand times. The world around him slowed to a standstill.

Nothing moved—not the crowd on the street or the woman in the window. Even the morning breeze ceased blowing against his cheek. Beside him, Pekol's lifeblood glowed ethereally beneath his skin. Riam could trace the lines of it through the man's body. There—right in the sweat-stained crease below Pekol's armpit where it glowed the brightest—that's where he'd stab the man. That's where he'd pay him back for his beating, and for the guard and Doby and Stick. Riam burned with the need to tear the glow from Pekol's body, to end his string of violence and murder. Anger and loathing bubbled up inside him. It consumed him.

Pekol must pay for his crimes. Ever so slowly, while the world remained frozen around him, the knife slid free, pulled by a hand that was now steady and firm.

Riam heard his uncle's voice inside his head, as clear as if he stood among the crowd around them. *Is this really honest anger, or is it revenge? Is it worth throwing everything away?*

Riam paused.

Is it desire, or is it what should be done? Gairen's memory asked.

Couldn't it be both?

Is it worth my sacrifice? Gairen asked.

Riam knew the answer to the final question from the past. If he executed Pekol, the crowd around him would drag him straight to a warden. He couldn't do it. Not here. Not in the middle of the street where it would waste his uncle's sacrifice. That would serve only revenge, and he needed to serve more than that or he was no better than Pekol—a slave to his own desires. The knife stopped just before the top of the hilt cleared the bandage.

He let go of his anger, and the world crashed back to

normal around him. The glow faded. He sagged and nearly collapsed. What strength he'd gained from his rest at the inn was gone.

He pushed the knife deep under the bandage and made sure it would stay hidden.

"I'm sorry, Master Raker. It won't happen again." The woman curtsied behind the window frame.

"Might visit you anyway. Words don't mean much from a whore."

"Fallen's truth. It won't."

Pekol thought it over and nodded. "Lucky it's such a fine day and I'm in a pleasant mood."

Riam knew the way Pekol worked. He'd let her believe everything was settled and then he'd be back to snatch away her relief and confidence, like he'd done with Doby's hopes for freedom. The woman was as good as beaten and didn't even know it.

Riam couldn't watch anymore. He let his eyes wander to the high-peaked, wood-slatted roofs that surrounded them. Billowy white clouds floated in the sky beyond them—the type that teased farmers, giving them false hope but never giving them the satisfaction of rain. They were a fitting match to his plight.

If it hadn't sunk in before, it did now. The world truly was unfair. Here he stood on the street with the most evil excuse for a man he'd ever met, yet he was the criminal, without ever doing anything worse than being thrown off a boat, and all he could do was watch. He needed to do something, anything. He shook off Pekol's hand and collected the rubbish the woman had thrown, hurling it into the wagon as hard as his injuries would allow. *I should have stabbed Pekol and gotten it over with, then run for the inn.*

"Come on, boy," Pekol said.

Ignoring the clouds and the people and his own regret, Riam limped along beside the cart, using a sidewall for support. Without it, he would have collapsed. No, it most assuredly wasn't a good day. His side and nose hurt like the Fallen, his face felt puffy and swollen, and his arm numb. Fear for Stick plagued him. Not to mention the shit and piss that covered his clothes. That pretty much summed life up—shit and piss wrapped in unfairness.

"Finding that broken chest before anyone else came

along and snaked it off my lanes is the cream on the cake today, boy. Don't know who'd throw it out, but it'll turn a few coins," Pekol said over his shoulder.

Riam wasn't sure if Pekol expected a reply or talked to himself. Pekol did a lot of the latter, and it wouldn't pay to join the conversation. He glanced over at the chest in the corner of the cart. It was a small thing, dark brown and polished, with sturdy iron hinges—the type used for storing money or valuables. They'd found it on Tinkers' Street before the sun came up. Riam doubted anyone would throw it out. Likely, a thief left it after breaking it open and stealing whatever it held inside.

"I'll bet I get ten dregs for it in the square, even with the damage. Anything can be fixed with the right tools and a little money." He looked back at Riam. "Well, almost anything." He cackled.

The laugh grated at Riam's nerves. "Yes, sir," he said. He had no idea about the value of the chest. In his life he'd never held more than two dregs. There were, however, lots of things that could not be fixed with money. The guard at the gate could not be fixed. Nola could not be saved. His uncle couldn't be returned. Money would never hold sway over his desires, and once he became a Draegoran, money wouldn't matter at all.

"Why the face?" Pekol asked. "You've got a look about you I don't much like. Thinkin' on something too hard for your own good." The cart stopped. "It's the coin, isn't it? You want some of the dregs the chest will earn."

"No, sir," Riam said, thankful for the halt that allowed him to rest.

"Is it the lesson I gave you?" Pekol tilted his head to the side and rubbed at his bottom lip. "I'll tell you what, I'll give you a dreg if I clear ten. That ought to take your mind off feeling sorry for yourself. You can spend it in the square. Laws don't much apply there. After that, if you work and do as you're told, we can put this whole thing behind us."

Riam started to refuse. Things would never be back to right, not unless Pekol miraculously fell into the pit.

"Thank you, sir," he forced himself to say instead. The words were false, but the coin would give him an excuse to move around the square and ask questions without Pekol getting suspicious. He forced himself to grin, as if the money made amends for everything the man had done.

Satisfied, Pekol yanked on the arms of the cart, starting it moving again. "You're lucky to have a raker as generous as I am. You know that, don't you, boy? Sollus-touched lucky."

"Yes, sir. Sollus has truly blessed me," Riam said. He rubbed at the knife in the sling.

Pekol made his ten dregs. Thirteen to be exact, from none other than Sadal, the dark-skinned Arillian who ran the square. Nobody else offered more than seven, and Riam had worried that he wouldn't get his dreg. But then, from across the yard, Sadal locked eyes on the chest and walked away from his conversation with a tall raker as if the man didn't exist.

Pekol could smell desire like a marcat smelled a sage hen. "Fifteen," he said, before the Arillian's robes stopped swaying with his steps.

Sadal put up a halfhearted argument, but there was no doubt Pekol would get the dregs. The question remained if Riam would get his promised share.

Riam took a risk and made sure he stood in the way when the money changed hands. Pekol cursed at him for being underfoot, but grudgingly kept his word and flipped a coin at him before heading off to join a group of rakers who gambled with dice. Sadal remained, turning the chest this way and that, examining the broken latch and the design on the cracked and chipped surface.

"Is it really worth so much?" Riam asked. Sadal would turn a profit on the chest sure as the wind blew, and Riam knew it would be more than double what Pekol made.

The Arillian pulled his beady eyes away from the chest. "It's not always the item itself that has value. Sometimes, it's the story of where it came from that fetches the highest price. The truth of a thing is worth more than gold to those who desire it." He glanced at the bandages on Riam's arm. "But you already know that, don't you? To those who search, I think your story is worth far more than this box." He snapped the lid shut and Riam jerked a step backward, startled. "But it's not a story I'd profit from, so I'll remain out of it." He winked and tucked the chest under his arm. "For now, anyway, but I would find a way to disappear if I was a young churp who fit the description of a boy the Wolves are looking for."

He looked past Riam and spied a raker entering the yard. "Ah, more business," he said and hurried away.

An odd man with odd words. No doubt he was even more conniving than Pekol. Riam half thought the Arillian already knew his glyph was gone somehow. *There's no way he could know that, but what was that part about the Wolves? Did he mean the Wolves are looking for me? That didn't make sense. How could they know who I am?*

Riam closed his fist on the dreg in his hand. He needed to hurry. No telling how Pekol would fare with the dice. If the man came back empty-handed, he wouldn't think twice about snatching the dreg back.

He wanted to go to the raker who'd given Stick his freedom. The man had another churp—a girl about Riam's age. She might have spoken to Stick or at least seen him yesterday.

It wouldn't do for Pekol to notice he went to her first, so he moved instead to the line of carts adjacent to her wagon. He worked his way down them, feigning interest in shoes on one cart and then at a pair of worn breeches on another. He pretended to be unsure about the breeches in case Pekol was looking. He'd come back and buy them to replace his soiled pair.

He risked a glance toward Pekol. He needn't have bothered being so careful—the man knelt and threw dice into a large clay bowl. Riam heard the rattle across the square. Groans broke out around the group, and Riam heard Pekol's hoarse cackle as he snatched a coin from each of the other gamblers.

"Seen Stick?" Riam asked while rummaging through the back of a cart. It held nothing but ash and broken plates.

A soot-stained churp on the back of the cart shook his head. "Not since yesterday."

Riam continued working his way through the carts and wagons, avoiding the one filled with waste from the butchers. He could hear maggots writhing in the back when he passed. A hollow-eyed churp sat on the driver's bench. The boy stared straight ahead, holding the reins of the single horse that pulled the wagon slack in his hands. Maggots wiggled in his hair. Riam shivered. He'd seen the boy before. He never spoke or moved on his own, just sat waiting to be told what to do next.

"You're back," the freckle-faced girl at Stick's old wagon said. "Thought maybe Pekol had done you in like Doby."

Riam couldn't remember her name. He waved at his sling. "He nearly did."

She brushed the stringy hair from her face. "I saw him beat you. You don't survive long here without knowing when to keep your mouth shut," she said in a low voice.

"Have you seen Stick?"

"Not today. I couldn't believe it when he showed up here after being set free. Idiot doesn't even realize Peke's got it in for him."

Riam felt a pang of guilt. *It's my fault.* Stick's only real flaw was kindness. "That's what I'm afraid of, that Pekol's done something to him. I haven't seen him, and Pekol's got a lot more coin than usual."

She looked around nervously. "Keep your voice down." She moved up close to him, oblivious to the smell of the chamber pot he'd spilled down his front. "You don't want to be heard by any of the other rakers making an accusation like that."

Riam nodded. "Keep a lookout for Stick, will ya?" he asked quietly. "And let me know if you see him."

"If he's smart, he's already left the city. If I were you, I'd be gone, too. You've a better chance running than you do with Peke."

She turned back to her wagon and climbed up a wheel to the back. "Don't have nothing you'd want to buy," she called out.

"Thanks anyway," Riam said.

He used his dreg to buy the breeches, even though they were worth a lot less. He even talked the raker into throwing in a loaf of stale bread so he wouldn't go hungry all day. He ducked behind a wagon and changed before returning to the cart.

"The day keeps getting better," Pekol said, walking toward him. He opened his purse and dropped a handful of coins inside. "Time to go to the pit. Best get it done."

Riam looked at the purse. Innocent people were dying, and Pekol was getting richer for it. Riam had one, maybe two, days to find Stick and do something about Pekol, and that was if no one figured out his glyph was gone or if the Wolves didn't find him first.

CHAPTER 34

Another day went by, and Riam felt a little better.
Grantor's Street was mostly empty, with only chamber pots and little in the way of refuse outside the
shops. They were halfway down the street when Jami came
out of the bakery. He held a cloth sack in front of him.

"Here's your order, Peke."

Jami came within arm's reach, and Pekol snatched the
sack from his hand and undid the drawstrings.

They stopped for it every third day or so, and Pekol always double-checked the contents of the sack.

"Two loaves and two sweetcakes." Jami looked at Riam,
taking in his injuries and the sling. He stepped back out of
Pekol's reach.

Pekol opened the sack and fished around inside before
grunting. He pulled the bag closed and hung it on a hook
on the front of the cart.

"So, Peke, about the favor . . ." Jami's nasal, high-pitched
voice trailed off. He took another step back from Pekol,
moving closer to the shop. He looked ready to bolt back
inside should Pekol get angry. "We're even after last night,
right?"

"We're even on the favor."

Jami sagged in relief.

"Although you still owe me for the charm."

"Ah, come on. You said I could have it for helping."

"Never said it was free. I said the favor would make us even. The charm is extra."

The door opened, interrupting their conversation. Master Silva stood in the doorway. His wide curling mustache was frosted in white, and his apron was a canvas of flour and sugar-splattered lines that could have sat next to an artisan's painting two streets away. He wasn't a big man, but he was bigger than Pekol. He held the door open with one hand, and a heavy rolling pin in the other.

"You've ovens to clean," he told Jami.

"Yes, sir." Jami ducked underneath Master Silva's arm and into the shop.

"You pay for your bread and keep moving next time, raker. The boy doesn't need to waste his time talking when there's work to be done."

"Boy owes me for a charm."

"That true?" Master Silva asked without taking his eyes off Pekol.

Jami's head poked out from behind the baker. "He said I could have it."

"Give it to me," Master Silva said.

"But . . ."

"Now!"

Jami fumbled something from around his neck, and Riam was sure he saw a flash of blue before Jami dropped it onto the baker's palm.

Master Silva looked at it and frowned. "Here." He held out the charm toward Pekol. "Take it and stay away from my apprentice."

Riam couldn't see the charm properly, only the leather thong it hung from draped over the man's hand. *Could it be Stick's?*

"It's not the charm I want. It's the dreg that's owed for it."

"The boy has no need for a Church of Man pendant."

"Not my problem. A deal's a deal," Pekol said. He thumbed the handle of the knife at his waist.

"There was no deal!" Jami yelled from behind Master Silva. "I'm not lying. He said I could have it. I didn't even know what it was."

"Boy says there was no deal, then there was no deal." He

tossed it through the air and into the back of the cart. "Move on. You're keeping the customers away with your smell."

Riam wanted to dive into the cart after the pendant. Instead, he didn't so much as glance toward it. He didn't want to attract Pekol's attention.

"No need for insults. Give me the dreg the boy owes me, and I'll be on my way. Otherwise, you can cart your own throwings to the pit."

Master Silva brandished the wooden rolling pin in front of him. "The only thing you'll get is this pin upside your head before I make a complaint to the district warden. I pay my taxes, and you'll collect whatever I put out front."

Riam slid closer to the cart, putting a hand on the side-wall the same as he'd done all morning for support.

The two men stared at each other, neither backing down.

"Here's your dreg," Bortha said, walking up to stand between the two. He flipped a coin toward Pekol, who let it spin by him without reaching for it. The dreg bounced on the street and landed behind Pekol.

"I don't want it from you." He thumbed toward the baker. "I want it from him."

"What does it matter where it comes from? Money is money." Bortha walked over and picked up the coin. "Now, quit being stubborn and take the dreg."

There was something different about the innkeeper. *The belt and knife.* Bortha wore a knife at his side, one Riam had never seen. The tip nearly reached the man's knee, and by the size of the sheath, it was wider than Riam's hand.

The knife didn't escape Pekol's notice either. "Been a long time since you wore that. It's not on account of me, is it? If I didn't know better, I'd think you were thinking of moving against me."

Bortha let out a forced laugh. "Not unless you're thinking of trying to kill me first." He put a hand on Peke's shoulder, turning him away from Master Silva. With his other hand he shooed the baker away.

Master Silva lowered the rolling pin. "Get the cart away from my shop," he said while moving back inside.

"When I'm good and ready!" Pekol snapped back.

"What good does arguing with that oaf do you?" Bortha said. "You've a full purse I see, your streets are easy today by the load in the cart, and soon you'll have a full belly with wine to wash it down with if you come by the inn. I've a job if you're interested—the kind of job we used to work together."

Riam's hand fell from the cart and he almost gasped aloud. *What is Bortha doing, inviting Pekol to the inn? What job could he possibly need that monster for?*

The skin around Pekol's eyes scrunched up. "Yesterday you were willing to fight over the churp, and now you've a job for us? What are you angling at?"

"Call it a change of heart. The inn's not doing so well, and you got me thinking. Then, yesterday afternoon, I overhear two customers discussing a shipment. I could use the money."

"Where? What kind of shipment?"

"Not here. Come by the inn after you make your turn at the pit. Then we'll talk."

Pekol tilted his head and rubbed his upper lip on his bottom teeth.

"Don't give me that look." Bortha held up his hands, showing his open palms. "Honest, I'm not up to anything but trying to make some easy coin for the both of us. I don't have the friends I used to for this type of work. I need you."

"Never trust a man who says he's being honest," Pekol said.

"When have I ever betrayed you, Peke? Never. Sure, we've had our falling-outs, but when it's come to what matters, we've always stood by each other."

"You're still here!" Master Silva yelled from inside. "I told you to move away from my shop."

"Shut up, Silva, or I'll let Pekol come in there, and I'll swear to the warden you started it."

Pekol smiled at that. "You should let me go in anyway—show him he's no better than me."

"There'd be blood, and then the warden would get involved. It's not that I really care about what happens to you, but I do need your help. What do you say? It'd be like old times—even better than going to the fights."

"All right. I'll come by the inn and listen, but you'd better not be jerking me about to protect the baker's runt."

"You've nothing to worry about. The job is real. I'll see you this evening." Bortha turned to leave, then paused and spun back around. "One more thing. Do you mind if I take your churp with me? There's no use taking him to the pit. You'll end up carting him back when he can't make it. He can muck out the stables instead."

Pekol's jaw tightened up. "So that's what—"

"No, that's not what this is all about. Take him if you want. I don't care, but take a look at him. If he walks to the pit and back, he'll be unable to muck out my stalls. It's been days, and I'd prefer to spend the evening discussing the job over a table and wine, not a pile of horse shit."

Pekol looked from Bortha to Riam, trying to gauge if they were in on it together.

Riam did his best to look as weak as possible—not that it took much effort. Bortha was right. Even though he'd made it yesterday, he didn't think he could do it again today.

Pekol rubbed his teeth on his lip some more while he thought. He wasn't going for it. Riam knew it. He would make him try and walk to the pit and back.

"Fine. Take him. But if he's not there when I get back, or you double-cross me, by the Fallen, I'll burn the inn down around you."

"There's no need for threats, Peke. He'll be there."

"He'd better be."

"Come on," Bortha said to Riam. "You've stalls to clean."

"Yes, sir." Riam took a step away from the cart. *The charm!* He'd almost forgotten it. He couldn't let Pekol dump it in the pit. He stepped up to the cart and grabbed the charm. "Since nobody wants it," he said, limping past Pekol. It took all the courage he had to look straight ahead and keep from wincing in anticipation of Pekol's backhand.

Bortha laughed. "Seems you haven't quite broken his spirit yet."

"You'll pay for that, boy," Pekol said.

"Relax, Peke. I already paid you for it."

Riam continued limping toward the inn. He looked down at the charm in his hand. It was exactly as he remembered it—painted blue and white with a sliver of yellow for a pupil—just like the one Stick wore. *But is it the same one?* If all the members of the Church of Man wore the pendant, he had no way of knowing for sure if it belonged to Stick. He wanted to believe it didn't, but in his heart, he feared it did. *It couldn't be a coincidence, could it?*

Something else occurred to Riam—the man who'd released the wasps in the timber yard had worn the same charm. That's where he'd seen it before. *What exactly is the Church of Man, and what is Stick's connection to it?* The world felt like a big bag of puzzle pieces with none that fit together.

Bortha caught up to him. "Come on. We haven't much time. Someone else is looking for you."

Riam and Bortha hurried back to the inn. Serina lounged against the table in the kitchen gnawing on a rib she held between both hands. She wore a soft, white shirt that buttoned down the front and was too large for her small frame—a man's shirt—yet it still clung to her body in a way that made Riam's heart speed up. The bottoms of her breeches were unbuttoned from her calves to her knees. Grease and flakes of meat surrounded her lips, but this did nothing to detract from her beauty. If anything, it made her more attractive.

Where did that come from? He'd never had those thoughts about Loral. Of course, Loral didn't have breasts like Serina, and she'd certainly never shown them to him. Riam fanned himself with his good hand. It'd suddenly become very hot in the inn.

Serina slid up onto the table and crossed her legs. Her toenails were a dark orange. Riam had never seen painted toenails before. They made her feet look nice. He wished he had shoes to hide his own dirt-stained feet.

What is wrong with me? He had more important things to think about than how Serina looked.

"Serina, can you go somewhere else to eat? I need to speak with Riam."

She lowered the rib from her mouth. "Why?" She licked grease from her finger.

"Because, for one thing, I need to talk to the boy about something I don't want you involved in, and two, because I'm afraid he won't hear a thing I say while you're here for him to gawk at."

Riam groaned. *I'm not gawking.*

"Really?" Serina said. She turned her large brown eyes toward Riam and opened and closed them slowly while continuing to lick at her fingers. Her long, purple-tinged eyelashes floated up and down seductively.

Riam felt his face flush.

She laughed.

Great. Now she's laughing at me.

"Serina, please."

"Fine, but I don't see why I have to leave. I already know you're helping the churp." She jumped down, nimble as a cat, and padded out of the kitchen.

"Let me see the charm," Bortha said as soon as she left.

"You think it belonged to Stick?"

Bortha held it up before him. "I don't think so. I think it's a different one. See the sliver of yellow?"

Riam nodded.

"It seems larger than the one Stick wore." He handed it back to Riam.

"What's it for?"

"Members of the Church of Man wear it. It represents the eye of a Fallen."

"But I thought the Church of Man didn't worship the Fallen?"

"They don't. The eye is supposed to represent that the Fallen serve us now, not the other way around, or some such."

"That doesn't make sense," Riam said.

"When it comes to the Church, nothing makes sense." The creak of a floorboard came from the hall beyond the kitchen. Bortha tilted his head. "Come on, we'll talk while we take care of the stalls. I was serious about that, and Serina can't listen in on us there."

When they left the inn, Bortha continued from where he'd been interrupted. "The Church would kill all the Draegorans if they could. Then we'd be on the wrong end of several thousand Esharii blades with an Arillian army right behind them, and neither of them would have to do a thing because the Covenant would tear itself apart before they arrived. They would just march in and sweep up the pieces. I'm no fan of the Draegorans, but I'm smart enough to know that we need them in the grand scheme of things."

Bortha handed Riam a shovel and moved the wheelbarrow in front of a stall. It didn't take much time for them to clean the first stall and add fresh straw. Bortha did most of the work.

"Listen, Riam. I didn't bring you out here for a lesson on the Church. Helping you is becoming too dangerous. There's a Draegoran looking for you. He came by the inn this morning. Described you pretty well and asked when 'the boy who cleans the stables' would return. I stayed out of sight and let my wife do the talking. She's never seen you, so she couldn't lie to him. I caught a glimpse when he left. I've never seen him before, so I don't think he's a district warden here in the city, but he was high-ranking. Any idea who he is?"

Riam was clueless. *Who would be looking for me? Maybe someone from the island, after they'd found out I'd gone missing from the boat. Was it the Wolf Sadal mentioned?* He shook his head. "I've no idea."

"I think it's about time you told me who you are."

Riam looked away, pretending to find a place for the shovel. "No one," he said. He placed the shovel against the stall door.

Bortha leaned back on his heels. His face tightened, giving it the same hard look as when he'd stared down Pekol.

Riam swallowed and took a deep breath. Despite the warning from the cooks, he owed Bortha. The man had risked his own welfare to help. The least he could do was tell him the truth. "You were right. I have the blood—you guessed that already. The one who tested me turned out to be my uncle. The Esharii killed him."

It became easier once he started, and it felt good to let free everything he'd been holding back. He told Bortha about the outpost and the attack by the Esharii, about his trip down the river and being pushed off the boat, and about his rescue by the strange couple who'd drugged him.

"The last thing I remember was them warming me by a fire and then I woke up in the cell with the glyph on my arm. After that, you know the rest. Pekol bought me out of the cell."

Bortha continued to stare at him, waiting for more.

Riam swallowed. "Well, you probably know that Draegorans are linked to their swords and that they draw power from them. I somehow took control of one of my uncle's swords—something no one's supposed to be able to do. Ever since then, I've been able to do things, but it's hard because I don't know what I'm doing. I'm just sort of stumbling through, figuring things out, and it drains me when I try anything because I don't have the sword."

"What kinds of things?"

"Not much. I mean, I can see things differently, like the spirit inside people, and today I learned that I can make it so that everything slows down around me."

"And that's everything?"

"Well . . . I think I sort of caused an explosion when an okulu'tan attacked us with his magic. Oh, and I ran down two Esharii with my horse, but that wasn't magic. Like I said, I'm still trying to figure it all out."

"And the sword?"

"It went into the river with me. I can still feel it, sort of, but I'm not sure where it is exactly. It seems to have moved and gone farther away. I think there is a limit to how far away I can sense it, and it's right near the edge."

Bortha raised his eyebrows questioningly.

"That's all of it. I'm not important—just another recruit for the regiments." That was it. He'd told Bortha everything, even though he'd been told not to, but he had to trust someone.

Bortha let out a short nervous laugh. "Most men never see an Esharii, and you've come face-to-face with them and survived. That alone makes you intriguing. Your abilities, however . . . those make you dangerous."

"I'm not dangerous. I can barely walk."

"For now, but I know one thing. Nobody likes the threat of someone stronger coming along behind them. I don't know everything a Draegoran can do with his magic, but if you can do powerful things that no one else can at your age, I promise you, you're a threat. And you're underestimating yourself. Anyone who can fight an okulu'tan with magic is someone to be feared."

"I don't want to be feared. I want what my uncle wanted for me, to go to the island and to become a Draegoran and help people, but I'm not doing that until I know the truth about Stick." He didn't tell him he had another goal now. *I couldn't live with myself if I escaped and allowed another churp to take my place . . . and Pekol will get another if I'm gone.*

Bortha rubbed at his chin and pursed his lips for a time. "Then you have quite the problem," he said finally, "and I'm afraid I can no longer help you if you won't take my advice and leave."

Riam sighed. He didn't even get angry. *I should have known the man would betray me, like everyone else.*

CHAPTER 35

"You have to leave," Bortha said, "and never return."
They were back in the kitchen. Not a glass earlier, the smell of grease and herbs, the hint of lye
used for cleaning, and the faint traces of Serina's perfume
that hung in the air had all been part of something special—
something warm and caring. With a single phrase Bortha
had severed his connection to the only place he felt safe.

"I don't understand."

"I needed to know why the Draegoran was looking for
you. Now I know. He'll have no interest in the inn or me
once you're gone." He took an apron off a peg and slipped
it on.

"But what about Stick? What about Pekol?"

Bortha would not meet his eyes. He pulled utensils from
a basin and shook off the excess water before hanging them
in their places on a rack that dangled from the ceiling. He
used more force than he needed to, and they banged and
clattered as he hung them. "Stick is probably on his way to
the Green Isles, and after I do the job with Pekol, we'll be
square again. That leaves only the Draegorans and you. I
have no intention of putting my nose into that snake den,
when all that needs to be done is for you to leave."

"But you said you would help."

"I am helping. Anyone else would have minded their own business or asked the Draegorans if there was a reward or, worse, let Pekol grind you to nothing in the first place." He wiped a hand on his apron and pulled a small pouch from his pocket. He tossed it to Riam. "There's thirty copper dregs inside. That's enough to buy a horse and get you a long way away from Parthusal or to buy a berth on a ship headed for Arillia. I don't want to know which you choose. Either way, you leave the city tonight and you don't look back. Forget the island. Nothing good comes from getting involved with those demons. If I had a son on the island and a daughter working Maiden's Fare, I'd rescue the son first."

Riam pushed his chest out, holding his ground and refusing to give in to Bortha's suggestions. "I told you, I'm not going anywhere till I know Stick is safe, and I'm going to get rid of Pekol."

"Grow up, boy." He threw a ladle down on the counter. It bounced off and along the floor. "Do you really think a twelve-year-old is going to stop that bastard?"

"You could help," Riam whispered.

"Dammit, boy. I'll deal with Pekol in my own time."

Riam could go straight to the island. Forget the sword, forget Pekol, forget everything, and become a Draegoran. The exact advice Gairen had given him. "Think of nothing else but becoming a Draegoran if you want to survive." *Perhaps it's time I listen.*

Riam stretched the fingers of his left hand wide. Surely the damage could be fixed on the island. It might be the only place it could be fixed. The Draegorans there were far more powerful than a twelve-year-old boy who didn't know what he was doing.

And Bortha was wrong about the Draegorans. Not all of them were bad. He had a chance to become one and prove it. He wouldn't waste it by running away and hiding, but he had to find out the truth about Stick and stop Pekol first. *What sort of Draegoran would I be if I began my training by ignoring an evil that deserves to be stopped?*

The purse sat heavy in his good hand, the leather stiff and clean—a new pouch. Bortha had planned for this before coming to get him. He recognized the gift for what it was—the innkeeper's way of easing his own guilt. He threw the purse onto the butcher-block table. It slid to a stop near the edge. "Keep it. You're not responsible for me. I am."

Riam stomped out the door, trying to look more confident than he felt.

He made it to the stable gate. He didn't open it. Instead, he stopped in front of it. An iron latch held the wooden gate closed. Once he flipped it open, he was truly on his own. *Maybe Bortha is right. Maybe I've been fooling myself, thinking I can stop Pekol.* A pair of hay hooks and a pitchfork hung on the rough rock wall. There were empty pegs for the rake and shovel they'd left by the stalls. The hammered metal of the hooks cast long shadows down the wall. An idea formed—one that didn't involve using the knife against Pekol. He already knew he couldn't stab the man in cold blood. He raised his head and pulled the gate open. He knew what he had to do.

"Wait," Bortha called. "At least take this." He came toward Riam holding a different purse out in front of him. It was oiled and stained from use.

Riam shook his head no. He wouldn't let the innkeeper buy him off.

"It's only a few dregs and the charm. If it was Stick's, which I don't think it was, he'd want you to have it. The money is for the work in the stables. You've earned it. Take it and buy new clothes. Whatever you decide, you can't do it in those rags."

Riam wanted to walk away again, to walk out the gate without the money and never look back, but the innkeeper was right. He needed the money. He'd pay the man back one day. He reached out slowly, fighting his pride.

"Don't come back to the inn." Bortha didn't let go of the money until Riam nodded his agreement.

He should have thanked Bortha—the man had done more for him than anyone else in the city, and he had a wife and an inn to worry about—but Riam couldn't do it. He couldn't get past the thought that the innkeeper had a duty to do more, that everyone around him had the duty to do more than walk blindly by those who suffered.

He took the purse and strode out the gate without another word. He didn't have much time until dark.

"Out of my shop, beggar," the narrow-faced tailor said.

"I'm not a beggar," Riam replied. He was lucky to find the tailor still open this close to sundown. The shop sat in an area that was far more expensive than he would have liked, but at least it was in a narrow alley and free from passersby. More importantly, it sat far enough from Pekol's lanes that Riam wouldn't be recognized. And it had one more advantage. Riam had asked around. The district wardens used the shop.

The tailor leaned over the counter and looked at Riam's stained trousers and bare feet. The blackened eyes likely didn't help his appearance. "And I'm the high landowner of the city. Get out before I take a rod to you. I don't help beggars or churps."

Riam kept the muscles of his face tight. He couldn't let the man know the truth of his guess. He placed a silver dreg on the counter. It made a crisp clacking sound on the wood.

The tailor rubbed at a thick mustache with a finger. "So you're a thief, then," he said, "and hiding the wardens' brand under a sling. Money's no good here if you're marked."

"There's not a glyph on my arm," Riam said. He had no desire to show the man the stitches and cuts with no way to explain them without suspicion. He placed a second dreg on the counter . . . *clack*.

The tailor glanced past Riam to the empty shop, as if the front door might open at any moment and reveal a trap.

"I'm running away. My grandfather likes to hurt me. I need proper clothing—breeches, a tunic, and a pair of sandals." Riam placed a third dreg on the counter. "That's more than enough."

It surprised Riam how easy it was to mislead the man. Somehow lies were easier when they were half-truths.

"No shoes here. You'll have to go to a cobbler."

"I'm sure you've an apprentice who could get them. I don't have a lot of time." Riam pretended to look around nervously, as if scared. Under the circumstances, it wasn't difficult.

The tailor watched, expecting Riam to place another dreg on the counter.

Riam kept his good hand at his side, two more dregs

hidden in his palm. He wanted to appear desperate, but not too desperate. The amount of money on the counter was already a fortune for what he was asking.

The tailor glanced at the dregs on the counter again. "I suppose I could measure your foot and have her find a pair, but they won't be new."

"As long as they fit and everything's ready tomorrow at this time."

"Tomorrow? Not possible. I'm far too busy to . . ."

Riam pressed a fourth dreg on the counter.

The tone of the tailor's voice softened as soon as the coin appeared next to the others on the wood. "Well, I suppose I wouldn't be showing the Fallen's charity if I didn't help a boy in danger."

Riam coughed into his hand. "There's one more thing. I need them to be the grays the Draegorans buy for recruits."

"You have to do it, Jami. I'm the only chance you have to get out from under Pekol. Once he has it in for someone, he never lets them go—ever. He'll wait years for his revenge if he has to," Riam said.

They stood in back of the bakery, in the shadows near a corner of the building where there were no windows, so they wouldn't be overheard. The secluded spot smelled of wet flour and smoldering wood. A fine coat of ash packed the cracks between the cobblestones.

Jami rubbed at his forehead. "It was only a charm."

"It's not the charm he cares about. It's control . . . and revenge against anyone who slights him. Look at Doby and Stick. He killed Doby because he lost control over him, and I'm afraid it might be too late for Stick. There are others he's hurt. I've helped him clean up his handiwork."

A guilty look crossed Jami's face, and he didn't argue that Stick might still be alive. He knew something—maybe it wasn't about Stick, but it was something that worried him. If he had anything to do with Stick's disappearance, Riam would never forgive him.

"But if you fail, he'll make you talk, and he'll know I was in on it."

"If I fail, I'll go into the pit, and he won't know a thing."

"He'll suspect something. He emptied the barrel two days ago."

"It's just a barrel. Nothing unusual about that. Besides, he'll be too tired to think of anything by the time we arrive at the shop. You don't even have to see him. All you have to do is make sure it's full and out front when we come by—"

"But there's hardly anything in it!"

"—and it has to be full of something he can't sell. I need it to be heavy so that he's worn out from hauling it around all day."

Jami raised his hands in the air in protest. "What am I going to put in it?"

"You'll figure it out. You'd better, if you want to be free of Pekol."

Riam felt a little guilty. Pekol might actually let the incident go, but there was no way to tell for sure. He decided to push Jami a little further. "And don't forget about Master Silva."

"What?"

"Pekol might forgive you for the charm, but he won't forgive him for facing him down. What will you do if Pekol goes after him?"

Jami let out a wailing groan. "This is all my fault. If I'd done my chores like I was supposed to, I never would have owed Pekol a favor. I never would have helped him with—" His eyes opened wide, and he clamped his mouth shut.

He'd been about to say Stick. Riam knew it. He grabbed Jami by the shoulders. "Helped him with what?"

"You were injured . . . he needed help with . . . a body."

Riam closed his eyes.

"I think he wanted me to see it—to scare me."

The muscles in Riam's jaw tensed. Anger welled up inside him, speeding his heart.

"It was like he was showing it off— Ow! You're hurting me." He tried to shake off Riam's hand.

Riam squeezed tighter and brought his face in close to Jami's. "Yet you still took the charm and helped him dispose of the body." The fire inside him grew, the same as it had with Pekol on the street. This time, Gairen's voice didn't stop him. He shook the small apprentice hard enough to rattle his teeth. "What is wrong with everyone in this city? No one cares about anyone." He let go with his good hand and grabbed the knife from the sling.

Jami squirmed to get away.

Riam held him in a firm grip with his numb hand. The familiar orange glow manifested itself inside Riam's vision, outlining Jami's body and exposing the flow of life within the apprentice.

"You helped get rid of Stick, someone you knew. You're as guilty as Pekol." Riam brought the knife up. He couldn't think of anything except making Jami pay for what he'd done.

"Stick?" Jami said from behind his hands. "It wasn't Stick. It was a woman!"

"What?" The anger melted away. *What am I doing?* He dropped the knife and it clattered to the stones. He let go of Jami.

The apprentice collapsed to the ground, tears running down his cheeks. "I didn't do nothing wrong. All I did was help him remove the body of a woman to pay off my debt. It's part of what rakers do," he sobbed. "It was just some woman."

"Then where'd the charm come from?"

"I don't know. It was in the cart when he came to get me. He laughed when I asked for it and said I could have it."

Riam's stomach heaved. He didn't know how far he would have gone if Jami hadn't spoken up. "I'm sorry," he mumbled.

"It was terrible, Riam. Her face caved in and her teeth broken. Who would do such a thing?"

Riam knew exactly who. He picked up the knife. Nothing would stop him tomorrow.

It began raining a glass after dark—a downpour that flooded the cobblestone streets. Riam huddled under an eave near the cart. It did little good. No matter which way he turned, the wind splattered rain in his face. The alley turned into a river.

The rain continued to pound him as the deluge grew, bringing the water's edge closer. Soon he would be sleeping in it.

"This is stupid," he said to himself. *There has to be a better place to wait out the rain.* The awning across the street called to him. The shopkeeper would never know.

He limped his way out of the alley and across the empty street. Crates lined the wall beneath the awning. He found a narrow gap and slid between two. There was enough space behind them to turn sideways and squeeze into a sitting position with his shoulder against the wall. It was cramped, but at least it was out of sight and out of the rain. He leaned his head against the wood and shivered.

Sometime later, the splatter of footsteps woke him. The rain still fell, echoing off the roof of the porch. He pulled his legs in tighter. While no one had ever said a word to him sleeping in the cart or walking back from the inn, he didn't want to be caught lying in front of a store like a beggar.

The footsteps stopped short of the alley. He peered from behind the crates. In the dim light that filtered from upstairs windows he could make out a figure at the mouth of the alley. It wasn't Pekol. Riam knew the hunch of his shoulders like the back of his hand after so many days following him down the streets. It wasn't Bortha either.

Something long and narrow caught the light. *Is it the Draegoran from the inn?* He pulled his legs in closer.

The man disappeared into the darkness of the alley. Whoever it was, they were definitely looking for him. *There's no other reason for anyone to go down the alley in a storm at this time of night.*

Riam pressed himself in tighter behind the crates. He still had the knife with him, but it would be of little use. He slid it out of the sling anyway. He'd wrapped the leather thong from the charm around the metal handle, and his grip on the knife was so tight that the charm bit into his hand.

The sound of footsteps splashing came again. They stopped directly in front of the porch where he hid.

Riam didn't risk another look. His mind screamed at him to run, even though it made no sense. If he crawled out, he'd be caught. He closed his eyes, straining to listen. Nothing—only the rain drumming on the wood above him and the splatter of it hitting the street. *What is the Draegoran doing?*

He felt something push at the edge of his awareness—

similar to the okulu'tan but softer. This time, he didn't fight back. Instead, he pressed himself harder against the wood, willing himself to be unseen. He thought of the water on the street, flowing around objects in its path. *Let it go around me like the rainwater.* He tightened the muscles of his body, as if he could squeeze himself smaller. *I am a raindrop the air moves around but does not penetrate.* He felt the Draegoran's power wash past him, searching and probing.

The muscles around his eyes hurt from closing them so tight. Time slowed. Each raindrop on the roof above pounded like a drum. The pressure around him grew stronger. He held his breath, afraid that if he didn't, he would be discovered. His muscles burned.

The probing ceased, and the splash of footsteps returned and then faded. Riam waited until he couldn't hear the Draegoran's steps anymore. Then he waited a bit longer for good measure. At last he relaxed and sagged against the crates, panting and trembling. The rain tapered off.

One more day and he would be gone. It would all be over, one way or another.

CHAPTER 36

"Kyden Verros?"

Verros opened his eyes. No trace of morning light penetrated the window. *Which meant very good news . . . or very bad.* He sat up and rubbed at the corners of his eyes with his knuckles. "Well, out with it, Roshan. What has you plodding into my room in the middle of Faen's darkness?"

A flare of light followed a metallic rasp, and the glow of a lantern chased long shadows up Roshan's face. "You said to inform you the instant we found the boy."

Verros twisted left and right, loosening his muscles in his morning ritual. His knees and back hurt with the pain of age whenever he woke, but it would fade once up and moving. Pushing himself to his feet, he grabbed a wide belt off the back of a chair and wrapped it around his waist. Once secure, he slipped his knife out from behind his pillow. He brushed his fingers softly over the crystal in the pommel. The slightest trickle of heat flowed up his arm and into his chest. He shivered. While there were many things the power could be used for—such as warming his body against the chill morning air—reversing the consequences of aging was regrettably not one of them.

Sensing nothing out of the ordinary across the web of

his regiment, he stuffed the knife into his belt and yanked his robe from Roshan's outstretched hand. "We have him, then? Where? Out with it." He pulled the robe over his head. Sometimes, he hated the way Roshan waited for him to ask questions before speaking. The man could bat an arrow out of the air with a sword, but somehow that speed didn't transfer to speech.

"Not yet. A message came from the city. Warden Hearst thinks he's found the boy among the churps. Says he'll gain possession of the boy soon and know for sure."

"Among the churps? How, by the Fallen, could that have happened?"

Roshan shrugged.

"Well, it doesn't matter what trouble the boy's gotten himself into—" Verros froze with the robe half buttoned. Hearst wasn't the type of man you assigned to a delicate mission. He ran the Red District for a reason. He was an enforcer, and good at it. Few broke the law or failed to pay taxes after they saw his work. "He knows I want the boy whole, doesn't he?"

"He knows, but it is Hearst."

Verros turned on him. "Roshan . . ." he said in annoyance.

Where others wilted under his temper, the big arms-master stood like a rock. "He knows better than to defy you, but if he figures out who the child is, there'll be blood. There's no way he'll be gentle with Jonim's whelp. Not after what happened on the ship. It's been ten years, but Hearst will never forget the death of every member of his taulin."

"He'll join them at the bottom of the ocean if he damages the boy permanently." Verros shoved the last wooden toggle through its hole on the robe. *Am I the only one who understands the significance of what the boy can do?* While many of his predecessors had been just as determined, none had held the vision to see what must be done—to plan out steps years in advance. And now Sollus had given him the final tool he needed to take control of everything, to return the Covenant to its former strength, and to put all those dirt-grubbing landowners back in their place—not only those rebelling in Mirlond, but all of them.

"There is something else. Another piece of news."

Again Roshan made him wait until asked. The man was exasperating. "And what news is that?"

"Master Iwynd disappeared from the outpost at Hath more than a tenday ago. Our man says he doesn't know where he went, but he packed all of his belongings, including that stupid arrow he keeps. Wherever he's going, he doesn't plan on returning."

"The council appoints that position. Iwynd may be the Owl's arms-master, but they'll take offense at him abandoning his duties—not that those idiots will do anything about it."

"He could be in the city already, or he could be steads away, searching along the river. There's a lot of ground between here and Hath," Roshan said.

Verros didn't doubt for an instant that Iwynd was already in Parthusal. "He's here, and that means Thalle plans on training new recruits again, or at least *one* new recruit. Which means he knows the boy is Jonim's son even without the letter we intercepted." *I won't let Thalle have him.* If the boy entered the Owl's training grounds, it would take an all-out assault to pry him loose. He wasn't ready for an open war. At least not yet—not until he had complete control of the council and the other kydens. *If Thalle knows what the boy can do, he'll risk everything to stop me from getting my hands on him. How can I use this against him? There has to be an angle.*

"Should I send the taulin waiting with the ship to reinforce Hearst? If Iwynd is in the city, I doubt it will take him long to find the boy. Hearst won't stand a chance alone against Iwynd . . ." Roshan thumbed his sword. ". . . or I could take more men into the city myself."

Verros knew where Roshan was going. "Not a chance."

Roshan stiffened. "If you don't think I can—"

"Oh, stuff your pride. It's not a question of if you can kill him. I need you here in case it becomes necessary to move against the Owls, not traipsing around the city trying to prove you are the deadliest man alive with a sword."

"It's not my pride I'm worried about. It is our men. I'm not keen on losing a single Wolf to the Owls—even if it is Hearst."

To someone who didn't know Roshan, the arms-master would have appeared as undisturbed and centered as always, but Verros knew the man like he knew himself. There was a slight lift to his chin when he was angry, and he blinked more. Roshan's eyes were fluttering like he walked in a sandstorm. He boiled beneath that calm facade at being held back and at the thought of losing Hearst needlessly. Verros didn't want to lose Hearst either, but Hearst's death would serve them well.

"Calm yourself. I don't like the thought of losing a senior warden, but Hearst is on his own. If he returns with the boy, then no harm done and we have what we want. If Iwynd is in the city and kills Hearst, then we have our reason to move against Thalle. No one will believe the Owl's arms-master is acting without his kyden's orders . . . and if he kills Hearst, then I'm more than justified in taking my grievance to the sand of the arena.

"But I was wrong about one thing. You *will* go to the city. Take a half-troop and don't let a ship depart unless you have personally searched it. Capture the boy. Iwynd, too, if he kills Hearst. We need the boy, and if Iwynd doesn't return, his kyden, as his first-line commander, will have to answer for his crime. But for Fallen's sake, don't kill him. If the death glyph appears next to his name on the rolls, the council may decide that justice has already been served.

"Instead, he must simply disappear. Once we have the boy and I've eliminated Thalle in the arena, then you can do whatever you want with Iwynd."

Kyden Verros rolled his shoulders and stretched to the side. *Removing Thalle and Iwynd would all but eliminate the Owls as a threat, and I'll be that much closer to turning my attention on the Stonebreakers.* The thought made his back hurt a little less. The idea that he might lose in the arena never occurred to him. Sollus was on his side.

Eisha Ryn was an immense warrior with an iron will and the strength of a maston. When Parron sent him to gather men for the final battle, he traveled the north, subduing the wild tribes one after another, defeating each of the chiefs in single combat.

When the last tribe bent to his command, he gathered them all and hammered them into a single force that helped tip the balance in Parron's favor.

After the battle, when the land was scorched and sown with all the hatred Tomu possessed until it could sustain no living thing, Eisha Ryn led the remainder of his tribesmen across the ocean with the rest of the survivors of Draegora.

For his part in the battle, he'd been entrusted to carry the most precious treasure of the Draegoran people, but when the survivors landed, Eisha turned his ships south and was never seen again.

Though no one remembers the treasure, the Draegorans have never forgiven Eisha's people.

—Kyden Deedre's *Study of the Tribes*

CHAPTER 37

S trapped on her back to a pair of crossed logs, her arms
stretched out from her sides, Ni'ola floated on the Najalii.
Water-soaked ropes dug into her wrists and ankles,
but they kept her from sliding off the cross beneath her and
into the depths below. Blood trickled down her forearms
where they'd drilled into the bone to place the tan'tari. *The
crystals must touch the marrow, where the blood is produced,
for the strongest joining to the spirit.* The thought came from
a distant memory, and when she tried to recall more, its origin scattered like a wisp of smoke.

The crystals would not help her predicament either. The
okulu'tan had drained every bit of power they possessed
before embedding them beneath her skin, and to her dis-
tress, they'd left the incisions open. The only thing that
might help was the lake below. She felt a vast concentration
of power within the water. With it, she could close the
wounds in an instant, but whenever she tried to draw that
strength into her tan'tari, she could not penetrate the surface of the water. She'd tried to reach it a dozen times before giving up. She simply didn't have enough strength to
break through the barrier. *Is this the test? If so, I've already
failed.*

Above her, a swath of bright stars went from horizon to

horizon across a cloudless sky. There was no moon. This was Faen's night, and not even a sliver of Sollus would make an appearance in the sky. Beneath her, the lake hummed with a power she could feel but could not reach. The sound of the okulu'tan chanting in a deep, slow rhythm came from the bank. If not for the pain of being tied to logs and having her arms sliced open like a gutted fish, it would've been peaceful.

Ni'ola's mind, however, was anything but peaceful. She'd known her body had changed, but she hadn't known how drastically until viewing her reflection at the village. She looked to be about eighteen, if not older, and her face had thinned so much that she looked more like her mother than the girl she'd been only days ago.

Li'sun had given her a simple explanation. "For every day you lived in a future possibility, your body aged that same day here in the present."

By her estimate, she'd spent at least six years traveling the ways. Six years—gone—and all she could remember were a few scattered glimpses. *What good does it do if I can barely remember anything—only enough to be confused?* It wasn't at all like Ri'jarra had explained before bonding her to Ky'lem.

Ni'ola drifted in frustration, watching the stars move along their journey west. She spotted the constellations she knew—the Sword and the Wreath, the Stallion, the Necklace, Peidon's Goat—and more than one falling star streaked across the horizon. While they were not actually the Gods of Light descending as her father had told her, they were still a symbol of their sacrifice, and she thanked the Fallen appropriately after each. Occasionally, a fish or turtle broke the surface, splashing soft waves in her direction.

Ni'ola tried to reach the power beneath her once more with no change. Whatever blocked her remained—an impenetrable stone wall. She pounded the back of her head against the wood of the log. It was infuriating. None of her memories told her what to do. She'd racked her brain searching, but the few recollections that came were like the one about tan'tari being set into bone. A quick thought as if it were a forgotten memory, and then the origin of it fading from her mind before she could grasp it. At times, the memories came three or four in a row and other times there were none—and when they did come, they made no sense. She would never be able to trust her thoughts again.

Li'sun had been little help. "I can give you no lessons, asha'han, until you become an okulu'tan. All I can tell you is to fight when the time comes. Fight for your life."

His words were useless. There was nothing to fight, so Ni'ola did the only thing she could do, drift and listen to the chant and the hum of the lake as her lifeblood leaked from her arms.

The night passed on. She was cold—colder than she'd been in the mountains with Ky'lem. The world felt distant to her, and the hum of the lake had grown louder. It called to her now. She knew a way to pass the barrier. It would be easy. Simply let go—let her spirit sink beneath the waves that lapped against her body—but to enter this way would be a one-way journey. Something lay beneath the surface that would not share its power. Something that wanted her. Something that needed life to wake and fight the enemy it had opposed since the beginning of creation. It would take her spirit for its cause, and it would not allow her to detract from that goal. Giving in to its call would mean surrendering her life.

Do not give in, asha.

"Ky'lem," she whispered. She reached out to him.

He moved quickly, ignoring the pain from his healing body. He favored his leg, but it did not slow him. He moved with reckless abandon for one so injured.

It is too late. I don't know what to do. I think I am dying.
No. I will be there soon. You must hold on.
The lake needs me.
I need you!

He burst out of the trees along the shore. She felt the crunch of the rocks beneath his feet and the blood pound within his chest.

She wanted to draw strength from him, but she couldn't bring herself to do it. Li'sun had said not to draw from him while his oya'sha was weak. She would not kill him to save herself.

The call below grew more insistent—strong and comforting, like her father reaching to hug her and tuck her under the covers after a long day. If she gave in to the power beneath the water, it would consume her, but she understood its need. She wanted to help it gain strength to fight the enemy.

I will die with you if you give in. Fight it! I am almost there. He sped up, even though his muscles and lungs burned with exhaustion.

She could resist no longer. *I am sorry, Ky'lem.* She took a last breath, ready to give herself to the water.

A second form came out of the darkness, slamming into Ky'lem and knocking him from his feet. She felt the pain of a blade biting into his side. He tumbled among the rocks and lay panting on his back, his own knife lost in the fall. A figure climbed on top of him.

"It is almost over. I will not allow you to help her, pachna," a nasal voice said.

Jal'kun straddled Ky'lem. The young spirit-taker who'd argued for her death brought the blade down toward Ky'lem's throat.

"No!" Ni'ola screamed. She thrashed at the ropes. *He is mine!*

Even in his weakened state, Ky'lem was not helpless. He had the training of a warrior, where Jal'kun did not. Ky'lem's hands came up and locked onto Jal'kun's wrist, stopping the blade's downward arc. He brought a knee up at the same time, using it to buck Jal'kun up and over his head.

Jal'kun flipped forward onto his back. The two men lay head-to-head—Jal'kun's hand holding the knife and Ky'lem's holding on to Jal'kun's wrist.

The two rolled along the shore before separating and climbing to their feet. Ky'lem was slower and his breathing was labored, but he pulled himself up into a fighting stance.

Ni'ola could see none of this with her eyes, but she felt it through the bond as a blind woman listens and feels.

"I continue to underestimate you, but that was the last time," she heard Jal'kun tell Ky'lem.

She felt Ky'lem spit. "So you've finally shed your cowardice enough to fight your own battles."

"Again, you are mistaken, Ti'yak. It is the other oku-lu'tan who are cowards. I'm doing what must be done to prevent this abomination. I served Ri'jarra faithfully and listened to his insane whispers for years. Only I know the truth of his visions. I should have been his ent'lai, not this asha'han."

Ky'lem lowered his center of balance, preparing for the okulu'tan's attack. "Come then, spirit-taker. I am not the asha'han you threaten with your knife."

"This?" Jal'kun held the knife up and laughed. He ran his finger along the edge, and it came away wet with Ky'lem's blood. "Why would I use this?" He tossed the knife through the air to Ky'lem and licked the blood from his finger. "Now that I have the taste of your spirit, I'll rip the life from your bones."

Jal'kun waved his hand, as if cutting a puppet's strings, and Ky'lem collapsed to the ground.

Ni'ola screamed and beat at the surface of the lake with her mind. The water around her boiled and steamed, but the power beneath defied her grasp. She felt Ky'lem's spirit weaken as Jal'kun drained the life from his body.

"Nooooo!" Ni'ola screamed. She threw everything she had at the barrier. It bent, further and further, until at last, with a deafening explosion of water and steam, it gave way. Ni'ola filled with power. The tan'tari beneath her skin blazed like torches, lighting the water around her in an eerie red, and her eyes blazed with fire.

She bent the power to her will, forcing it to strike at the okulu'tan before he could kill Ky'lem. Light, bright as the noon sun, shot from her hands in two narrow beams that raced over the surface of the lake.

Jal'kun's head snapped up. The two beams struck an invisible shield. White-hot power splashed around the edges, but the shield held.

She remembered the old spirit-walker's lightning and pulled more power from the limitless depths of the lake. It threatened to overwhelm her, but she didn't care as long as she saved Ky'lem. She let it flow through her body and hurled it out over the okulu'tan. Lightning, jagged and blinding, struck down at Jal'kun. Thunder boomed out over the lake.

Jal'kun staggered backward and fell to one knee. His shield flickered. "Not possible . . ." he gasped. Sweat beaded his forehead. "I will not be defeated by an asha!" He rose unsteadily to his feet, his shield growing solid once more.

She struck again and again, pounding at his shield, but Jal'kun held her attack at bay. She could not draw more. She was dangerously close to shattering her tan'tari, and if that happened, Ky'lem would be dead.

What do I do? Call the wind as Ri'jarra did against the Draegorans? A funnel in the sky would be of little use against Jal'kun. There were no clues from the ways to help her. *Think! There must be a way to defeat him.* She had unlimited power to draw from in the water.

The water . . . and Ri'jarra. There was something about the old spirit-walker and water. She dug for the memory and realized it lay in her past, not her future. Ri'jarra's only lesson rose in her thoughts as if she stood next to him in the pool once more. *"All waters are connected to each other. Too few okulu'tan remember this lesson."*

Ni'ola sent beams of molten energy beneath the surface of the lake. They flowed toward the shore, but instead of rising when they reached the bank, they dove under the land until they were beneath Jal'kun.

The ground rumbled, and Jal'kun searched around in confusion. He did not adjust his shield. It proved to be his undoing. A pillar of light erupted from the ground beneath him and rose to the heavens. Jal'kun screamed.

Ni'ola could hear his flesh sizzle and pop and smelled roasting flesh through Ky'lem. When she was certain he was no more, she let the power go, and the light extinguished, returning to the darkness of the night. Before she let the power fade completely, she used it to fill Ky'lem and to heal her own wounds. The wounds on her arms closed and mended, and she made sure to heal her eyes this time before letting the power go. She sagged against the ropes that held her, exhausted. The cool water of the lake washed against her body. She had nothing left.

All was quiet. The voices of the okulu'tan had ceased, their chant abandoned.

Sensing her weakness, the power of the lake struck. It wanted the energy she had taken returned, and it wanted her. An invisible hand took hold of her spirit and dragged it down into the depths.

The coolness of the water became suffocating and hot. She fought it, grabbing for anything that would help. The power gripped her tighter, sucking at her life. She tried to pull the energy of the lake back to her, just as she'd done to save Ky'lem, but it was closed to her now. So she pulled at the only other thing she could feel, Ky'lem.

Greedily, she tore away the oya'sha she'd replaced and

used it to hold off the power of the lake. It could not take her, but neither could she escape its grasp.

Ky'lem gasped, and his eyes rolled back in his head.

She would kill him if the stalemate continued. They would both be lost. "Is that what you want, our deaths?" she yelled.

Lightning crackled over the water, raising the hair on her body. The power continued to pull at her, and she drew more strength from Ky'lem to hold it at bay. "You cannot have me!"

With a deafening clap, a burst of lightning exploded over the water. When it faded, the power in the lake eased back below the surface. The hum was also gone, no longer calling to her. Ky'lem lay on the shore.

Ky'lem! Don't die—not because of me. Please, wake up.

He stirred and coughed. *Ni'ola?* The query was faint, but he lived. She could feel the wonder and awe in his mind and, behind it, pride.

CHAPTER 38

Pekol jumped when Riam pulled himself out from beneath the cart. "By the Fallen, boy. Don't startle a man like that."

Riam stood and straightened the sling, making sure the knife remained hidden. He faked a wince for Pekol's sake. He no longer needed to wear the thing, but he had to keep up the pretense. He still had no feeling from his elbow down, but it didn't stop him from using the arm. He picked up a handful of wet straw and used it to wipe black goo from his fingers. "I was checking the axles. I think they need to be greased after all the rain. The wood looks swollen."

The axles did need it, but not from the rain. He'd used his knife to scrape out all the grease he could reach. Then he'd pushed mud and dirt in its place. Pekol would be worn out by the end of the day, which was exactly what Riam wanted.

"Rain's never bothered the cart before," Pekol said. He rubbed at the thin coat of whiskers along his jawline.

Riam shrugged. "It rained something fierce last night. The water was all the way up to the bottom of the cart."

"Didn't seem that strong." He looked Riam up and down. "But you do look like a drowned marcat," he said and let out a cackle. The laugh was forced. "You stayed with the cart all night?"

Riam gave him a wide grin. "Never let it out of my sight."

"No one bothered it?"

"Who would bother an empty cart? Though come to think of it, I did hear footsteps once. Must have made a wrong turn because they turned around as soon as they came to the end of the alley."

Pekol's forehead wrinkled.

If Pekol knew about the Draegoran coming, Riam imagined he must be very confused. If the stakes of the game they were playing were not so high, he would have laughed. He needed to keep the raker off-balance.

"Did you meet with Bortha?"

Pekol's confusion turned to suspicion. He cocked his head. "Nothing you need to know about, and you'll forget about that conversation." He curled a hand into a fist. "I don't need to remind you who's in charge, do I?"

Riam dodged around the back of the cart. "No, sir. I didn't mean anything. I'll keep my mouth shut and work like I'm supposed to." He cowered down and put a hand over his face protectively. "You're the raker, I'm the churp. I know my place." He looked at Pekol between his fingers. He might have overdone it.

The mad-dog look faded from Pekol's eyes. "Good. Let's get going." Pekol moved to his place at the handles, grabbed them, and pulled like any other day. The axles squealed as the cart rocked forward, but it didn't move. "Push on the back. Once they loosen up and dry some, it should be fine."

Riam used his good arm to push. The cart groaned and screeched, but it barely moved. He'd done too good a job. The wheels were frozen. This part of the plan had been an afterthought, something that might even the odds if it came down to a fight. If Pekol climbed underneath, he'd know what Riam had done. Pekol might actually kill him here in the alley. Riam pushed harder, throwing all his weight into the effort, even using his "injured" arm. His feet scraped at the wet cobblestones.

With a loud shriek, something broke free and the wheels turned.

"That did it. Keep pushing. It'll get easier," Pekol said over his shoulder.

The cart rolled a little more smoothly by the time they turned the corner onto the street. Riam eased off, letting Pekol take most of the effort.

The morning continued this way, with Pekol shouldering the load and Riam pretending to push whenever Pekol glanced back in his direction. Anytime they stopped, Riam scurried to complete his tasks as fast as he could. He wanted to get the cart loaded, and he didn't want to give Pekol the chance to rest. Once they made it to the pit, he would make his move when Pekol struggled to empty the barrel Jami had prepared. Riam didn't want to do this, no matter how much he disliked Pekol, but good people had to stand up for those who could not.

Riam grabbed a chamber pot and walked to a sewer drain. Before coming to the city, he would have believed that pushing a man over a cliff and calling it an accident was cowardly and unfair. He had no such qualms about fairness anymore, at least not where Pekol was concerned. Ask the gate guard or Doby or Stick. None of them would care if they were alive and had a second chance. Besides, it really wasn't any different than when his uncle had executed the prisoners back in the town where they'd discovered Nola. He thought his uncle Gairen would have approved.

He'd daydreamed yesterday that he'd get answers about Stick from Pekol before the man died, but that was a fantasy that would get him killed. No, he would remove Pekol quickly and settle for justice. Then he would go to the island where he could serve something greater, something good.

Riam placed the pot back on the doorsill and moved to the next shop. Soon they would be at Master Silva's bakery. So far there hadn't been a thing worth taking to the Square, which was good. Riam needed enough time to return and retrieve his clothing from the tailor and be gone before anyone complained of refuse in the street or unemptied chamber pots.

They rounded a curve in the lane and came within sight of Master Silva's shop.

He couldn't see the barrel. Jami had failed him.

He held a curse on the tip of his tongue, just short of saying it out loud, when the crowd parted. There it sat, up against the wall right where it always did. Thank the Fallen. Jami had done his part after all.

They made their way building by building toward it, stopping at each so Riam could collect the waste of shop owners and merchants. Riam's heart beat faster the closer they came. *Please let Jami have filled it with something that could not be sold.* Without the barrel, Pekol would sit back and make Riam empty the cart. There would be no opportunity to catch him unprepared.

The cart clunked to a stop in front of Master Silva's shop. Normally, this was the best-smelling spot on the street—the strong odor of baking bread always made Riam hungry—but today, a sharp, tangy smell floated on the air.

"Morning, raker," Master Silva said, stepping out of the doorway. His voice was absent of the disdain he usually reserved for Pekol. He moved toward the barrel. "Let me give you a hand since your churp is injured."

Fallen's mercy! Master Silva would create a scene if he noticed something out of place with the barrel. Riam looked for a place to flee. He might get away if he made it down the closest alley and into the crowd on the next street before Pekol could catch him.

Pekol let go of the cart handles and rubbed at his shoulders. Beads of sweat ran down his temples and his chest heaved. He cocked his head to the side and looked at Riam.

Riam shrugged. When Pekol turned back to Master Silva, Riam shuffled to the side, putting the cart between him and the bakery.

Master Silva stepped in front of the barrel and scratched at his head. He glanced to the wagon and back.

"What's wrong?" Pekol asked.

Riam took two steps backward, getting as much of a head start as he could without it being obvious. He could still retrieve his new clothing and get to the island. Pekol would never think to look for him near the docks. He took a third step back.

"I think you should bring the cart closer. The barrel is full of olives. It's still going to be heavy."

"Olives?" Both Riam and Pekol said at the same time.

"Whole barrel went bad."

Pekol rubbed at his chin. "Olives, you say . . ."

It couldn't be luck. Jami must have tricked Master Silva. "It happens. Sometimes they sour and you don't know it till it's opened. Can't sell 'em. Can't eat 'em," Master Silva said.

Pekol frowned. "Why not?"

"Because they're rotten, you fool. They'd make you shit your guts out. Can't even give 'em to the piggeries. It'd poison the whole lot."

Pekol frowned. "I'll have to go straight to the pit because of the weight. Means I'll have to make two runs today." He obviously didn't want to take the olives if he could get nothing for them in the square, and he certainly didn't want to make two trips with a cart already difficult to pull. He muttered curses to himself as he moved the cart closer.

Master Silva looked right at Riam. "It's also inconvenient for me. I'm out twenty dregs' worth of olives."

The two men strained and grunted with the barrel, and they almost dropped it when Pekol stumbled, but they managed to get it into the cart.

"Come on, boy," Pekol said. "You're going to have to help me, and no cryin' about your arm or your side. I know it doesn't hurt as much as you're letting on."

Riam took his place behind the cart.

"Ready?" Pekol said.

"Yes, sir."

Pekol lifted and they both strained against the weight. The cart creaked forward.

"I'll have something for you if you return this afternoon," Master Silva said.

Pekol took the words to be directed at him, but this time, there was no doubt in Riam's mind. Master Silva had been looking right at him when he spoke. He'd said "if" not "when." Jami must have told him what he planned.

Master Silva gave Riam a curt nod when he passed.

It was hot, and Riam was sweating profusely by the time they made it to the pit. The smell of the piggeries was as overpowering as the first day he'd come here—maybe worse since Pekol didn't give him a scarf to cover his nose and mouth. A slight breeze hit him, making the stench worse. There was no getting used to it, no matter how many times he came here. Fortunately, for better or worse, this would be his last trip.

Two children, dressed in little more than rags, ran toward them, their baskets swinging wildly in their eagerness to collect food for the pigs.

Riam always hated to see the children who scavenged the rakers' carts and wagons. The oldest he'd seen couldn't be more than six or seven, and these two were no different. One was a boy and the other a girl, although even this was difficult to tell with all the dirt and muck that clung to them and matted their hair.

"Git!" Pekol waved them away. "Nothing in this load for ya."

The children slid to a stop, kicking dust into the air. They eyed the cart, trying to puzzle out if they were being lied to or if they would get into trouble for not checking the cart themselves.

"I said, git!" Pekol picked up a rock.

The taller of the two children, the boy, stood protectively in front of the girl while she backed away. She had open sores on her arms and legs that oozed clear fluid.

Pekol threw the rock. It smacked the boy on the shin, and he jumped and squealed before running off after the girl.

"They're like dogs," Pekol said. "Don't understand anything but food and pain."

No, they're like me. Orphans forced to work as slaves. They simply had no family to care for them.

Watching them climb through a wooden fence, Riam's old life didn't seem nearly so bad. *A few beatings are a small price to pay for food and shelter.*

No . . . that was wrong. That was his fear talking.

His grandfather murdered others and deserved his fate — same as Pekol. The fear subsided, replaced by anger. It filled him, pushing aside all other emotions. One way or another, Riam's life as a churp was coming to an end.

No other rakers were here, and now that the children were gone, there was no one else in sight. All he had to do was catch Pekol off guard for a moment.

Pekol pulled the wagon to the usual spot. It seemed to take forever to cross the yard.

"Tie the cart off," Pekol said.

He watched as Riam measured the length of rope and cinched it to the stake, but he didn't watch when Riam climbed underneath.

Riam pushed the hook between the axle and the underside of the cart, making sure it wouldn't catch if the cart started rolling back into the pit. When Pekol was unloading the barrel, he'd give the cart a push, and it would take Pekol with it over the edge—an accident if anyone asked. He slid out from under the cart.

"Done, sir," Riam said.

Pekol glanced underneath the cart, but there was no way for him to spot what Riam had done without getting down on all fours—which he never did.

"Let down the gate on the back of the cart. I can't lift the barrel by myself, so we'll turn it on its side and tie it off, then dump the contents with the rest of the refuse by tilting the cart back."

Curse the Fallen! He needed Pekol in the cart.

Riam slid sideways along the narrow space of ground between the back of the cart and the ledge. He leaned out enough to look down. It was a long way to the bottom. The world suddenly felt wobbly, trying to throw him over the edge. He shivered and turned away. He fumbled the latches on the gate, and it fell open with a thud.

"Now sit on the cart handles so that it doesn't tip back while I work on it."

His plan might still work. All he had to do was wait for the man to get near the back end and let the cart flip back. Riam's heart pounded and his hands were sweaty.

Pekol climbed into the cart and walked the barrel halfway back.

A little farther. Just a little more.

But Pekol stopped. He dumped the barrel over, and a flood of olives tumbled out. He used his knee to pin the barrel against a sidewall and tested the balance of the cart, making sure it would not tip back. "Hand me one of the other ropes so I can secure it."

Riam grabbed a rope from another tie-off stake, dragging its metal hook along the ground, and gave it to Pekol.

The raker snatched it from his hand and wrapped two loops around the barrel before tying it to the side rail with a square knot. He jumped out of the cart and wrapped the

long end of the rope around one of the cart handles to secure it. He fumbled with the excess rope that held the hook
and settled with leaving it piled on the ground.

Riam's only other option rested in the knife he carried.
Now was his best chance for that if he was going to do it—
while Pekol bent over the cart handle. He slid the knife out
of the bandage and into his hand. He stepped up behind
the raker. All he had to do was strike, just as Bortha had
told him, and it would be over. No one else would ever be
hurt. He grabbed at the power that had served him before.
Nothing came. The world didn't slow. The orange glow
didn't fill his vision. He tried another approach. He felt for
his link to the sword, trying to pull some spark of energy
that would serve him. Nothing. He would have to do this
on his own. He raised the knife, ready to plunge it into
Pekol's back.

He tightened his grip till his hand shook, but he couldn't
get himself to bring the knife down. He wanted to, but all
the reasoning that had brought him to this moment fell
apart. No matter how terrible the man was, Riam couldn't
bring himself to stab a person in the back. Even Gairen had
faced his grandfather when he killed him.

"Are you going to try and stick me, or just stand there
holding the knife in the air?" Pekol said.

Riam jumped backward, his heart thumping so hard he
could feel it in his ears. *How had Pekol known?* The man
hadn't even looked back. He remained hunched over, putting a last cinch in the knot.

"I figured you'd try and use Bortha's knife today." He
stood and turned toward Riam. "I've spent my life on the
city streets. I'm smart enough to notice when someone is
carrying a blade, boy."

Riam glanced at the sling, now dangling empty.

"It's not where you carry it, it's how you carry it. Folks
that carry a weapon act a little different—more mindful of
certain movements and more protective of the location—
especially if they are new to carrying it. Plus, they act more
confident, as if having a slim piece of sharpened steel will
protect them. More often than not, it only gets them into
trouble."

He stepped forward, faster than Riam could react, and

batted the knife from Riam's hand. It tumbled through the air and bounced off a rock with a dull clank.

Riam tried to run, but Pekol snatched him by the hair and slung him in a wide arc that spun him around and slammed him against the cart.

"Did Bortha put you up to this, sending a boy to do his dirty work?"

"No. I took the knife. Bortha doesn't even know I have it," Riam blurted out.

Pekol backhanded him across the mouth. "You're lying. That's one of Bortha's throwing knives. He keeps them strapped to his forearm under his shirt. Knew I couldn't trust him. Should have done away with him a long time ago. Well, I'll settle with him before the sun sets."

"No!" Riam said. "He gave me the knife to protect myself. That's all. He didn't say anything about using it against you." It wasn't exactly a lie. Bortha had never said Pekol's name when he gave it to him.

Pekol rubbed his bottom teeth against his upper lip, deciding what he was going to do next.

I should have used the knife in the city when I had the chance. Pekol would kill him for sure now.

"Where were you last night when Hearst came for you?"

"Hearst?" Riam asked, confused by the change of subject.

"The district warden. The one who added time to your sentence. He was suddenly curious about you yesterday— enough to have him pounding on my door in the rain. I told him right where you were. He should have found you. You've been sneaking off at night, haven't you? After all I've done for ya."

"I was there. I saw him," Riam said.

"Don't lie to me, boy." Pekol tried to catch him with another swing. Riam dodged. He didn't escape the blow completely, but it struck him with far less force than the first.

"I'm telling the truth," Riam said in protest. "I slept on the other side of the street among the crates at the mercantile to get out of the rain. He didn't see me."

"He would have known you were there."

"It's the truth." He wasn't about to tell Pekol about his powers or how they'd hidden him from the Draegoran.

Pekol glanced behind him again. "Well, he'll be along soon. We can sort it all out when he arrives."

"He's on his way here?"

"Oh, yes." Pekol pulled out the knife he kept in his belt. "But that doesn't mean I can't have a little fun first. Told me to keep you alive, but that leaves me a lot of leeway." Pekol let out a cackle that turned into one of his coughing fits.

Riam scrambled over the front of the cart faster than Pekol could recover. When he crawled to the back of the cart, his weight sent the back down and the front end teetering upward. The contents of the cart slid toward the back, adding more weight. The back of the cart slammed to the ground, dumping refuse out the back and over the edge of the cliff.

Riam nearly went with it, grabbing the edge of the cart just in time to keep from going over the back. The bitter tang of olives filled his nostrils as they poured over and past him. When enough weight emptied, the front of the cart crashed back to the ground.

Pekol came around the side toward him, and Riam dove over the opposite side and crawled underneath the cart. They played chase like this for a time, Pekol circling back and forth with Riam moving to the opposite side underneath to stay away. Finally, Pekol stopped.

"Come out, boy. I promise. I won't touch you."

"Like you promised Doby he would go free?" Riam said. Pekol would never keep his word, and even if he did, it wouldn't do Riam any good—Hearst was on his way here. He had to find a way to escape.

"That boy got what was coming to him."

"Right. And the woman you killed? She deserved it, too, right?"

"Shut your mouth—"

"Or what, you'll kill me? A little late for that threat."

Pekol knelt beside the cart, slashing the knife back and forth at Riam.

Riam stayed well out of reach. He looked at the fence to the piggery. He might be able to make it if he could get Pekol to crawl underneath the cart. "Let's not forget Stick while we're talking about what everyone deserves. Of course, it's only women and boys you touch. When it comes to men like the guard, you have someone else do your killing."

"You'll beg for death when I catch you, you little shit," Pekol howled and scrambled around the cart.

"Oh, no. The great killer of whores and children is going to beat me again."

Pekol made a strangled noise and yanked the front of the cart up by the handles, tilting it high into the air.

Riam scrambled back, getting tangled in the ropes used to tie the cart off.

Holding the cart tilted up and the knife out in front of him, Pekol moved hand over hand toward Riam. He snarled, spittle dripping from the corners of his mouth and his upper lip curled back to expose his teeth like a dog. He jabbed the knife at Riam.

If not for Pekol's awkward position, Riam would have been skewered. Riam tore at the rope wound around his leg and his hand closed on the metal hook. He dodged a wild slash from the knife.

In desperation, Riam pulled at the power within himself and swung the hook with all his strength.

A rush of energy flowed through his body, powering his swing as if Sollus himself was behind it. The hook sank deep into Pekol's thigh.

Pekol let out a howl and fell backward, dropping the cart. One of the handles smashed down on his face.

Riam dove for the hook on the second rope before Pekol could recover and aimed a blow at the man's head.

Pekol got an arm up to protect himself, and the hook drove through his forearm. He struck back with the knife, slicing Riam's arm.

Riam rolled away and leaped to his feet. He didn't feel the wound—the slash had found his numb limb, but it still bled profusely.

"You're going to pay for this," Pekol said. He dropped the knife and took hold of the hook in his forearm, trying to work it free.

Riam had to do something. He searched frantically for the knife Bortha had given him but didn't see it, so he did the only thing he could think of. He rammed the cart with his shoulder and pushed with everything he had. The wheels didn't want to turn at first, but when the cart started rolling, there was no stopping it. It went over the edge of the pit.

Pekol didn't get the hook out in time. The rope jerked him violently by the arm toward the cliff. He slid toward the edge until the anchor line hooked to his leg snapped taut. A loud pop was followed by a tormented scream.

Neither hook tore free. Pekol lay stretched on the ground, the weight of the cart pulling him by the arm toward the cliff and the anchor stake holding him by the leg. His arm twisted and stretched. Blood leaked from both wounds.

Pekol's scream tapered off. He sucked in a breath. "For Fallen's sake, boy, help me," Pekol said. His bottom jaw shook. Spittle ran from the corner of his mouth.

"Why should I?" Riam said.

"Take my purse. Take anything you want. Just help me . . . fuck, it hurts." He fumbled for his purse with his free hand and tore it from his waist. He tossed it limply in Riam's direction.

The rope shuddered and Pekol's arm stretched even more. He didn't scream again, but he bit his upper lip hard enough that his teeth went all the way through and his eyes bulged.

Riam turned away.

"Help me, please," Pekol whimpered.

Riam couldn't take it. He searched the ground around him until he found Bortha's knife.

He paused. "Tell me where Stick is first," Riam said.

Pekol let out a delirious cackle. His head lolled to the side.

"Tell me, and I'll cut you free." Riam held the knife up in front of Pekol's face to get his attention. "Did you kill Stick?"

"No," Pekol said. "I gave that useless shit to Hearst. He'll get exactly what he deserves." He giggled and jerked.

"You're a monster," Riam said.

"No one with a glyph gets away. Not Stick. Not you. Not anyone. Wolves won't allow it."

Riam pulled the bandages off his arm and held it out for Pekol to see. "Well, I guess it's a good thing I don't have a glyph anymore."

The stake holding Pekol and the cart began to tilt forward with the weight, threatening to pull free of the ground.

"Hurry! I've answered your questions."

"Yes, you have." Riam moved to the anchor stake and worked at the rope with the knife.

"What are you doing?"

"Cutting you free. Good-bye, Pekol."

CHAPTER 39

Riam didn't take the main road back. He made his way through the fence and the piggery, and across the sprawling farms and rolling hills that lay outside the city instead. If anyone paid attention to him, no one said anything. It took longer than he wanted, but he couldn't take the chance of running into Hearst on the road.

At a farmhouse he tore a section of cloth from a shirt on a clothesline to bind the cut from Pekol's knife and used the rest to make a new sling. No one saw him take it, but he was no thief, despite what the glyph on his arm had indicated. He left a few dregs for the owner to find and threw the old sling in a ditch. It didn't take long before blood seeped through the new one, but there was little he could do about it.

The wound was a small price to pay to rid the world of Pekol. He had no regrets—the raker deserved his fate—but his actions weighed heavily on his thoughts.

No matter Stick's fate at the hands of Warden Hearst, at least his fellow churp had been avenged. Although it didn't solve anything, it brought some measure of justice and completeness to the loss. If Riam ever visited the Green Isles, he'd find Stick's mother and tell her the fate of her son and that Stick had planned to return home to make amends.

He used a different gate to enter the city. The guards were curious about his injury, but they waved him through after he paid the fee and told them he'd come to the city to find a mediker. From there, he made his way to the bakery. If he were smart, he'd go straight to the island by way of the tailor. If it wasn't for the money from Pekol, he would have, but he owed Master Silva for the olives, and he couldn't leave the debt unpaid.

He came up the alley to the back door of Master Silva's shop. The soot-stained tiles made him pause. He'd almost killed Jami here. That had never been his intention, but the power, when it came, fueled his desire to fight. No, fight wasn't the right word. The power wanted him to kill. It'd been the same on Maiden's Fare with Pekol and at the pit when he'd held the hook in his hand. At first, he'd thought it was simply his anger, but the more he thought about it, the more he knew that there was something more going on. That scared him. *Was this desire what made the Wolves so dangerous?* He remembered the timber yard, when he'd wanted to touch the blade to the dead body. He swore the events were connected, but once again, all the answers were on the island.

"Riam! You're alive," Jami said through a window. He disappeared, and a moment later the back door to the shop banged open. "I thought sure you were a goner and that Peke would return alone."

"Pekol won't be coming back," Riam said.

"It's done, then?" Master Silva said from the doorway.

Riam nodded. "I can't stay long, but I didn't want to leave without paying for the olives. I know there was nothing wrong with them." Riam dug through Pekol's purse. "Twenty dregs for the olives, that's what you said. I'm sorry I couldn't bring the barrel back."

"For Fallen's sake, don't worry about the money or the barrel. Doby was a good boy, despite what he'd done to earn his sentence. So was Stick. Having a glyph on your arm isn't meant to be a death sentence. Supposed to do your time, learn your lesson, and move on. People like Pekol have twisted it all around."

"No, take it," Riam said, shoving the money into Master Silva's hand. "I won't be needing it. I don't mean to be rude, but I need to be going. I don't want to put you in any danger."

Master Silva took hold of Riam's wrist. "That's fresh blood on your sling. You don't need to be going anywhere until someone's had a look at it."

"Pekol cut me pretty good, but I can't stay. The district warden is looking for me, and maybe a few other Draegorans along with him. If any of them find you helping me . . . well, I don't know what will happen, but it won't be good."

"I know about that. A Draegoran came by after you left for the pit asking questions. It wasn't Warden Hearst, and I didn't recognize him, but he was high-ranking. I'm guessing there's more going on than the fight between you and Pekol."

"I have to go. He might return."

"Bah. I've already answered his questions. He won't be coming back, but we'll keep you here behind the shop to be safe." He turned to Jami. "Go and fetch a mediker. The old one Bortha uses. He knows how to keep his mouth shut." He passed Jami a few of the coins Riam had given him. "Pay whatever he requires to hurry and keep quiet about it."

Jami dashed off down the alley.

"Sit down on the bench. I'm going to lock the front door."

Riam didn't want to explain the old injuries or how he'd removed the glyph. Jami and Master Silva were kind people. The less they knew, the better it would be for them. He looked in Pekol's purse. A good thirty dregs remained inside. He pulled out five more and placed them on the bench—more than enough for wasting the mediker's time.

He wished he could stay and say good-bye. It was ironic that of all the people he'd encountered since being tested, Pekol had been the only person he'd actually said those words to.

Riam used Grantor's Street to leave the bakery. Despite the risk, it provided the quickest way to the tailor's shop. He needn't have worried. This late in the afternoon, the streets were filled, and it was easy to scurry along the edge of the crowd. With the rags he wore, people went out of their way to avoid him.

A shopkeeper sweeping the steps to his store recognized Riam. He looked at his chamber pot and frowned. "Where's Peke?" he asked.

"He'll be late today. He had to make an extra run to the pit because of the baker down the street." Riam waved back the way he'd come and kept moving before the man could ask more questions.

True to their bargain, the tailor had Riam's clothes and sandals ready.

"Draegorans see you in these and you're sure to get their attention."

"I'm counting on it," Riam said.

"Thought you said you was running away."

"I am, but you have to run somewhere to leave another place behind."

"Hope you know what you're doing."

"Me, too." Riam dug into the purse and handed the man an extra dreg. "Thank you for the clothes. Where's the closest mediker and a place to get a meal and a bath?"

After a bowl of stewed meat and scrubbing himself twice in a tub, Riam felt whole again. It was amazing the difference a few bites of food and a bath could make. He smiled halfheartedly at that. Gairen had used almost the exact same words after the fight with the wasps. He'd been right. The bath washed away the smell and filth of Pekol and of being a churp.

Instead, he smelled like marigold and sage from the ointment the mediker sold him. The woman had sewn his arm up without a word about his injuries once Riam paid her enough for her service and for the salve she said to use twice a day for a tenday. All Riam had to do now was figure out how to get on a boat to the island without the Wolves finding him.

"Late, aren't ya?" the young woman who took the empty bowl from his table said. She was pale with freckles and a slightly upturned nose, and her hair was haphazardly tied back. Thin, stray locks stuck out in all directions.

"Excuse me?" Riam said.

"I asked if you were late. The tests were done more'n two months ago."

"I'm from Nesh. It took a while to get here."

She snorted. "I'll say."

"I got lost."

"You travel all that way by yourself?" She seemed impressed.

"Not all the way, but I was for the hardest part."

"Well, I'm sure they'll still take you once you get to the pier."

Riam sat up straight. "The pier?"

"The one reserved for the Draegorans. You can't miss it. It's the big stone one with an iron gate and Draegorans milling about." She winked at him.

Is it that simple? After everything that's happened, all I have to do is show up at a pier?

"Thank you." Riam jumped up from the table and dug an extra dreg from his purse.

"What's this for?" she asked.

Riam shrugged. "Taking the time to talk to me."

She tucked it away. "Wish everyone gave me extra."

Riam paused at the door. "Ummm . . ." He held his hands up, pointing questioningly down the street both ways.

She laughed. "Keep to this street all the way to the end, then turn left on the coast road. You won't miss it."

"Thanks."

It was farther than he thought it would be, but he enjoyed the walk. He hadn't seen much of Parthusal, and now that he was free, it seemed as if he were seeing the city for the first time. He passed rows of houses, some small and packed close together and others large with high walls and gates. There were fountains and statues and gardens, bakeries and open markets. Colorful awnings shaded the entrances to shops, and the smells changed with every step, from grilled meats to exotic perfumes. Even the crowd felt different—no longer oppressive and uncaring. People smiled at him or called to him to look at trinkets and goods. City guards took notice of his gray clothing and nodded in respect.

All in all, his newfound freedom gave him a sense of wonder and awe he hadn't felt before. The city really was a magnificent place, and that was without catching a glimpse of the keep or the Temple of Sollus he'd heard about from the other churps. He chuckled at the memory of going into town with his grandfather. It had always been something special. Now, it would be like going back to the pit. *Well, maybe not that bad.* Home didn't quite smell like the pit, and he wouldn't mind seeing Magistrate Ferrick again.

A hand grabbed his arm roughly. "Well, if it isn't our missing recruit. I've been looking for you."

Hearst's voice nearly made Riam wet himself. He yelled out and tried to tear free, but Hearst squeezed his arm hard enough to make Riam stand up on his tiptoes.

"None of that, boy." Hearst jerked Riam forward, maintaining his hold and walking Riam down the street like a puppet. "I'm not going to hurt you unless you make me." He looked at Riam's clothing, noticing the grays for the first time. "It seems you were already headed to the island. Well, I'm here to help you along."

How did Hearst find me so quickly? In a city this large, it couldn't have been dumb luck.

"You're a surprising young man," Hearst said. "I thought you'd be long gone from the city once I found Pekol at the bottom of the pit, but I double-checked the inn to be sure. Bortha had to be persuaded to let me read his thoughts.

"That was an impressive piece of work you did on Pekol, by the way. He was a ruthless little bastard, but he had his uses. Maybe I'll have Bortha take his place. That'll set a nice example for the rest of the district."

Riam didn't respond. He wasn't sure if Hearst really meant the last part about Bortha or if the man meant to break his spirit. Hearst seemed a lot like Pekol in this regard—ready to do things for spite if he knew they would hurt.

They came to the coast road. Docks stretched out from the land's end like fingers. The smell of fish hung in the damp air, and gulls squawked from perches atop roofs and beams. Hearst turned them to the right.

"The pier is the other way," Riam said.

"Too many eyes from the other regiments there."

Whatever the Wolves wanted with him, it wouldn't be good. He searched for a means to escape but saw nothing that would help. Not a soul on the road would interfere with a Draegoran escorting a child in gray. He had Bortha's knife, but he held little faith that it and whatever power he could summon would do him any good against the strength of a full Draegoran. He was caught, and there was absolutely nothing he could do about it.

The crowd parted ahead of them, and Riam's mouth fell

open. There in the middle of the street stood Master Iwynd. A small leather pack sat beside him. The people around the Draegoran gave him a wide berth, forming an empty pocket on the busy road. Hearst yanked Riam to a stop.

Riam sagged with relief. They hadn't parted on the best of terms, but Master Iwynd was still a welcome sight.

"You're going in the wrong direction, Hearst. The recruits go by way of the pier."

"I have my orders," Hearst said.

"As do I," Iwynd said. He drew the same longknife Riam had seen him carry back at the outpost.

Traffic halted, with the people around them backing away to give them more space. By the wide eyes of the crowd, a fight between Draegorans was not something they were used to seeing.

Hearst licked his lips. "The boy—"

Master Iwynd leaped forward. Hearst let go of Riam's arm and attempted to draw his sword. It didn't clear the scabbard before Master Iwynd buried his longknife in the warden's chest.

Master Iwynd grabbed a fistful of Hearst's clothes and pulled him close. "Just so you know, the boy is Jonim's son."

Hearst's eyes widened. He snarled and shook.

Iwynd twisted the knife and shoved it harder against Hearst's chest before letting go.

Hearst's legs gave out, and he slid off the blade to the ground.

A woman screamed and dropped the package she carried.

Master Iwynd scanned the crowd. As if he'd issued a command, people went back about their business.

Hearst's body withered and darkened.

Master Iwynd tsked his tongue and shook his head. "Always draw your weapon when your opponent does, especially when you know he's faster than you."

Riam swallowed. "Yes, sir."

"Get his sword. We don't have much time. He's not the only one looking for you. The district is crawling with Wolves." He retrieved his pack and threw it over a shoulder.

Riam looked for something to wrap around the blade to keep from touching it, like Gairen had done back in the timber yard. Seeing nothing, he pulled his sleeve down over his hand and reached for the sword.

"You don't need to do that. It's safe. Once a Draegoran dies, the crystal goes dormant."

Riam still avoided touching it and used his sleeve to slide the blade back down in its scabbard. He unbuckled the belt and tugged it from beneath Hearst's body. He ignored the stares of the people who passed by. "Why are you here?" Riam asked.

"You'd rather I was back in Hath?"

"That's not what I meant."

"I know, but there will be time for conversation later. I told Hearst the truth. I have orders from your grandfather, and we've a ship to catch."

His grandfather? What is Master Iwynd talking about? The man is dead.

CHAPTER 40

K y'lem's head lay in Ni'ola's lap. The rings from his beard filled a bowl by his side, and Ni'ola combed through the rough, wavy hair with her fingers, applying mint-scented oil. There was an unusual fondness to the gesture, like a mother caring for an injured child, yet it was he who was the elder, not her.

In his old life, Ky'lem had experienced a similar scene every sundown—lying in a longhut much larger than this one with his wives and daughters unwinding the rings from his beard and oiling the hair before sleep. Ni'ola's hands felt both similar and different. In her touch was the innocence of his oldest daughter, Mi'lae, the strength of his firstwife, Tsi'shan, and the awe and wonder of his youngest daughter, Chy, who was not yet old enough to take her mother's surname.

What bizarre dream have I entered? He'd certainly never expected an outcome such as this when he joined the warband to go north over the mountains. He'd expected to gain stature in the tribe—maybe another wife. But this was no dream, and his wives were no longer his to claim. He was a pachna now, serving a spirit-walker unlike any who'd touched the sacred lake before her.

Ky'lem reached up and grasped Ni'ola's wrist, as if to

confirm this reality. He rubbed his thumb over the scar that ran the length of her forearm—proof of her abilities. He felt the roughness of the scar compared to the rest of her dark skin and the hard lump from the crystal that allowed her to use the magic.

"Li'sun says you will not die, as long as I keep you strong until your spirit has recovered," she said in a hoarse voice. Dark circles hung beneath her eyes. She'd held him, cradled in her arms, for more than a day and a night—only leaving to relieve herself or retrieve food, and even for those necessities, she'd balked at being gone from his side.

Her red pupils brightened, and a surge of warmth passed through his body. She was in nearly as bad a shape as he was, but she was determined to keep giving him her strength.

"Enough. Leave me be." He knew how tired she was, and he didn't want her to drain what little strength she'd regained. He sat up, and Ni'ola used the opportunity to check the moss-caked wound from Jal'kun's knife. He pushed her hand away. "I've been stabbed many times, some worse than this, and survived." It wasn't true. An injury such as this would have meant a long, painful death if she hadn't repaired the damage to his insides.

The warmth faded, and her hands moved to the back of his shoulders, examining the older wounds, the ones left by the mergols.

"They remain clean and cool to the touch. There is no swelling below the surface," she said.

Mergols were filthy animals, and their talons carried the rot with them. Even with the wounds closed by magic, they needed watching. "More scars to match the ones on my face," he said, pointing to his cheek and torn ear.

"I like the scars. They make you look fearsome." Ni'ola massaged at the knots in his muscles. "A servant once told me that scars are there to remind us who we are and what we've been through, and you have been through much."

"They only remind *me* that I'm getting too old and slow to get out of the way of things that wish me dead."

She pushed his head to the side playfully. "Too old and slow? What other warrior carries the skins of three Draegorans from a single raid?"

He laughed. *How quickly things change.* Not long ago he'd been repulsed by her touch, by her dark skin and her weakness, and he'd been humiliated at being bonded to a foreigner and an asha. Now she spoke as one who'd been with the tribes her entire life, and she made him feel he still served the people. He didn't know if it was the bond that made him feel such devotion or the strength she'd shown against the mergol and Jal'kun. He supposed it didn't matter. He would give his life for her—something he would have been incapable of doing for a woman before leaving on the raid with the old okulu'tan and Pai'le, even for his firstwife.

"It itches," he said, scratching at the moss on his side.

"That is a good thing. It means the wound is healing," Li'sun said from the doorway of the hut.

"It would be far less annoying if you simply used magic and saved my body the effort."

"I could. So could Ni'ola with a few lessons. But natural healing is stronger, and there is no hurry." He held a gourd with a stopper in the top in one hand and a small sack in the other. He lifted the gourd up. "But I have brought something that will help."

Ni'ola's hands shivered against his back. "The palic is foul," she said in his ear. In the Esharii language, the words had a double meaning, applying to both the medicine he carried and advice he gave.

Li'sun laughed. "Not this time. Today I bring something better—honeyed wine. We have gained a new spirit-walker, for better or worse, and a fearless pachna along with her. Normally, there would be a feast, but with Ky'lem's wounds and your . . . uniqueness, we will forgo the usual celebration."

"Do not dance around the truth like an Arillian merchant, Li'sun," Ni'ola said. "A celebration would anger those who believe as Jal'kun did and it would create resentment among those who remain unconvinced I belong here."

"Forgive me." Li'sun bowed his head. "Your words hold truth where mine do not, but even for me it is difficult. I still see a foreign asha'han when I look at you, but that is not who you are. This will be your greatest strength and, I fear, your greatest weakness."

"Might as well rub poyla pepper in their eyes now so they get used to it. Her place is here," Ky'lem said. Ni'ola served the tribes now. Ky'lem knew this like he knew how to breathe—the bond gave him unquestioning certainty. He would not let these men treat her like an outsider, no matter who they were. She had earned her place.

Li'sun shook the wine. "Will you still share a drink with me? Here alone, we may still celebrate."

Ky'lem had no reason to say no. So far, Li'sun had been their ally. Why, however, was the question he wanted answered, and this would be a good opportunity to learn the spirit-taker's motives. He looked to Ni'ola for her approval, although there was no need. He felt it through the bond. Ni'ola nodded anyway, for Li'sun's sake.

Li'sun removed his sandals before stepping onto the multicolored rug that lined the floor. From the bag he carried, he withdrew two crudely hammered cups. The edicts were very clear. An asha'han was not permitted the strong drink until she married—all knew this. Li'sun refused to let his eyes fool him a second time and, after setting the first two down, withdrew a third cup. "You are no longer an asha'han or a foreigner. You are an okulu'tan and a servant of the people," he said, placing the cup down next to the others.

Ky'lem agreed, and even though he knew the truth of the words in his heart, it still surprised him a little. He wouldn't have believed it a short time ago, but his view had changed rapidly over the past several days. It had always been ability that counted with him, and Ni'ola had proven herself a powerful okulu'tan, but more than that, in facing the mergol alone, she'd proven herself brave enough to drink with any Esharii. *It will take a thousand years to convince Pai'le and the other tribesmen to agree, but I will find a way somehow. I must if I ever want to unite the tribes.*

Li'sun poured the wine. "A smaller amount for our new spirit-walker. I am not trying to be rude or doubt your strength, but you are not accustomed to fermented drink." He passed a cup to each of them.

Ky'lem drained his in two deep swallows. It was a strong wine, pleasant and sweet, and it brought a warmth similar to Ni'ola's magic to his chest.

Ni'ola looked from the cup to Ky'lem and back.

"It is customary to drink deeply from the first cup. It shows trust in the host," Li'sun said.

Ni'ola snorted. "There is no need to school me in Esharii customs," she said with more than a little vehemence in her voice. She met his eyes and held them. "Perhaps I *don't* trust you."

"I . . . well . . . that is . . ." Li'sun stammered.

She laughed. "My delay was not due to mistrust. I was contemplating how much my life—and my body—have changed." She examined the liquid a moment longer before putting the cup to her lips. When she did, she didn't stop drinking until she'd downed it all.

She is brave and strong for one so young, but she will need that strength in the coming days. Jal'kun is not the only spirit-taker who will challenge her. Together, they would overcome those who opposed her. It was what lay after them that remained unclear to him . . . and there was still the command to marry her one day—and the second one about her child. He turned his mind to the itching of his wounds to keep from betraying his thoughts.

Ni'ola slapped the cup down in front of her. The honeyed wine was sweeter than she remembered, but behind the sweetness came a rush of fire that burned her mouth and throat. She did not let it show on her face. She could not afford to show weakness in front of Li'sun, or to any of the other okulu'tan, for as long as she trained in the village. The Esharii despised weakness above all else.

"I know you have little trust for us, but Jal'kun did not act on behalf of the village," Li'sun said while refilling the cups. "He should not have interfered with the test."

"He did more than interfere. He tried to kill both of us before we arrived . . . twice." It was more than Jal'kun and his attacks that made her wary of the okulu'tan, and even though she had a few small memories of Li'sun teaching her in the future, it was not enough for her to truly trust him yet.

Li'sun frowned. "I thought as much when we found the bodies of the mergols. It was too much of a coincidence that the beasts chose to challenge one another at the same time you traveled nearby. Unfortunately, I had no way of knowing who controlled them."

"It makes no difference," Ni'ola said. "It was all part of

Ri'jarra's plan. He knew Jal'kun would attack us. Just as he knew I would not pass the test on my own. He planted the seed of weakness in Jal'kun's heart long ago. It's almost funny. I was failing. I could not break through the barrier. If Jal'kun had simply let things be, Ky'lem and I would be dead."

"But—" Ky'lem started to protest and stopped. Confusion and disbelief flew across the bond. It was too far-fetched for him to believe.

"It is true, Ky'lem. The old spirit-walker still manipulates us from the great beyond."

Li'sun nodded. "As I said before the test, many who've prepared for years fail to survive, but Sollus aided you in the fight—whether that was through Jal'kun or Ri'jarra is irrelevant. It was Sollus's will for you to succeed."

"I still don't understand this test," Ky'lem said. "You tie a wounded person to a log and place them on the lake, and if they survive, they are okulu'tan. It makes no sense."

"That is because you do not feel Parron's hunger. An okulu'tan must be able to resist the call. If he cannot, then his life is forfeit."

"Parron? What do the Fallen have to do with the lake?"

Li'sun looked to Ni'ola and raised his eyebrows questioningly.

Ni'ola was confused. The okulu'tan was asking her for something with that look, but she had no idea what.

A smile flitted across Li'sun's lips. "So you don't know all of our customs. I confess this pleases me. I was beginning to worry at how much knowledge traveling the ways had given you. You traveled far. Too much knowledge too quickly and . . ." He paused uncomfortably for a moment. ". . . let us say that those who remember too much from the journey are easily confused and must be kept locked away for the good of the village—their insanity can be quite dangerous."

Ni'ola's eyes widened. "Are you saying that these memories will make me go crazy?" She knew that those who traveled the ways were a little unstable—it hadn't taken long with Ri'jarra before his death to know that—but the memories so far seemed more of a nuisance than a danger. Many were helpful.

She felt Ky'lem shudder at the thought of her losing touch with the world around them.

Li'sun held up his hands. "Hopefully, it will take many years for this to happen, but if you travel the ways again, it will accelerate. Ri'jarra was the only spirit-walker known to have made three ventures without going insane. The mind cannot handle so many conflicting realities. It protects itself and blocks all but the strongest, but as time passes, the memories escape. The insanity and confusion are the price for that knowledge."

There was an uncomfortable silence. "You needn't worry yet. You have many years ahead before it catches up with you." He handed the refilled cup to her.

Ni'ola took it eagerly. She'd had moments of confusion already, and Li'sun's words did little to put her at ease.

"Back to your question," Li'sun said. "It is up to the okulu'tan how much his, or *her* in your case, pachna knows. I was asking for permission for Ky'lem to remain while we discussed the truth of the Najalii. It would be rude to speak of it in front of him without asking."

Ni'ola sat up straight. "We will have no secrets from each other." She was sure of the statement, but a pang of something slipped from Ky'lem. It was gone before she could examine it. *Guilt or fear? Is he keeping something from me, or does he think I keep something from him?*

Li'sun interrupted her thoughts. "Your people—"

"Former people," Ni'ola corrected. "The people north of the mountains are no longer mine."

"I meant no insult. Your *former* people believe in Sollus and respect the Fallen, but many truths have been lost."

"Of course they respect Parron. He and all the other gods gave up their immortality to save the worlds of man. Although Draegora was ruined before Parron could stop Tomu, the Dark God was prevented from destroying everything."

"That much is truth," Li'sun said, "but examine the memories you share with Ky'lem from the moment of your bonding. They might give you some of the pieces you are missing."

Ky'lem's knowledge agreed with Ni'ola's words. The beliefs of the Esharii and the northerners were much the same, though his knowledge was more detailed. The Gods of Light had imprisoned the dark ones from the universe and, for time immeasurable, governed among the heavens in peace. Then the dark ones had escaped.

To fight them in the heavens would have destroyed the stars and the worlds beneath them. It was Parron, greatest of the gods, who decided the only way to save the universe was for them to give up their powers. So they'd fallen, dragging the dark ones down with them to the worlds of man, leaving behind only the weakest of their kind, Sollus and Faen. Parron and his counterpart Tomu fell to this world, bringing their war to Draegora.

The two gods fought from one end of the continent to the other for a hundred years, destroying everything in their path. At last, when no city remained and all men stood on one side or the other, the final battle came. When their armies met, the two Fallen held nothing back, each unleashing everything within their grasp to defeat the other. The clash of their might left Draegora a wasteland.

The northerners believed the Fallen were consumed in the destruction. This was a lie. The Fallen did not die. They were simply drained—becoming empty shells that now rested, rebuilding their strength for the day they would rise to fight again.

"So if the Fallen are not dead, why haven't they shown themselves in the last thousand years?" Ni'ola asked.

"Forgive my irreverence, but I have wondered the same thing," said Ky'lem.

"But they have," Li'sun said. "It was Parron's hunger for life you felt in the Najalii. You are connected to him, in nearly the same manner you are bonded to Ky'lem, and you have been since the day Ri'jarra linked you to the crystals."

"But Parron fought for good. What I felt in the lake wanted me dead!"

"No. It wanted your oya'sha. Your life is simply irrelevant."

Ni'ola spread her arms and sloshed wine onto the rug. "That's the same thing! Why would the Fallen God of Light want us to die?"

"The two gods drained themselves in the final battle. When at last the fighting was over and Parron's army had defeated the followers of Tomu, they found the Fallen lifeless upon the ground, their hands upon each other's throats— only they were not dead."

"Why didn't they kill Tomu if he was helpless?" Ky'lem asked.

"Spoken like a true warrior," Li'sun said. "Each of the Fallen had children who were given the ability to share the power of their fathers. They commanded armies and fought with such strength that none but another child of the gods could stand before them. When the final battle came, there were many, but in the end, only eight survived, all children of Parron. The eight tried to kill Tomu, to end the struggle once and for all. Yet no blade would penetrate his skin. Rocks cracked against his body and failed to crush him. He could not be drowned because he did not breathe. Even the hottest flames failed to burn a single hair on the god's head. Nothing could be done. After days of attempting all manner of death, the eight held counsel. The people were preparing ships to flee the desolation of Draegora, to take their followers to this side of the world. It was decided the Fallen would be carried with them.

"The two most trusted children were given the sacred duty of carrying the Fallen's lifeless bodies. Eisha Ryn was entrusted with Parron, but something happened on the voyage. Sollus gave Eisha Ryn the gift of traveling the ways, and he learned much before the fleet arrived. In the dark of night Eisha Ryn stole away, escaping south, to this land. He ordered his ships burned so that they would not be found and marched his people overland, to a vast lake surrounded by the huts of the people. Once there, he ordered that Parron be entombed beneath the water."

"The Najalii," Ky'lem said. "The lake of life."

"Yes. The lake was already sacred to our ancestors, even before Eisha Ryn and his people arrived."

Ni'ola felt Ky'lem's thoughts. *Could this be true? Are we no different than the gray demons—the descendants of the vile invaders who'd spread their seeds across the land? Was Eisha Ryn, the first great leader, revered by the tribes, truly a Draegoran?* The thought struck at his heart like a blade. It was a betrayal of all he knew.

"But this doesn't explain why he tried to kill me," Ni'ola said.

"Patience. I am nearly done. The descendants of the Fallen drew power from their fathers when needed. But the bond went in both directions. Each held unique strengths to use in battle, and for every life they took, they fed power back to the father. Those who survived were the last of their kind, but they passed on the ability to their descendants.

"You are one of their descendants, as am I, and so also are the other okulu'tan and, sadly, the gray demons as well. The connection to Parron through the blood is what gives both of us our power, and in turn we feed him the lives of our enemies."

"You still haven't answered the question. If I am one of Parron's descendants, why does he want me to die?"

"The Fallen are like vast deserts, desiring the rains to bring life back to them. In his long sleep, Parron knows he is stronger than the dark one, but the gap between them narrows. Because of the gray demons' corruption and the lives they feed him, soon Tomu will be stronger, and Parron is desperate to awaken before this happens. He would take all our lives if it allowed him to rise before Tomu."

"And the dark one, where was his body placed?" Ni'ola asked, even though she could guess the answer.

"Tomu's body was placed on a lifeless island and guarded by the other children. In their weakness, their descendants bonded with the dark one. If the gray demons are not stopped, they will destroy us all with their betrayal, and that time comes sooner than any of us would like."

Li'sun pulled a small book from the bag he carried.

"This is the journal of Eisha Ryn, where he wrote his memories from traveling the ways. Only a spirit-walker is allowed to possess it, unless there are none, and then it falls to the spirit leader to hold it until the next arrives. It contains the original edicts, and it has been passed down for a thousand years. Each of those who have traveled the ways has added their words. It is the reason I allowed you to be tested." He flipped the book open to a page that was marked and read—

"Let no female descendants be trained in arms or spirit until the rebirth nears, for a woman's place is not among those who do battle, but with the people, and her duty is bound in continuing the blood."

"That is from the edicts, but scrawled beneath it, in another hand, are these words—"

"So shall it be until Tomu stirs and the child marked by Faen travels the ways. She will name the Sko'dran, and her arrival marks twelve—"

"Ri'jarra left this page marked with the cloth when he passed the book to me before leaving."

"Twelve what? Years?" Ky'lem asked.

His heart raced. Mentioning the Destroyer of the Night sent such a flare of longing and desire from Ky'lem across the bond that Ni'ola's own heart pounded with his.

"It is not known. There are other references to an asha'han becoming an okulu'tan, but none so direct as this one, and none mention the word twelve.

"In truth, I'd hoped Parron would take your spirit on the lake, and that these words were from a future that never came to be. It is too late to hope for this now. You must lead the people to the Sko'dran," Li'sun said.

Ni'ola shivered with fear. There was something else there, buried in her memories, about the reference to the child marked by Faen. She shook her head, as if the movement might jar something loose. Nothing came. For the Sko'dran, she had more than enough memories of the death that would follow his arrival. They wanted her to name him. *How do I do that?* How could she name the warrior who would lead the Esharii over the mountains, and not just a warband or a tribe, but all of them—every man, woman, and child who could hold a spear? *How many would be lost in such a war?* Not only from the tribes but also from her former people. It would be thousands . . . no, hundreds of thousands. *And they want me to be responsible?* She couldn't bring herself to do that, no matter how much she'd already come to think of herself as Esharii.

Ky'lem's thoughts were her opposite. He wanted her to name him to this position with his whole soul. *I am bonded to a madman—no, they are all mad!* There had to be another possibility. She believed everything Li'sun said, but she would not do this.

The ways held thousands of possibilities. Certainly this could not be the only path. She looked back and forth between them. Li'sun's smile, meant to calm her, was menacing, and Ky'lem's eyes were full of lust and desire. *It will not be me. I will not be responsible.* She pushed herself back toward the wall of the hut to get away. The drink made her mind fuzzy, but one thought remained clear. *I will never name this Sko'dran. Never.*

CHAPTER 41

M aster Iwynd led Riam down narrow alleyways, paralleling the coast road. A musty brine smell, similar to the olive barrel, hung in the air, making Riam's nose itch, and through the gap between the over-hanging eaves, he could see gulls circling above them. At each cross street, Master Iwynd paused to spy around corners before dragging Riam through the crowd and into the next alley. Riam dodged all manner of refuse as they hurried down the backstreets, from broken crates to rotting fish, and even a suspicious lump that resembled a body wrapped in sheets. The few men and women who passed moved warily in the shadows, and they kept their eyes to the damp paving stones and their business to themselves when they passed Master Iwynd. Riam thanked the Fallen he hadn't been a churp in this part of the city.

Master Iwynd stopped behind a shop and drummed on the door. Little marked the place from any other. It held a plain, sturdy door, and like the rest of the buildings they passed, the two-story wall facing the alley stood barren of windows. The only indication of what lay inside were bits of rope scattered on the ground and piled against the wall. Riam bent and picked one up. Thin and frayed, it had the look of being too long in the sun.

The bolt to the door clunked loudly in the quiet of the alley. The door opened a hand, and a slim, mustached face peered out. Whoever the man was, he stood less than a hand taller than Riam, only coming to Master Iwynd's shoulder.

The man swung the door wide and waved them in, craning his neck to look up and down the backstreet. "The front door is barred and there's none here but me. I sent Olanda to the market and gave my apprentices the day off, like you told me." The man was as thin and lean as he was short. Without the mustache, he could pass for a young man with the right clothing.

"Thank you, Engvale," Master Iwynd said as soon as the man closed and bolted the door behind them.

The inside of the shop wasn't large, but it wasn't small either—about the size of Bortha's common room. Nets crowded the room, making it feel jumbled and confining, and winding through the room felt like walking through a giant bird's nest. Nets hung from the ceiling, were strung from hook to hook along the walls, and lay heaped in mounds on the floor. A heavy fishing net covered a wooden frame down the center of the room, and on each end of the frame, the net lay piled as high as Riam's waist. In a corner, a stack of rope spools towered to the ceiling. The odor of must and brine permeated everything, and beneath it, there was the smell of fish and burnt hair. The floor, where visible, was stained with water spots and candle drippings.

"Course, as soon as I closed, I had more people knockin' than I do in a tenday. That's the way of things. When you want something, it's never there, and soon as you don't, it's everywhere you look." The reedy man coughed into his hand.

Master Iwynd removed a small purse from his belt. "That will more than cover the loss to your business."

The man weighed the pouch in his hand. "That it will, sir. That it will."

"What have you seen?"

"The Wolves are stirred up, that's the Fallen truth. Never seen 'em so thick. I don't know what they want, but there's at least two taulins moving up and down the coast road. There's another one to the south near the Wine Docks and a fourth near the Scissor Docks. Don't know how many there are to the north. None of 'em have come to the shops, though. Their eyes are set to watchin' the street and the piers."

"*The Dolphin's Lady* is ready?"

"They're still loading a few things, but all the big cargo came in yesterday and none of the crew had shore leave last night. They won't be happy about that."

"Inform the captain it's time. If it's not loaded already, it isn't coming with us. We sail as soon as he gets the harbormaster's clearance and a towboat set to pull him from the docks. I want the ship ready to leave the moment we board."

"Yes, sir."

Engvale scurried to a front window and eased the curtain back, checking the street out front before ducking out of the shop. Master Iwynd barred the door behind him and dragged a rope spool to a spot where he could sit and peer around the edge of the curtain.

Riam flopped down on a pile of nets.

"We've a little time," Master Iwynd said. "*The Dolphin's Lady* won't be ready for at least a glass, maybe two. Engvale will let us know when it is time to move. I've used him to watch the docks for years. He's a good man. For now, you can tell me where you've been. The story is you jumped from the barge and ran away."

"Ran away?" Riam laughed. "I didn't run away. That bastard Tannon and his friends threw me off the barge."

"Go on," Iwynd said in a voice that doubted Riam's words.

To prove his side of the story, Riam sped through the events since leaving Hath, from his time on the barge to the fight with Pekol. He left nothing out. The old Draegoran didn't interrupt or make any judgments, only nodding and asking questions about how and when Riam had used his newfound power.

"You did well. A man like Pekol would have gone on killing. Let me see your hand." He squeezed Riam's fingers hard enough to create spots of white and watched the blood return. "I've never heard of anyone removing a glyph in such a manner."

He let go and shook his head. "The whole arm is completely invisible to my sight, as if there's no spirit in the limb, which is impossible. I'm glad I found you, if for no other reason than to try and heal it."

"How *did* you find me?" Riam asked. "You were re-building the outpost when I left."

"A much simpler story than yours. I sent a letter to your grandfather with Captain Karlet. Gairen asked me to do it. I told him no, but I changed my mind. Later, when you didn't arrive with the other children, your grandfather sent me searching for you. That's when I discovered the Wolves were looking for you. I knew they'd bring you to the island in secret, so all I had to do was find their ship and keep watch. They don't know I've secured a ship of my own—a fast one, prepared for a long journey."

"Is the island so far away?" Riam asked.

"We're not going to the island."

The abrupt finality of the words made Riam's head spin. For months he'd remained fixed on getting to the island to keep from giving up. In one quick response, Master Iwynd had torn the rug from beneath his feet. "What do you mean, we are not going to the island?"

"What I said. We're not going to Doth Draegoras. You'd never survive the training."

Riam stood up and faced the arms-master. "If I'm strong enough to make it through Pekol and the Esharii, I can survive the island." *Master Iwynd thinks I'm not good enough. I will prove him wrong.*

"Sit down. I'm not questioning your ability. You've far more strength than you know. What I'm saying is that the Wolves will never allow you to wear the glyph of another regiment, and we can't allow you to wear theirs, so there is no going to the island."

"But . . . but . . . ." Riam sputtered.

"There is no arguing the decision. It comes straight from your grandfather."

Riam slapped his leg in frustration. "You keep saying 'my grandfather' like I understand, but he's dead . . . and I don't even know why the Wolves are looking for me or why they want me, or why we can't go to the island. Gairen wanted me to become like him, and I made a vow that I would. None of this makes any sense."

Master Iwynd rubbed at his temples, as if trying to avert

a headache. "I'm sorry, boy. I've been at this so long I forget what it's like to be young and blind to the world. There's a reason Draegorans don't have wives and give their children up to fosters, and you're the Fallen's evidence why those rules exist."

He took a deep breath and let it out. "Every male Draegoran has the duty to spread the blood, but they are not supposed to do more than . . ." he looked uncomfortable as he searched for the right words, ". . . to do more than gift their seed upon the women of the Covenant. A long time ago, when Master Thalle, the kyden of Owl Regiment, was a warden, he had two children—your father, Jonim, and your uncle, Gairen. He wasn't supposed to know who they were, but he did, and once he knew, he made sure they were trained as Owls. You don't need to know that story. Those were mistakes made long ago, but he followed the rules in all other matters afterward, and he never let the knowledge of his children interfere with his duty. Gairen was the same way, right up until your father's death. That's when he became obsessed with finding you."

Riam bristled at the casual mention of his uncle not following the rules. Gairen had saved him from a miserable life with a miserable old man. "Gairen believed in me, and he wanted me to become a Draegoran."

"No. Gairen wanted your grandfather to go back on his decision to stop training replacements, but he can't. After speaking with him, I agree. But I didn't say you wouldn't be trained as a Draegoran, only that you won't set foot on Doth Draegoras. Not until your training is complete anyway—which it never will be if you don't meet my expectations."

Riam's chin snapped up. "You're going to train me?"

"That's what I'm trying to tell you. I trained both your father and your uncle, and if I can make swordsmen out of those two, I can do well enough by you."

Riam suddenly felt ashamed. He'd lost Gairen's swords. How could he train without them? "What about Gairen's blades? Don't I need them?"

"Forget the swords. They're gone. Kyden Verros, the commander of the Wolves, has them both. You've got Hearst's sword, and it's a decent enough weapon, if a bit long for my liking. We'll have to figure out how you took control of Gairen's and bond you to this one once we're far enough away that others won't be able to sense the weapon's location. But you'll learn to use it properly before we worry about that."

They were quiet for a time as Master Iwynd watched the street through the window.

Trained in secret. What would that make me? He wouldn't be a real Draegoran without the glyphs from a regiment, which made him wonder why Master Iwynd was going to train him at all . . . unless he wanted something. *There is more going on than the old Draegoran is telling me.*

"So, if my grandfather doesn't want any more Owls to be trained, why are you training me? Why not let the Wolves have me? Which, I suppose, leads to the question I asked before—why *are* the Wolves looking for me?" Riam shivered at the thought of the Wolves catching him again. He remembered Hearst's cold voice, threatening to brand Bortha and put him to work on the streets.

"When Gairen asked me to write the letter, he was right about one thing. You must be trained. But he was right for the wrong reason. I'm not going to give you a history lesson, that will come later, but the reason behind the Wolves' search is the same reason you were able to take Gairen's sword—the strength of your bloodlines."

"Gairen told me about how we are supposedly descended from the Fallen. That doesn't seem possible."

"Oh, he was telling the truth. We are—you, me, and every member of the regiments. Eight of Parron's children led the survivors of the Fallen's war to this land. Being descended from one of those eight is what gives us the ability to link with a catalyst—the crystals you see in the pommels of our weapons—and the number of bloodlines a person carries is a good indication of how strong they will be. Since one of Parron's children fled south with his followers and joined with the Esharii tribes and another was killed in a war with Arillia before siring any children, there's never been a Draegoran descended from more than six of Parron's children."

"Wait . . . that would make the okulu'tan who attacked us Draegoran, the same as you, wouldn't it? He was using magic," Riam blurted out.

"In a sense, yes, though I wouldn't say that in the presence of a tribesman unless you mean to fight and kill him. To return to the question, though, there has always been the hope that a child descended from all eight bloodlines would be born."

"But you just said that was impossible, that one of the original eight had no children before he died."

"As far as anyone knows, he didn't sire a child, but there have always been stories—rumors of a pregnant woman taken by the Arillians. There are others that say she fled inland."

"What does this have to do with me and the Wolves?"

"Kyden Verros is one of a handful of Draegorans who are descended from six of the original children, and his abilities are uncommonly strong, even among them. He is, by far, the strongest living Draegoran—nearly as strong as some of the first generations. Because of your ability to take control of Gairen's sword, he likely believes you are descended from seven—maybe even all eight—and he'll stop at nothing to have you under his control. If he's unable to do that, he'll want you dead. That's how the man sees the world. You are either an opportunity to expand his power or a future obstacle."

"Are you saying that I might be descended from all eight?" Riam asked, terrified of the response.

"Doesn't matter. I think the rumors and legends are just that, rumors and legends, but your grandfather and I both believe you'll be at least as strong as Verros. Regardless, it's what you did with Gairen's sword that matters. No one has ever severed another Draegoran's link to the crystal. It's this ability that has me training you in secret."

"But why? I mean, I want to be trained—it's all that's kept me going since Gairen died—but how will I learn to help people if I never go to the island?"

"I'm afraid your life will never be like other Draegorans. I'm to train you for one purpose, to break Kyden Verros's link to his crystal. Once this is done, you will help your grandfather and our allies, the Stonebreakers, make certain there are no more recruits trained on the island— by any regiment—ever again."

"You're saying you want me to stop the most powerful Draegoran alive! Not only that but help bring about the end of all the Draegoran regiments by preventing them from training recruits. Why would I want to do that? The Draegorans keep the Esharii from invading and protect those who can't protect themselves."

Master Iwynd looked troubled. He stared at Riam, obviously deciding how much more to say. "Because we have lost our way, and Kyden Verros must be stopped."

Riam was silent for a time. He frowned.

Master Iwynd mistook the look on Riam's face for worry about the Wolves. "Think of stopping Verros the same as stopping Pekol, only on a much grander scale."

That doesn't help much. Stopping Pekol nearly killed me.

"Trust me, when I'm done training you, no man will be able to stand against you with a blade. That, along with help from the Stonebreakers, should get you close enough to destroy Verros's link and allow your grandfather to take control of the council and the other regiments."

He eyed Riam up and down. "Speaking of training. We need to change your clothes. If you walk out of here in the gray clothes of a recruit, you'll bring the Wolves running. I should have thought of that earlier."

They stripped off Riam's shirt and fouled his breeches with tar and dirt. Master Iwynd tore the hem out of the bottom and cut a few holes in the seams to give them the appearance of long use.

The whole time, Riam worried about Master Iwynd's words. It wasn't a man with a blade he worried about, but the strongest Draegoran who'd ever lived and the army of Wolves who followed him.

On the other side of the harbor, and four hundred steads out to sea at four degrees south of east-by-northeast, rested the Isle of Doth Draegoras. Originally a landmass of bleached-white rock without a tree or shrub living on its surface, it was now a fortress, with a warren of hallways, training yards, barracks, smiths, gardens, and all manner of workshops that dealt with the art of combat and war. A high stone wall surrounded the island, with six square towers spaced evenly around its length. Atop each tower, a colorful pennant snapped and danced on the wind—six symbols marking six regiments, each created by the six children of Parron when they established the Covenant and charged themselves with guarding the tomb of a fallen god.

In a room near the top of one of these towers, the one with a wolf's head centered on a deep orange background, Kyden Verros leaned over a map of the island. Next to it was another of Parthusal. Figurines stood at various locations on the maps. With him were his executive officer, Master Florren, the master-of-training, Master Phen, and the master-of-the-rolls, Master Allon. Three senior wardens stood behind them. These men were the regiment's senior officers currently on the island, except for the two troop commanders who remained with their men. Kyden Verros's aide, a half-warden named Ovyne, sat at a desk nearby capturing the details of the meeting on paper.

"As soon as I felt Hearst's death, I gave the order to move. Warden Dolan's troop is at fifty percent strength, since he has a half-troop detached to Arms-master Roshan in Parthusal. His remaining half-troop is here," the executive officer, a gaunt-faced man with a square jaw, gray at his temples, and a receding hairline, pointed to a figurine with a narrow baton, "spread out to cover the island's dock and the two small beaches on the southwest side.

"Warden Hoeple's troop is also split in half, with a half-troop on the wall, concentrated on each side of the Owl's tower," he tapped each side of a marker on the map, "and the other half-troop is in a training hall not far from the Owl's main entry." He tapped the final location and stood back. "Even if Master Iwynd and the boy make it past Master Roshan, there's no way for them to reach the Owl's tower, and we will move on the old Owl as soon as we have Iwynd and the boy in our possession."

"Good. Any trouble with Hound or Bloodhammer?"

"None, sir. At least not after I explained that Master Iwynd had killed Master Hearst and we were simply there to prevent him from returning to his regiment. They are watching us closely, but neither will interfere unless the council tells them otherwise. The Ironstrikers will stay out of our way, and it's fifty-fifty on whether the Stonebreakers come to the old Owl's rescue. Their ties run deep."

"Wait," Master Allon said. "When was Hearst promoted to master? I didn't vote on it, and it certainly wasn't approved by the council." The master-of-the-rolls puffed out his chest when the others looked at him, but all he succeeded in doing was highlighting his weight. Where the other officers in the room were crisp and disciplined in their appearance, Master Allon was unkempt. His robe was slightly wrinkled, and his white mustache and goatee too long, with hair hanging over his mouth so that the ends were between his lips. It made the man look like a goat when he spoke.

In his prime, Kyden Verros knew Allon to be a formidable soldier, and his loyalty to the regiment was without question. Twenty years ago Allon had been made a master after crushing a rebellion in Thae before it turned into a full-blown revolt. He'd left a trail of bodies dangling across the Free Cities of Thae and replaced a dozen landowners before the people had finally acquiesced. The years away from the mainland as master-of-the-rolls, however, had made Allon's body and mind soft. Verros could tolerate that. It was the softening of his spirit that bothered him, but he had plans to remedy the condition.

"I promoted him, Master Allon—posthumously. It's about time the regiments took back some of their authorities from the council."

"Well, even if you get the other kydens to agree, it still requires a vote from us." He looked at the two masters beside him, but neither was unwise enough to complain about power already lost.

Kyden Verros sighed. Master Allon didn't see it—he'd always been too confined by rules. Rules, though, could be changed. "We are at war, Master Allon. I won't waste time holding votes on routine issues that are clearly command decisions. But I am glad you broached the subject. I'm making several changes to simplify the way the regiment operates. There will be no more votes by the masters on anything. I, and I alone, command the regiment." He nodded to the senior wardens. Two of them drew their swords. His aide stopped writing, his hand frozen over the paper.

"Do you take issue with that?" He almost wished the man would disagree. He'd be forced to kill him, but it would be nice to see some of Allon's former spirit return before he died.

Master Allon hesitated for less than a heartbeat. He was languid, but he wasn't stupid. "I obey, my Kyden."

"Good, because I am sending you to take command of a special expedition at North Keep. I want you to probe the Esharii tribes to determine their current strength and to find out what they are up to after the recent attack at the outpost in Hath." Fighting the Esharii would bring Master Allon's former spirit back . . . or get him killed. Either way, the issue of his weakness would be solved. Most likely, he would get a lot of soldiers killed with poor decisions before the problem was resolved. He sighed. He'd need to send a note to the master at North Keep with instructions to limit the damage. "You leave tomorrow. I want the names of three wardens you recommend to replace you as master-of-the-rolls before you depart."

Master Allon's eyes grew round, and he looked from one cold face to the next. He had no friends or allies here. He was weak, and his penchant for sticking to the absolute truth of Draegoran law had alienated many of them. To his credit, he adjusted his belt and pulled himself up straight. His heels snapped together, and his fist thumped over his chest in salute. "Yes, my Kyden."

With a nod from Kyden Verros, the senior wardens sheathed their blades.

The conversation was interrupted by a knock at the door. "Enter!" Master Phen called.

A young armsman entered, breathing hard from running up the stairs of the tower. He saluted between gasping breaths. "Your pardon, Kyden Verros . . . Kyden Blane has ordered you to attend an immediate session of the council."

"Took him long enough," Master Florren said with a chuckle.

"Your pardon, gentlemen. I must go and 'explain my actions' to my peers once more. They won't be so smug when I bring charges against Master Iwynd and Kyden Thalle for killing Master Hearst." He smiled. "Master Roshan had better not kill Iwynd. If he does, you'll have company on your mission, Master Allon."

Kyden Verros stopped in the doorway. He should say something more. It was never good to leave his senior officers with threats and vague worries eating at their thoughts.

"Gentlemen, once I challenge and kill Kyden Thalle, our forces will move against the remaining Owls, and once they are no more, the Stonebreakers and the end of the council will be our next targets. Our regiment will take control of this island and all the lands of the Covenant, and we will teach the landowners the fear and respect their grandfathers held when they heard the word *Draegoran*. Make sure our men are ready. I will not tolerate failure from anyone, and those who serve the regiment with distinction will receive their due rewards. Those who do not," he looked pointedly at Master Allon, "will be removed."

CHAPTER 42

Master Iwynd let out a deep breath and leaped up from the spool. "Engvale has returned," he said, hurrying to pull the crossbeam from the door. The relief on his face and the speed at which he flung the door open contradicted his normally calm exterior. Riam supposed that waiting and doing nothing were not things a master did very well.

The small-framed shop owner slipped inside.

Master Iwynd put a hand on his shoulder. "All is ready?"

"Sir, the ship is set. They are securing it to the towboat as we speak." He looked to the floor, not meeting Iwynd's gaze. "Forgive me for saying this, but you will not make it. There is a taulin from the Wolf Regiment at the entrance to the Scissor Docks, and they do not appear to be leaving anytime soon."

Master Iwynd didn't hesitate. "It is not your fault, Engvale. You've done well, but I have one more task for you. I need you to take the boy to the ship. My presence will attract the Wolves like blood among sharks, but they won't look twice at Engvale the net mender and his apprentice making a delivery."

Riam didn't like it. Every time he was separated from those he trusted, terrible things happened. Unfortunately, he had no say in what Master Iwynd commanded, and even if the old Draegoran would listen to him, he had no other ideas to offer. "But how will you get to the ship?"

"You worry about playing the apprentice, boy, and let me worry about that."

Engvale's head bobbed up and down while he eyed Riam up and down. "You match Harran's build and hair color well enough, but you'll need to lose the sandals. Mine go without unless they are wearing their Tenth Day clothes. I'll get one of Harran's shirts." He ran up the stairs to the second level.

Is the world against me? He'd worn the new clothes— clothes he'd earned and paid for himself—less than a day, and already he was back to going barefoot and his breeches ruined. He pulled a sandal off and flung it into a corner. Things would change once they reached wherever they were going. He had to believe that. Master Iwynd wasn't Gairen, but he seemed a decent man. He was risking himself to help, and even if he'd been ordered to do it, that still counted for something. Of course, if Master Iwynd was telling the truth, Gairen wasn't any better and had only been using him as well. He threw the second sandal harder after the first. *Faen take Master Iwynd for spoiling something else I believe in.*

Master Iwynd pinched at his bottom lip and his hand tapped the hilt of his longknife. His brow creased as he watched Riam.

Whatever the motives behind Master Iwynd's actions, he worked to make things right. *Was it fair to ask for more than that?* Riam froze at the thought. *Did any of the reasons really matter, so long as they accomplished what was right?* He shook his head. There was something flawed in that way of thinking, but he couldn't place his finger on it. The reason people did things mattered just as much as their actions.

Master Iwynd let go of his lip and tousled Riam's hair— an awkward gesture, and certainly unexpected from the callous old Draegoran. "Ease up on all the worrying. We'll get you out of Parthusal and things will be better—maybe not easier, but better."

Engvale returned and tossed a tan shirt at Riam. He pointed to a net that ran the length of the wall. "We'll take that one. It's bulky enough to hide your face with it on your shoulder, but not so heavy that the two of us can't carry it. It was made for the shallows, but the Wolves won't know the difference."

"You'll need to hide Hearst's sword somehow," Iwynd said. "I want the boy to keep it with him."

Engvale frowned, but a simple net mender did not argue with a Draegoran. He moved quickly, searching the shop until he found a few barrel staves and an old piece of canvas. He wrapped the sword and staves together to disguise the shape and tied the bundle with rope. "That will do."

By this time, Riam had the shirt on. It was plain and coarse, but it was clean.

"Let's go." Engvale handed the parcel to Riam and grabbed the front of the net. Riam tucked it under his arm and grabbed the back.

Master Iwynd opened the door for them, and without a word, they were moving. The door to the shop closed with an ominous thud.

The net wasn't heavy, but the way it dangled around Riam's feet forced him to shuffle along the stone street to keep from tripping. About the time he finally had the rhythm for it, they were at the entrance to the Scissor Docks. One look at the docks explained the name. Two long, wooden piers stretched out like the open end of a pair of scissors. They were wide enough that several small wagons traveled up and down their lengths, delivering and receiving goods. Here and there, booms swung nets and pallets to and from the ships. The piers weren't as busy as the street, but they were far from empty.

The Wolves stood at the mouth of the docks, spread out like rocks against the slow current of people eddying around them. No one could enter without moving past one of them. After so much time with Iwynd and Gairen, the Draegorans looked far less intimidating than the taulin on the plains. He had no doubts about their ability, though. With the power in their swords, those five could handle fifty men in the blink of an eye if they needed to.

"Who's the boy?" a female Draegoran said. She had short hair, nearly shaved, and it was obvious she led by the number of glyphs adorning her skin. Like the others, the fierce head of a wolf stared out from the left side of her neck.

"My apprentice."

"You have proof?" she asked.

A second Draegoran made his way over to them. "How long has he been your apprentice?" He was much younger than the woman, and he'd probably never used a razor on his chin in his life. If he had, he hadn't been using it for very long. There was, however, a coiled tension in his movements, like a snake prepared to strike. His youth would make him no less dangerous.

"He's worked in my shop for nearly two years. Don't know how I can prove it."

"Anyone nearby who can vouch for him?" the female asked.

"Every shop along the docks knows him. Go ask any one of them about Harran. You'll get an earful on how he shamelessly chases their daughters. But if you will forgive me, I am late. This net must be on *The Perseverer* before she sails, or I don't get paid."

The female Draegoran squinted while she examined Riam. "What happened to his eyes?"

While it'd been several days since Pekol's beating, Riam's eyes remained discolored and dark. He tried to look uncaring that at any moment the Wolves were going to figure out the truth and drag him away. "Not my fault if a girl is promised but still wants to flirt with me," he said, hoping his face didn't turn red.

The female Draegoran arched an eyebrow.

"Her mother thought otherwise," Engvale said.

Both Draegorans laughed.

"I was only flirting." Inside he wanted to protest the false words. He'd never flirted with a girl in his life—well, not unless Loral counted. *But that hadn't been flirting, had it?* He'd certainly liked spending time with her, at least until she'd blabbed his secrets to Tannon and gotten him thrown from the barge. He certainly missed her far more than he was angry with her—especially the way she'd pressed against him for warmth while sleeping. He felt his face flush.

"We have a saying where I was born in Thae, 'What the

daughter does, the mother did.' This is what makes them so protective." The young Wolf winked at Riam.

"We have another saying where I am from," the female said, glaring at her subordinate. "'An undutiful boy will prove an unmanageable husband.' He should honor and respect her commitments without having to be chased away like a thief."

Riam stiffened at the reference. He was no thief, even if he'd served as a churp for being marked as one.

"Sir, ma'am, if you please. I must deliver the net," Engvale said. "The ship will depart at any moment."

The female taulin leader turned to Engvale as if she'd forgotten him. "Ah, yes. You can go, but the boy stays here."

"But I must get the net to the ship."

"Drag it, or go and get someone from the ship to help. Either way, he doesn't leave my sight. While I believe you, net mender, I'm not taking any chances—not with my arms-master in charge."

Engvale looked from one Draegoran to the other, as if to protest, but held his tongue. Nothing could be done that wouldn't seem suspicious.

"Go ahead, sir," Riam said. He dropped his end of the net but kept the package with Hearst's sword. "I'll hold this until you return." He moved as slowly as his nerves would allow to the edge of the pier and climbed to a seat on the first pylon. Even though calm on the outside, his heart pounded in his chest. *What am I doing?* Instead of getting away from the Wolves, he was plopped down in the middle of them.

Engvale looked around helplessly. Riam gave him a shrug. Seeing there was nothing more he could do, he began dragging the net down the left pier.

People came and went under the Draegorans' watchful eyes while Riam waited. All it would take would be for one of the Draegorans to ask someone passing that knew Engvale's apprentice and he would be discovered. Apparently, their conversation had been convincing, because the Draegorans largely ignored him, only glancing back occasionally to be sure he was still there.

He'd been sitting there for a quarter of a glass when the young Draegoran shouted. "There!"

Riam searched the crowd for the reason behind the man's outburst, and there, eight or nine shops down the street, stood Master Iwynd. He stood at a corner talking to a boy that matched Riam's height. *Who is that?*

"Mandal, you stay here and watch the Scissors." The female Draegoran drew a thick, curved saber. "The rest of you with me."

The others drew their weapons and followed. They did not run, but they moved with steady purpose. The crowd spread out wide of the advancing Wolves, opening a path to Master Iwynd.

The Wolf left behind—the young one who looked like he'd never shaved before—edged away from the entrance to the Scissor Docks with his hand closed tightly over the hilt of his sword. He watched his fellow Wolves, obviously eager to be part of any action. He never so much as glanced back at Riam.

If Riam was quiet, he doubted the Draegoran would remember he was there.

As soon as the other Wolves were halfway to Master Iwynd, the unknown youth sprinted away and disappeared around a building. Master Iwynd drew his longknife and turned on the advancing Wolves.

Riam was off his perch and had to catch himself, or he would have been standing next to the young Draegoran for a better look. While he knew Master Iwynd was good, Riam wasn't sure how he would fare against four opponents. Especially when those opponents held blades double the length of his knife.

The Wolves were almost to Master Iwynd. The old Draegoran was giving him an opportunity to escape. He backed down the pier one step at a time, expecting the young Wolf to turn around at any moment. He was, however, far more worried about Master Iwynd than he was about himself.

A woman's scream and the ring of steel hitting steel decided Riam's next move. He wasted no more time worrying about Master Iwynd. He turned and darted down the dock. At any moment the young Wolf would notice his absence. He imagined footsteps pounding after him and ran faster.

Sure enough, he hadn't gone twenty steps when a yell came from behind him. "You, boy! Stop!"

The pier ahead wasn't empty. Aside from the numerous people who were either loading ships or traveling about their business, there were stacks of barrels and boxes, pallets piled with heavy-looking bags, and several wagons filled with goods. Riam had no idea which of the dozen ships before him was *The Dolphin's Lady*.

"Pardon!" Riam shouted as he dodged around a wagon and jumped over a trunk a man had just put down. No longer his imagination, he could hear the young Wolf running behind him. The bundle Riam carried slowed him down.

He cut close to the edge of a stack of crates. He caught movement to his right and threw himself to the left. His foot caught his other leg and he tripped, sending the bundle flying and him tumbling. When he came to a stop, he pushed himself up to see Engvale standing atop a box and holding the net out before him.

Riam had no time to ask what he was doing. The young Wolf's footfalls grew louder and Engvale cast the net an instant before the Draegoran rounded the crates. There was no time to dodge the unexpected throw no matter how fast the Draegoran's reflexes. The net covered him completely, tangling in his legs and taking him down to the wooden planks far harder than Riam had fallen.

Engvale gave the young Wolf no time to recover. He jumped from the box and pulled a belaying pin from where it was tucked into the waist of his breeches.

Snarled up in the net, the struggling Wolf could not draw his sword or defend himself. Engvale brought the wide, heavy end of the pin crashing down on his head. A hollow thunk echoed down the pier, and the Draegoran collapsed in a heap. Engvale gave the Wolf a second blow, and by the smacking sound, Riam didn't believe the young Draegoran would ever wake. The workers around them scattered and pretended they saw nothing.

"Go. The ship is the third on the right. I'll catch up." The net mender lifted the lid on one of the crates and pulled at a handful of netting, dragging the Wolf with it.

Riam shivered, imagining the young Draegoran's rotting body delivered to some faraway port. He felt sorry for whoever opened the crate later. Turning away from the grizzly scene, he scooped up the bundled sword and made his way down the dock as fast as his feet could carry him.

He couldn't read the words painted in swirling letters, but *The Dolphin's Lady* was easy to spot. The front of the ship held a carving of a woman with one arm around a large fish and her other arm pointed forward. It was also the only ship swarming with activity. Men coiled ropes, checked tie-downs, and scrambled up and down the rigging.

"We sail now," the captain said as soon as Engvale arrived and ushered Riam across the gangplank.

"But Master Iwynd isn't here yet!" Riam said.

"Lad, I was paid to take you to Arillia, and I was told to sail the instant you were on board. The old Draegoran threatened to take my soul if I didn't, and he said nothin' about waitin' for him. You're here, so we sail, and that's that."

"But—"

The captain turned to his men. "Cast off and signal the towboat to pull us out. Kari, stow the gangplank."

Engvale grabbed Riam by the shoulders and pulled him in close. "I must go. Master Iwynd will follow close behind, I am sure of it. There is a trader I buy from in Hammisal named Feyza. Find her, and she will help you." He passed Riam the pouch of coins Master Iwynd had given him. "Take this."

Riam pushed it away. "I have money."

"No. Take it." Despite his words that Master Iwynd would follow, Engvale looked worried. "You do not know how long the wait will be. You may need it."

Riam nodded. "Thank you, Engvale. I hope the Wolves don't catch you."

"No one on the pier will say anything, and my apprentice will swear he was here today if anyone asks. Besides, I am only a simple net maker who witnessed a fight near the docks—who would question me about a missing Draegoran?" He smiled, flaring his bushy mustache and exposing stained teeth before running down the gangplank.

"Good luck to you, child. May Sollus watch over you on your journey," he called as the ship pulled away.

Riam watched the pier, hoping that at the last moment before it was too late Master Iwynd would come running. He never did.

The captain stood beside him. "It'll be fine, lad. You'll see. A smooth sea never made a skilled sailor."

Riam stood with the captain on the aft deck of the ship, still looking back at Parthusal. Above them, crewmen scurried up the rigging to untie the mainsails. Riam wished he could join them. From that height, he would be able to see the entire coast road. While the odds of him even recognizing the Scissor Docks from halfway across the harbor were poor, and even poorer for spotting any trace of Master Iwynd, he felt guilty for not at least trying.

The truth was, however, that it did not matter. There was nothing he could do regardless of what he saw behind them. Master Iwynd had to be alive, and he would find a ship to follow them. Doubt nagged at him though. *What if Master Iwynd didn't escape the Wolves? What will I do alone in some far-off land I know nothing about?* He groaned at the thoughts and images that formed in his head—of being forced to clean filthy alleyways and pisspots, of maggots and rotten food, and of hunger and fear. He set his mind. *By the Fallen, I will never go back to being a churp. I'll die before becoming a slave again.*

"Why the sour face, lad?" the captain asked. "From here, the city is beautiful. Parthusal," he went on, "it is like a wife. She is the most beautiful when duty forces you to leave her behind or when you return after being gone on a long voyage. It is the time between that wears a man down. Stay away too long, and you forget her. Stay with her too long and her blemishes and foul habits grind upon your soul. That is why I love the sea. The sea never loses her beauty."

Riam gave the captain a lopsided smile and scanned the horizon. He had to agree—at least about the sea. Where the city might be larger and grander than anything he'd ever seen, the concept of so many people living together was easy to grasp—it was like home, only bigger. Nothing in his memory compared to his first real look at the ocean. The vastness of it, stretching out to the horizon ahead, mesmerized him.

The must-and-brine smell was still there, but now that they were out on the water, it was almost pleasant. With the sun high behind them, the ocean reflected lines of orange-and-red sunlight back into his eyes, making the waves flutter like rolling flames that hissed against the ship's hull. A multitude of birds circled above them or dove down into the water to come bursting back out in a fountain of sparkling droplets.

There was something more, too. Something Riam could

sense but not see, hidden under the surface, like the quiet, forceful strength behind Master Iwynd's eyes. Riam couldn't tell exactly what it was, only that it was so powerful it made him feel small and insignificant. He stood frozen, lost in the water's raw strength.

"You've never seen the ocean before, have you?" the captain asked.

"No."

"Well, close your mouth. You won't be so astonished when you start puking your guts out for the fish."

One of the sails caught the wind, and it snapped like a whip.

"We've the broad reach of the wind. Drop the towline!" the captain yelled. "Hold the sails low till we're free, then let 'em fly. We'll be running with as much speed as she'll do."

"Make way to the beak!" a sailor yelled at the others on the middeck as he dodged between them. He took the stairs to the foredeck three at a time before scrambling to the nose of the ship to free them from the towboat.

Riam watched the crew work, but his mind remained on other things.

After all he'd been through—the attack by the wasps, the battle at the outpost, the long days of cleaning the streets for Pekol—he wasn't going to the island. He was headed to a place he knew nothing about, and he was alone. That scared him to the center of his bones, but there was also a kind of freedom that came along with it very much like when Gairen killed his grandfather and dragged him from his home—a feeling that the worst of things were over and that a new path opened before him.

In Arillia, nobody would know him. There would be no Draegorans or Esharii trying to capture him, there would be no long-lost family members trying to use him for their cause, and there would be no crazy talk of the Fallen and their bloodlines. If Master Iwynd never came, he had money enough to buy an apprenticeship somewhere and live a normal life if he desired. The future lay open to him, and he was free.

These were pleasant thoughts, but he didn't really believe any of them. He'd had the rug pulled from beneath him too many times now to believe he would ever be free of the regiments. He'd gained some distance and freedom, but that was all. He remembered Bortha's words, "If you can do things no one else can, you're a threat." The Wolves and the Owls, maybe the other four regiments as well, would always be looking for him, either to use him or prevent others from using him. His grandfather expected him to return and defeat the leader of the Wolves, a task that seemed impossible. The Wolves wanted to add him to their rolls. Someone, even if it was not Master Iwynd, would find him.

The loud pops of the sails snapping taut above him pulled Riam from his thoughts. The world lurched as the wind-filled sails drove the front of the ship down into the water. Riam lost his footing and stumbled to the railing. Mistaking his reason for being there, the men in the towboat waved their hats and yelled out Sollus's blessings to him on their way back to the city and their families.

CHAPTER 43

Kyden Thalle, commander of Owl Regiment, signed his name and placed the long-feathered pen down on his desk. The words on the paper before him blurred together in the weak candlelight. He stoppered the inkwell and rubbed his eyes. He was tired. Tired of conspiracies and maneuvering, tired of secrets . . . tired of the lies. Everyone important to him would soon be out of reach of Kyden Verros and the Wolves. Both of his sons were dead, and Master Iwynd would be setting sail with Jonim's boy shortly, if they hadn't already departed. His regiment now numbered less than fifty, although no one else knew this but the Owl's master-of-the-rolls, and Kyden Thalle had sent him, against his strong objections, off to evaluate the rebellion brewing in Mirlond. Kyden Thalle's fingers moved from rubbing his eyes to massaging his temples.

Under fifty—from a regiment that once numbered in the hundreds.

He ran a hand through his thick white hair and looked around the room, at the scrolls stacked neatly upon the shelves, the books of varying height and multicolored spines seemingly stored at random, and the odds and ends that remained from more than four-dozen kydens and nearly a thousand years.

All will be gone. Fallen help me, but I was not wrong.

He leaned forward and blew on the ink, drying it so that it could be folded up and sealed. He didn't have much time, and he didn't know why he'd wasted his remaining moments writing the letter to Jonim's son. The boy might never receive it, but he'd handled things poorly with Gairen over the years and would not leave things unfinished.

He read it over one last time.

Son of my son, blood of my blood,

If you hold this letter, then you've escaped the coffin that is this island. I do not seek to explain my decisions and do not require your forgiveness, but I fear I do owe you at least a semblance of a reason for sending you away—for sending all of you away. Master Iwynd likely told you that you are to be trained for a single purpose, but that was merely a pretense to move you both beyond the reach of Kyden Verros. I have lost both my sons, and I have no desire to see either you or Iwynd in the ground beside them. I also have no desire to see you used by another regiment, a weapon for their continued shortsightedness.

There is no easy way to say this, so I'll come to the point of this letter. There is no great plan for saving us all from the greed and hubris of the Wolves. For that, I am afraid it is already too late.

Long ago my mind was opened by an Esharii spirit-taker who spared a young and desperate half-warden and helped him save his closest companion. When I became kyden, the seed planted by the tribesman allowed me to discover the true depths to which we have betrayed our cause. I vowed never to train another recruit, that I would not add another source of strength to the enemy our regiments were created to stand against, and that I would do all in my power to reduce the number of Draegorans across all the regiments. I have done unforgivable things to prevent recruits from obtaining a crystal, but for you I go back on my word. I will not leave you helpless in the battle that may come during your lifetime. Your training is my parting gift. May it serve you well.

If you choose to return to the lands of the Covenant, there will no longer be an Owl Regiment. The Hounds and the

Bloodhammers will fall in behind the Wolves, even to the peril of their own ranks. Sheep who watch their brethren eaten and believe it will never be them. The Ironstrikers are reclusive and only desire to be left alone with their books and their forges. As long as they keep producing blades, the Wolves will tolerate them. If Kyden Blane and the Stone-breakers remain, he is a man you can trust, but I fear his regiment will be next. They are all my failures—for even though I've shown the other kydens the truth, they refuse to acknowledge it. I could not convince them that the regiments must be ended. I also underestimated the depths of Kyden Verros's hunger.

The best advice I can give you is to remain absent from this land. Learn a trade. Find a wife one day. Do whatever you desire. I free you from this curse. You owe us nothing.

Kyden Thalle nodded to himself and stood up from the desk. The words would have to be enough. He'd made his choices long ago, both right and wrong, and he would face the endgame when Kyden Verros challenged him. He ran his hand over the pommel of his longknife. He did not hold on to any illusions that he might win. He hadn't drawn any power into the blade for years, and Verros would not accept any form of submission save death.

His aide, Half-warden Tuon, stepped into the doorway and knocked lightly on the open door. "Sir, you asked for this." In his hands he held a folded red pennant, recently removed from where it flew over the tower.

Tuon wore his black hair short and nearly flat on top, the opposite of what most others favored. Thalle thought of Tuon as a boy, but he was only a few years behind Gairen. Strong-willed and always willing to fight, he'd chaffed at being Kyden Thalle's aide while his peers commanded scouts along the Esharii border.

"Yes. Thank you."

Tuon set the pennant down on the desk and turned to leave.

"Wait."

Kyden Thalle tightened up the folds to make it smaller and placed the red pennant in a wooden box, making sure it lay smoothly within. He folded the letter, sealed it carefully using blue wax and the candle, and stamped it with his sigil before placing it reverently on top. He started to close it, but as an afterthought placed the seal he'd just used inside the box as well. He eyed the room, but he could see nothing else he desired to pass on. He flipped the lid closed and locked the box.

He held both the box and the key out to Tuon along with a purse full of coins. "Take the box and depart for Parthusal immediately. There, you are to find the first ship bound for Arillia. You will locate Master Iwynd in Hammisal and present the box to him and letter within to the boy he trains. You are to tell no one where you are going, and you will serve Kyden Iwynd until he sees fit to release you from his service. Do not return without finding them."

"Sir, with respect," Tuon said hesitantly, "if it's to be open war with the Wolves, my place is here watching your back."

"Your place is where I tell you it is, and your duty is to do what I tell you to do. Must I remind you of your oaths to myself and the regiment?" He didn't like being harsh with Tuon, but he had no time for explanations.

"Yes, my Kyden." The half-warden saluted and reached for the box.

Kyden Thalle held tight a moment, preventing the half-warden from pulling it out of his grasp. "You will proceed from this room straight to the dock and order the boat waiting for you to cast off. You will make no stops and retrieve none of your possessions. Understood?"

Tuon nodded, but he refused to meet his eyes.

Kyden Thalle released the box. "Go. Depart through the kitchens and the servants' quarters. All other routes are blocked."

Tuon's mouth was set in a grim line, but he said nothing. His body was rigid as he gave Kyden Thalle a final salute. He turned and was gone.

Kyden Thalle took a deep breath and relaxed. The final piece on the board had been moved. He pulled his longknife from its sheath, set it on the desk, and sat down to wait for Kyden Verros and the Council. He was sure it would not be long.

EPILOGUE

(A Return to the Beginning)

Convinced the Draegoran and Ferrick were not returning, Lemual eased his way out of the barn. He'd heard the men approaching as he unsaddled and brushed down Clod, the old bay they used for pulling the plow and their small wagon into town. When he'd spied Ferrick, he'd almost shouted to the magistrate, that was, until he saw the man in gray. He didn't know what the Draegoran wanted with Father, but Lemual wasn't about to interfere. He'd stayed in the barn and kept quiet, even when he watched Riam dragged from the house and taken away. He felt a pang of guilt for that, but he could not have stopped it.

Cautiously Lemual moved toward the house. "Father?" he called out.

There was no reply.

"Father, are you there?" he called again when he reached the porch.

Hesitantly, he walked to the front door and stepped inside.

A sandglass later saw Lemual driving the wagon down the ruts that led from the farm to the main road. When he reached the intersection, he pulled back on the reins and brought Clod to a stop.

He looked left, in the direction of Stillwell, where he'd spent the morning ordering supplies. Then he looked right, the opposite way, in the direction of Cove and the coast. For months he'd stopped here, thinking that one day he would turn right and never look back. He'd never been able to do it. He'd made a promise to his sister the day she died.

With Father dead, he was now free of that promise. He'd packed what few clothes he owned, food, and everything of value he could find in the house and barn into the wagon. The purse at his waist held the two gold dregs left on the table and the few coins his father kept hidden away. Lemual glanced one more time to the left before turning Clod in the opposite direction toward Cove. Some might call him a coward, but there was nothing more he could do for his nephew.

ACKNOWLEDGMENTS

I can't possibly thank every person involved with hammering this story into coherent shape, but I'll do my best. If I've forgotten anyone, my apologies for the slight. First, my deepest thanks to my agent, Jennie Goloboy, at Donald Maass Literary Agency for her unwavering support and commitment to both myself and her authors, and to Fleetwood Robbins for his developmental input and ideas.

To my beta readers, critique partners, friends, family, and ardent supporters who've trekked through variations or portions of the book, Danielle Hinesly, Jason & Jamie Krenkel, Jennifer Della Zanna, Colleen Davis, Tiffany Reynolds, Tasha Kreger, Rachel Robins, Stephanie Dunn, Tiffany Avery, Miles Watson, Melissa Freeman, Alison Wallace, Jen LaVita, and Jamie Pelzer, thank you for your time and priceless suggestions.

A huge thank-you to my two mentors back in my MFA days at Seton Hill University's Writing Popular Fiction program, the late David Bischoff, who continually pushed me to swing more sharpened bits of metal around in my stories, and Timons Esaias, who very candidly forced me to recognize the worst of my bad writing habits.

To my family, thank you for all the time you've sacrificed to my writing madness. You've always believed in my work, and the journey would be empty without you.

And finally, profound thanks to Sheila Gilbert and DAW for allowing me to join the family.

Tad Williams

The Last King of Osten Ard

"Building upon the revered history of *Memory, Sorrow, and Thorn*, Williams has outdone himself by penning a 700-plus page novel that is virtually un-put-down-able.... Williams' grand-scale storytelling mastery is on full display here. Not just utterly readable—an instant fantasy classic." —*Kirkus Reviews* (starred)

"Tad Williams is a master storyteller, and the Osten Ard books are his masterpiece. Williams' return to Osten Ard is every bit as compelling, deep, and fully rendered as the first trilogy, and he continues to write with the experience and polish of an author at the top of his game." —Brandon Sanderson

"What got me the most about this new one, the thing that felt the best, was not the book's considerable literary merits but its power to muffle the outside world for the time it took me to read it." —Tor.com

The Witchwood Crown: 978-0-7564-1061-2
Empire of Grass: 978-0-7564-1062-9

To Order Call: 1-800-788-6262
www.dawbooks.com

DAW 52

E. C. Blake
The Masks of Aygrima

"Brilliant world-building combined with can't-put-down storytelling, *Masks* reveals its dark truths through the eyes of a girl who must learn to wield unthinkable power or watch her people succumb to evil. Bring on the next in this highly original series!"

—Julie E. Czerneda

"Mara's personal growth is a delight to follow. Sharp characterization, a fast-moving plot, and a steady unveiling of a bigger picture make this a welcome addition to the genre."

—*Publishers Weekly*

"*Masks* is simply impossible to put down."

—*RT Book Reviews*

MASKS
978-0-7564-0947-0

SHADOWS
978-0-7564-0963-0

FACES
978-0-7564-0940-1

To Order Call: 1-800-788-6262
www.dawbooks.com

DAW 191

Don't miss any of the exciting novels of
Marshall Ryan Maresca

MARADAINE

"Smart, fast, and engaging fantasy crime in the mold of Brent Weeks and Harry Harrison. Just perfect."
—Kat Richardson, national bestselling author of *Revenant*

THE THORN OF DENTONHILL	978-0-7564-1026-1
THE ALCHEMY OF CHAOS	978-0-7564-1169-5
THE IMPOSTERS OF AVENTIL	978-0-7564-1262-3

THE MARADAINE CONSTABULARY

"The perfect combination of urban fantasy, magic, and mystery."
—*Kings River Life Magazine*

A MURDER OF MAGES	978-0-7564-1027-8
AN IMPORT OF INTRIGUE	978-0-7564-1173-2
A PARLIAMENT OF BODIES	978-0-7564-1266-1

THE STREETS OF MARADAINE

"Think *Ocean's 11* set in Maradaine, complete with magic, violence, and plenty of double dealing."   —Bibliosanctum

THE HOLVER ALLEY CREW	978-0-7564-1260-9
LADY HENTERMAN'S WARDROBE	978-0-7564-1264-7

THE MARADAINE ELITE

"A grand adventure—and some last-minute revelations promise plenty of entertaining twists to come."   —*Locus Magazine*

THE WAY OF THE SHIELD	978-0-7564-1479-5

DAW 213

Bradley P. Beaulieu

The Song of the Shattered Sands

—◆—

"Fantasy and horror, catacombs and sarcophagi, resurrections and revelations: the book has them all, and Beaulieu wraps it up in a package that's as graceful and contemplative as it is action-packed and pulse-pounding." —NPR

TWELVE KINGS IN SHARAKHAI
978-0-7564-0973-9

WITH BLOOD UPON THE SAND
978-0-7564-0975-3

A VEIL OF SPEARS
978-0-7564-1636-2

BENEATH THE TWISTED TREES
978-0-7564-1460-3

WHEN JACKALS STORM THE WALLS
978-0-7564-1462-7

"Çeda and Emre share a relationship seldom explored in fantasy, one that will be tried to the utmost as similar ideals provoke them to explore different paths. Wise readers will hop on this train now, as the journey promises to be breathtaking." —Robin Hobb

"*The Song of the Shattered Sands* series is both gripping and engrossing." —*Kirkus*

To Order Call: 1-800-788-6262
www.dawbooks.com

DAW 202